Anya
Unbound

Dan Carruthers

For Wes
Fond memories of the
Yukon from another
Yukoner

Dan

 FriesenPress

Suite 300 - 990 Fort St
Victoria, BC, V8V 3K2
Canada

www.friesenpress.com

Copyright © 2017 by Dan Carruthers
First Edition — 2017

All rights reserved.

ISBN
978-1-5255-0071-8 (Hardcover)
978-1-5255-0072-5 (Paperback)
978-1-5255-0073-2 (eBook)

1. FICTION, CHRISTIAN, SUSPENSE

Distributed to the trade by The Ingram Book Company

This story of Anya is fiction. Yet many young girls and boys in this world are living in bondage to sex traffickers. I hope that my story draws attention and resources to this issue.

It is my hope and prayer that those who read this story will see that there is hope in the person of Jesus Christ. I encourage you to call on His name; He will set you free.

> *"the spirit of the Lord is upon me, because He anointed Me to preach the gospel to the poor. He has sent Me to proclaim release to the captives, and recovery of sight to the blind, to set free those who are oppressed,"* (Luke 4:18; New American Standard Holy Bible)

Acknowledgements

The consistent encouragement of the *Millarville Church Writing Group* and its leader, Prof. Bill Bunn, helped produce this story. Thank you; I never thought I'd write a novel. I am grateful to my wife, JoAnna, for the prayers uttered on my behalf as I made this journey. I thank my Lord for His inspiration and guidance.

Anya
Unbound

Chapter 1

A figure darted into the forest as Sean's truck rounded the corner. "What on earth was that?" He slowed his truck and pulled off the gravel road. He was sure it was human; too small to be a Sasquatch. Sean laughed to himself as he came to a stop in a cloud of dust. Who would be way out here?

He walked along the edge of the forest stopping to listen and looking for a sign that what he thought he saw was real. Why had he left Jesse at home? Sean knew how to track animals and was alert to any subtle sign a creature might leave as it made its way through the Yukon wilderness but his dog Jesse was the ultimate tracker. He stooped to examine footprints in a patch of silt left from the spring runoff. Definitely human, fresh and about a size seven sneaker he guessed. He entered the forest and walked in the direction indicated by the footprint. "Is anyone here?" he called. Silence except for a chattering squirrel. Strange, he thought, whoever it was they didn't seem to want company. "I know you're here," he shouted, "I'm going back to the truck but I'll wait a bit in case you need a ride. It's okay to come out. I won't hurt you."

Sean sat in the truck. His mind pondered reasons why a person would be on foot this far from civilization. There was almost no traffic on this piece of road that ended in a dead end if you didn't have four-wheel drive. He didn't see any vehicles broken down on the road but he supposed there could be one further on in the direction he was going. He poured himself a coffee from the thermos. *"Why would they be so secretive anyway?"* he wondered.

It was one of those soft and bright fall days only the Yukon wilderness could produce. The sun beamed through the windshield of the truck making the cab uncomfortably hot. He rolled down the windows and leaned against the driver's door. The silence hung in the fragrant autumn air as his eyes scanned the green and gold forest for any sign of movement.

The Yukon was a notorious hiding place for criminals trying to evade the law. Maybe he was stalking a criminal. That would explain their secretiveness. The thought caused him to lift his Marlin from the gun rack on the back of the truck cab. He scanned his immediate surroundings while levering a .45-70 cartridge into the chamber then laid the gun on the seat where it was available if needed. Leaning back against the door he smiled thinking how small this criminal was with size seven shoes.

Sometimes Indian families would go berry picking alongside roads. They would drop off the older kids at various berry-picking spots and pick them up later. Maybe this person was just one of those shy native teenagers. Then again, berry season was over so this theory didn't hold much water.

The movement of the willow branch caught his eye and focused his gaze. He knew it wasn't a bird; he could feel someone watching him. He sat still, listening, staring at the forest wall alert to any sound, movement or unnatural image. Nothing. Maybe they're playing hard to get. "You can come out, I won't hurt you," he called through the open passenger side window. "What's your name? Mine's Sean." He waited, unmoving, his eyes scanning the forest for any sign of a person. *"Maybe they need to see me."* His face brightened at the thought. He glanced at the rifle. Leaving it on the seat, he climbed out the driver's-side door and walked around the back of the truck where he leaned against the truck box and called again, "Here I am. I'm here to help you if you want. I don't mean you no harm."

Sean's eyes widened in surprise but he didn't move for fear of spooking her. She was young, maybe just out of her teens. Like a cat watching for dogs, she took slow, deliberate steps while her head twitched to the right and the left. In her right hand, she grasped a stout stick of fire-killed pine about three feet long. "You're safe. I won't hurt you. Are you okay?" Sean's voice conveyed a tone of gentle concern. He continued to stare in disbelief at the thin form approaching him. Her blonde hair with bits of vegetation caught up in the tangles reminded Sean of a squirrel's nest. Her torn, once-white blouse hung out of the waistband of ripped, loosely fitting and faded jeans. The sight begged the question *"was this a fashion statement or something more sinister?"* As she drew closer, he could see tracks of dried tears carved through the dirt on her bony cheeks. The sight caused his words to catch in his throat; "My name is Sean, what's yours?" He felt the awkwardness of his smile but he wanted to relieve her obvious fear.

She grasped the stick as if it was her turn at bat. "Don't come near me or I'll hit you with my stick." She glanced about as if expecting some kind of ambush. Sean raised his hands in an attempt to convey his innocence and submission. He could discern her mind wrestling with the situation, *"should she trust this stranger or should she retreat to her desperate refuge in the forest. No, she couldn't survive alone in this wilderness; she would take the chance."*

"Can we sit in the truck please?" came the accented, polite but tremulous response.

"Sure, you bet," Sean replied as he turned to open the passenger side door for the girl. She lurched backwards raising her stick when she saw the rifle on the seat, her eyes wide in fear.

"It's okay, I'll put it away. I wasn't sure who you were." He apologized as he slid the rifle off the seat and wrapped it in a tarp in the truck box.

The faded, dry bloodstains on the back of her blouse caught his attention as she climbed into the truck. Sean shut the door behind her and walked around the front of the truck making certain she could see him.

Her eyes followed his every move but she felt strangely secure inside the cab of the truck. The stick, like the stuffed bear from her childhood, provided a measure of comfort even though she didn't feel threatened by the stranger. He was different; his words were soft, almost calming and he kept his distance. But, could she trust him? Not yet.

Opening the driver's door, Sean started to climb in wondering who this girl was and what came next. "You stay over there!" she ordered. Sean stopped halfway into the cab of the truck with one hand on the steering wheel.

"I can't drive if I stay here," he protested.

"Oh, okay, you can sit but I've got a stick so don't you try anything!"

"Look lady, I'm not going to 'try anything'," his voice betrayed his irritation, "I'm not forcing you to ride with me. You can get out anytime you want." He took his place behind the wheel. The girl lowered her eyes and pressed her body into the door in response to his rebuke. He silently kicked himself for his outburst as he watched her recoil in pain. This girl was hurting. "Sorry, roll up your window, the road's dusty. Where can I drop you?" He spoke gently and passed her the plastic juice bottle full of water and one of his homemade cookies. There *was* no place to drop her that he knew of.

"No! Please, don't leave me alone!" Sean's eyebrows arched as he turned to face the girl. Her pleading and frantic eyes locked with his. "Can I stay with you and your family?"

Her fearful reaction to his question caused Sean to scan their surroundings once again. *"What's with this girl?"* he thought.

"Settle down, your safe and no one is going to hurt you," Sean's voice was soft and calm. "Yes, you can stay with me, it's just me and my dog but you're welcome. I still don't know your name."

"Anya. Can we not talk?" she whispered. He watched her take a long drink from the water bottle. Her hollow cheeks swelled as she stuffed the cookie into her mouth.

"Okay, we don't have to talk," he agreed trying to place the accent in her speech. East European he thought, Slavic? He started the truck, shifted into gear and turned onto the road.

Chapter 2

Anya might have been secure in the silence but for Sean it loosed a stampede of thoughts, mostly questions. This girl was obviously scared of something or someone and, if he had to guess, he would say it was someone that did her a lot of harm. He watched her in his peripheral vision as the eyelids in her expressionless, dirt covered face drooped then suddenly jerked open before falling again. The warm cab filled with the stench from her body. This girl needed sleep, a bath and probably a lot more.

She bolted upright when he reached behind his seat. He pulled out a blanket and handed it to her. She hesitated then grasped and pulled it onto her lap where she folded it into a cushion positioning it behind her back. Leaning against the door, stick in hand, she squirmed and continually repositioned herself trying to avoid falling asleep. It didn't work.

The truck slowed and turned off the gravel road onto the narrow track that led up the side of the valley towards a mountain. Anya jerked awake; her wide, bloodshot eyes filled with terror searched her surroundings as she raised the stick against her unseen demons.

Sean persisted in a concerned stare until he got her attention. "It's okay; this is the road to my place. We'll be there in half an hour." His voice was tender and soft like a father would speak to a daughter awakened by a nightmare.

She leaned back into the seat drawing her knees up to her chest and looked straight ahead in silence, chewing on her lower lip.

The big 4x4 pickup wound its way up the narrow track through the forest gaining almost a thousand feet in elevation above the valley floor. On occasion, the mountain revealed itself through openings in the forest. The sun was seeking a place to hide behind the mountains of the coast range when Sean wheeled the truck into the yard. Its golden glow reflected off Pancake Lake and the windows of Sean's cabin. The cool air sliding off the mountain heralded the coming night.

Jesse came bounding up to the truck happy to see his master. Sean bent to give him an ear rub and an affirming greeting before leading him to the other side of the truck where Anya was getting out, one hand firmly gripping her stick. Jesse wagged his tail as he nosed Anya's legs to confirm her identity. Dropping her guard, she leaned over to pat him then, with a spasm of latent yearning, she crouched and wrapped her arms around his neck. Without warning, she released the dog, stood upright and held her stick in front of her. Her red eyes glared at Sean.

Sean ignored her glare. "Well this is it." He pointed to the log cabin as he grabbed a gunnysack from the truck box. "You just met Jesse. Come on in, we'll get the stove going and get you settled."

The cabin was large by Yukon standards. He built it himself hauling logs from the surrounding forest. It sat on the gentle south slope of a large bowl containing a small lake. The spring-fed lake had no official name and no fish but Sean called it Pancake Lake. It provided abundant water and contributed to the serenity of the setting. Beyond the lake was the mountain and in the far distance, the coast range separating the Yukon from Alaska.

He opened the heavy wooden door ushering his guest into the cabin. The smell of gun oil and wood smoke hung in the air. Sean had been cleaning his guns the night before. The odour of gun oil would dissipate but the smell of wood smoke was a constant. They entered the large kitchen. He cooked his food on an old black, wood-burning stove sitting in the corner. An airtight, wood-burning heater sat in the middle of the house where its radiant warmth could flow throughout the cabin during the cold and dark winter months.

Anya stood silently against a log wall, shivering, stick in hand, while Sean lit the Aladdin oil lamp hanging over the kitchen table and started a fire in the cook stove. The pine kindling crackled its welcome. He noticed her shivering. "Won't be long and you'll be warm and toasty," he promised, "come and I'll show you where you can sleep." She followed him to the guest bedroom where he pulled aside the curtain that acted as a door. He lit the bedside lamp for her and showed her how to blow it out. A wardrobe and chest of drawers took up most of one wall. A washstand with a large pitcher and bowl decorated with blue painted flowers stood under a window framed with blue curtains. The single bed made of logs stood against one wall. A quilt his mother had made for his bed when he was a boy adorned the store-bought and comfortable mattress. He pulled back the quilt and sheets to allow the bed to warm. A colourful rag rug covered the plywood floor next to the bed.

"I'll be in the kitchen fixing supper. It's warmer by the stove but you can stay in here if you want." Sean left her and retreated to the kitchen where he stoked the fire with more wood. After filling the kettle, he put on a pot of coffee. When the coffee was ready, he poured himself a cup and sat watching the darkness settle over Pancake Lake. "How ya doin' Anya? Coffee's ready if you want a cup," he called. There was no reply. "Anya?" Still no reply. He got out of the chair and walked to the guest room knocking on a log to announce his presence. He heard sobbing.

"Can I come in Anya?" he asked as he approached the door. The sobbing stopped. He poked his head around the doorpost. Anya lay on the floor in a corner of the room in the fetal position clutching her stick. He went to her side thinking she was injured. The stick slashed toward him as she rose up screaming. His body twisted in defense but the stick connected with his shoulder as he retreated from her fury. He stood bewildered on the other side of the room watching the frenzied girl beat the air with her stick, screaming at him as she backed into the corner. *Dear God, what is happening to this poor girl?* he silently prayed. *Help her Lord whatever it is.* Anya collapsed onto the floor sobbing, her body shook but it wasn't from the cold. "Please Anya, I want to help you, I will never hurt you." Tears began streaming from

Sean's eyes as his heart went out to the broken soul lying on the floor. He stood in silence rubbing his shoulder, watching the girl from the forest.

* * *

"Open the door and get Sydney," he shouted as he approached the squalid, concrete block building. The young girl in his arms was unconscious. "*God's mercy*," he thought. The heat and humidity weighed on him more than the thin, fragile form in his arms. Mostly he staggered under the weight of her soul.

Darkness came quickly in the tropics promising some relief from the oppressive sun and heat of the day. The shortcut had taken him into the squalid sex-trade district that he knew all too well. He had followed the screams to a building that he knew served as a tourist brothel. Pretending to be a customer, he started calmly up the flight of stairs where a wiry Asian man stood at the top holding an AK47 rifle. His Krav Maga training kicked in when the man pointed the rifle at him. In an instant, he stepped to the side grabbing the barrel of the gun and pulling with all his might. The man fell forward losing his grip on the AK, tumbling down the stairs and coming to rest against the wall at the bottom. There was no movement.

Clutching the rifle, he ran to the room where the screams had now ceased and kicked in the door. A very fat, partly naked and very white man lay on the mattress beside an Asian girl partially clothed in a thin yellow dress stained with blood. Her eyes were closed and she didn't move except for the rising and falling of her chest as she breathed. She looked to be no more than 12 years old but he found it difficult to guess the age of Asians. Sean, still holding the rifle, strode up to the man whose eyes grew wide before suddenly going blank and lifeless. The girl didn't move.

* * *

After a few minutes, Anya raised her head. Her tear-filled eyes met his as she shivered and sobbed, "I'm sorry. You are not a bad man."

Sean was incredulous. *"Jekyll and Hyde,"* he thought. "It's okay Anya, I forgive you. I'm so sorry that you have been hurt. Please believe me when I say I want to help you even if I don't know how. I am going back in the kitchen; you come when you are ready. It's warm in the kitchen."

Chapter 3

Supper could wait, he needed time to think and pray. Besides, his shoulder ached; she had a good swing.

Jesse lay at his feet while Sean sipped his coffee trying to stop his mind from re-hashing the recent past and, instead, consider the present. She was in his house and he brought her here. He could have refused but the look of terror in her eyes told him he had no choice. Should he have left her on the side of the road? Of course not. Maybe she's mentally ill; she sure acts crazy. Maybe he should have turned around and taken her to Whitehorse. Maybe he should still do that; he didn't need some deranged girl living in his house. Damn it! What's done is done, now get on with it.

"Lord, I think You have a hand in this. I hope You do because I'm in over my head. Please help me to know what to do and say to this girl. I leave it in Your hands."

Sean could feel her eyes. He turned to see her leaning into the kitchen as if seeking permission to enter. "Come in Anya. Sit here by the stove, it's nice and warm." He tried to sound inviting while directing her with his hand to the comfortable chair opposite his.

She shuffled across the floor dragging her stick, her body reeking as it shivered. The shuffle told him she was in physical pain. The smell told him she needed a bath.

Her frail body slumped into the overstuffed chair. He held back tears as his eyes examined the ragged, tortured creature facing him. She sat in silence staring at Sean. The stick lay impotent against her leg; her eyes vacant testifying to a vanquished soul. He met her gaze with tear-filled eyes. "You are very tired aren't you?" he ventured. She nodded. "What can I do for you Anya?"

"Do you think I could have a shower?"

The spoken request surprised Sean. "Uh, well, I don't have a shower, but I can fix a bath for you if you want?"

"I would like that." She looked into his wet eyes.

"I'll heat up some water and we'll get your bath going then we'll have some supper. Would you like that?" asked Sean. Anya nodded her head in appreciation while her hands played with each other in her lap.

It occurred to Sean that Anya had no change of clothing. As for toiletries, she couldn't even brush her teeth if she wanted. He put the graniteware boiler on the stove to heat then went to the guest bedroom. He opened a dresser drawer and laid a pair of men's flannel pyjamas on the bed for her. Retrieving the soft terry-cloth bathrobe from the wardrobe, he laid it on the bed alongside the pyjamas.

Sean lit a lamp and rustled around in the bathroom coming up with a brand new hairbrush and toothbrush. He laid out a big, soft bath towel, a washcloth and face towel along with a bar of Ivory soap.

"You're welcome to use my shampoo, in fact you can help yourself to anything," said Sean as he re-joined Anya in the kitchen.

"Thank you," came the timid reply. He noticed that she no longer shivered.

Sean poured buckets of hot water into the old tin bathtub and left another bucket beside the tub for rinsing. "There you go – have at 'er," said Sean turning and closing the door as he left the room. "I'll start supper." The bolt on the door slammed shut.

Sean brought in the rest of the supplies he had bought in town and stowed them in their proper places. The sun had set and darkness was cloaking the land. Jesse was looking for his supper so he tended to his companion while imagining a supper menu for him and Anya. Pork cutlets, roast potatoes and fresh green beans that arrived in Whitehorse on the mainliner yesterday. Homemade applesauce would be a nice addition. There was just enough of Sean's famous apple-orange-cranberry pie left for dessert.

The warmth of the cook stove greeted Anya as she appeared from the bathroom wrapped in the bathrobe, her hair in a turban and the stick in her hand. Sean immediately noticed her bare feet.

"You need some slippers girl." He went to his bedroom and returned with a pair of heavy wool socks that he only wore in the winter. "Don't have any slippers for you but here, put these on, they'll keep your tootsies toasty." He grinned as he handed the socks to Anya.

"Have a seat." Sean motioned towards the armchair in the corner of the kitchen. "Can I get you something to drink – some water, juice, milk while you're waiting on supper?"

"Do you think I could have a glass of juice?" She answered as if she was somehow unworthy of the offer. She settled into the comfortable chair laying her stick across her lap.

"Coming right up," said Sean. He retrieved a carton of cranberry juice from the propane refrigerator and poured a glass for Anya. As he handed it to her, he noticed bruising on her neck and a recent cut on her forehead. He caught himself staring as images from his past once again flooded his mind.

* * *

Sydney, a nurse, and her husband, Ben, retired military, left their comfortable lives in Brandon, Manitoba to live in a dark and derelict district of Phnom Penh, Cambodia. Their teenage daughter, buried in a cemetery near their hometown, died of a drug overdose while working in Canada's sex trade. She was the token white girl in a stable of Cambodian and Vietnamese girls.

Ben held the door open as Sean squeezed through the narrow opening. He squinted in the stark fluorescent lighting of the room. Sydney, dressed in her pyjamas, trotted down the stairs directing Sean to the examination room and ordering Ben to bring a pan of hot water. He laid the battered little girl on the smooth, white sheet covering the examination table.

The light revealed so much more than what he had seen in that room in the brothel. Although still unconscious, her closed eyes and long eyelashes suggested a measure of peace. Upon closer examination, the ruse was exposed. Bruises covered her neck and a swollen cheek confessed to a blow to her face. Her small hands showed signs of abuse through work or self-defence or both. Broken and split fingernails and still open, infected cuts were scattered over her hands and feet. She was thin, much thinner than a girl of her stature should be, and probably undernourished. Sydney motioned for Sean and Ben to leave the room. Her parents probably sold her he thought. Dad wanted a new motorbike or maybe they just had too many mouths to feed. Sean would never know the truth.

Sean Carson was on his way back home via the Orient when he met Ben in a Phnom Penh noodle shop. He thought 10 months in Israel working on a kibbutz was a sufficient distraction until he met Ben and Sydney and heard their story. They invited him to stay and help, no strings, so he did. That decision saved his life. And, the lives of many others.

Chapter 4

"Shut up and drive. I'll take care of them; it's your job to get them to Snag."
John glared at the driver of the Kenworth 900.

The crane dropped the container on the trailer. Wimp finished securing the four corners and jumped into the cab of the truck finding his way into the sleeper. They stopped briefly at the gate where the driver passed the paperwork to the attendant.

"Have a good trip," he waved and slid the window shut as the Kenworth rolled away from the gate. He didn't hear the banging on the walls of the container over the roar of the Kenworth's diesel.

* * *

Sean finished setting the table happy for the opportunity to use a tablecloth that only came out on special occasions. Its red and white, checkered pattern cheered the comfortable ambiance of the kitchen. He hoped it would do the same for his guest.

Setting the warm serving bowls on the table, he invited Anya to join him for their meal. Bowing his head, he thanked God for the provision in his life, and added a special thank you for introducing him to Anya. He silently asked for God's direction on how to handle his situation.

"Now you help yourself Anya, take all you want, there's lots," Sean invited. *"No, he would let her stay,"* he thought, *"she needs quiet and rest more than a bunch of people asking questions and poking her; at least for now."*

Sean watched Anya load her plate, devour it and load it again. Her behaviour, gaunt face and thin frame told Sean that she had suffered some measure of food deprivation in recent days, probably weeks.

He tried to make conversation over their meal but she ignored him seeming to prefer her food to his company. When she finished her second plate, she pushed it away, glanced at him then muttered, "Thank you." She stared at her hands folded on her lap,

"You're welcome Anya," said Sean, "we have dessert too, would you like your pie warmed up?"

"Yes please," she replied without looking up.

"Let's sit over there." He motioned to the armchairs. "We'll have our pie and coffee in comfort."

They ate their dessert in silence except for the clicking of their forks against the china and the occasional crack coming from the firebox of the stove. He wished he knew more about the stranger in his home. Sean didn't want to pry while at the same time he was genuinely concerned for this mysterious girl that had entered his life. He could see that she was beginning to relax. Perhaps she was beginning to trust him and her surroundings or maybe it was simply fatigue. Either way, conversation was not her strong suit.

"Now you go to bed whenever you like," said Sean breaking the silence. He had no doubt she was desperately fatigued and needed rest. "I'll do the dishes and put things away, you just relax."

"Thank you, I would like to go to bed, I am very tired." She handed him her plate as he rose from his chair.

"Okay, goodnight Anya. You are safe here; no one comes by except my friends. I'll look in on you before I go to bed if that's okay with you."

She stared at him, her eyes wide, then, lowering her head she said, "Yes, I guess that will be okay. I have my stick."

He ignored her reference to the stick. Sean felt relieved as he watched her shuffle towards her bedroom dragging her stick. He found Anya's reluctance to talk stressful. Her physical and mental trauma was profoundly evident and her presence disrupted his otherwise peaceful life. He didn't resent her; he just didn't know what to do with her. Like most men, he wanted to fix her, to see her healthy and whole. Did she have any family or friends that could care for her? It might be a while before he was privy to that information. In the meantime, he would do his best to help her find the kind of peace he enjoyed. He knew he would need help; patience and sensitivity were not his best character traits. Yes, he needed help but he knew where to find it.

Jesse came in from his evening constitutional and the two of them got ready for bed. Jesse jumped up on the bed while Sean took his pyjamas from under the pillow and put them on. He quickly glanced into Anya's bedroom to check on her. The lamp was still burning. She was lying still, breathing softly, her blonde hair draped over the pillow, her stick lying alongside her body. The Bible that had been on the bedside table was now lying on the bed next to her. He stepped into the room to blow out the lamp then retreated to his own bedroom.

Most of Sean's prayers that night focused on Anya and her condition. Finally, he asked, "Lord, help me to understand Anya's situation and use me to accomplish Your purposes in her life. I know I'm a hard man Lord, but please make me gentle for Anya's sake while she is here." He blew out the lamp and quickly fell asleep.

Chapter 5

"Nieeeeeeee, proszę, I'll be good, I promise! Stop, Stój!, ahhhhhhhhhhh!" Anya's screams startled Sean and Jesse to full wakefulness.

Sean grabbed the flashlight and together they were beside her bed in a flash. "It's okay Anya, it's me, Sean, you're safe."

She continued screaming in a foreign language then turned and began pounding him with her fists as he knelt beside the bed. The stick and flashlight rolled onto the floor. He finally gripped her wrists and held her down speaking gently to her while she writhed and contorted her body trying to escape his grip. After a few minutes, she began to relax probably from exhaustion. When he released her wrists, Anya gripped his hand with both of hers; the other personality emerged. He couldn't see her in the darkness but he could feel her body shaking the bed.

"Let me light the lamp, Anya, everything is okay," he said as he pried her fingers off his hand.

"There, that's better. See I'm here, it's me, Dad, I mean Sean." A powerful memory broke through a wall he erected a long time ago as he spoke soothing words to Anya. That little girl was also terrified when he knelt to comfort her, only that one, his daughter, died in his arms. He squeezed his eyes tightly shut to stop the tears from coming.

* * *

It had been over five lonely years since Sean lost his wife and daughter in a car accident. They had been attending a guide and outfitting convention in Las Vegas. Gina, his wife, had taken their daughter shopping while he met with some of his industry friends. They were supposed to meet for a late lunch. It happened right in front of him as he lounged on a sidewalk bench in front of the hotel waiting for their return. Gina died instantly according to the coroner. His other beautiful treasure, Felicia, died in his arms waiting for the paramedics. She was 12.

The accident had left a huge hole in his life that he had filled with grief, hopelessness and anger. He felt like he had entered a dark cave where bitterness enveloped his whole being. Loneliness imprisoned him and there was no escape, or so he thought. At first, Sean buried himself in his work trying to cope with his grief and loneliness. He sold his house in town and moved to his cabin on Pancake Lake. His friends tried to reach out to him in his grief but he became more reclusive as the months passed. Then, he was gone.

* * *

She began to sob into her pillow. Extending his hand, he let it rest lightly on her back alert for another attack. Her body shook in spasms but she didn't reject his touch. He could feel the scar tissue on her back beneath the flannel pyjama top. The turmoil in his own mind settled as he prayed in silence, *"what comfort can I give to this terrified girl from the side of the road."*

He didn't know how much time had passed before Anya fell asleep. He pulled the covers up around her shoulders and laid the stick beside her fragile form before leaving the room. "Lord, I can't handle this," he whispered. "You've gotta help me, but more than me, You've gotta help this girl. Comfort her. Heal her Lord. Please make her well in body and mind."

Chapter 6

Sean slid out of bed dressing quickly as he shivered in the cold. Winter was looming. After letting Jesse out, he started a fire in the stove trying to avoid disturbing Anya who was still sleeping. He slid the kettle over the hot spot and put fresh coffee in the drip pot then prepared a pot of porridge adding a handful of fresh crowberries. Sean bought oatmeal in 80-pound sacks; next to his Sheltie, Jesse, it was just another manifestation of his Scottish heritage.

Jesse finished his breakfast then lay at Sean's feet. It was Sean's habit to read his Bible in the morning and to commit his day to the Lord before eating breakfast. He lounged in his favourite armchair looking out the bay window as he sipped his coffee. Mist drifted over the surface of Pancake Lake as the sun's golden glow warmed the landscape. The sight caused him to reflect on the condition of his heart – a famous, possibly fictional Scot, Rob Roy, once remarked that his countrymen were *"well known, and more remarkable for the exercise of their intellectual powers than for the keenness of their feelings; . . .[they are not easily] influenced by the enthusiastic appeals to the heart and to the passions."* Yet, Sean knew he could call on his Lord, Jesus, to soften his heart just as God did for the warrior King David in the Old Testament. "Lord, help me to be gentle and humble like You. Let Anya know *Your* gentle spirit in me."

* * *

Fall was his favourite time of year even though it was the busiest. Winter would soon arrive and a wise man would make himself ready. Sean sometimes guided hunters in the spring and fall and fishermen in the summer. When things were slow, he would do odd jobs as they came along. Sometimes he would work with friends who had a company that built log cabins. He was financially comfortable because of the settlement from the accident that took his family. He didn't really have to work but he wasn't that kind of man.

Guiding for the fall was over. It was just a week ago, Jerry, the client from Ohio, was his last hunter of the season. He killed a trophy moose thanks to Sean. By now, he was home telling stories about his adventures in the northern Yukon but there was a point when Jerry wasn't sure he'd ever see his home again. After he had taken his moose, Sean came down with a virus of some kind that not only seriously disabled him but also threatened his very life. Jerry was fearful that his guide would die and leave him alone in the wilderness.

They spent the night at a spike camp in the Hart River country. The morning light was gray and a cold wind blew out of the north. The sky brooded over the valley and occasional snowflakes drifted by as Sean dragged himself back to the cabin after checking the horses. Something was wrong; he had a splitting headache and he was cold and weak. By the time they finished breakfast he knew they had to get out of there. It had started to snow and Sean was getting ready to die. Jerry was scared. He feared that Sean would leave him in the wilderness where he'd die of starvation, freeze to death or the wolves would get him.

With Jerry's help, Sean managed to get their outfit on board the packers before they set out for the base camp. Normally a two-day ride they had to make it in one. The wind was picking up the snow and driving it into their faces as they wended their way along the trail. The snow was deeper each time they stopped to rest and the challenge greater still to get back into the saddle. The saddle horn was the anchor keeping Sean from drifting off his mount while Jerry's periodic queries into his condition kept him conscious. The trail had become invisible and darkness settled in. *"Where was the camp? When in doubt, let your horse do the thinkin',"* Sean thought.

He squinted into the snowy blackness searching for a sign of refuge. Hopeful hallucinations tormented him until that special moment when a light appeared, endured and became his beacon. His horse picked up its pace and Sean knew they were almost there. The porch lantern lit up the door of the cabin and, from the window, a soft, flickering yellow light testified to the warmth within. He fell from the saddle. When he awoke he found himself in the Dawson hospital.

* * *

Now, Sean was back home busy cutting, hauling and stacking 10 cords of firewood after which he would shoot a moose or caribou for his winter meat. Another couple of cords and he'd be done with firewood ensuring a comfortable and warm cabin when the mercury fell and the snow piled high. This year he thought he'd take a caribou from off the mountain. A small herd of the woodland subspecies lived and moved along the range that stretched from Pancake Lake to Carcross. Red meat supplemented the pork and chicken he bought from local growers. He also traded with his Alaskan friends on the coast, caribou and moose for halibut and salmon.

A loud crack from the stove lifted Sean from his reverie. The morning fire chased the chilled air out of the cabin and the smell of coffee permeated the small space he called home. Perhaps this is what roused Anya from her bed. As she poked her sleepy head around the corner, Jesse rose to greet her. Wrapping the bathrobe around her, she shuffled into the kitchen. Sean noticed that she wasn't carrying her stick.

"Good morning Anya." Sean stood and smiled at her wondering if she had any memory of her night terrors. "I'll get you a pitcher of hot water so you can wash up."

"Good morning Sean, Jesse." She spoke words tinged with confidence and couched in peace instead of fear as she crouched to rub Jesse's ears and hug his neck. "I really have to pee. Where's the toilet?"

Sean chuckled. "Take Jesse with you, slip on my boots by the door and follow the trail to the right of the porch, can't miss it."

"Really?" she said with a doubtful tone.

"Yup, really," Sean replied with certainty.

Chapter 7

Later, they sat in silence enjoying their coffee after a breakfast of toast and porridge. Anya turned from looking out the bay window and faced Sean across the table. "Thank you for being there for me last night."

"That's okay Anya," he replied. "Do you remember what you dreamt?"

Anya turned away to look out the window again. After a moment of silence she said, "I could clean your cabin if you want?"

Sean played along, "Do you think it needs cleaning? I thought I did a pretty good job of keeping it presentable."

"Oh no, no I didn't mean that," she flushed red.

Sean laughed. "I know you didn't, just teasing you."

"Anya, I know you don't have other clothes and I'd rather not see you get into those dirty rags you were wearing. You're welcome to make up an outfit from my wardrobe; we're about the same height. Might be a little big on you otherwise but heck, who's gonna see but me and Jesse. What do you think?"

"Thank you. Burn my clothes, I don't want to see them ever again!" she snarled.

The outburst startled Sean.

"I'm sorry. It's just . . . " Anya looked down at her coffee mug.

"Tell you what, let's go have a look at my wardrobe and you can pick out whatever you like, kinda like a shopping spree - in a hardware store." He chuckled.

Anya smiled as she rose to accompany Sean. His heart leaped at the sight of her smiling face.

Anya picked out a blue wool plaid Pendleton shirt, one of Sean's favourite 'go-to-town' shirts.

"Is this okay?" she asked politely.

"Nice choice, exactly what I'd have picked," Sean replied with a smile, "goes great with your eyes." She smiled back.

Unlike the shirt rack, the choice of pants was severely limited: denim jeans or a couple of pairs of heavy wool, army surplus, winter pants. She chose a faded pair of Levi's with a label promising a size 30 waist and 32 leg.

"I can't offer you much in the way of under garments, but help yourself," Sean said as he opened the top drawer of his dresser.

Anya chose a white, almost new cotton t-shirt, two pairs of black cotton briefs and two pairs of grey, light wool socks.

We'll plan a trip to town soon and we'll get you some real girl clothes," said Sean.

Anya's face drained to a pallid bone white as she turned to look at the wall.

Seeing her response, Sean wasted no time offering an alternative. "Or maybe I can get Reina to pick something up for you and drop it by next time she's out this way."

He changed the subject. "Look, I've got firewood to get in so why don't you just make yourself at home with Jesse, try on your new clothes, read a book, listen to music or just relax. I'll be back around noon to check on you. Don't worry about anybody calling 'cause the phone is in my truck and my friends are the only people who might come by. If you need me for anything just send Jesse; he'll fetch me right quick." Sean donned his jacket and laced up his boots. "See you soon Anya – you're safe, don't worry."

When he was out of sight of the cabin, he stopped the truck and grabbed the microphone for the radiotelephone. "Whitehorse radio, this is YJ7085, over."

"Hi Sean, how are you, haven't heard you for a while," said Brenda, the radiotelephone operator.

"Hi Brenda. Been up in the Hart River country. Just finished my last hunt and been busy getting ready for winter. How you doin' - over?

"Doing fine. Dave and I are planning a trip to Hawaii this January. Really looking forward to it - over."

"Good for you guys," said Sean. "Brenda, can you get me 383-6487 please?"

"I'll see if Reina is by, stand by one," said Brenda.

"Reina here, go ahead."

* * *

Sean first noticed Reina at church. She was hard to miss. He didn't pay a lot of attention as he was busy looking after his fishermen clients. Then, Pastor Ray introduced them at a church trap-shooting event a year ago last August. Reina was a shot gunner if he'd ever seen one; no duck was safe from her 20 gauge Ithaca Featherlight. Their mutual love for shooting and the outdoors gave them something to talk about. Soon they found themselves seeing more of each other as the months went by.

Reina came to the Yukon direct from Mexico. She was a nurse and had no difficulty immigrating. She lost her husband in a storm at sea. He was a fisherman. She noticed an advertisement in a hunting magazine seeking nurses to come and work in the Yukon. The government must have thought there might be some nurses who enjoyed hunting. Having no family, she sold her modest home in La Paz and headed to Whitehorse, the capital of Canada's Yukon Territory.

Sean thought that if all nurses looked as good as Reina the hospitals might have a few more patients. Dark Spanish eyes the color of good Scotch whiskey watched over a nose and mouth sculpted by God Himself. Long, thick dark hair framed the features that first drew Sean's attention. Reina kept herself fit through her outdoor pursuits. Her toned muscles subtly embraced her frame yielding a figure worthy of any glamour magazine.

* * *

"Hi Reina, Sean, how you doin', sorry I missed you yesterday, hey, are you going to be at home next week - over?"

"Si, senor, planning my Spanish courses for the winter, you coming in?" she answered.

"Yeah, wasn't planning on it but something's come up and I think I need some help - over."

"Always here for you Sean, what's going on?" she queried.

"I'll tell you when I see you."

"You know I hate it when you do this. Why don't you come by for lunch - over?" Reina and Sean were getting to be more than friends and she welcomed opportunities to spend time with her favourite student.

"Thanks, I'll see you in a week or so, maybe a Wednesday, gotta finish getting my firewood. I'll let you know. YJ7085 clear." Sean hung the mic' on the hook and Reina huffed over his abrupt end to the conversation.

The image of the girl standing in his kitchen flashed into his mind as he put the truck into gear. Felicia would have been about her age he thought. His life would change if she stayed – this orphan, this lost soul. She would be safe here but from who? Maybe Reina could help discover her story. He saw the terror in her eyes and the painful movement of her body. What or who was she afraid of? What had they done to her?

Chapter 8

The peace of the forest embraced him as he sat on the stump procrastinating in the cool air. The calls of the chickadees blended with and soothed his anxious thoughts – God's grace and he knew it. His chest swelled as he inhaled; this was *his* home and he was glad for it. Could he once again share it with another?

He looked up at the standing dead pine tree – his immediate goal. Soon his body would be wet with sweat. He removed the heavy wool shirt covering a black cotton tee before stretching his muscles and bending to pick up the chainsaw. The roar of the engine silenced the forest and his thoughts.

* * *

Travel and reckless pursuits failed to fill the void in Sean's life. The emptiness remained. He was angry with himself. It overflowed, affecting undeserving others in his life, further aggravating his loneliness. He tried to find some solace in the Holy Land where he hoped to find God. But, his spiritual muscle continued to wither as his fleshly muscle grew taut and solid. Obeying the Jewish Law turned him off; like the Jews, he could never be truly obedient. He refused to enter into the elaborate religious exercises meant to atone for his sins. Still, the Hebrew God of the Bible appealed to Sean – he seemed personal and caring, if he could only find a way to meet him.

India was more disappointing. Hindus had too many gods to choose from, all demanding and hateful not to mention, ugly. Worshipping a stone figure was not his cup of tea. Hinduism aimed for an impersonal oneness with the cosmos or Universal Soul (Brahman). Indians too seemed to be looking for God.

His last hope before returning to the Yukon would be the mysterious orient, the home of Buddhism. His troubled soul looked forward to the promised enlightenment and peace at the feet of the Buddha. But, once again, his quest led to disappointment. He discovered that Gotama's original teaching, distorted and corrupted over time, resulted in a multifaceted religion. Buddha (Gotama) is not God and he rejected any subservience to one supreme God. His teaching emphasized the vast vacuum in human experience but he offered no way to fill the hole. He left men without God and without hope.

Sean encountered several forms of Buddhist religion. All denied reason and logic with the aim of being "one with the ball" as the golfers say. Like Hinduism, Buddhism sought some kind of impersonal oneness with the cosmos, a denial of self. To reach this state of 'nirvana' you must lose yourself, your identity as a human. You do this through multiple re-births. Earning merit (Karma) or meditating on silly riddles (koans) that attack your capacity to reason help you along the way. The product of this belief system was lives enslaved to demons and a striving to earn merit. Fatalism and hopelessness abounded. Then he met Ben and Sydney.

Ben and Sydney were Christians working the streets of Phnom Penh, Cambodia. They helped young girls escape lives of sexual abuse and human trafficking. When they introduced him to this human carnage, occurring on the streets of many Asian cities, he found an outlet for his anger. It wasn't a healthy outlet but an outlet nonetheless.

He began to understand his own condition as he worked alongside this gentle and compassionate couple. He saw how his guilt, self-hate and anger held him captive. It robbed him of the life that God wanted for him just as evil men robbed these young girls of their lives. Ben and Sydney encouraged him to read his Bible. There he discovered that God was seeking *him*. Christianity wasn't a religion. He didn't have to invent elaborate ways to find or please God, or achieve nothingness. It was about a loving God reaching out to establish a relationship with *him*. Ben and Sydney helped Sean understand God's promise of freedom not bondage because of what Jesus did on the cross.

When Sean arrived at his home in the Yukon two years later, he was a new man. God healed the gaping hole in his soul, replacing it with a hope and a future. He began attending a small church on the Alaska Highway. There he came to know the love of God not only in his life but also in the lives of others like him. God's promise was true. He was beginning a new life, an abundant life through the sacrifice of Jesus Christ for his sins.

* * *

Reina, along with a couple of others, were taking a counselling course from Pastor Ray. He knew that Reina could be good for Sean and was hopeful that they would hit it off, and, they did. Sean accepted Reina's invitation to enroll in one of her Spanish courses over the winter. She forbid her students to speak English in class causing Sean no end of frustration but his high school French and Reina's personal attention mitigated his language learning disability. The one-hour drive each way in the dead of winter three times a week was worth it. Reina always made him supper at her place and she was happy to have Jesse as a guest and student.

Reina quit full-time nursing after a few years. She filled in for other nurses when she was available as the need arose. Her work as a counsellor through the church kept her busy and every year she taught Spanish at the local college.

Last spring she flew into Sean's fishing lodge to attend to a man having heart problems. Sean's plane was down so he called his friend Arnie on the HF radio and got him to contact Reina and see if she could help. Arnie flew her in and she nursed the stricken angler back to health. He survived and Sean shipped his mounted trophy Grayling to his home in Florida. Reina got a mess of fresh grayling for her service but she had to do the cooking.

They began seeing each other more often. Reina was like a fresh breeze. She lifted Sean out of his loneliness and back to the person he used to be and the life he enjoyed. Others could see the love they had for one another but they could also see that Sean was a little slow on the uptake. Deep down he loved her but something hindered his expression of that love.

Chapter 9

"Hello Anya and Jesse!" Sean called loudly as he walked toward the cabin not wanting to surprise Anya. Anya was still jumpy and he didn't want to startle her and possibly get another beating with her stick, besides it was a northern courtesy.

The door opened and Jesse launched toward his master. Anya stood in the doorway looking like a cross between a runway model and lumberjack or, more accurately, a scarecrow. Sean's face broke into a broad smile at the sight. His shirt hung on her meagre frame in the same way it did on the wire coat hanger. She had used one of Sean's bandanas as a belt to hold up her jeans and tucked the bottoms into the heavy wool socks that almost reached her knees. Her outfit could have accommodated two Anyas but he was hopeful that his cooking would begin to put some meat on her bones.

"Well aren't you the prettiest lumberjack I've ever seen," he said acknowledging the almost universal feminine sensitivity to personal appearance.

She recoiled from his remark, a scowl on her face then she flushed red and a faint smile emerged. "What is lumberjack?" she said with a quizzical look on her face.

"I guess they don't have them where you come from," he said, prying just a little, "come on in and I'll show you." Sean ushered her back into the cabin.

He dug out a volume of his fifties-vintage Book of Knowledge and showed Anya photographs of men falling trees in the forests of Canada during the first part of the century.

"Oh, *drawl*," she said with a strong accent.

"What language is that Anya?" asked Sean.

"It is Polski, Polish," she said.

"Are you from Poland Anya?" Sean was careful how he asked.

"Yes," came the curt reply signalling that further questioning was not welcome.

He felt like he was living with two different personalities; one he was getting to know, the other appeared and disappeared like a wolf in the forest.

"Let's have some soup for lunch, and then I have to go back out and cut more wood."

Sean warmed the pot of homemade hambone and bean soup on the cook stove while Anya thumbed through the pages of the book. He put some buns in the warming oven then joined Anya at the table.

"Those are loons." He noticed her looking at the pictures of the great northern water bird with the haunting call. "Have you ever seen or heard a loon Anya?" She shook her head.

"Well maybe one day I can show you one. They are quite beautiful and their call is just wonderful to hear on a quiet summer night. You know they carry their little ones on their back when they swim to protect them from predators." Sean loved talking about the creatures that inhabited the Yukon wilderness.

Anya looked up from the book and stared into Sean's eyes. He took a step back ready to deflect whatever was coming next. Instead, he watched her eyes fill with tears but not so much that they spilled. These tears were different, not like the ones that followed her raging outbursts. He could see that this girl was full of tears, some that she either couldn't or wouldn't let fall.

* * *

A year ago, on the other side of the globe, a lonely soul awaited her freedom. Tomorrow she would be free to live a different life, a life as an adult in the real world. She delighted in those rare occasions when the matrons escorted the girls on brief tours of the world outside the walls. The experience overwhelmed her senses. With little context for interpretation, they left her confused like Alice in Wonderland. Even so, she revelled in the new sensations, and, through her love of books, context began to bloom.

Since she was two years old, the matrons tended to most of her physical needs. The rest of her languished in a lonely place where she ached for something she didn't know and couldn't understand. Vague memories and the books she read teased her with images conjured from her impoverished imagination. Words on a page hinted at something wonderful but even a dictionary proved futile in her search for understanding and relief from the ache.

Tomorrow they would give her some money and directions to the offices of the Ministry of Labour and Social Protection where she would get a job and help in finding a place to live. She was excited about embarking on a new life while, at the same time, anxious about finding her place in this foreign world.

Anya lay awake trying to imagine what it would be like to get up when she wanted and go to bed when she felt like it. What would she eat? Her heart raced. Sometimes the matrons would make her help in the kitchen but only with simple, mundane tasks. Now she would have to learn to cook and to buy her food at a store. Was she ready to meet the challenges that awaited her? She thought of her friend Kazia. The thought soothed her. Kazia would be with her and together they would get along.

Until now, her physical world was small, constrained by tall stone walls and cold bureaucracy. For 14 years she knew little change in her world. That morning she rose early as she did every morning when the dorm matron rang the harsh clanging bell. She slipped out of her nightgown and into the grey, bibbed dress that all the girls wore every day for a week. A clean dress, underwear and a nightgown appeared on their beds every Sunday morning. She and Kazia stood together in the line, jubilant, whispering about their imminent freedom. They picked up their bowls of watery soup and a piece of crusty bread and retreated to the table in the corner where they always ate together. After breakfast, they filed into the classroom where they spent most of the day. The bell signalled the end of classes and the two girls parted to attend to their assigned chores. This week Anya used a treadle sewing machine to stitch patches on already worn out linens. Kazia dug potatoes in the garden.

Tonight's supper was special. It was a celebration of the 'graduation' of the five girls who were about to leave for the outside world. The server ladled a thick red meat sauce over Anya's plate of sticky pasta. She picked up a bun on her way to join Kazia at their table. The meal was tastier than usual and Anya returned for a second helping.

After supper, the two girls squeezed hands and departed to their respective dorms. Anya looked forward to early evening play times and her quiet time before bed when she read her books. But, tonight was different. She left her book on the nightstand and whistled softly. Tonight was a time to say goodbye to old friends.

The patter of little feet announced the arrival of her rat friends that shared her cubicle. The two rats sat on the shelf above her pillow and took turns nibbling on the morsels of bread that she held in her fingers. Their ears twitched and twisted towards her voice as she told them of her dreams of living in the real world. She shared her anxious heart as one would do with a mother or father. After the bread was gone, she thanked them for being her friends and apologized for leaving them. When the lights flickered, the two animals scampered away leaving Anya alone. No one ever read a bedtime story to Anya. No one ever hugged her, or kissed her goodnight. The dorm went dark. She lay sobbing into her pillow. Tomorrow she would leave the familiar and only world she ever knew.

Chapter 10

He called out as he always did when he approached the cabin. Jesse and Anya met him at the door. Jesse got a pat on the head and Anya a smile.

"I made coffee!" she offered as they sat at the table. Sean detected a measure of pride in her announcement.

He watched her retrieve the coffee pot and pour the steaming, dark liquid into his favourite mug before joining him at the table. Jesse curled up on his rug. She was gaining weight and her golden hair almost glowed in its new lustre. The cut on her face was healing and the bruising on her neck and face had disappeared. Most times she was quiet and gentle, speaking little, staring out the window, sometimes crying for no apparent reason. On other occasions, without warning, she would turn on him like a panther, screaming while beating him with her stick or fists before collapsing onto the floor in tears. Later, she might apologize but sometimes she acted as if nothing happened.

He noticed that her crying spells were less frequent. She would engage in conversation but she guarded her words and simply ignored some questions Sean posed. Her stick spent most of its time leaning against the wall by the bathroom, accessible, but for the most part, inert. He was pleased with what he saw but still concerned over what he couldn't see.

"I was thinking," she said, "maybe I could get out of the house tomorrow and get some fresh air. Maybe I could be a lumberjack."

Sean faced her and chuckled at her suggestion.

"Okay," he said, "tomorrow you can come with me if you're feeling up to it. I'd like to see a little colour in your face and some fresh air would do you good." Anya's pale face stretched in a broad smile and she did a little bounce on her chair. "I won't be a bother, I promise," she cooed.

Anya's smile always buoyed Sean's spirit, but he knew enough about emotional trauma to stay alert. "You won't be a bother Anya as long as you feel strong enough; I'll enjoy your company." Sean grimaced at his first taste of her coffee.

Anya sat at the table opposite Sean watching him. She was grateful that Sean had taken her in but she couldn't understand why he let her stay. His behaviour confused her much as her own did. Why did he put up with her? Maybe he would beat her if she continued to misbehave. Maybe he would kick her out, abandon her. No, he was different, she felt safe with him; he always forgave her and treated her nicely; could she trust him? She still wasn't certain.

She knew he liked his coffee. Perhaps brewing a pot of coffee might somehow atone for her bad behaviour. She wanted to express her thankfulness for the safe haven Sean had provided. She didn't want to be a burden to him; she wanted to help where she could.

"Is it okay?" She had noticed his reaction to the brew. He tried to hide it.

Sean looked up from his mug. His eyes locked on hers. "Have you ever used one of these Anya?" he asked pointing to the coffee pot simmering on the cook stove.

"Well no, but I thought I would try," she replied looking at the floor.

"Anya, look at me," he ordered, "that's great, that's a spirit I appreciate. You keep trying and thank you for thinking of me." Sean's stern countenance morphed into a reassuring tender smile as he looked into her eyes.

Anya smiled back as she squirmed in her chair.

"Do you like to bake Anya?"

"I don't know. I've never baked anything."

Sean rose from his chair and went to the counter where he withdrew a card from a recipe box. He handed it to Anya and sat down. "It's completely up to you but if you want to try baking some cookies that is a recipe that will tell you how." He hoped she would take the challenge. Taking charge of a task and completing it would help her feel more in control of her circumstances. Besides, his cookie supply was running low.

Anya stared at the card. "I don't understand." She turned the card so Sean could see it from across the table and pointed at it.

"Oh, I see. Those are abbreviations for quantities." He explained the meaning of cups and teaspoons showing her the tools she would need to make the cookie dough.

"I will try," she announced.

"Good for you Anya, I'll be back this afternoon for a cookie." He got up and left.

* * *

The weather had turned cold but the sun was still strong, perfect for cutting firewood. Sean liked to work in his shirtsleeves, the exertion kept him warm. The girl from the forest continued to dominate his thoughts as he felled standing dead trees. He bucked them into stove lengths but decided to leave some of them for tomorrow when Anya would help him.

Despite her intellectual prowess, Sean saw a naivety in Anya. She seemed well read but limited in life experience. She was 17 years old, but in many ways, she acted like a younger girl but with a strong and determined spirit. The coffee episode spoke volumes to Sean.

Sean was helpless to attend to Anya's hurts. He knew that Anya needed a woman to confide in; Reina needed to meet this girl. He knew Reina would know what to do. First, he had to convince Anya to come to town with him where medical resources would be available. He was working on her but she remained resistant.

He threw the last log onto the pile in the back of his truck and climbed into the cab. The truck rolled and lurched along the old trail towards his cabin where he backed up to the woodpile. He stacked his morning's labour alongside the nine cords piled in his wood yard. *"Almost done; get a caribou and old man winter can do his worst,"* he thought.

* * *

"Anya, Jesse!" he shouted as he walked up the path to the cabin beginning to feel the cold through his sweat-soaked shirt. The door opened and Jesse burst through to greet his master. Anya stood in the doorway smiling; Sean smiled back.

"I have cookies Sean!" She clapped her hands together. "Come and see."

An image of his daughter flashed in his mind then faded. He felt a wave of warmth flood his body; his heart smiled along with his face.

Chapter 11

The morning dawned bright with a heavy mist on the lake and frost on the ground. The cook stove freely gave up its warmth to the kitchen where they sat at the table watching the sun warm the scene outside the bay window. "I am happy today Sean," said Anya as she finished her porridge.

"And why is that Anya?" said Sean.

"Today I get to be a lumberjack!" she trilled.

"Well let's start slow, maybe you can be a lumberjack *helper*." Sean tried to sound encouraging.

* * *

It had been over a week since this mysterious orphan entered his life. Sean glowed when she said that she was happy; a girl her age should be happy. Her physical and emotional state seemed to be improving. Sometimes, like today, she acted like nothing had happened to her. The rages and bouts of depression had grown less frequent. Sean had called Pastor Ray asking him to check missing person's reports; there were none. He still didn't know much more about her than when he first found her on the side of the road. Did she belong to anyone? Did she have a family? Why is she so fearful? All he knew was that she was an abused 17 year old from Poland. His heart broke on those nights when he would hear her sobbing in the darkness.

Today was special and it was good to see Anya so excited. She appeared to be physically healthy except for bouts of phantom pain. She had gained weight since she arrived losing the 'scarecrow' image she once presented. Her face was now full, almost radiant, especially when she smiled, which was much more often now. She hadn't had a night terror for two days and she hadn't beat him with her stick for several days.

Tomorrow he would ask her to accompany him to town. He'd mention it in passing to get her thinking. She seemed much more at ease since she had been at his cabin but whenever he mentioned a trip to town, it seemed to resurrect hidden fears.

His motives centered on her welfare. He wanted Anya to meet Reina. He thought that maybe the presence of a woman in her life would calm her and encourage her to be more forthcoming. He also hoped that Reina could get Anya to consent to a physical exam. She wouldn't acknowledge her hurt and Sean was helpless to find and treat the source of the pain. Reina could help her find needed clothes and personal items and he wanted to locate her family if she had one.

* * *

The changing colour of the leaves in September heralded the arrival of fall in the Yukon. Nights grew colder; during the day the air was often crisp with frost on the ground in the mornings. The sun seemed to burn brighter as the season advanced as if trying to forestall the season that would turn the land into a frozen prison.

The truck and its three lumberjacks bounced along the old wood cutting roads first made back in the 30's when the area was logged with horses. Although still low in the sky, the sun beamed through the windshield warming the occupants in the cab of the truck. Jesse sat in the middle of the seat alert for grouse often seen along the way. Anya rested her hand on his neck.

"Here we are," Sean announced as he pulled the truck into a clearing and turned off the ignition. "Now I want you to stay alert when I fall a tree, most of the time they go where I want them but, stuff happens, and you don't want to be in the way if it does. I'll let you know when I'm ready to fall one – I'll shout 'timberrrrrr'. If you want to sit or go for a walk with Jesse, he doesn't like the saw, you go right ahead but don't stray too far. I'll call you when it's time to load up the truck."

Anya nodded her understanding. She and Jesse strolled a little way down the road where they sat to watch Sean drop the standing dead spruce tree he had his eye on. The saw roared to life then fell back to a staccato idle as Sean walked to the base of the tree. He surveyed the tree from different angles deciding that he could drop it close to the truck. He made his undercut then looked to see where Anya and Jesse were sitting watching. After making his back cut, he shouted, "timberrrrrrrrr". The tree made a loud cracking sound and began to lean in the direction of the truck. Sean gave a push with his free hand and the tree crashed to the ground breaking off all the limbs on one side. Anya clapped, Jesse barked and Sean took a bow.

After limbing and bucking the tree into 16-inch stove lengths, they loaded the pieces into the truck box and went in search of another one. Both Sean and Anya worked up a sweat. Anya, hair hanging over her now ruddy face, looked tired but healthy. She winced as she climbed into the truck. Sean reached across to open the glove compartment and rummaged through the contents until he found an elastic hair 'thingee'. He handed it to Anya who noticed an unusual reverence in his action. "Here, this will keep your hair out of your face." The tone of his voice was abrupt as he returned to guiding the truck down the trail.

By noon, they had filled the truck box with rounds of firewood. "Let's take a break and go have some of that good soup and a cookie," Sean announced. Jesse's ears perked at the mention of 'cookie' and he barked his approval. Anya smiled and nodded her head with enthusiasm at his suggestion.

At the end of their day, Anya placed the last log on the huge pile beside the cabin; the firewood-gathering season was officially over and it was suppertime. "Let me get a picture of you and Jesse beside this pile of work". Anya and Jesse sat side by side on a corner of the woodpile. "Smile," Sean ordered. Jesse's ears perked up. "Now, one more with all of us." He mounted the camera on the tripod, set the shutter timer and ran to stand beside the other lumberjacks. Anya's smile lit up her face displaying her perfect teeth.

Tears welled as he struggled to contain the joy he felt knowing that she had a good day.

After a supper of baked salmon, wild rice and asparagus, the three lumberjacks lounged in the kitchen. The John Denver song ended and the tape machine clicked off. Jesse licked out their empty bowls of rice pudding while they listened to the fire crackle in the stove, their aching muscles soothed by its radiant warmth. The night was clear and a full moon rose over the Coast Mountains reflecting off Pancake Lake.

"It will be cold tonight." Sean pointed to the moon. Weather forecasting was natural for those who lived close to the land. Their lives assumed the rhythm of the seasons assimilating the cues that foretold the future of land, sky and water. Should they choose to ignore the signs they did so at the risk of personal peril.

"Did you enjoy your day Anya?" Sean looked over at the weary girl in the ponytail stretched out in the armchair.

"Oh yes. You live in a nice place. I was glad to help you after all you've done for me. I am tired though."

"And so you should be. This was your first busy day after your time of rest. You look much healthier Anya and it was good to see you enjoying the work. Thanks for your help."

"I will sleep well tonight." He could hear hope in her voice.

"So Anya, you've had some time to think about it; are you coming with me tomorrow?" Sean pretended disinterest so as not to arouse fear in Anya. It seemed to work.

"We will go to your friend's house?" she asked.

"Yes, Anya. You don't have to go anywhere you don't want to and Jesse will go with us. Reina is a wonderful lady. I guarantee you'll love her. She's a great cook and her house has a shower!"

Anya came to attention. "I would really like *that*."

"Then you'll go?" Sean looked for a commitment.

"Yes, I will go."

"Wonderful. We'll pick up some clothes and things for you while we're there. We'll leave right after breakfast."

Anya sat silently, her head down, as if thinking. She lifted her head and looked at him. He saw that the joy in her countenance was replaced with narrow, questioning eyes and tight lips. "Why are you doing this?" Her voice was curt, demanding.

"Doing what, taking you to town?"

"No, why do you treat me the way you do?"

"Why would I *not* do this?" Sean replied as his eyes challenged hers.

"You don't know me Sean. You don't know what you've let in your house."

Chapter 12

He stared at the mystery sitting across from him, pondering her remark.

"I think I know enough Anya." His voice was reassuring, welcoming. She felt the pleasure in his response as if he didn't care *what* she was. "You, my dear, are fearfully and wonderfully made by the hand of God, how could I not care for you?" He paused giving her time to ponder his remark while watching her countenance change. "Anya, are you familiar with the Holy Bible?"

"Yes," she said, looking down at hands busily trying to distract her from the question. "Tonight, when you go to bed, take a few minutes and read Psalm 139. God wants to talk to you Anya. The Bible is His love letter to you. You can't *make* people love you Anya, but you can *let* them love you."

Later, Sean lay in the darkness of his bedroom listening to Anya turning pages in the Bible. He heard her reading quietly, repeating a passage as if trying to understand. He prayed for her.

The words Anya read seemed to embrace her soul. They comforted her as no words had ever done. She felt God's love for her and knew a peace as she had never known. She slept.

* * *

It was still dark when Sean and Jesse stepped onto the cold cabin floor. Sean was excited that Anya was coming to town with him. He was confident that their visit with Reina would yield a breakthrough of some sort; he just didn't know what it would be. After breakfast they climbed into the truck and started for town. Jesse lay on the seat resting against Anya's leg.

"What is this river?" She sat bolt upright, eyes wide as they approached the bridge crossing the river.

When Anya was nervous, she fidgeted and withdrew into herself like a coiled spring held in place by something unseen. The smallest event could trigger a paroxysm of terror or an outburst of spitting venom.

"It's called the Teslin River." Sean glanced at her with a puzzled look on his face. "Do you know this river Anya?"

"No!" Her eyes betrayed the lie. Sean watched as she searched the landscape like a mouse would do before venturing from its nest. She was looking for something or someone. She began to cry and moan as if in pain curling into the fetal position against the door of the truck.

Sean pulled the truck off the road and shut off the engine. He watched and listened to her sobbing, angry that he could do nothing to take away whatever pain she was feeling. He prayed quietly as the minutes passed. Soon she composed herself and sat upright. He handed her his bandana to wipe the tears from her face and tried to smile a consoling smile. He wanted to reach out and hug her but he knew better.

"You have a great day ahead of you Anya. Reina and I will be with you. We want you to enjoy yourself, have some fun." Sean tried to distract her, take the pressure off the spring, but to no avail.

Jesse lay with his head on Anya's lap. Her hand rested on his neck. When she stroked the dog's head Sean watched the tension leave her neck and shoulders. Soon they turned onto the south access entering the city of Whitehorse. They drove along the Yukon River at the base of the clay escarpment turning right en route to Reina's house in Riverdale. Jesse sat up to look out the window and barked in recognition of his second home. He jumped out when Sean opened his door and ran to greet Reina standing in the doorway. Sean walked around to open the door for Anya as Reina rubbed Jesse's ears in welcome. "Such a gentleman," Reina commented on the move with a hint of sarcasm.

"Reina, I present my new friend, Anya. Anya, this is Reina, the goddess I spend all my time talking about."

Reina rolled her eyes before reaching out to hug Anya. "I am so glad to meet you Anya, come on in, all of you." She gave Sean a questioning glance as she guided Anya through the door with her arm around her tiny waist.

Jesse went immediately to his bowl of water on the kitchen floor. After satisfying his thirst he left for the back yard through the special 'dog door'. Reina ushered Anya to a chair at the kitchen table while Sean grabbed the coffee pot off the stove and set it on the cast iron trivet in the middle of the table.

"Could I use your bathroom Reina?" Anya asked with desperate shyness.

"You sure can, let me show you." Reina led Anya down the hall to the bathroom.

"What's going on?" she whispered forcefully upon returning to the kitchen.

"I found her," he whispered back. She's been with me for a couple of weeks."

"You *found* her?" Reina was incredulous. "Where? Under a tree?"

"I'll tell you later. I don't know what's going on but she needs help Reina. She's scared spitless, been abused, physically, mentally and maybe sexually. Her body is hurting and I think she should have a physical exam. Her emotions are fragile and she needs to be able to trust us; she needs lots of loving care. She's wound tighter than a drum when she's in a strange place. At the cabin she's much more relaxed with me and Jesse."

Sean heard the bathroom door open. In a voice louder than normal, he asked Reina, "What's for lunch, I could eat a bear." Anya joined them at the table.

"Do you like enchiladas Anya?" Reina asked in a friendly tone ignoring Sean.

"I don't know what it is," she replied in a timid voice.

"Well, you can smell them cooking. They have chicken and tomatoes, garlic, salsa, onions and cream all wrapped in a tortilla. You try it and if you don't like it you don't have to eat it, we'll get you something else."

"Thank you Reina."

"Let's have coffee and you and I get acquainted. I already know that guy." Reina waved her hand towards Sean.

Sean sat without speaking watching Reina perform her magic then excused himself to throw the ball for Jesse in the back yard. By lunchtime, Reina and Anya were talking as if they knew each other.

Chapter 13

Reina leaned out the back door and announced lunch was ready. Sean and Jesse re-joined the girls in the kitchen.

"After lunch I'm going to get Anya some clothes and stuff but she wants to stay here with you," Reina declared. "I think Anya should spend the night with me."

"Yes ma'am, I think that can be arranged," Sean replied, "are you okay with that Anya?"

"Yes, you are a nice lady Reina." Anya smiled.

"You tell *him* that!" Reina nodded her head at Sean.

Anya looked puzzled at her remark. "Will Sean stay with us?" She looked to Reina then Sean.

"No, I have another place I stay, but I won't be far away and Reina will make sure you are safe. Try not to worry Anya, you are in good hands."

"Does Reina have a gun like you?"

Sean and Reina looked at one another.

Reina put her hand on Anya's shoulder. "Yes I do Anya. Why don't we have lunch?"

After lunch, Reina measured Anya in all the correct places while questioning her about colours, styles and brands of clothes, not that Whitehorse offered much of a selection. Anya looked puzzled as if Reina was speaking a foreign language.

"I'll be back in a couple of hours. You go ahead and have that shower. I'll leave you a robe and fresh towels. Help yourself to my shampoo and stuff. We'll have another talk when I get back."

Anya stood watching the beautiful Latin lady that had welcomed her into her home. Deep within she felt the desire to embrace the lady and to feel Reina's arms around her. "Thank you Reina, you are good to me." Anya's voice trembled with emotion. It was becoming increasingly evident that the young girl had not experienced much human affection and kindness in her life. She always accepted her lot as if it was normal and what she deserved. The behaviour of these two people challenged her view of herself. She was confused. After she had read the Bible passage Sean showed her, she began to wonder about who she was, especially in God's eyes.

"See you in a bit," Reina replied as she hurried out the door.

Anya headed for the bathroom.

Sean decided to use the quiet-time to work on his pistol, a CZ 75B. He wanted to smooth out the trigger and he thought he should do it while in town in case he screwed it up. If he did he could call on his gunsmith friend, Ted, to fix whatever damage he might do.

He spread an old white terry towel on top of newspapers on the kitchen table. Retrieving his Czechoslovakian-made 9mm pistol from his bag, he fieldstripped it on the towel. The trigger assembly came out in one piece and he took care not to lose any of the tiny springs and pins when he removed the sear. After about half an hour of rubbing on 400-grit sandpaper and repeated inspection of his work, he was satisfied with the slightly reshaped and polished surface on the sear. Next, he removed the hammer assembly and polished a couple of surfaces with a diamond hone. After reassembling the hammer and trigger, he said a short prayer and pulled the trigger. "Wow!" he exclaimed, "much better in both single and double action." He couldn't wait to try it with live ammo.

Sean prided himself in his shooting ability and the quality of his firearms. He was a natural when it came to shooting but strived to maintain his skill by spending many hours and many rounds practicing with rifle and pistol. Pistol shooting challenged his inherent skill but thanks to constant practice, he consistently led the pack of fellow shooters. Tactical skills were his latest challenge. While in Israel he trained with some IDF reserve soldiers, a privilege he would never forget. He and Reina joined the tactical handgun league in Whitehorse and both grew proficient in shooting in real-life scenarios. His CZ was his favourite pistol but Reina preferred her Sig Sauer 226.

The sound of the garage door opening signalled Reina's return. Sean helped her unload the bags and boxes from her Jeep and put them in the living room. Dropping the last of the boxes, he walked into the kitchen to see Reina glaring at the oil-stained towel on the table. "What's this?" She turned to scold him but he was ready for her. "I put down newspapers, it's my towel and I'll clean it up right now."

"You better mister," she ordered as Anya came into the kitchen wrapped in a bathrobe.

She walked towards Sean but stopped when she saw the pistol on the table.

Sean saw the fear in her eyes. "Nobody is going to hurt you Anya, I'm putting it away." Reina looked on in astonishment.

Anya suddenly relaxed and approached the table. She stood looking at the black pistol lying on the towel, inhaling the scent of gun oil.

"Can I hold it?" A confident and determined look was in her eyes as they locked with Sean's. The fear in her eyes had disappeared. She continued to look purposely at Sean waiting for his answer.

"Ah, sure," he stammered, "do you know anything about guns?"

"No, but I want to." Her voice hinted at an underlying, hidden sentiment. Sean handed her the empty gun with the slide locked back. She held it briefly and gave it back to Sean.

"Are you okay Anya?"

"Yes. Bad men hurt people with those," she declared.

Chapter 14

It was like Christmas as they gathered in the living room. Anya stared at the bags and boxes then turned to Sean as if seeking an explanation. He nodded and smiled signalling his approval for her to begin opening the packages. Sean and Reina sat beside each other on the couch delighting in Anya's response as she opened each item. Sometimes she let out little squeals of delight over what she found inside a box or bag holding the garment up and showing it off. The black bra came out by mistake when she pulled the blouse out of a bag. She quickly stuffed it back in and pretended no one saw it.

"I got you some bush clothes and winter boots too in case you decide to hang around this bushman for a while. Winter's coming and you will definitely need one of these." Reina pushed a large box towards Anya.

Inside was a red bomber-style parka. It had a coyote fur-trimmed hood, goose down insulation and a cotton/polyester outer shell. Anya put it on and stood revelling in its luxurious warmth. Sean stood and pulled the hood over her head tightening the drawstrings and leaving her face framed in the fur trim.

Anya stared at him then fell to her knees crying. Sean stepped back, looked at Reina and raised his hands in a gesture questioning what he'd done to provoke such a reaction. Reina wrapped her arms around Anya and, looking at Sean, mouthed, "It's okay, not you."

Reina stayed kneeling on the floor comforting the sobbing Anya. She looked at Sean and in a quiet voice said, "Why don't you take this stuff into the guest room and go get us a pizza for supper."

He saw the wisdom in her suggestion. Sean gathered up the items scattered about the room and removed them to the guest bedroom. He and Jesse left the two women embracing one another on the floor.

Jesse and Sean returned a few hours later with a hot pizza and a big bottle of Pepsi. He had stopped for coffee then visited T&Ds General Store to browse the gun rack and pick up some more ammunition for his pistol.

Reina had set the oven at 150° F so he put the pizza along with some plates in to stay warm. Reina came into the kitchen from the guest bedroom.

"She's fine – well, mostly. It wasn't you. Well I suppose it was in a way. Anya is overwhelmed, confused and grateful for your caring for her. I don't think anyone has cared for her in a long time, if ever. You are a good man Sean and I thank God it was *you* who found her, but that girl is in rough shape. She agreed to let me examine her. I took a vial of blood that I'm running over to Carol at the lab to process right away. I'll be right back. She's got a surprise for you so make sure you're surprised!" Reina threw on her coat and rushed out the door.

Sean sat at the table sipping a glass of Pepsi. He heard the bedroom door open and turned to see Anya standing in the hallway.

"Wow!" Sean sat back in his chair staring in shock and awe. "What happened to that lumberjack I used to know?" No longer was she wearing his clothes. Now she wore real girl clothes.

She blushed, feeling awkward in the new clothes. Anya was dressed in designer jeans secured with a black, rhinestone-studded belt. She wore a Spanish-styled, high neck blouse under a black embroidered bolero jacket. Her long blonde hair shimmered as it fell over one shoulder as if it didn't care. She smiled as she walked across the room and stood at the table in front of Sean. "I have never had such nice clothes. Thank you for caring for me."

Sean smiled back. "You are worthy of care dear girl. You look very nice in your new clothes Anya. I think there was a bit of truth in what you said about me not knowing what I allowed in my house. You look like a model." Sean gushed over what Reina had done for Anya.

Reina returned in time to see the awed expression still on Sean's face as he was talking with Anya.

"Cleans up pretty good doesn't she?" Reina put her arm around Anya's shoulders.

"And you're quite the cleaning lady my dear!" Sean's eyes showed his appreciation as they met Reina's eyes. "Thank you Reina for doing this for Anya, you are a sweetheart." Anya wrapped her arms around Reina's waist and hugged her.

"Can I get a picture of you two?" Sean asked as he slipped the camera out of his shirt pocket.

The two girls posed as if they were models in a photo shoot as Sean snapped pictures.

Chapter 15

"So how did she get to be here in the Yukon?" Sean asked.

"I don't know, she clams up when I ask, but I don't think she's here legally," replied Reina. "Her past life explains her responsiveness to your care for her Sean; she grew up in an orphanage. I don't think she has ever experienced any love in her life and certainly no close family life, so her time with you has left her confused. She has never known a father and the women in the orphanage were not what you'd call 'motherly'. She is fearful of men, another story I'm sure, which accounts for her struggling with trusting you. I was pleased to see her acknowledge and express appreciation for your care for her; that is a huge step. It tells me that she trusts you more than you know. She has grown comfortable with you but she has difficulty making sense of your behaviour, how you treat her and me. I doubt she has ever witnessed a husband/wife or father/daughter relationship and has no idea how men and women should properly relate to each other. It's important that we are steady in our relationship with each other and her and alert to her needs."

They sat at the kitchen table talking quietly over coffee. Anya was still asleep in the guest room so they were careful not to wake her. They both noted the progress they saw in Anya's demeanour during her short time with Reina. She had shared some things with Reina, which she refused to talk about with Sean. Still, she agreed at Reina's urging, to allow Reina to share with Sean. They were both pleased at Anya's response to her new clothes but it spoke loudly about her past. Her enthusiastic engagement in the board game they played after supper surprised Sean. She interacted with them as a young girl would with her parents. It felt good to see her relaxing and trusting more.

Reina discovered that Anya had no family. She grew up and went to school in a state orphanage in Gdansk, Poland. The ZOMO, a communist secret police organization, killed her parents during the period in the eighties when uprisings against communist rule were common. She was two at the time. No living relatives could be found and, if they existed, they didn't find her. Instead, according to the orphanage records, a woman named Irena, perhaps a friend or neighbour, left her at the orphanage. She lived the only life she has known, until recently, within the walls of that orphanage. On a child's sixteenth birthday, the orphanage releases them to fend for themselves. Anya, worked for an American tourist company in Gdansk and over the year that she was there she improved her English. She tried to immigrate to America but she was too young and couldn't meet the other conditions necessary.

"There's more," Reina went on. "I examined Anya, with her reluctant permission. There is evidence of beating in the recent past with a stick or perhaps a whip of some kind. She has marks on her back and legs from the beatings and the red welts from recent abuse are still evident. Her ribs are bruised but not broken and her breasts show signs of trauma probably from some kind of tool, maybe a pair of pliers. I took pictures in case we need them in the future. She wouldn't tell me anything about what happened to her, who did it or why. She is not only traumatized but also suffering from considerable shame. She can't understand why we would embrace her the way we do; she has a poor self image and believes she is unworthy of our attention."

Sean's hands formed fists supporting his head as he leaned forward staring at the tabletop. "She was hiding from whoever it is that beat her." He now understood her behaviour when they first met on the side of the road. "I found her at 42 mile on the Pike Lake road. She ran across the road and hid in the forest but I managed to coax her out. She was scared Reina, scared really bad. I never saw anybody on the road that day but you know that isn't unusual out there."

"Should we call the police?" Reina asked full of concern.

"No, not yet. They'll treat her first as an illegal immigrant, lock her up and deport her, then they might, I say *might*, try to find her abuser or abusers. No, let me see what I can find out." Reina could see the cogs turning in Sean's brain.

The phone rang. Reina picked it up before it could ring again. "Okay, thanks Carol, I'll be right over." She hung up the phone. "That was Carol from the lab. The results from the blood sample are ready for pickup. I'll be right back." Reina put on her jacket and left.

It was over half an hour before she returned. "I stopped to pick up some antibiotics," she confided. "She's going to need them."

"Why, has she got some kind of infection?" queried Sean.

"You were right, she's been sexually abused and she has a venereal disease. The antibiotics will clear it up but I don't want you to mention this to her, she probably has no idea that she's infected and we should leave it that way." Reina enunciated carefully so there would be no misunderstanding.

"Damn!" Sean scowled and turned away from Reina. "If I find that SOB . . ."

Chapter 16

Reina put her arms around Sean from behind. "I understand how you're feeling." She could feel his body shaking with rage. "You see her as you would see your own daughter if she were alive today and you can't bear to see her hurt."

He turned in her embrace and embraced her back. "Thank you Reina. You are special to me; I can talk to you, you listen and you always understand. You are a woman of wisdom and you have a wonderful heart. I so appreciate what you are doing for Anya - and, me."

Anya stood at the door to the kitchen watching her caretakers embrace one another.

Sean released Reina. "Good morning glamour puss! How'd you sleep Anya?" Sean's greeting expressed his genuine happiness in seeing her looking bright and healthy.

"Glamour puss?" Anya repeated with a puzzled look.

"He just means you're looking good this morning. You must have slept well?" said Reina.

"Oh, yes. The bed is so cozy and warm and your house is peaceful like Sean's."

Reina hugged the young girl. "I'm so glad you had a good rest Anya."

Anya hugged her back. "I like it when you hug me Reina," she whispered, "Is that okay?"

Tears welled in Reina's eyes. "Yes Anya, that is okay. I like hugs too." She kissed Anya on her cheek. "I'll start breakfast. Why don't you try on some more of your new clothes and surprise us." Reina smiled.

Anya smiled and retreated to the guest room while Sean and Reina prepared breakfast. Reina put on a fresh pot of coffee and began preparing her famous home fried potatoes. Sean set out cloth napkins and place mats hand quilted by Reina. He arranged the silverware and filled each crystal goblet with real orange juice; he, like Reina, hated the phony stuff. He retrieved the jar of Robertson's Special Edition marmalade that Reina was careful to keep in her pantry for when Sean came by. He also put out a small crystal dish of wild raspberry jam that he and Reina had made from berries they picked earlier in the fall.

"Don't forget the salt and pepper," said Reina as she handed him her Mexican mementos. Shaped in the image of characters from a Mariachi band he placed them on the table knowing how important they were to her. "Sean, will you butter the toast while I finish the eggs," Reina asked.

"I'm on it," he replied as Anya walked into the room.

She looked so much healthier in decent clothes that fit her. The tattered pink sneakers were gone, replaced by a pretty pair of white loafers. The long-sleeved white blouse tucked into her blue jeans accented her slim figure along with the brown leather belt with engraved silver buckle circling her tiny waist. A string of blue beads hung around her neck and another on her wrist enhancing her glacier-blue eyes.

"Lovely Anya, you look just lovely in that outfit," Reina remarked while Anya blushed. "Have a seat, breakfast is ready." Reina dished out the bacon, home fried potatoes and scrambled eggs with cheese onto the warm plates. Sean served the plate of buttered toast.

Sean and Reina exchanged pleased looks as Anya engaged in the conversation over breakfast. As long as the subject didn't close in on her personal life she seemed relaxed and comfortable. After breakfast, they took turns over their coffee volunteering ideas to fill their day.

"Can I stay another night," Anya asked Sean. "Reina wants to show me how to sew quilts."

Winter was on his mind and a weather change was imminent. Sean wanted to get his meat in before the weather got much colder and the snow began to fall. He looked at Reina who shrugged her shoulders signalling agreement with anything he decided.

"Tell you what, I've gotta go and get that caribou so why don't you stay here with Reina until I get back. I shouldn't be gone for more than three or four days. What do you think Reina?" Sean offered.

"Would that be okay with you Reina?" Anya asked with a humble tone in her voice.

"Anya, I would love that. I enjoy your company. Besides, then I won't have to help drag that smelly caribou off the mountain." She smiled at Anya with a sideways glance at Sean. Anya bounced excitedly in her chair smiling at Sean. "Tomorrow's Friday and I have to teach a class at two. You could come with me if you want Anya."

"Okay, that's settled. I'll leave after lunch, but, before I go, we need to have a talk little girl." His look and the serious tone of his voice startled Anya. Reina looked down at the napkin on her lap as the smile on Anya's face drained away. Sean tried to soften his words with a smile.

"Reina, Anya, let's go in the living room," Sean said as he rose from his chair.

Anya was visibly nervous, even fearful as she sat on the sofa beside Reina. Sean walked up and knelt in front of Anya extending his hands palms up. She reluctantly put her hands in his. His hands were rough but his voice was soft and kind and she didn't pull away. "Anya, I want you to know that I care for you very much and I will never intentionally hurt you. Reina told me you said it was okay for her to share with me what you told her about yourself. I'm so sorry for the loss of your parents and the life you endured in Poland. You have missed so much in your life and I know about your abuse and hurt." Anya looked down at her hands held gently by his. Reina had her arm around her shoulders.

"Anya, Reina and I serve a loving, caring God, our Father who is in heaven. Through His son Jesus, the Christ, He promised those who believe in Him a new life, an abundant life. He promised to redeem that which the enemy of our souls has stolen from us. Some years ago, I lost my wife and daughter in a car accident; the enemy stole them from me just as he stole your mother and father from you. After, like you, I lived a lonely life filled with a lot of pain." Sean looked at Reina seeking approval for his words. She nodded.

"I have a new life because I believe that God sent His son Jesus to die for my sins and fulfill His promise of an abundant life. He has given me a church family and Reina to help in my healing. Now, He has entrusted me with your life, for how long I don't know. God wants to heal you Anya and I believe He has chosen Reina and me to help do that." He paused to let his words hit their mark. Sean put his hand under Anya's chin and lifted her head to look into her eyes. They were once again full of tears that had yet to spill over.

"Anya," he continued, "Will you tell me how you got here and who hurt you?"

Anya sat pondering his question. After a few minutes she nodded her head. "Thank you for loving me, both of you. I feel safe now but I know they are looking for me. If they find me they will take me away again," she said with resignation.

"We won't let that happen Anya." Sean's voice was firm.

"The American woman, Dixie, at my place of work in Gdansk, she said she would take me and my friend Kazia to America. I was so happy because I had tried and it was impossible. I didn't have the correct papers and I was too young. I couldn't get a passport and nobody in the government would help me so I went with Dixie. She took me to the port in Gdansk where she introduced me to a man named Anthony who worked on a big ship. He was a bad man but I didn't know that, I trusted Dixie. She said that he would look after me until we arrived in New York." Anya's face began to disfigure in her distress.

"He never looked after me or took me to New York!" She began to cry. "He sold me like I was a loaf of bread to other men on the ship. They raped me!" Anya fell onto Reina's lap where she wept, yelping loudly like an animal in severe pain.

Sean knelt beside her, one arm around her convulsing body, raging in his helplessness. *"God help her!"* he cried out in silent prayer.

It was almost an hour before Anya began to regain her composure. Her tear soaked face and reddened eyes looked into Reina's face begging for acceptance. Reina took her face in her hands, kissed her gently on the forehead and told her how much she loved her. Anya hugged her neck, whispering, "Thank you, thank you Reina. I didn't mean to. I didn't want to. If I didn't they would beat me."

"It's not your fault Anya." Reina tried to reassure her. "Sean's going to get you a glass of water and I want you take some medicine that will help calm you."

Sean retrieved a bottle from the medicine cabinet. He filled a glass with water and grabbed a spoon from the silverware drawer. Reina poured a teaspoon of the liquid from the bottle. Anya swallowed the sweet, milky fluid washing it down with a mouthful of water.

"Do you want to tell us more Anya?" Reina asked.

Anya squirmed on the couch as she looked at her hands folded in her lap. She pushed her hair back over her shoulders, rubbed her eyes and replied, "Yes."

"After many days the ship stopped in a place called Churchill. There were other girls on the ship just like my friend, Kazia and me. They put all of us in a big steel box and gave us a blanket and a large bottle of water. We used buckets for a bathroom; no food. I could tell that we were on a train for one day but then they moved the box onto a truck. Sometimes the truck would stop and someone would pass a few stale buns through the door. I never saw people when the door opened, just trees or fields." She stopped and drank from the glass but avoided eye contact with Sean and Reina.

"I think we travelled on the truck for three or four days never stopping for long at any place. We tried making noise and yelling but I don't think there was anyone around to hear. The day you found me, I had been running all night. The truck stopped by a river, the river we went by on our way here, where they let us out. We stayed there all day and we spent the night in an old building. They tied us up at night. They told us not to try to escape. We were in the wilderness and there was nowhere to go. Even if we got away, they said the wolves would kill and eat us. They had guns."

"Who were these people?" asked Sean.

"I don't know. There were three of them. One they called John and another they called Wimp but I don't think that was his real name. I never heard the name of the other one but he was Polish."

"Would you recognize the truck or the men if you saw them again?" Sean pursued.

"Oh, yes. The truck was orange with black squares painted on the doors probably covering a name. It was big with a long nose and the word Kenworth on the side. The big box sat on a trailer attached to the back of the truck. It was blue with doors in the back and one on the side. It had letters on the side painted over with blue paint but I could tell the name started with an 'M'."

"I will never forget the men. They hurt us. They caught Irenka and me when we tried to escape – they beat us both with ropes and with a stick. They raped Irenka and did awful things to her body until she fell asleep. They forced us to watch then they grabbed me by my hair to do the same. I fought them but they held me down. I screamed from the pain and, Kazia, my friend from the orphanage, threw a piece of firewood and hit the one on top of me. He fell off and I jumped up, ran to the river, and jumped in. I could hear screams coming from the building but I swam as fast as I could. I'm not a good swimmer. I could hear the gunshots and see the bullets hitting the ground around me as I ran into the forest. Kazia saved my life when she threw that log. I left her. I left all of them. Now I am free and my friends are still with those bad men. I'm so sorry." She began to weep.

"It's over Anya, you're safe and we're going to look after you and ask God to help us find the others. It wouldn't have done any good to go back; you couldn't have done anything to help the others. Anya, you need to forgive yourself as God forgives you or you will never have any peace; God will help you if you ask Him. Perhaps your escape will help us to find them. Never forget that we love you and we won't leave you alone. None of this is your fault Anya. We know that and God knows that. Now it's your turn to believe it." Sean's words were full of authority and Anya believed him.

Chapter 17

His exertion climbing the mountain in the cold air crusted his beard with ice. It had been over an hour since he left the cabin but he was now above the tree line. The yellow and red leaves from the willow and birch bushes littered the ground mixing with the green moss, lichens and rocks. He left his pack and other gear at the tree line where stunted spruce trees provided shelter. The site was his favourite campsite on that side of the mountain. A small spring provided water and he found firewood without much effort.

Sean crept through the mist covering the sub-alpine zone like a soft wool blanket. It was here that the small herds of caribou hung out. The mist limited visibility but it would burn off soon as the sun rose higher in the sky. He stopped, crouching low, not moving as his eyes strained to identify the shapes ahead of him. He counted five phantoms moving slowly in the grey mist unaware of his presence. Cows and calves he guessed.

He sat on the bed of moss and raised his personally tuned Cooey Model 10 to his shoulder resting his elbow on one knee. Looking through the Redfield three-power scope, he verified that two cows had calves and the other was a dry cow. He moved the safety to 'fire' and took a deep breath. The air was slowly leaving his lungs when the shot destroyed the silence of the morning and echoed off the mountain peak ahead of him. The custom loaded 30.06 cartridge sent a 150 grain Silvertip bullet spiralling at 3000 feet per second towards the target 150 yards away. The cow dropped where she was standing, her neck vertebrae shattered. The others disappeared into the mist. Sean brought the rifle down from his shoulder and waited.

He had achieved his immediate and most difficult objective. His thoughts veered from the caribou carcass and the mountain to the two people who meant the most to him. Was Anya still at risk from the men who had held her captive? Would they seek her out? She thought they would, despite his assurances. Her fear remained rooted in her soul, robbing her of the joy she should know as a young girl. Was he being naïve? If they were trafficking in young women, it was quite possible they would want to recover Anya. Each girl was worth a lot of money, the main incentive for the kidnappers to deliver her to their scumbag customer in good condition. It was possible that she could go to the authorities with information that could land them in jail – and Anya deported.

Sean knew from personal experience that evil people victimized Asian women in this way. Businessmen from Korea, China, Taiwan and other Asian countries consider it good luck to have sex with a virgin. Then there were the other scum from Europe and North America. The pimps of these traumatized and shamed women would sell them to a brothel or other human trafficker. They force those who get pregnant to abort or they wait and sell the child when it is born.

The cow, fat and in good condition, would dress out at maybe 250 pounds. Sean cut the throat allowing the blood to flow then laid his daypack on the ground and moved the carcass so the head was upslope before gutting the animal. He kept the heart to make jerky but he wasn't a liver man so he left it for the ravens and maybe a wandering wolverine. He partially skinned the animal, spread the rib cage and inserted a stick to hold the chest cavity open and speed cooling. He would have all the meat hanging in his work-shop by tomorrow afternoon he figured.

He leaned his rifle against a birch bush and sat with his back against a rock. The coffee and Anya's oatmeal/chocolate chip cookie revived him. The mist was burning off and he could see blue sky above. His prayer was answered, a nice animal, first day out and close to home. Since the kill was so close to home, he decided to pack out the quarters and the neck rather than bone it. He could get half the carcass and maybe the neck out before supper if he used the pulk. The lightweight, plastic sled worked well above tree line but not so well in the trees. That's where he'd transfer the load to his pack frame.

He remembered Jim, a friend with the coastguard in Alaska, telling him that certain commercial fishermen collected substantial bonuses transporting women to mainland Alaska from offshore ships; once landed they were sold into sex slavery. The coastguard was stepping up their patrols but the Gulf of Alaska is a huge body of water. The victims, he said, don't have any legal status, usually don't speak English and are fearful of police, some of whom are corrupt. Most suffer psychological, sexual and physical abuse. Even if rescued they are deported where they suffer from social alienation and stigmatization in their home countries. Their home governments offer little or no assistance and the victims often become involved in drug trafficking and other criminal activity. Depression, guilt, self-blame, anger and sleep disorders are common for victims subject to these stresses. Without support, severe hopelessness can lead to suicide. The traffickers and pimps, if caught, often get off without any jail time, and are back in the game soon after their release.

Sean saw evidence of these pathologies in Anya. By God's grace, she would heal and she would come to know the life God intended for her to live. But, what about the other girls that were with her? Sean pondered the question. Anya was suffering from survivor's guilt and it was taking a heavy toll on her mental health. *"Anchorage or Fairbanks, I'll bet that's where they are going,"* he thought. Maybe they have already disappeared into the blackness of the underworlds he knew existed in those cities. If not, he decided, he needed to find them before their captors found Anya.

The realization that Anya may not be as safe as he thought replaced his mission to secure fresh meat for winter. Reina might also be at risk. He had to get to the truck where he could call Reina and warn her of the possible danger. Loading both hindquarters into the pulk, he started down the mountain.

* * *

"We can't hang around here any longer; she's gone, probably died from a bullet or exposure in the bush." Marik was restless, tired of their fruitless searches for the girl called Anya. "Besides, we still have the others and it's dangerous staying here. Even in this wilderness, word can get around. We need to move."

"Shut up Marik!" Marik shrank back from John's harsh response. Wimp remained quiet in keeping with his nickname. They were all stressed and he didn't want to stir up John's wrath any further. "She's alive, if she wasn't we'd have found her body by now. Marik, you and I are going to town. I'll ask around in case she's hanging out there. Wimp, you stay here and watch the girls."

Marik started the Kenworth. He let it idle while he dropped the legs on the trailer, disconnected the brake and electrical lines and pulled the release on the hitch. Pulling ahead, he left the trailer in front of the abandoned building once used as a base for mining company prospectors. John joined him and they started for Whitehorse.

The orange Kenworth tractor pulled into the parking lot in front of the YMCA building. They figured she would go to some place that took in homeless and destitute people and the YMCA was one such place. John went to the front desk where he described Anya to the receptionist claiming that she was his runaway niece. She hadn't seen any girl fitting the description but referred him to the hostel at the other end of town. Nobody had seen her at the hostel either. Marik and John had lunch at a prominent but low-end restaurant on Main Street where John asked various staff and patrons if anyone had seen his 'niece'. No luck.

He doubted that she would go to the police. As in Poland, she wouldn't trust them and she'd know they would deport her. She might be safe for a while but back in her own country, without any support, evil men would victimize her again. The police didn't take people like her too seriously. They saw her as street trash and bringing her captors to justice was not likely to be successful given their connections to organized crime. Besides, once she was back in Poland there was little incentive to pursue the matter further. She would end her years in a brothel from a drug overdose or worse.

Chapter 18

Reina put her briefcase on the desk and removed the corrected exams. Nancy and Roberta were already in their seats so she introduced them to Anya as a friend visiting for a few days.

Anya took a seat near the back of the room watching the other students file in and take their seats. She imagined herself as a student one day then put the thought out of her mind. How could a person like her ever hope to be a student in a nice school like this?

* * *

Reina, he remembered, was teaching at the College today; did Anya go with her? The mossy terrain of the alpine zone was damp from the fog and allowed the pulk to slip smoothly over the ground. He stopped at the campsite and picked up his pack frame before continuing down the mountain. The trail through the trees was made of exposed soil and rocks, which made pulling the pulk more of an effort. Finally, he stopped and tied one of the quarters onto his pack frame. Sitting in front of the frame, he put his arms through the straps and leaned forward. His leg muscles strained to bring him to his feet. He stood and bent forward to adjust the 70-pound load of meat and bone onto his shoulders while fastening the hip belt.

Sean arrived at the cabin half an hour later. Although the load was heavy, the trail was downhill and he wasn't even winded. He hung the hindquarter in his workshop to continue to cool then walked to the truck to call Reina. "Whitehorse radio, this is YJ7085 over."

"Hi Sean, what can I do for you?"

"Hi Joan, I'm calling Reina at 383-6487 please."

"Stand by." He could hear the phone ringing. "Sorry Sean, no answer, maybe she's working today."

"I'll try later Joan, thanks, 7085 clear."

Where was she? His selfish thoughts said she should be at home to answer his call. He started back up the mountain. The exercise eased his anxiety as thoughts that are more rational occupied his mind. Maybe they were out shopping or maybe she went to the College early. Either way he couldn't do anything more so he might as well pack out the caribou.

Almost an hour passed before Sean loaded the other quarter onto his back and started back down the mountain. After hanging it beside the first one, he tried Reina again – still no answer. Pushing foreboding thoughts out of his mind, he turned and walked to the cabin. He'd have some lunch before starting back up the mountain. He sat at the table sipping the thick, hot soup studying his thoughts and contemplating the rest of his day. If he continued at this pace he could have the entire carcass hanging in his workshop before dark. He tried phoning again but still no answer. As he started up the mountain, he asked God to protect his dear ones.

* * *

Reina and Anya arrived home where Jesse expressed his enthusiasm over their return. "Let's have a coffee and relax before I make supper," said Reina. "You feed Jesse and I'll make the coffee."

* * *

The sun was low in the sky by the time the quarters were hanging in the workshop. His body was weary and he would hurt in the morning. He decided that the stress of worrying about Reina and Anya was taking its toll. This time Reina picked up the phone.

"Hi Sean, where are you?" Reina's voice was calm but expectant.

"Hello my dear." The anxiety began to drain from his body and his voice. "I'm still at the cabin. Got a nice cow caribou and just finishing up but won't see you until tomorrow, over." Sean stretched out on the seat and leaned against the door of the truck.

"Wow, that was fast, where'd you shoot her, over?"

"In the neck," he chuckled to himself anticipating the reaction.

"You know what I mean!" came the impatient reply.

"I shot her about an hour and a half from the cabin on the north ridge, maybe a half hour from our campsite." It felt so good to be speaking to the love of his life.

"Look, I've still got one more piece to pack out. I'd better get moving but let me speak to Anya before I go will you, over?"

"Okay, here she is."

"Hi Sean, I miss you." The tone of her voice confirmed her feeling of aloneness despite being with Reina.

She *missed* him? He laughed to himself; maybe she missed beating him with her stick. "Hello Anya, I miss you too but I'll be back tomorrow. Is everything okay? Over."

"Oh yes, I'm enjoying my visit with Reina, we went to the College today, over." Sean jerked upright and took a deep breath before replying.

"I'm happy for you Anya. How about you tell me all about it tomorrow. Put Reina back on will you?" Sean asked.

"It's good to hear your voice Reina. I'll see you soon but, Reina, I want you and Anya to stay home tonight and tomorrow and keep your doors locked. Don't open the door to anyone you don't know. Do you understand, over?"

"Yes, I understand. What's wrong Sean?" Reina's voice was laden with concern.

"We'll talk about it when I get back, just do as I ask and try not to alarm Anya," Sean was firm.

"Okay, you know you can count on me Sean. Get back soon will you, over."

"I will. 7085 clear."

Three Whisky Jacks were sampling the gut pile when he arrived at the kill site. The temperature dropped as the sun disappeared behind the Coast Mountains. He retrieved the neck of the caribou and started down to his campsite. The neck made good stew meat and hamburger and he wasn't leaving it for the scavengers. At the campsite, he loaded his camping gear into the pulk and tied the neck onto his pack frame. As it turned out, he wouldn't be spending the night.

Carrying his rifle, he started on his last trip off the mountain. The trees of the forest turned the twilight into night as he left the alpine meadows behind him. He knew the trail but he was careful to avoid tripping over roots and rocks. The moon lit the last of his journey home. He walked along one of the old logging roads silently praying for the safety of his loved ones. The cabin came into view promising nourishment, warmth and rest for a weary body. Only God could attend to his thoughts.

Chapter 19

In the afternoon Marik and John stopped at the Whitehorse Inn for a drink. They continued their inquiries about Anya but to no avail. Their young waitress suggested they check out the local college campus where lots of young people gathered. John didn't think Anya would go to such a place but they were at a dead end so he decided to stop in on their way back out of town.

Marik did a double take. "That's her! In the Jeep." He pointed to the Jeep driving out the exit of the college parking lot as they entered the lot at the other end.

"Follow her," shouted John, "but stay out of sight or she'll recognize the truck."

The two men sat in the truck watching the house as the twilight gave way to the darkness of night. They parked on a street where they could see the front of Reina's house with its large picture window. The two women inside were oblivious to their watchers.

"There's only the two women," Marik observed. "We could just grab her and put the other one out of her misery. She's too old anyway. She'd slow us down and complicate things."

"Shut up and listen! This is how we'll do it," ordered John as he screwed the silencer onto the muzzle of his Colt .45 semi-auto.

The sound of splintering wood and Jesse's barking shattered the silence as the back door swung open and slammed against the wall. John shot Jesse at point blank range as the dog raced to challenge the intruder. Reina never made it out of the kitchen. He kicked Jesse's body down the basement stairs, stepped over Reina's body and ran down the hall to where Anya was hiding. The bathroom door flew open in response to the force of his boot.

Anya screamed as he grabbed her by the arm and forced her roughly down the hallway and into the kitchen. The sight of Reina lying on the floor evoked hysterical screams as she fought her abductor trying to go to Reina. John pushed her onto the floor face down, his knee in her back. He wrapped duct tape over her mouth and around her head muffling her screams. Securing her wrists with duct tape, he dragged her back on her feet and pushed her out the door into the cold darkness. Marik and the Kenworth were waiting behind the fence in the back lane.

* * *

Sean lounged in his favourite overstuffed chair trying to finish First Samuel before going to bed. He wasn't finding much peace in his prayers and the story of David's life in the Bible was far from comforting. Perhaps he'd find his peace in the arms of Morpheus now beckoning with a vengeance. *"Just two more chapters to go, I can make it."* He wasn't one to leave a job half finished. The crackling of the fire and its blanket of warmth was taking its toll on his weary body and troubled mind. He got up and drank a full glass of cool water from the earthenware crock before, refreshed, returning to his chair and David's story. *"David would soon be home with his family where he would find rest from battling his enemies."* By the time his eyes read verse three he was sitting upright in the chair, eyes wide in disbelief. He read it again, aloud, *"When David and his men came to the city, behold, it was burned with fire, and their wives and their sons and their daughters had been taken captive* (1Samuel 30)."

* * *

75

The Kenworth idled down the laneway without lights to avoid detection. The forest on the right and the fences lining the other side of the lane helped absorb the sound of the engine. John strapped Anya onto the bunk of the sleeper as she continued to struggle. Reaching the street Marik soon had the tractor up to speed and pointed in the direction of the Alaska Highway.

"So what did you do with the other one?" Marik shot a curious glance towards John.

"She won't be a problem, just drive." John's reply was terse and disinterested as he glanced in the mirror to see if anyone was following them.

Chapter 20

The Highway was dark befitting the lonely land of Canada's Yukon. Few people lived in its vacant vastness; most resided in the capital city of Whitehorse. Traffic too was sparse, semis heading north to Alaska. They too would soon be on their way to Alaska with a valuable cargo of human flesh. They had lingered too long in Marik's view but John seemed obsessed with finding Anya. Marik thought he was atoning for the guilt he seemed to feel for letting her get away in the first place, taking out some of his guilt on him and Wimp. Now that she was back, they could finish their delivery, collect their reward, and retreat to some obscure, warm country with good beaches.

The tractor lurched and dipped as it left the gravel road and turned onto the track leading to the abandoned building. The mining company had built it to house summer prospecting crews scouring the surrounding mountains for signs of minerals. Now a derelict, the building was unsuitable for habitation especially during a Yukon winter. Wimp stood next to the door of the shack holding a small battery operated lantern. High-pressure air rushed from the brake system signalling the end of their mission. Marik turned the key and the diesel rattled into silence.

John opened the curtains on the sleeper and released Anya from the bunk straps. She twisted her body into an upright position just as John pulled her up and guided her out the door and down the steps to the ground. Pushing her roughly, she stumbled into the shack led by Wimp and his lantern. When John cut the duct tape a foaming torrent of curses spewed from her defiant mouth. She fell next to one of the other girls, his big hand almost breaking her jaw when he slapped her across the face. "Shut up you bitch! You've caused us enough trouble." Pain seared her brain and blood flowed into her mouth and down her chin, as she lay unconscious on the warm body of another lost soul.

* * *

It was still dark when Sean rolled out of bed and onto the cold floor. Pain swarmed the muscles in his legs as he stood and reached for his clothes. Dressing himself helped relieve some of his stiffness. Forcing himself to stretch, he made his way into the kitchen where he stuffed a handful of moose jerky into the breast pocket of his shirt before filling his thermos with cold coffee left over from the day before.

He was ready for winter but there was still something important he had to do after getting in his winter meat supply. Sleep had finally come but not until early in the morning defying his earlier attempts to rid his mind of ominous thoughts. Those same thoughts now renewed their torment as he laced his boots.

The truck started despite the cold. He knew they were on the precipice of winter with its short days, long nights and piercing cold. Sean grabbed the microphone and tried to call Reina. Again, no answer. It was Saturday. *"Maybe they stayed up late and turned off the phone so they could sleep in,"* he thought. The truck continued bouncing down the track towards the main road as Sean tried to hang the mic on the swinging hook.

* * *

"Get them up and feed them," John ordered, "as soon as they're done we're leaving this hole."

Marik went to start the Kenworth. When he returned he helped Wimp ladle warm baked beans into waxed paper bowls and pass them out. The girls, waking from their troubled sleep, crowded close to the old tin stove. They sat, blankets around their shoulders, eating their meagre breakfast in silence. Orange flames licked the sides of the stove through holes eaten out by rust over the years providing a warm glow to the black interior of the shack. Anya's aching, swollen jaw and bruised tongue made it difficult to eat. Kazia sat close beside her.

Marik and Wimp loaded the big steel container with a bottle of water from the river and the bags of day-old buns Marik brought back from the bakery in Whitehorse. Marik climbed into the Kenworth. He tossed the sleeping bags and garbage bags full of clothes to Wimp who threw them into the container. The weather had turned colder so they bought cheap sleeping bags at the local general store. Sweaters and wool shirts from the Salvation Army thrift store would further help to keep their cargo from freezing

John escorted the girls one by one to the derelict outhouse before loading them into the container. Shivering in the cold, they quickly donned the warmer clothing and climbed into the sleeping bags. The heavy steel door slammed shut leaving them in darkness once again.

Marik backed the tractor into the trailer until the hitch engaged then gave it a slight forward tug to check the security of the connection. Jumping out of the cab, he connected the glad hands and electrical cable. After he checked the operation of the trailer brakes and lights, he yelled to John that all was ready

The delay caused by Anya's escape allowed colder weather to settle over the Yukon but they had yet to see any snow. Even if they got snow, it wouldn't complicate the delivery of the girls to their client as long as it wasn't too deep. They couldn't risk entering Alaska at a conventional border crossing so they would be using an aircraft to move their cargo over the border unseen by authoritative eyes.

John walked ahead to check for traffic on the main road; it was deserted as usual. He waved to Marik and the truck lurched forward along the dirt track. As it climbed the incline onto the gravel road, John jumped onto the lower step, opened the passenger door and climbed in. Marik worked through the gears as they gained speed. At the junction with the Alaska Highway, they turned north heading for the long deserted community of Snag, notorious for recording the coldest temperature in North America, -81.4° F, on February 3, 1947.

Chapter 21

Sean drove a little faster than usual. The sun was rising, although it had yet to show itself. Snow-capped mountaintops began to glow orange betraying its presence somewhere over the horizon. He watched the grey morning light disappear as the light of a new day advanced down the valley sides. The truck slid in the gravel as he negotiated a curve but he confidently controlled the skid and brought the vehicle back on track. His mind was awash with thoughts of Reina and Anya. Was the verse he read last night just a coincidence or was God speaking to him?

He turned onto the Alaska Highway. After shifting into fourth gear and getting up to speed, he poured himself a cup of cold, strong coffee and began to gnaw on a strip of jerky. For some crazy reason he pondered his passion for jerky. Displacement behaviour they call it. He liked to make jerky from the fine textured, dense muscle of the heart, especially a moose heart. It was important to trim away any fat before cutting long strips about half an inch wide and immersing them in the bowl of his special marinade. There the marinade worked its magic as the meat wallowed in the dark, fragrant bath. After a day or two, he would spread the strips of heart muscle on the oven racks. Leaving the door partly open and keeping the fire low, he'd wait until they were dry and impervious to decay.

The smoke from countless chimneys rose straight into the still air as Whitehorse residents stirred from their sleep and began their day. He regretted his early arrival. It would spoil the girls' Saturday morning sleep-in.

Maybe he should have breakfast at the Airport Chalet, a motel and restaurant complex on the Alaska Highway opposite the airport, and delay his arrival at Reina's house. He hangered his Cessna 180, nicknamed 'TJ', at Arnie's Aviation across the road from the Chalet. He could check and see if Arnie had finished the changeover from floats to wheel skis. No, he dismissed the thought. He needed to be sure they were safe; after all, didn't he promise Anya that she *would* be safe? They could sleep-in on Sunday.

Reina's Jeep was in the driveway so he pulled alongside it and shut off the engine. Jesse would start barking any second announcing his arrival to the sleeping girls. The dog knew the sound of Sean's truck but Sean didn't hear any barking. He unlocked the door and slowly pushed it open so he wouldn't hit Jesse who would be on the other side. Jesse wasn't there, nor was Reina.

"I'm back!" Sean announced his arrival but the silence continued. He could hear the furnace fan but he could feel a draft of cool air. Maybe they were in the yard and left the back door open. He mounted the stairs into the living room then turned and entered the kitchen. In an instant, he was in disaster triage mode kneeling beside Reina who was still lying on the floor. He confirmed that she was breathing so he felt for a pulse while he scanned her body for any sign of injury. A crust of dried blood in the hair at the top of her head caught his eye, as did the smeared blood on the floor where her head was resting. Her pulse was slow but strong, a good sign.

Fearing what he already knew he covered Reina with his coat and raced through the house looking for Anya. The broken bathroom doorframe caught his eye. On his way into the basement, he saw the splintered frame of the back door and the body of his beloved Jesse lying at the bottom of the stairs. He cleared the rest of the stairs with one leap kneeling and praying that his dog was alive. Jesse was dead. The bullet had gone through his chest exiting his back where it broke his spine. He died instantly. Anya was gone.

Reina began to stir as he tried to soften the dried blood on her scalp with a cloth soaked in warm water. She showed no other signs of injury or shock but he began to uncover the path carved by the bullet where it skidded along the top of her skull. An inch lower and she would probably be dead. Sean sat on the floor holding Reina on his lap as he leaned against the kitchen counter. His voice was soft, tender as he tried to reassure her that she would be okay and that he was there to help her. She opened her eyes and looked into his.

"What's your name?" he asked.

"Reina." Her reply was feeble but confident and clear. "My head aches and my shoulder is sore. Where's Anya? Did he take her?" She started to sit up but he pushed her back down.

"I need to check you for concussion. Lie still." He used his hand to cover her eyes one at a time and watched the response of her pupils when he removed his hand. "Good, I don't think you have a concussion."

"Honey, you've been shot but you will be okay. You probably fell on your shoulder but nothing is broken. Anya is gone, I'm sorry." Sean didn't mention Jesse. "I'm going to help you up and move you onto the couch. Do you think you can stand?"

"Yes, just hold onto me," she whispered.

Sean helped Reina onto the couch where she was content to sit upright against a pillow. He noticed two bullet holes in the wall as he guided her out of the kitchen. "Thank you Lord for bad shots," he prayed.

"Sit here while I get my beard trimmer, some bandages and stuff," Sean ordered.

When he returned, he shaved the hair around the wound trying not to intrude into the wound itself. It had stopped bleeding. Despite being a superficial wound, he could see the skull and bone splinters, which he removed with a sterile gauze pad and tweezers. The bullet had torn up some of Reina's skull but had not penetrated. Next, he soaked a gauze pad in hydrogen peroxide and swabbed the wound and surrounding skin. He applied a thin film of antiseptic cream to the wound and its edges and applied a large bandage completely covering the wound. A gauze strap around her head and under her chin would keep the bandage in place with minimal pressure. He stood back and examined his handiwork before bending to hug her. "I'll bring you some water and a couple of ibuprofen tablets."

He returned and crouched in front of her. "How are you feeling now?" he asked watching her down the pills.

"My head and shoulder are sore but I guess I should expect that. The pills will help with the pain. But, what about Anya?" her voice broke and her face contorted as she fought back tears.

"I don't know Reina. I need you to tell me what happened. Can you do that?" Sean struggled to control his rage as he listened.

Reina nodded her head and began to relate the events she remembered until the point where she lost consciousness. She recalled seeing the man shoot Jesse before he pointed the gun at her and fired. Then, all went black.

"Where's Jesse?" She could tell by his face that he was gone. "I'm so sorry Sean. I know how close the two of you were. He was always by your side through those years of grieving, I'll miss him too." Tears flowed down Reina's cheeks as she extended her arms to embrace the seemingly stoic man kneeling at her feet. His face twisted as he accepted her care and leaned towards her hugging her waist. He began to sob quietly. Her hands held his head as she shared Sean's grief over the loss of his friend.

His sobs weren't just for Jesse; he had betrayed Anya. He wept for her also. Those old feelings of self-hate began to show their ugly presence. He crumpled on Reina's lap under his burden of guilt. He knew he needed to forgive himself but he had to take care of some things first.

Chapter 22

"Arnie, this is Sean. Hey, how are you doing with the changeover on TJ?"

"All done Sean, finished it last week. She's topped off and ready to fly when you are. Sorry I didn't call, got busy with other stuff."

"No problem Arnie, me too. I'll be by later this morning." Sean hung up the phone and turned to Reina.

"What are you going to do?" she asked without trying to disguise her anxiety. "We need to call the police Sean."

"No!" His reply was immediate and emphatic leaving no doubt about his unwillingness to entertain her suggestion.

"Sorry," he tried to apologize for his response. "We can't involve them Reina."

"But why, we are dealing with murderous criminals trafficking innocent girls," she pleaded with him.

"Yes we are," he agreed, "and that's exactly why we aren't going to involve them."

"I don't understand," she moaned.

"Reina, you remember my fishing buddy Jim in Juneau?"

"Yes."

"Jim and I have talked at some length about this evil business. He is involved from the enforcement side but he knows the reality of the outcomes and those outcomes are not pretty." Sean began to explain.

"I worked with some people in Cambodia who helped women and girls caught in the net of traffickers and pimps. The scum of the earth make bags of money off these women and girls. To them, they are nothing more than commodities, chattels sold to the highest bidder. I saw the incredible damage done to these girls. And, I saw the amazing healing that can happen with dedicated helpers working in God's Spirit. I've also seen the complete lack of concern by others, including the police and other government agencies. We, in the west, look at the sex trade as an industry that needs protection. Our governments even pass laws protecting the so-called 'rights' of women to be degraded, abused and killed. Why would I turn to such an authority to 'rescue' Anya and the others? Besides, they will deport the lot of them and they will die in the hands of the same kind of people. I might as well kill her myself. I won't do it!"

"I hear you. So what are you planning to do?" Reina continued.

"Arnie's got TJ on the wheel skis so she's ready to go. I'm going to try and find that truck that Anya told us about. It's gotta be bound for Alaska and there's only one road this time of year; Top of the World is closed. They wouldn't go to Haines; that's a dead-end. I want you to keep the HF radio on while I'm gone."

Reina looked puzzled, "So what are you going to do if you find it?"

"I don't know. Pray?" He answered with another question.

Sean threw his gear into the back of the plane and did a quick walk-around trusting that Arnie had everything in order. The little Cessna started without a problem. He scanned the panel; all the needles pointed where they should. Receiving clearance for taxi, he eased the throttle forward and steered the plane to the button on runway 32 while filing a note with Flight Services.

The air was cold, crisp and calm. He acknowledged the clearance for take-off and firewalled the throttle. The little plane leapt off the runway into the thick air as if happy to be back in its element. Sean had modified TJ by adding a STOL (short take-off and landing) kit including wings with drooped leading edge cuffs. The larger, 285 horsepower engine and three bladed Hartzell propeller further enhanced its performance.

About a thousand feet above ground, Sean lowered the nose a little. He pulled the throttle and prop back to 24 square and set up the little plane to continue its climb-out at cruise speed. He pointed the nose towards Haines Junction.

The truck could be in Alaska by now if they drove all night. It was about an eight-hour drive to the border at Beaver Creek. It closed at eight in the evening and didn't re-open until eight in the morning at this time of year. Sean levelled off at 6,000 feet leaning out the mixture, closing the cowl flaps, and trimming up for straight and level flight. At this altitude he could see traffic on the Alaska Highway and an orange truck pulling a large blue box would be hard to miss.

The drone of the engine somehow calmed his mind, giving place to new thoughts and questions. How did they expect to pass through customs and immigration with a container full of screaming females? US Customs always inspected freight entering from the Yukon. I suppose they could just shoot or kidnap the officer; there was usually only one on duty during the winter. Too risky, it wouldn't be long before some other traveler came by and reported the scene. Hiding a Kenworth and Sea-Can isn't that easy even in Alaska. The off-duty spike barricades would deter them from trying to bust through the border. Finally, there were no other routes over the border, at least none that would accommodate their rig.

Smoke from houses at Haines Junction caught Sean's attention. He glanced to his left letting his eyes follow the ribbon of gravel until it disappeared into the Coast Mountains. No way would they take that route. Haines was a small fishing and summer tourist town served by one road and the Alaska State Ferry system. Their rig would attract a lot of attention at the border. Freight came into Haines by ship not truck so their presence would be suspicious. If they managed to clear the border inspection, unlikely, they would need to silence their human cargo while on the ferry. Even then, the ports along the route were mostly small fishing towns except for Juneau. Juneau was a town of fewer than 30,000 people; not a great market for the goods they have for sale. Jim had told him that any trafficking intercepts the Coast Guard made were destined for Anchorage and Fairbanks, not Juneau.

Sean adjusted his heading, pointing the nose of the plane to Burwash Landing near the north end of Kluane Lake. Traffic on the Alaska Highway was sparse this time of year, most of it commercial vehicles. He had seen two semis in a hundred miles. Neither matched his target rig. His thoughts returned to Reina and her condition after almost losing her life.

"Reina, this is TJ, are you by?" he spoke into the microphone of the HF radio.

"TJ this is Reina, you're 5 by 5, go ahead Sean." Her voice sounded clear and healthy.

"How you doing love? Still got a headache?"

"Nope, pills took care of that. I'm a little tender as you can imagine but the pills work fine," replied Reina. "I'm staying awake with no problems. Had some breakfast and a cup of coffee then did a quick fix on the back door. Find anything?" She was careful about how much information she transmitted, as the frequency was open to the public.

"Nothing. Just passed the Junction and heading to Burwash now. I wanted to check up on you. I'll call you again when I get to the White."

"Okay Sean, thanks for your concern. Talk to you soon. Love you. I'm clear."

Sean hung the microphone back on its hook, relieved to hear that Reina was doing well. "Thank you for saving her Lord." He mumbled his gratitude.

A fresh fall of snow dusted the landscape beyond the Donjek River in sharp contrast with the brown mantle further south. Winter was beginning to envelop the Yukon. Wellesley Lake, off Sean's starboard wing, appeared a vivid sapphire blue against the snow-covered landscape. As he crossed the White River, Sean glanced to his right toward the abandoned settlement of Snag, famous for being the coldest place in North America. An orange truck hitched to a blue box sat next to the airstrip.

Chapter 23

He kept the aircraft straight and level not wanting to draw attention to himself. At least three people milled around the truck but there was no sign of the girls. He guessed they were still in the Sea-Can. Sean could see one set of vehicle tracks in the snow along the Snag road. The unblemished snow on the airstrip told him no plane had used the strip. This was how they were getting the girls across the border, by aircraft.

"Reina, this is TJ, are you by?" he spoke into the microphone.

"TJ, Reina, go ahead," came the reply.

"All's well here, found the box we lost, how you doing?" Sean was careful with his words.

"I'm fine, when are you coming home?" Reina understood what Sean was saying and she was nervous about what might happen.

"Could be a while. I need you to do something for me if you're up to it?" he queried.

"I'm fine Sean. What do you need?"

"Get the motor home out of Bob's yard and drive it to Sheila's." There was silence on the other end.

"Are we going camping?" she struggled to produce an authentic laugh.

"Sort of, pack your gear and *lots* of food. Bring some *extra* clothes; you might need them. Wait at the lodge with Sheila when you get there, got it?"

"Okay, I'm getting the message. Be good and maybe I'll see you for supper. Reina clear."

Reina knew Sean had found the truck but what came next she could only guess. She was anxious to see him and to help in any way she could but her first priority was to pray.

Sean buzzed the small community of Beaver Creek flying low over the few buildings fronting the highway. The airstrip was about a mile north of town so if you wanted fuel or a ride to town it was a good idea to get Don's attention before you landed. The little plane gained altitude and looped back to line up on the runway. Sean put the craft onto the ground and taxied to the fuel tanks where Don was leaning against his truck. Shutting down the engine Sean climbed out and greeted him.

"I was just leaving when I heard you buzz town," he said as he extended his hand. "Are you coming or going?"

"Doing a little scouting before the snow gets too deep." Sean tried to sound nonchalant as he lied. "I might have some wilderness tourists lined up for next year so I'm looking at my options in your backyard." Sean climbed onto the wing and Don passed him the fuel hose and nozzle.

"How's business?" Sean made neutral conversation hoping to avoid probing questions. Don owned the only service station and general store in town and he had the contract for the fuel concession at the airport.

"Slow, always slow this time of year," replied Don, "had a good summer though so that'll take us through the winter. In fact Belle and me might take a trip to Arizona after Christmas."

"Now there's a plan. Great time to get out of the cold and dark. Nice country too, different but nice." Sean tried to encourage Don. He and Belle never went anywhere but now they were getting older they seemed to be spreading their wings with the help and encouragement of their daughter who lived in Whitehorse.

"Hey, you wouldn't have a 4x4 I could rent for the day?"

"Sure, you can use my truck, no need to rent," Don offered. "Drop me off at the store and she's all yours."

After finishing fuelling TJ, Sean moved her off the apron and secured her on the tie-down area. Grabbing his backpack and rifle, he climbed into the truck with Don and they headed for town. Don topped off the dual tanks on the truck while Sean visited with Belle in the store. He had to decline her invitation to supper as he wasn't sure what the rest of the day held for him. He took a rain check, bid her goodbye and walked out to the truck where Don was serving gas to a traveler. "Say Don, can you spare a Five-Star? It could get real cold in a hurry this time of year."

"Sure, stand by and I'll get one." Don wandered into the store and returned with a large duffle bag containing the legendary sleeping bag.

"Thanks Don, might see you later tonight but I'll make camp if I'm too late," Sean called out the window of the truck. He rolled away from the gas pump and onto the Alaska Highway heading south for the Snag road. The bright sun had melted the skiff of snow off the highway except in shaded spots. He made good time, passing the Enger Lakes after ten minutes of driving. The Snag cut off was just ahead. He pulled off the highway onto the gravel road leading to the abandoned settlement of Snag and stopped. The tracks of the Kenworth and its trailer were the only ones visible in the light covering of snow. The airstrip was a good 12 miles ahead and Snag, or what was left of it, another three miles farther on.

He drove a short distance so he wouldn't be visible from the highway then stopped. Lifting the engine hood, he pulled the wires off the horn and the switch for the backup and brake lights then returned to the cab where he disabled the automatic interior light. Since it was an older model truck it wasn't equipped with daytime running lights. The heavily sprung four-by-four jerked and lurched along the unmaintained road at a leisurely pace. Hunters and the occasional curious tourist were the only visitors since they decommissioned the town and the World War II airstrip in the late 1960s. Although abandoned, the strip was still useful in case of an emergency and the old buildings offered meagre shelter if needed. Sean and other pilots continued to use it as they had need. His thoughts focused on the encounter that lay ahead; he needed to gather intelligence before he could decide on a course of action.

The road took a sharp turn to the east telling him he had maybe a mile and a half to the airstrip. The forest continued to hide his presence. When the road turned north again he knew he was close and began looking for a spot to park the truck. He backed into a break in the trees and shut off the engine. He sat, watched and listened. After 15 minutes, he opened the door and slid out of the truck with his daypack and rifle. Instead of closing the door, he let it rest against the latch. He took his pistol from the pack and slid it into the holster on his belt then removed the binoculars, hung them around his neck and tucked them inside his jacket. Slinging the pack onto his back and grabbing his Marlin, he began walking through the trees in the direction of the airstrip.

The shallow layer of snow helped muffle his steps as he worked his way slowly through the forest. He stopped frequently to listen and scan his surroundings. The air was still but he heard no sound. The forest grew brighter as he approached the edge of the large cleared area that surrounded the airstrip. At the edge of the trees, he scanned the open area now littered with waist-high willow and birch bushes. There were footprints in the snow down the middle of the airstrip with spruce bows laid out at intervals along the track. To his left, about 400 yards away, he could see the Kenworth with its trailer and Sea-Can parked at a right angle to the strip. Another 200 yards beyond the truck were the old buildings and airport tower. Smoke curled from a chimney.

Through the binoculars, he watched a body with a pistol in a holster on his hip move past a window in the old building. He saw another man sitting and smoking; he had an AK47 rifle propped against his body. There was no sign of the third man. The side door of the Sea-Can faced south, away from the buildings; there was no lock on the latch and no sound came from its interior. Sean scanned the cab of the Kenworth hoping to locate the third man but it appeared empty.

He moved through the trees along the edge of the clearing until he ran out of cover about fifty yards from the truck. Scanning the buildings from his new vantage point, he located the third man. He appeared to be sleeping on a makeshift bed near the smoking man. Waiting for the pick-up plane to arrive and load their illicit cargo he surmised. Rustling sounds came from the Sea-Can.

Sean took some photos and pondered the situation, developing a plan and considering the contingencies that needed to go with it. If the girls remained quiet and the latch and door of the Sea-Can didn't make too much noise he could get them out of their prison without their captors hearing. The men were at least 200 yards away on the opposite side of the Sea-Can. He needed to act fast as the pick-up plane could arrive at any time.

Leaving his pack and rifle in the forest, he ran across the clearing using the truck to hide his progress from anyone looking his way. He stood beside the drive wheels at the front of the Sea-Can listening and watching for any sign that the men had heard or seen him. All was quiet except for the muted, intermittent sounds of the girls moving inside the steel container. He lifted the handle of the door latch and rotated the cams pausing to listen and watch before allowing the door to swing open. "Anya, it's me! Stay quiet; no sound!" His whispered command was strong but muted by the interior of the container.

Chapter 24

Reina waved to Bob as she backed her Jeep up to the motor home where she could unload the groceries, bags of clothes and her gear. Bob ran a truck rental business. He and Sean were long time friends and he let Sean park the motor home in his fenced yard. They had put the vehicle up for winter storage not planning to use it again until spring. The big diesel engine started and idled roughly while Reina stowed the groceries and other items. The water and holding tanks were empty but she decided to leave the antifreeze in the plumbing system until she got to the lodge at the White River crossing; she could flush it and fill the water tanks there if necessary.

Reina parked the Jeep, locked it up then went to the office where Bob was sorting keys behind the counter. "Hi Reina, how you doing young lady? Heading south for the winter?" he joked while pointing to the motor home idling in a cloud of blue smoke.

"Hi Bob. No nothing like that, actually I'm heading north. Sean's scouting some country for next year's clients and asked me to drive up and meet him."

"Well you've got the weather for your trip. Pretty nice fall so far but winter's just around the corner."

"I don't expect to be away too long. Should only be gone a couple of days. See you when I get back Bob." Reina turned and left the office.

She did a quick walk around the vehicle to ensure all was in order for the trip. Sean had done a complete maintenance and check when they put it away for winter but it was always a good move to look for anything out of order before a trip. She eased the 34-foot machine onto the Alaska Highway and headed west towards Haines Junction, an hour and a half away. She would stop and top up the fuel tanks there then continue on to the lodge at White River, another 3-hour journey. She was confident Sean would be there when she arrived

* * *

Anya fell on her knees, leaned out the door and wrapped her arms around Sean's neck. He pushed her back and stared into her tearful eyes, "Later Anya. Thank God you're okay. Reina is okay, she's alive. Listen Anya! Look at me!" Her wide, wet eyes focused on his. "We have to get you all out of here quickly but you *can't* make a sound. Are the girls all able to walk?"

"Yes, but some don't have good shoes." Anya's voice trembled. "I am so happy Reina is okay."

"We don't have far to go but we have to move fast and everyone has to be *quiet*." Sean emphasized 'quiet'. "I want you to lead the girls altogether straight ahead and into the forest." He pointed to where he left his pack and rifle. "I will follow you." Anya addressed the girls in Polish as they crowded around the door watching and nodding their heads in understanding.

Sean took some more photos then he and Anya helped the girls climb down from the Sea-Can. He directed them to stand beside the drive wheels of the truck where the men in the building couldn't see them if they happened to look their way. Some of the girls were shaking and crying quietly while others tried to console their sisters. Without warning, one of the girls became hysterical. She broke away from the girl trying to calm her and rushed to the open door of the container screaming in Polish. Sean tackled her, slapping his hand over her nose and mouth. Together they fell into the snow where a few seconds later she went limp.

Anya rushed to her side. Sean assured her she would be okay and ordered her to go back and calm the others, many of whom were crying. He used his binoculars to check on the men in the building. The man with the rifle had come outside and was looking around. Sean motioned for Anya to keep the girls quiet and still. Sean continued to watch the man with the rifle as the girls stood frozen and trembling in the snow. Finally, he turned and went back inside the building.

"Anya, what was that about?" Sean whispered angrily.

"She was afraid they would catch us and kill us," Anya explained, tears streaming down her cheeks.

"Look, I know you are all scared but we need to be *quick* and *quiet*. I'm counting on *you* Anya." He held her shoulders and looked into her eyes. "I want you to lead the girls to the forest. I'll bring this one. Can you do it?" She nodded her head.

Anya led 11 girls at a slow run across the clearing and into the forest while Sean watched the men in the building through his binoculars. They appeared oblivious to what was going on at the truck.

He hoisted the unconscious young girl over his shoulder in a fireman carry and ran across the clearing. "Anya, look at me. I need you to explain to the girls that if those guys go after us they are to scatter in different directions and find a place to hide." He paused to verify that she was paying attention. "When they feel safe to move they are to go to the south end of the airstrip but stay hidden in the forest." He pointed to the spot. "From there they have to make their way east, where the sun rises, until they come to the river. Tell them to stay near the river but still in the forest and I will find them." Anya made sure the girls understood his instructions while trying to reassure them that it was unlikely the men would chase them.

He handed his pack to her. "Can you carry this?"

"Yes, I will carry." Sean noticed that a calm, confident attitude replaced her state of agitation.

Picking up his rifle, Sean told Anya to have them follow him, no talking. The girl on his shoulder felt lighter than a caribou quarter. The thin cover of snow on the ground made for easy, hushed travel. It also made for easy tracking so they needed to keep moving. Sean loped through the trees like a wolf. He tried to set a pace but still had to stop on occasion to allow the girls to catch up. Three of the girls wore light slip-on tennis shoes that filled with snow, soaked their socks and froze their feet. To their credit, they didn't complain and kept up with the others.

After 20 minutes, they arrived at the truck. The excitement and the run had actually helped warm their emaciated bodies. Sean motioned for the girls with the poor shoes to climb into the jump seat in the truck cab. He lowered the one on his shoulder onto the front seat where she began to stir. Anya reassured her and helped her into the back seat admonishing the other girls to keep her calm. He started the truck and turned on the heater fan before speaking to Anya. "We've got room for you and two more girls in the cab, the rest will have to ride in the box. You decide who goes where."

Anya spoke to the girls in Polish while Sean spread the canvas tarp on the bottom of the truck box. Six of the older girls climbed into the box snuggling with each other to stay warm. Sean spread the big Arctic Five-Star sleeping bag over the girls, the image recalling memories from happier times of his daughter's sleepovers. He climbed into the driver's seat and made a quick visual inventory of his cargo. Four girls shared the jump seat behind him; Anya and two young, terrified girls sat scrunched together beside him. "This is Blanka and Halina." The girls looked at Sean with wide, fearful eyes. Anya said something in Polish and they nodded. Anya sat beside him, her face full of questions, eyes pleading with him to tell her they were safe. He was beside himself with relief that Anya was once again safe. Against his better judgment, he put his arm around her shoulders and brought her close, kissing her forehead in reassurance. His conscience reminded him of how he failed her not many hours ago. She didn't fight him and he spoke no words.

As the truck warmed, the smell of dirty bodies filled the cab but he seemed to be the only one who noticed. They covered the 12 miles of road back to the highway in silent apprehension but in good time. No one followed. Sean stopped and checked on the girls in the truck box. They huddled together under the sleeping bag relieved to be free from their prison.

Climbing back into the cab he tried to put the girls at ease telling them through Anya that no one was following. He took Anya by the hand and smiled, "you'll see Reina pretty soon." He turned the truck onto the highway and headed south. He knew Reina would still be on the road. His mind turned to the next problem; in less than an hour he would have to explain 13 Polish girls to Sheila and Sam at the White River Lodge?

Chapter 25

The White was beginning to freeze up. Driving across the bridge, he could see the shelf ice forming along the shores. Its flow had receded considerably from peak summer flows. The river got its name from the glacier flour and other sediments that entered the stream at its glacial headwaters in the St. Elias Mountains to the west. These contributions coloured the water a milky white.

The White River Lodge originated from the staging site on the south side of the River during the construction of the Alaska Highway in the 1940s. Sheila and Sam owned the lodge for over 40 years. Well known for their hospitality, they and their huge Malamute, Bozo, provided a welcome service to those travelling the highway, especially those forced by severe weather to seek refuge. In recent years, they shut down the operation for a good part of the winter when traffic was sparse, but they would never turn anyone away. Sean's fishing lodge was not far away and over the years he came to be best friends with Sam and Sheila.

Sean pulled off the highway following the gravel driveway around the back of the Lodge where several small log cabins stood in a line overlooking the river. Many years earlier he and his wife and daughter had helped Sam build these cabins. He parked the truck between two of the cabins out of sight from the highway, shut off the ignition and slid out of the cab.

Immediately Bozo bounded over to greet him and inquire of his cargo. He helped Anya out of the truck introducing her to Bozo then directing her to let the girls out the passenger door while he attended to those in the truck box. Sam had been bucking up some logs for firewood but he now stood watching in disbelief as Sean drove up and unloaded his passengers.

"Hi Sam," Sean called across the yard over the sound of the idling chain saw. "Got room for some guests?"

Sam shut off his saw and walked over to Sean and the girls where he removed his glove and extended his large hand to Sean in greeting. "Good to see you. Kinda late for you to be up this way isn't it?" he queried while surveying the crowd of shivering girls. Sam could see by the appearance of the girls that something wasn't right.

"Sam, I've got a situation and I need you and Sheila to help me."

"You know you can count on us Sean, but let's get your girls into the lodge where it's warm." He ushered the girls towards the back door of the lodge.

Sam and Bozo led the way. The hand-made wooden door swung open on four large hinges that protested under its weight. Sam held open the door as Bozo and the girls stepped into the small mudroom. A subtle smell of wood smoke permeated the warm, moist air that filled the space. Wood fires heated the lodge over the years and the log walls became imbued with the smoke that escaped while tending the firebox. Coat pegs lined the dark walls, some supporting well-worn coats and hats while others waited their turn to serve. An assortment of boots and slippers lined the base of one wall. "Sheila! We got guests. Sean's here with his girls." Sam announced chuckling as he led the way into the spacious living space of the Lodge.

"What girls? Sean doesn't have any girls, just Reina. Be there in a second," a voice replied from the kitchen.

The girls stood in a tight mass of bodies in the centre of the room quiet and apprehensive, unsure of their situation and the strangers surrounding them. Blanka and Halina stood as one in a tight, protective embrace. Bozo circled them puzzling over the strange smells yet eager to identify each one. Anya stood apart, beside Sean, holding onto his arm.

He turned to her. "Anya, tell the girls that they are safe here and these people are going to help them. Tell them Bozo won't hurt them, he's friendly." Anya obediently addressed the girls in Polish while Sam directed them to the odd assortment of comfortable, overstuffed chairs and sofas littering the large room. Before the girls could respond, Sheila came through the kitchen door. She came to an abrupt stop, her mouth opened and the dishtowel she was holding fell to the floor as her mind tried to explain the scene before her.

"Meet Sean's girls!" Sam swept his arm before the company of dirty, smelly and dishevelled females huddled together in her living room.

"Hi Sheila, good to see you again and thanks for taking us in." Sean walked over and hugged his stunned friend. "I'd like you to meet my friend Anya and her friends."

Anya extended her hand. Sheila took it in both of hers then, released from her shock, embraced Anya with a warm hug. Looking into her eyes with a broad smile and her own discerning eyes, she greeted Anya, "Welcome to our home." She turned to look at the rest of the girls. "Sean's friends are our friends, have a seat and make yourselves at home." Anya translated while the girls drifted into the chairs and sofas. "Sam, put some wood on the fire!" she ordered, "these folks look cold." In obedience, Sam opened the door of the barrel stove, allowing a wisp of smoke to escape, and pushed a couple of logs on top of the coals.

"What can I get you to drink?" Sheila scanned the crowd with a welcoming smile. Sean looked at Anya but she was non-committal.

"How about some tea and hot chocolate Sheila?" Sean offered. "I see the coffee's on as usual, motioning to the large pot sitting on top of the barrel stove. And Sheila, these girls are very hungry, can you rustle up a snack?"

"Good as done, why don't you come into the kitchen and give me a hand." Sean knew she was looking for more than help with the drinks.

"Give me a minute Sheila and I'll be right there. Sam, come with me." Sean gave his friend a meaningful look as the two went back outside. When they were out of earshot, Sean explained what had just happened and the need to be alert in case the bad guys came looking for the girls.

"Why don't we call the cops and let them take care of them?" said Sam.

"I'll tell you why Sam," Sean sighed.

Chapter 26

The distant drone from the engines of the approaching DC3 brought Marik and John outside while Wimp continued to sleep. Scanning the sky to the north they searched for the aircraft they knew would soon release them from the burden of the 13 girls in the Sea-Can. Marik pointed to the silver object reflecting the sun as it began its descent. Aircraft crossing from Alaska to the Yukon land at the Beaver Creek airport to clear customs but the remote wilderness and lack of radar facilities invited exceptions for those not wanting to declare their presence.

"We've got to get those girls ready to load," ordered John. "Go get Wimp. I don't want any delays. We'll turn over the girls, collect our money and get outta here." Marik ran toward the abandoned building where Wimp, wiping the sleep from his eyes, met him at the door. "Come on, the plane's here. We've got to get the girls loaded as soon as it lands."

* * *

Sean briefed the couple on his situation while Sheila busied herself preparing tea and hot chocolate. It wasn't the whole story but it would do for now. He needed to prepare them for the aberrant behaviour they would most likely see in the girls. He explained the potential danger associated with the girls noting the shooting at Reina's house and describing the three men and their truck and trailer. The threat of danger fazed neither one; instead, it served only to fortify their commitment to help. Sheila expressed concern over the physical condition of the girls and the shabby, dirty clothes they were wearing. He told her that Reina was on her way in the motor home and would be bringing clothes for the girls. She would examine each of them but, in the mean time, he suggested they could all do with a bath. Sheila nodded her head in vehement agreement.

Sean returned from checking the highway and the area surrounding the lodge. Sam placed a tray of oatmeal-raisin cookies, 16 ceramic mugs and two thermos pots of hot liquid on the coffee table in front of one of the sofas. Sheila followed with cream, sugar and a pot of honey. Anya invited the starving girls to help themselves, which they did with zeal and politeness. Some of the girls offered thanks in timid English and made remarks about the comfort of the lodge and the size of Bozo. Anya explained that they could all speak English, some more than others, but they were shy in using the language. Polish is their mother tongue, she explained.

Anya told Sam and Sheila the story of how evil people had deceived them, brought them to Canada and were planning to sell them into the sex industry. "This is a big, lucrative and sordid business," said Sean, "traffickers make lots of money off these girls. They are valuable commodities. The low-life thugs who trap and sell them have a lot at stake and they won't hesitate to kill anyone who interferes with their operations. They tried to kill Reina when they came for Anya." He went on to caution them about saying anything to anyone about the girls and to be wary of the three men who may be looking for them. "I'm not sure what to expect," he said, "they could go looking for the girls and if they do we should expect them to come here. We need to prepare in case they show up. I suggest that we put the girls upstairs tonight. It's possible they might just abandon the operation, give up and try again with some more girls."

"What about the people that are buying the girls?" asked Sam.

"Good question Sam. I don't know who they are but if I had to guess I would say they are an organized crime group probably east European – bad people probably making money off the oil workers. That was my experience in Asia and my friend in the US Coast Guard tells me that all of their intelligence points to organized crime with Russian connections. They recruit losers like the three thugs who trapped these girls and use them to accomplish their nefarious purposes with promises of big payoffs. They are valuable as long as they have the goods, otherwise they are expendable."

"Okay, enough about the bad guys," interrupted Sheila. "Let's let these girls clean up for supper. Anya, come with me, I'll show you where things are and you can coordinate the clean-up while I get the roast in the oven." Sheila had experience as a drug and alcohol counsellor and knew how to engage victims of abuse. It was important, she knew, to help the girls gain a measure of control over their lives. Simple gestures like making a shower available were important. She led the way up the creaking stairs and along the hallway. She showed the rooms to the girls and pointed out the metal grates in the floor that allowed warm air from below to flow into the rooms. Each room could sleep two guests and came with two bathrobes. Anya encouraged them to find a roommate. She pulled down the window shades and closed the curtains as they went from room to room cautioning the girls to stay away from the windows.

There were three showers off the hall. Abundant water flowed from their well at over 15 gallons a minute and the propane-fired, on-demand water heater kept the water hot. Sheila asked Anya to gather the girls' clothing and she would wash them after supper. Anya startled Sheila when she told her to burn them instead of washing them. "That's fine with me Anya," she replied with full understanding of the rationale behind Anya's order. "If you need anything you just holler, I'll be in the kitchen." Sheila retreated down the creaking stairs.

Sean retrieved his pack and rifle from the truck and helped Sam fill the wood box next to the barrel stove. When they installed propane, he put a propane stove and small grill in the kitchen for Sheila. This reduced the amount of wood he needed to cut from when they used the old wood-fired range. The small diesel gen-set provided their electricity during the day and early evening but they often shut it down at night. Guests used flashlights or battery operated lanterns when the generator wasn't running but Sam and Sheila preferred kerosene lamps.

Sean sat on a stool in the kitchen peeling potatoes and talking to Sheila. He kept an eye on the highway outside the window. Sam came in with a big roast he'd cut off a hindquarter of the moose he shot a couple of weeks earlier and set it on the counter. "Thanks Sam. I don't have enough potatoes for all of us," she lamented.

"Reina will be bringing a load of groceries including potatoes so don't fret," commanded Sean. "If we're lucky she might even bring a newspaper and a pie or two."

Anya walked into the kitchen clothed in a white terry-cloth bathrobe, grey wool socks up to her knees and a towel turban. The sight of her brought back fond memories to Sean of when they first met. "Thank you for the shower Sheila, I feel so much better and probably smell better too." She tried to smile. "The girls are taking their turns and some are having a rest."

"Reina should be here soon. She'll sure be glad to see you Anya," said Sean. Anya came to his side and hooked her arm through his. "This is a pretty special girl to Reina and me," he said to Sam and Sheila. "I found her hiding in the bush on the road to my place, scared to death and looking like a half starved, flea bitten mongrel dog. God loves this little girl and He's got plans for her. Felicia would have been about her age if she . . ." He stopped talking, turned away from Anya and took a long sip of coffee from his mug.

"Who is Felicia?" Anya asked looking questioningly at Sean and then Sheila.

Sheila looked at Sam then back to Anya. "Sean had a daughter named Felicia but she died in an accident a few years ago. He lost his wife Gina at the same time," Sheila answered. "Felicia would have been close to your age by now."

Anya put her hands on his shoulders. He turned to her, "Anya, you remind me so much of Felicia, sometimes I forget you aren't her. You are Anya, I know that but I care for you as I cared for my own daughter. Please forgive me."

She hugged his neck. "Nothing to forgive. Thank you Sean for loving and caring for me and for rescuing me and the others."

"She is a sweet one Sean," remarked Sheila. "I'm glad she's got you to keep an eye on her."

"Someone's here!" Sam's concerned voice interrupted them. He and Sean ran from the kitchen and into the dining room.

Chapter 27

Through the large window, they could see the motor home. Reina was walking to the front door. They smiled at each other sighing with relief that their visitor was a friendly. Reina walked into Sean's arms where he embraced her longer than usual. "How are you?" Sean looked at the knitted watch cap covering her bandaged head. "It's so good to see you."

"I'm fine, long drive though. You found Anya and the girls didn't you? Tell me you did!" She looked past his shoulder and saw Anya standing, vibrating until it was her turn. They ran into each other's arms hugging and kissing each other full of joy.

Sean and Sam left the women to revel in their emotions while they unloaded the groceries, medical kit and other supplies from the motor home and carried them into the lodge. Once unloaded, he drove the vehicle around the back of the lodge and parked it beside the generator shed. Grabbing Reina's gear bag and shotgun, he returned to the lodge through the back door locking it behind him. Darkness was falling.

Anya and Reina carried the bags of Salvation Army clothes and footwear upstairs. She had bought items of personal clothing and other things like hairbrushes, toiletries and sweet treats and put them in individual daypacks for each of the girls. Anya took charge of distributing the items, encouraging the girls to sort out the clothing sizes among themselves.

Sheila was back in the kitchen peeling more potatoes. She smiled at the clamour coming from upstairs. Sam was in his favourite chair beside the barrel stove, a stack of magazines on the table beside him, reading the latest issue of the Yukon News that Reina had brought.

Sean placed the 'Closed for the Season' sign at the highway access in the hope of discouraging visitors and fastened the cable across the access. Once back in the lodge he drew the shades on all the dining room windows, turned off the porch and yard lights, and locked the front door. Wrangling dining room tables and chairs he created one long table to accommodate everyone for supper. "Sheila," he yelled, "have you got any candles for the table?"

"In the pantry. Help yourself," came the reply.

What looked like a new group of girls assembled in the living room. They stood with clean faces and combed hair in silence, fidgeting with their hands, self-conscious in their 'new' outfits. Inquisitive eyes searched their surroundings and the strange faces within. Anya spoke to them in Polish while they savoured the delicious smells that flowed from the kitchen. Blanka and Halina stayed close to Anya and her friend Kazia. Sean, Reina, and their hosts stood smiling at the girls trying to put them at ease. Anya took Reina by the hand and introduced her to the girls. One by one, they greeted Reina with tentative handshakes and a mixture of cryptic Polish and English phrases.

"Okay ladies, it's time for supper so let's go into the dining room and take our seats," announced Sheila.

* * *

The pilot lined up his plane with the runway. His experience in Vietnam made landing at Snag look like child's play. His co-pilot, not a pilot at all, braced himself for landing what he considered an antique aircraft on the abandoned airstrip in the middle of nowhere.

John was already at the truck when Marik and Wimp joined him. The sight of the open door on the Sea-Can caused the three men to stop and look at each other as if for an explanation. They bolted to the open door where the obvious slapped them in the face. "What the hell!" John was still looking inside the Sea-Can while Marik and Wimp were examining the tracks in the snow.

* * *

The girls were in awe as they took their seats at the table in the dimly lit room. The table clothed in white linen, sported full place settings for everyone. Five, tall red candles illuminated salt and pepper sets, baskets of warm homemade rolls, butter plates and small crystal bowls of pickles and horse radish. Sheila placed two large bowls of salad at each end of the table along with a small pitcher of her homemade salad dressing. "Sam, will you ask the blessing on our meal and our guests?"

All bowed their head. Sam began, "Lord, we know how much You love each of us and we want to thank You for Your love. This meal that you have provided is a token of that love as are these wonderful girls and our old friends that you have brought to our house. We ask for Your continued protection and blessing on each one here and on Your provision in our lives. Amen."

"Sean, Sam, you give me a hand with the food. The rest of you can start with the salad," ordered Sheila as she rose from her chair and headed for the kitchen, Sean and Sam following close behind.

Sean set two large bowls of mashed potatoes on the table followed by Sam's offering of two bowls of gravy. Two large platters of sliced moose roast joined the feast along with bowls of mashed turnip, glazed carrots and steaming broccoli. Sam filled each glass with clear cold water and offered his homemade wild cranberry wine to anyone who chose to take the dare. Reina and Sean were the first to hold up their glasses waiting for their portion of the rich red nectar familiar to their palates from past visits. Following their lead, the rest of the guests held up their glasses.

When Sam finished filling the glasses, Sean proposed a toast. Anya translated. "I am full of gratitude for the safety of these girls and my friends but mostly I am grateful for the privilege of serving a loving God; a God I can count on. To our Lord and Saviour, Jesus, be glory and honour." Anya repeated his words in Polish and all joined in savouring Sam's wine.

* * *

The gooney bird touched down and taxied towards the Kenworth. A large man with a pockmarked complexion and Latin features climbed from the plane with a canvas bag in one hand. He walked towards the three men at the truck. The pilot emerged from the door and walked to the tail of the aircraft where he relieved himself.

"I am here to pick up our goods. I trust they are in good condition?" said the man with the bag. He looked at John. "I have your money."

* * *

The absence of leftovers attested to the appetites of the girls and their need for nourishment. Sam dispensed coffee and tea as Reina and Sheila served ample slices of Sean's signature apple/cranberry/orange pie complete with healthy scoops of ice cream. Appreciative sounds filled the room as the girls relished the tasty pie.

After supper, the girls helped Sheila clear the table and wash the dishes despite her protests. She could see that they were weary in mind and body yet content in their safe haven. Anya, on behalf of the girls, asked permission to retire to their rooms. Sean had them gather in a circle as he led a prayer seeking peace of mind, safety and a sound sleep for all present. No one seemed to notice the sound of the semi passing on the highway, no one except Sean.

Chapter 28

It was late. The others had long since retired for the night. Sean sat in the armchair in the corner of the room draped in darkness. The flames, dancing behind the glass door of the airtight heater, cast their animated orange images on Bozo's torso as he lay stretched out on the well-worn rug. The lodge was quiet except for the soft tapping of the old, oak clad clock that once hung in the parlour of Sheila's childhood home in Nova Scotia.

He tried not to think, allowing the silence to soothe his tortured mind and affirm his need to know that all was well with the sleeping souls above him. Sleep was not on Sean's agenda. Instead, watchfulness took its place. Maverick thoughts threatened to distract his senses but he quickly reined them in. If he failed, Bozo was his backup. The dog's acute senses would detect any activity in or out of the lodge long before it alerted Sean.

He had been looking forward to a quiet, peaceful winter. Reina had never been to Cambodia but she expressed interest. Sean suggested a trip to visit his friends in Phnom Penh where they could help with their work with girls caught in the human trafficking underworld. Ironically, he now found himself immersed in this same underworld operating in his own backyard. After discovering Anya hiding in the forest, his quiet winter plans went out the window. She and 12 vulnerable others suddenly entered his and Reina's lives. Their captors were evil men who would kill to protect their chattels and Reina's head wound testified to their determination. He was determined to thwart any further attempts by these traffickers to regain control of the girls.

The loud crack inside the airtight brought Sean from his chair and Bozo to his feet. His vigilant mind translated the sound as a gunshot before realizing it was only the fire. He and Bozo resumed their peaceful poses allowing the adrenalin to dissipate and their racing hearts to resume a leisurely lope. Shortly after, Sean drained his mug of the remaining hot chocolate and rose from the chair. It was time to have a look around.

Bozo came to his side as he moved into the adjoining dining room. He raised the window shades and squinted in the bright moonlight that lit up the room through its many windows. He moved along its walls allowing his eyes to adjust to the brightness while scanning the grounds outside. Nothing moved, not even the shadows. Positioning himself in a corner, he stood still and silent, letting his eyes do their work. Bozo lay at his feet. After 15 minutes, he turned and moved back into the dark side of the lodge with Bozo bringing up the rear.

His parka hung in the mudroom. He slipped it off its peg and put it on as he unbolted the heavy timber door. Using his leg, he kept Bozo from running out as he eased the door open a little at a time. He scanned the surroundings bathed in the light of the full moon. The sting of the still, frozen air in his nostrils told of a marked temperature drop. He drew his pistol and slid outside along the back wall of the lodge. Bozo wandered across the yard and sent a stream of steaming pee onto a tree by the woodpile.

Sean stopped in a shadow and waited. Bozo cruised the grounds refreshing his markers and in the process signalling to Sean that all was well.

* * *

The men finished their breakfast in silence at the small diner attached to the motel in Haines Junction. John was attentive to the radio playing in the kitchen while searching the newspaper for any news about the shooting. Nothing. Strange he thought, but good. Marik attracted the attention of the cook who doubled as their waiter and pointed to his coffee mug. Grabbing the coffee pot from the warmer, the cook sauntered to the table and filled the three mugs with fresh coffee. "Where you fellas off to?" he tried to make conversation with the sullen group of men. John glared at him. "We'll have our bill now."

Marik and Wimp went outside to start the Kenworth while John paid the bill. The wind came from the west flowing over the mountains and moderating the temperature. They should have been thousands of miles away from here by now enjoying tropical breezes.

"What do you think he's going to do Wimp?" asked Marik as he turned the key and pushed the starter button. "Whoever took those girls is long gone, I think. We'd be wasting our time looking for them. Besides, if they went to the cops *they'll* be looking for *us*. I say we get rid of this rig and lay low."

"But where would they go?" replied Wimp. "Nobody's seen them along the highway."

"Maybe they headed straight to Whitehorse or even farther south. Probably drove all night." Marik watched the RCMP patrol car in his mirror. "Stay calm, the cops just pulled in."

"Morning," said John as he held the door open for the two officers entering the cafe.

"Good morning," they replied as they entered the diner without taking particular notice of him.

John walked toward the Kenworth trying not to draw any attention as the officers sat at a table next to the window. He joined the other two men in the cab of the truck. "Let's get out of here. Head for Whitehorse," he commanded Marik.

* * *

Sean and Sam were finishing their first mug of coffee when Sheila came down the stairs.

"Did it get colder last night or is it just my old bones?" she asked as she reached for the coffee pot.

"Minus 25 this morning. I plugged in the motor home," Sam replied looking at Sean. "Whitehorse is much warmer, zero according to the radio. Any of those girls up yet?"

"Not a sound. You boys stay quiet and let them sleep, they've been through hell."

The stairs creaked as Reina descended into the living room wrapped in a thick, blood-red robe.

"Morning my dear. Sleep well?" Sean rose and hugged her as Sam and Sheila bid her good morning. Sean had changed the bandage on her head and given her another ibuprofen tablet before she went to bed.

"Oh yes. I feel so much better and my head doesn't really hurt that much."

Sheila handed her a mug of coffee as she sat beside Sean on the couch.

"What about you? I didn't hear you go to your room. Did you stay up all night again?" Reina scowled at Sean who looked into his coffee mug without replying.

"So what's the plan Sean?" Sam asked leaning forward with interest trying to distract Reina from her question. "Looks to me like you've just about got a family in the making but you might need a bigger house," he muffled a laugh with his hand.

Sean's face flushed red. He didn't ask for this predicament but his life was now inextricably bound to the lives of 14 women, 13 of whom were highly vulnerable. For such a time as this, he thought. He was convinced God put Reina in his life to help him sort out the situation and strategically placed friends like Sam and Sheila along the path of his journey. He didn't mind the journey so much but he sure wished he knew where he was going.

"First off, I want you all to know how much I appreciate your love and friendship. God has put you here for His purposes even if we aren't quite sure what He's up to. I do know one thing for certain; He doesn't want any of those girls to perish. In fact, He doesn't even want their pursuers to perish and that's a hard pill for me to swallow. I don't know where those guys are and that bothers me – a lot. I admit that I half expected to see them last night but just as thankful I didn't."

His audience sat in silence attending to his words, watching him, waiting to hear the plan. The expectant looks on their faces caused Sean to adjust his position, lean forward and turn the tables.

"So, what do *you* think we should do?"

* * *

"Drop me off at that restaurant," John ordered. Marik pulled the rig into the parking lot of the Airport Chalet. "You two keep going. Hide the truck at the place by the river where we lost that girl. I'm getting another vehicle and I'll meet you there later in the day. We'll hold up there and figure out what to do." He climbed from the truck and went into the restaurant. The Kenworth eased back onto the highway heading south.

"Tell me, where would a fellow rent a truck around here?" John asked the waitress as she poured coffee into his upturned mug.

"Bob's Trucks, down the highway about half a mile" She pointed back to where they had come from. "Ask for Bob and tell him Trudy sent you, might get a deal this time of year."

John thanked her then, trying to act nonchalant, he asked, "You haven't seen a team of girls come by this way lately?"

"You mean a school team?"

"Yeah, a school team, about a dozen or so," he replied.

"Nope. Probably at the high school. You know how to get there?"

"No but I'll check when I get that truck. Thanks."

Chapter 29

Sean endured the silence by searching their faces with his own expectant gaze. Nothing. Reina looked at Sheila and Sheila looked at Sam. Finally, Sam shrugged his shoulders and agreed, "I'd sure like to know where those guys are too. I only like surprises on Christmas, Anniversaries and Birthdays." Everyone smiled, releasing some of the tension of the moment.

"Okay," said Sean, "here's what I want to do. I'll return Don's truck, take TJ down the highway, and see if I can spot that Kenworth. Sam, I don't need to tell you to stay alert, you know the risks associated with an unseen enemy. Reina, I don't think it's a good idea for you to be at home right now, they could return for some reason." Looking at Sam and Sheila he asked, "Is it alright for Reina and the girls to stay here a while longer, maybe a day or two?"

Sheila was quick to respond, "That's not any problem at all Sean, long as you need to. It's our privilege to be able to help out and, frankly, I think it would do those girls some good to just lie around, get some meat on their bones and enjoy feeling safe. I'm starting to enjoy the company." Sam nodded his agreement as Sheila headed for the kitchen to prepare breakfast.

"Thank you both. Your hospitality is legendary." Reina nodded in agreement.

"How's the airstrip Sam?"

"Flat but watch for moose," he smiled. The Lodge's airstrip was short and rough but Sean had landed there before. It worked if you came in slow.

"Okay, after breakfast I'll leave. Reina, can you get those blood samples you need and I'll drop them off with Carol at the lab when I get to Whitehorse?" Reina nodded. "Leave your HF on so I can keep you posted and you let me know if you need anything. Let's pray."

The smell of burnt toast somehow appealed to Sean. It always brought back distant and fond memories of visits to his Aunt Ruth's house on Sea Island. You had to keep an eye on your toast in those days lest it turn up black. Sheila busied herself in the kitchen, Sam dropped an armload of firewood in the wood box and Sean and Reina sat on the couch talking. Bozo, at rest on the rug, turned to look up the stairwell at the sound of stairs creaking under the padding of many feet. A choir of 13 white robed, radiant faced angels flowed into the room.

Anya, leading the procession, walked over to Sean and Reina where she gave Reina a hug then turned to Sean. "Can I have a hug?" He gave Reina a puzzled look. She smiled and nodded.

Sean rose from the couch and embraced Anya with tears in his eyes. "Good morning dear girl."

Sean led the welcoming committee by taking each girl by the hand and greeting them with a smile and a good morning. Sheila joined in the receiving line before retreating into the kitchen to finish preparing breakfast and check on the toast. Anya spoke in Polish and motioned to the chairs and couches in the room.

"Did you all sleep well?" asked Sean, glancing at Anya.

Heads nodded timidly. "They were so tired and stressed from yesterday," said Anya. "No bad dreams either."

"Breakfast's ready! Take your seats. Sean, Sam, give me a hand in here." Sheila commanded from the kitchen.

Reina ushered the girls into the dining room where the morning sun shone brightly through the windows. A glass of real orange juice (Sheila knew Sean wouldn't have it any other way) and another of water adorned each place setting. Small pitchers of half-and-half joined bowls of brown sugar, crowberries, low-bush cranberries and raisins on the table. Homemade raspberry jam sat beside the two baskets of hot toast covered with colourful tea towels. Bozo made the rounds receiving welcome pats and scratches from the girls as they took up their places at the table. Sean, Sam and Sheila soon appeared bearing trays filled with bowls of oatmeal and carafes of hot coffee and hot chocolate. Reina passed out a multi-vitamin pill to the girls and a small dish of yogurt asking Anya to explain that it was to help them regain their health.

After breakfast, they all sat enjoying their coffee or hot chocolate and talking among themselves. Sean interrupted, asking for their attention. He reassured them of their safety and encouraged them to rest and recover from their ordeal. He thanked Sam and Sheila for opening their home then reminded the girls that they were welcome guests and that their hosts wanted to serve them in any way they needed. Sam welcomed them to join with him in his chores if they wanted and offered to take them on walks for exercise and fresh air. Sean cautioned them not to venture out on their own. Sheila reminded them that she too was their friend and that she cared for them. If they wanted to talk she was available and if they needed anything she encouraged them to ask. She invited them to help her with chores around the Lodge if they wanted – no obligation.

Reina enlisted Anya's help in making sure the girls understood that they all cared for them and wanted to help in any way they could. She explained her background as a nurse and counsellor. Anya helped explain that over the next couple of days, Reina wanted to examine each of them to ensure they are healthy and that they receive any treatment necessary. As part of her examination, she needed a blood sample that Sean would take to Whitehorse for analysis. She asked Anya to have the girls meet her and Sean at the table across the room. The girls obediently lined up at the table where Sean and Reina withdrew a vial of blood from each thin, white arm.

When they were finished, Sean had everyone gather in the living room. He told them that he had to leave for a day or two but that he would return. He avoided explaining why he was leaving. Based on his earlier conversation with Sam, he reassured them that Sam and Bozo would watch over them and not allow any harm to come to them; they were in good hands. Sam was in charge and they were to obey him in all situations.

He stood and bid them goodbye. Anya gave him a hug and Reina walked with Sean to the back door of the lodge where he donned his parka and shouldered his bag. The two embraced while they prayed for each other. Reina handed Sean his rifle and watched him walk to the truck.

* * *

Belle was pumping gas into a car with Alaska plates when Sean pulled into the yard. He grabbed the bag with the Five-Star and waited for her inside where he expected to find Don. The store was empty.

The bell on the door tinkled as Belle entered. "Hi Sean, welcome back. How'd it go?" Belle greeted him with a smile as she slid out of her parka and mitts. "Sure got cold of a sudden." She went around the counter and put the money from the sale into the cash drawer.

"Successful, and thanks for the use of your truck." He didn't want to get into details. "Where's Don?"

"He's at the airport. He tarped your engine last night but wanted to put a heater on in case you came back today. Looks like he guessed right. You leaving? Oh, there he is now." Don drove up and parked in front of the office. The bell on the door tinkled as he entered.

"Hi Sean, good trip?"

"Real good. Thanks for the truck and the bag Don; I put them to good use. I gotta be leaving; can you give me a lift back to the strip?"

As they drove to the airstrip, Sean asked Don if he had seen an orange Kenworth tractor pulling a blue Sea-Can. He wasn't sure how he would answer any queries about his interest in such a rig. Don responded in the negative and didn't ask any questions. The rest of their conversation on the short trip revolved around the condition of bush roads and plans for Christmas.

Don pulled up beside TJ and left the truck engine running. The two of them pulled off the engine tarp and Don removed the electric heater he had placed inside the cowling. Sean did a quick walk-around then stowed his pack and rifle in the back before climbing in to see if the engine would start. It roared to life on the first revolution. Don signalled through the engine noise that he would loose the tie downs.

The men gave each other a short wave as Sean taxied toward the end of the runway. Needles were good on the run-up; air was clear, cold and still. The little aircraft climbed effortlessly in a gentle turn to a south heading. Sean climbed to 5500 feet and trimmed for straight and level flying. He called White River on the HF as he flew by to check that Sam's old Spilsbury was still working. They spoke briefly before signing off. The girls were lounging, reading books and magazines, playing with Bozo and visiting with Reina in her makeshift clinic. The news put his mind at rest, at least for a time.

Chapter 30

The flight turned out to be uneventful; no sign of the Kenworth. Sean landed at Whitehorse. He would leave the blood samples and Reina's requisition with Carol pretending that he was just the messenger in case she asked questions. He fuelled up and decided to grab some lunch at the Airport Chalet before running his errand and carrying on to Watson Lake. Leaving TJ at Arnie's he drove over to the Chalet.

The lunch crowd was gone and Trudy and Ted, the cook, were having coffee at the staff table when Sean walked in. They both greeted him while Trudy went to get the coffee pot.

"Having lunch Sean?" she asked. "We've still got some cutlets left if you're interested."

"Sounds fine Trudy."

She glanced at Ted who was already on his way to the kitchen.

"Say, have you seen an orange Kenworth hauling a blue Sea-Can?"

"Sure have. It came by this morning and dropped off a fellow looking for a bunch of high school girls, a sports team of some kind. He needed to rent a truck so I sent him to Bob's."

Sean perked up. "What happened to the Kenworth?"

"Don't know, it just carried on south down the highway. The guy had his coffee, read the Star, made a collect call to Fairbanks, paid and left."

"What did he look like?" Sean tried not to sound like a cop but he needed information.

"Big guy, over six foot, maybe in his '30s with short, dark hair. He wore a dark blue nylon parka. Had a scar on his cheek," she paused, thinking, "left one, quite prominent, maybe two inches long. What's up?" She looked at him, questioning him with her eyes.

"Oh, just a hitchhiker I noticed on the highway. I wondered if that truck picked him up." He lied.

Ted hit the bell getting Trudy's attention to pick up Sean's lunch order.

"Did you happen to hear what the guy was talking about on the phone?" Sean asked as Trudy put his lunch on the place mat.

"I wasn't really listening but from what I did hear it sounded like he was trying to get help to find something he lost."

Sean parked in front of Bob's office but left his truck running. After some small talk Bob confirmed that a man named John Dubicki rented a blue F250 4x4 super cab. The name was legit according to the Manitoba driver's license he presented. The man hadn't said where he was going but he headed south on the highway.

As he drove down the two-mile hill towards town, Sean tried to make sense out of the intel' he acquired. His hope that these men would leave the country after losing their cargo was starting to dim. Unless they left or the authorities put them away, the girls would continue to be at risk, at least from them. How long would they search for the girls he wondered? There were other risks too. The authorities, if they found the girls, wouldn't waste time deporting them back to Poland. Except for some compassionate intervention, their lives would be as good as over. The thought caused him to turn into the parking lot at the Federal Building.

He cleared the stairs two at a time making his way to Jay's office on the third floor. Jay Morgan was the Director of Immigration in the Territory. Jay and his family were close to Sean and his family. Jay's wife, Beth, and

Gina were best of friends and Nanette and Felicia were in the same classes at school. Sean had helped build their cottage on Marsh Lake where the two families spent many days together, swimming, fishing and enjoying their time at the Lake. After the accident, they tried to reach out to Sean but his grief put a distance between them. Upon Sean's return from Asia, the relationship underwent considerable healing to the point where Sean and Reina would spend time with the Morgans.

"Hi Betty, is Jay available?" Sean addressed the receptionist.

"Hi Sean, hold on and I'll see." She pressed a button and announced Sean's presence into the receiver. "Okay, he'll see you. Go on in."

The office door opened and a very tall, slim man in a dark blue suit stuck out his hand in greeting.

"What's up Sean?"

Sean closed the door behind him and sat opposite Jay. "Jay I'm here in confidence and I know I can count on you to honour that confidence." Jay leaned back in his chair open to whatever Sean had for him.. "I've got a hypothetical situation I need your advice on."

Sean painted a word picture of a human trafficking situation allegedly taking place in eastern Canada. The victims have been rescued and are about to be deported. He asked Jay if there were alternatives to deportation and, if there were, what conditions went with them.

"Well Sean, to be straight up with you, there are alternatives but they are seldom used. In most cases, deportation is the outcome. In rare cases if a subject had married a Canadian we review the case and if we find the marriage is legitimate, they can stay in the country. Another alternative, even less common, is for someone to nominate the subject based on humanitarian and compassionate grounds. I have seen this approach end positively but a good lawyer is important for success."

"Would you need a specialist immigration lawyer?" Sean asked.

"That would be my recommendation," Jay replied, "you should talk to Ron Vance, he's got experience in immigration law and can tell you what is required to make a viable case. I'll get Betty to give you a copy of the guidelines if you want."

"Who makes the final decision in the case of the humanitarian and compassion alternative?"

"The local director if it's straight forward. Such cases seldom make it to court. If approved, the subject is granted permanent residence status and can apply for citizenship at a later date."

"Thanks Jay, you've been most helpful." Sean got up to leave.

"Look Sean, you call me if you need anything else. I'll try to help as best I can." Jay's voice betrayed his insight into the conversation. He walked Sean out of the office and asked Betty to get him a copy of the guidelines he spoke about.

Sean walked the blood samples over to the lab where Carol promised to have the results available the next day. After finishing his tour of town without finding the truck that John Dubicki was driving, he decided he needed to talk with Pastor Ray.

Sean drove into the parking lot of the little white church standing quiet and empty alongside the Alaska Highway. He pushed open the door that he knew was always open. Ray said that open door is a reminder to Christians to keep their arms open to the lost just as the Lord's arms were open to receive him.

When Sean returned from Cambodia, this small church welcomed him despite the tatters of his past life still clinging to the new man birthed by his faith in Jesus Christ. Sydney and Ben, through their ministry to victims of human trafficking in Cambodia, helped him understand why he felt such a void in his life. They explained with the help of the Bible, God's Word, that *"while we were still sinners, Jesus died for us"* that we might know true fellowship with God, not religion, but relationship with a loving, caring God. Sean had come to realize that religions sought to seek an unknown god or gods through countless manmade rituals, belief systems and human efforts that put people in terrible bondage. With Sydney and Ben's help he learned that God wants none of that. The sinner is *"justified by faith"* and *"it is by grace that you have been saved, not by works, lest any should boast"*. God reached out through his Son to offer all who believe, freedom and life. Despite Sean's feeling of unworthiness, he learned that ALL are unworthy and that's why God sent his Son to rescue us. He came for repentant sinners not deluded 'holy ones'; *"Come just as you are"* as the song says, *"come all you who are weary and heavy-laden and I will give you rest."* Through faith, Sean had entered the Sabbath rest that God promised from the very beginning.

The light was on in Ray's office where he was working on some drawings for a construction project. His career as a draftsman helped supplement his small salary as a Pastor. Sean called out to him as he crossed the sanctuary.

"Hi Sean, you're back soon, did you get your caribou?" Ray invited Sean into his office.

"Oh yeah, got my wood and shot a caribou for winter meat. What did you and John do with that bear?"

"Made a whole lot of sausage and some nice roasts."

"Great, nice change. I'm sure you'll get your share of other people's moose and caribou anyway. Is Nancy back?"

"Yes, she's sorry to have missed you. She's up at the house if you've got time for a visit."

"I'll take a rain check Ray but I might be back to spend the night. I've got a situation that needs lots of prayer. I can't share the details at the moment but I wanted to give you a head's up and ask you and the congregation to pray for Reina and me."

"We can do that Sean. The Lord knows what you need so we'll just ask Him to take care of your situation in His way. Let's pray right now." Ray put his arm around Sean's shoulders and the two bowed their heads in prayer.

"I've got to run Ray. I needed to share with you even though I can't say much but I promise to keep you posted as things develop. Give Nancy and the kids a hug for me. Might see you tonight." He turned and left.

He drove across the highway to Arnie's where he fired up TJ planning to use the rest of the day to check out the highway to Watson Lake. Along the route, he made a short diversion to Pancake Lake then back to the Alaska Highway. That's when he spotted the Kenworth and the blue F250 parked beside the abandoned prospecting camp on the river. This was where Anya had made her escape. Her abductors had returned.

Chapter 31

The men huddled at the makeshift table next to the leaky, tin airtight heater. Cold air invaded through broken windows and holes in the walls where scavengers and vandals had removed the cladding from the abandoned camp building. They sat in silence, the mood sullen.

"Me and Wimp think we should forget about trying to find the girls and get out of this God forsaken land. Somebody has them, and they've probably talked to the cops by now. They will be looking for us, and there's only one way out of this place. If we don't make a move, we'll be trapped." Marik's voice was firm, but he had difficulty making eye contact with John. Wimp sat with his eyes locked on the flames licking the sides of the heater through a large hole.

"You're right Marik." John was emphatic. Marik's eyes grew wide as he turned to look at John. Even Wimp stole a glance. "We've got a lot invested in those girls but things are going to get too hot for us to hang around and try to find them, besides there's lots more where they came from. If the cops have the girls, they'll deport them and we might get a second chance at them. We have to get out of here now." John watched a wave of relief come over the faces of his colleagues. "If they can't find us they will give up as usual. I want you two to take the truck, head for Edmonton, and meet me at Leon's place. Find a place to hide the truck and trailer, the sooner the better. I'll return the pickup and catch tonight's flight to Edmonton." John stood up to leave.

"Okay," Marik addressed John's back as he watched him leave, "we'll leave soon as we finish our coffee."

Without warning, John swung around, drew his pistol and shot both men.

* * *

It was still early evening when he finally arrived at Ray and Nancy's house. Nancy had cooked him supper while he caught up with the kids, listening as they related recent events in their lives. Sean struggled to contrive a story to explain Jesse's absence. After a brief visit, he was ready for bed and retired to the guest room. All was well at the White but not here; he hadn't mentioned what he found. What was he to do? His prayer hung in the dark while he closed his eyes and fell asleep.

Morning came too early but the workings of his mind defeated any attempt to prolong his sleep. Where was that furry friend that bounded onto the bed every morning? The familiar surroundings and time of day revived memories of his friend and companion. Tears flowed as he buried his face in the pillow and convulsed in his grief. He missed Jesse. "Please Lord, release me from my grief. I'm tired of grieving lost loves. You have put others in my life that I have come to cherish, now they too are at risk; protect them. I know that might sound selfish but I want to see them live long and abundant lives for Your sake, not mine. Thank you."

Nancy had left a carafe of coffee in the kitchen for him. The coffee tasted so good, just as if Reina had made it. No breakfast though. He would drive to the Chalet and have breakfast there.

"Morning Sean, where you off to today?" Trudy filled his cup with restaurant coffee.

"Good question Trudy. Not sure yet." He was careful in answering, "Maybe take TJ and head south to Watson Lake on some business, then back here before dark. Can I get three scrambled, bacon and whole grain toast please?"

"Coming up." She topped up some other coffee cups before giving Sean's order to the cook.

He sat looking out the large windows towards the airport runway watching a student pilot do touch and goes. Sipping his coffee, he considered his next move. The wind was from the southwest, keeping the temperature warmer than usual for this time of year. It was much colder further north. It had dropped to -32 at the White last night according to Sam. Sheila and Reina were putting together a wish list for Sean to pick up and bring with him on his return. He decided to fly back to the prospector camp, land on the road and check out the situation on foot. Whatever he found would determine his next move.

Trudy returned with his breakfast and more coffee. "Remember that guy you were asking about yesterday?"

"Yes, what about him?"

"Well, he spent last night at the motel and had breakfast here. I guess he must have found his girls team at the school."

Sean tried his best to be calm and disinterested. "Is he at the school now?"

"Don't know, he headed north when he left." She turned to wait on other customers.

Sean wolfed down his breakfast, paid the bill and left a larger tip than usual for Trudy. He decided to check out the prospector camp first. The camp was barely visible from where he turned to line up on the gravel highway; he didn't want to draw attention to his presence. He noticed that there was no smoke coming from the chimney but the Kenworth was still there. TJ touched down and rolled into the approach for a Department of Highways gravel pit.

Grabbing his rifle, he patted the CZ on his hip and started on a lope along the edge of the highway. He crossed the bridge and entered the forest before the approach to the camp came into view. Silently, he worked his way through the spruce and willows on a carpet of moss until he could see the orange truck through the trees. He sat for at least 15 minutes listening and watching. The wind in the treetops was the only sound and there was no movement.

Moving closer to the abandoned building, he kept to the riverside where there were fewer windows and more cover. He crept out of the willows and crouched beside the wall listening for sounds within. All was quiet. He waited another 15 minutes but still there was no sound except for the wind. Crouching low, he made his way towards the front of the building where he could see the truck and trailer. Again, he waited. Nothing. Maybe they had all gone to town in the blue pickup.

He made his way to the open door and looked around the doorframe. Both men were slumped over the blood-covered table. Scanning the rest of the room, he entered and confirmed that both men were dead and had been for some time. He opened the door of the Kenworth with his gloved hand and confirmed that it was empty. Lastly, he checked the Sea-Can. It too was empty. *"No such thing as honour among thieves and perverts,"* he thought.

After taking some photos of the scene, he returned to his plane, quickly taxied onto the road and took off heading back to Whitehorse. With the permission of the tower, he did a flyby over downtown and the high school to see if he could spot the blue pickup. He didn't see it.

Sean asked Arnie to fuel up TJ. He'd be back later. "Don't leave it too late Sean; we've got some weather coming in."

Bob was outside fuelling the blue F250 pickup when Sean drove into the yard. "Hi Sean, that guy you were asking about came back and bought one of my trucks."

"What did he buy?" asked Sean.

"That little red Chevy step side 4x4. Nice truck and he didn't even dicker."

"Did he say where's he was headed Bob?"

"Said he was going to register and insure it then head to Alaska to visit friends in Fairbanks."

"When was that?"

"A couple of hours ago. How come you're so interested in this guy?"

"Remind me to tell you sometime. Gotta run. Thanks Bob." Sean jumped into his truck and drove downtown. He didn't see any sign of the red Chevy.

Parking at the general store, he reached for the microphone hanging in front of his windshield. "Whitehorse radio this is YJ7085, over."

"Hi Sean, how can I help you?"

"Hi Darla, can you get me Sam at the White River Lodge please?"

"Standby."

"White River, go ahead Sean,"

"Hi Sam. How's that wish list coming along?"

"Got it right here, got a pencil?"

Sam read off a long list of items ranging from various sizes of bush pacs to slabs of bacon and underwear. Sean took careful notes and promised to do his best to fill the order. "I hope to be back before dark, there's some weather coming in. How is it up your way?"

"We're good, clear air but it's cold."

"Okay Sam, give my love to the gang and, Sam," he paused, "Sam, stay alert, stuff's happening. 7085 clear."

Sean spent the next couple of hours gathering items from the list. Starting with the dry goods, he enlisted the store clerk, Tracy, to help gather the items on his list. He was fortunate to get a parka for each girl and felt-lined boots to match the list of sizes. Hats and mitts were not a problem but buying female undergarments challenged his devotion to their well-being so he left the task to Tracy. She amused herself kidding him about outfitting his new harem. Sean went along with the kidding but avoided explanations.

Tracy had one of the bag boys help Sean with an extra cart to assemble the grocery list. There were enough Americans living in the Yukon that you could always find a turkey in November. Sean bought four just in case they were still hanging out at the White when Christmas rolled around. Besides, you can never have enough turkey when you eat moose all winter. On the way to the airport, he picked up the blood analyses and the mail. Errant snowflakes fell on his parka as he transferred his cargo into TJ and completed his walk around.

* * *

John pulled into Destruction Bay and parked in front of the restaurant at the Talbot Arm Motel. A couple of men, locals, were drinking coffee at the staff table talking with a man in a white bib apron. The man approached John's table with a coffee pot and a menu. "Veal cutlets are the lunch special, you take cream in your coffee?"

"No. That sounds fine, I'll have the cutlets. Is that all anyone serves along this highway, he joked. Every time I stop it seems that veal cutlets are the special for the day." The man in the apron shrugged his shoulders, turned to replace the coffee pot on the warmer and went into the kitchen. He doubled as a cook and probably washed dishes and pumped gas as well. John got up and retrieved a newspaper lying on another table. Judging by the headlines it was a slow news week. His life should be so boring he thought. When the man in the apron returned with his meal, he asked how far it was to Fairbanks.

"You can count on eight hours."

"Is there any place to overnight on the way?"

"Oh, sure. A couple of hours further on there's White River Lodge, then the motel at Beaver Creek just before you cross the border. Beaver Creek might be your best bet; Sam closes down at White River for the winter. I expect he's already closed up by now. Your next option would be Tok in Alaska about a four-hour drive from here. Stay at the Mooseberry if you stop there. Border's closed at night. It's a lot colder north of here so keep your tank full."

"Thanks. Say, you haven't seen a bunch of young girls travelling this way have you?"

"Nope. Another one of those school sport teams?"

"Yeah." John sliced into his cutlet as the man in the apron re-joined those at the staff table.

He topped up his gas tank before pulling back onto the highway. The days were shortening and it would be dark by the time he reached Tok. As he approached the Donjek River he could feel the temperature difference even inside the truck. Only one vehicle had passed him on his way north; people didn't drive at these temperatures if they didn't have to. He turned up the fan on the heater. The bridge over the White River loomed in the distance. As he passed the entrance to the White River Lodge he saw the sign 'Closed for the Season' and a cable blocking the approach. A young girl with blonde hair appeared from behind the lodge and walked with a large dog toward the river.

Chapter 32

TJ climbed out on the southwest wind banking left and climbing until the DG read 300 and the altimeter 4500 feet. The extra weight was noticeable but the little plane trimmed neatly for a flight of less than two hours. A warm front was invading the Yukon from the Alaska panhandle. These systems promised lots of snow when they collided with the cold interior air but Sean was confident he could stay ahead of that collision until he reached the White. He saw no sign of the red pickup.

Buzzing the Lodge he swept low and slow over the airstrip checking for obstacles and the general condition of the dirt surface now covered in a couple of inches of snow. Satisfied, he set up for a short field landing. He touched down and rolled to a stop at the fuel tank. Sam backed his pickup close to the plane as Reina and Anya followed on foot wrapped in their parkas. Sean climbed out and stretched as the two girls embraced him with welcoming hugs. He hugged them back planting a good-to-be-back kiss on each cold cheek.

"Lot cooler here than Whitehorse," he remarked as he passed a box to Anya. "For you my dear."

Anya squealed and jumped as Sean passed another box to Reina. "And for you my dear."

Reina kissed him then joined Anya retreating to the warmth of the Lodge leaving Sam and Sean to finish unloading.

Sean opened the baggage door and began handing boxes to Sam. After loading the pickup, Sam drove to the back of the Lodge to unload while Sean topped off his tanks and taxied to the tie down area. He wrapped the cowling with the engine blanket and did a quick walk around before grabbing his rifle and heading for the lodge. The sky had clouded over and snowflakes were in the air.

The Lodge was bustling with activity as he stepped from the mudroom. Sheila was in the kitchen directing the girls as they unpacked and stowed groceries. She and Reina were making sure to keep the girls busy. Reina and Anya were on the floor sorting through the boxes of clothing, boots and pharmaceuticals arranging items in neat piles on which they placed bright yellow paper nametags.

"You didn't open your boxes," Sean observed as he stood looking down at them.

"We wanted to save them for later," replied Reina, "after supper we'll open them. I think the girls will be excited to see their new clothes. Do you want some coffee?"

"Thanks Reina, I'd love one." Sean sat on a couch while Reina retrieved a mug. "Hey Sam." Sean pulled a small box from his shirt pocket and threw it to Sam. "They were on sale so most of them were gone. I got the last box."

Sam caught the box of .223 cartridges with one hand. "Thanks Sean, I can never have enough of these and they're not easy to come by. What do I owe you?"

"I think it's the other way around Sam. Consider them a small token of my appreciation." He threw him another small box wrapped in colourful paper with a ribbon. "For your wife."

Sam smiled knowingly as he took the gift and went into the kitchen to give it to Sheila.

"Feels like Christmas," Reina remarked as she passed the mug of coffee to Sean.

Sheila came running into the room and headed straight for Sean. "Thank you Sean, you read my mind, I've always admired this necklace but never thought I'd own it." She reached over, hugged his neck and kissed his cheek before showing off her treasure to Anya and Reina.

"I think *Sam* should get the hug. He's the one who put me onto it." Sean nodded towards Sam.

Sheila hugged her husband and kissed him with delight. "Thanks Honey, I love it. You always knew I did."

"Okay, now I'm all excited, let's open our gifts too Anya." Reina smiled at Anya who nodded her head enthusiastically.

Anya untied the ribbon before removing the colourful paper that hid her gift – she had never received a present. On top of a leather-bound Holy Bible was a framed photo of her and Jesse and Sean sitting on the woodpile at Sean's cabin. Sean had embossed Anya's name in gold letters on the cover of her bible. Inside the cover was a handwritten inscription: *To my dear Anya, fearfully and wonderfully made, loved by God, and me, your friend forever, Sean.* Tears filled her eyes as she leaned over to hug Sean. Words were not necessary; the tears streaming down her cheeks said it all.

Reina's eyes watered as she watched Anya. She turned to Sean who invited her to open her gift. Anya slid closer to Reina. Wiping the tears from her cheeks, she watched with anticipation as she removed the ribbon and wrapping. A small, royal blue velvet box was inside another box. The room fell silent. Reina stared at Sean who smiled and nodded. She lifted the lid on the box revealing a diamond ring.

"I hope you know my love for you Reina; will you marry me?"

Sam whispered to his wife, "About time, don't you think?"

Reina's face beamed as she answered, "You know I love you too, and yes, I will Sean." A cheer went up from those looking on. Tears flowed as the two hugged each other. Anya couldn't contain herself and soon joined in their hug.

"Well, this is some special day," announced Sheila, "better break out the crystal. Sam you get a couple of bottles of your best cranberry wine. Let's toast this lovely couple."

Sean stood, his arm around Reina. He kissed her on the cheek. "I'll be right back. Gotta check the fuel drains on TJ for water in the fuel. I want to get it done before that weather gets nasty." He headed for the door.

"That's Sean, taking care of business, but I love him for it," Reina sighed and hugged Anya to her side.

"I love him too Reina, is that okay?" asked Anya.

"It sure is dear girl. And you need to know that he loves you too, like his own daughter."

* * *

The winter darkness had enveloped the land. Snow was swirling chaotically in the turbulence set up by the building and trees. At the airstrip, it slanted in the wind driving into Sean's face. Bozo stayed in the woodshed rather than join Sean and face the storm. The temperature had risen a little but the wind kept a body well chilled. Sean drained a small amount of fuel from each wing tank and was satisfied with what he saw in the plastic cup. On his way back to the lodge he did a tour around the grounds and out to the highway.

He couldn't see much in the dark with the heavy snow further reducing visibility. There were no vehicle tracks on the highway; who would be travelling in this weather anyway. He stopped at the woodshed to scratch Bozo's ears and load his arms with firewood; wood consumption would go way up tonight. His frozen face broke a smile as he thought about him and Reina becoming one before God. Their relationship was solid, full of love, confirmed by many others. Why hadn't he asked before? He didn't have an answer but it didn't matter anymore.

* * *

Sean joined the others in the living room. Sheila and Sam poured 17 glasses of wine using up one full bottle of Sam's famous wine. Sam whistled for attention before speaking. "I've known this man a long time. Haven't known Reina as long but let me tell you, you won't find better people under the northern lights than these two. I suppose Sheila and I have prayed for this engagement for a while. We, like so many others, saw these two as naturals for one another and it blesses my socks off to see them pledged to marry. Raise your glasses please. To Sean and Reina with God's richest blessings."

After the toast and congratulatory hugs, Anya rounded up the girls and invited them to find the pile of clothes with their name on it. She explained that the items were a gift to each of them to celebrate their freedom. She told them that starting tomorrow they would be having English classes using the small Bible that was included in each pile. Blanka, Halina and Celina stood quietly against the wall as the other girls went to their respective stack of clothes, boots and other items. Some of the girls modeled their colourful fur-lined parkas, mitts and bush pacs while others sat picking through the new clothing. For the moment, they forgot the pain and suffering of the last few weeks.

Reina and Sheila noticed the three girls off by themselves and went over to stand with them. Anya soon joined them asking them in Polish why they didn't go and see their new clothes. Reina and Sheila watched the girls grow agitated then angry. "They don't understand why you would give them such nice things; they think they are whores and want to go back," said Anya. Reina looked at Sheila. Both women recognized these feelings from their counselling experience with other victims of abuse.

"Anya, we need to go upstairs where they can talk. Can you get them to come with us?" Reina asked with tears in her eyes. Sheila announced that supper would be late and went with Reina, Anya and the three girls.

It was six o'clock when Sheila came downstairs and announced that supper would be ready in half an hour. Anya and Reina followed with the three girls. Anya asked the other girls to take their items to their rooms and get themselves ready for supper. The girls filled their arms and scrambled up the stairs to their rooms.

Sean and Sam watched in bewilderment as Anya sat Blanka, Halina and Celina in front of their pile of clothes. Reina told Sean and Sam that they were to present each of the girls with an item from their pile and remind them that they are God's creation and He loves and forgives them. The two men each knelt in front of a girl and watched intently as they spoke the words and offered an item from their pile of clothes. The girls doubled over in tears sobbing as Anya, Reina and Sheila held them.

Chapter 33

After supper, the girls helped clean up, then went to their rooms. Sean motioned for Reina and Anya to join him in the living room. "How have they been doing, the girls? That episode before supper was a bit scary."

"To be expected," replied Reina, "that is not unusual, especially if victims have been captive for a long time. That little exercise you helped with will do a great deal to assuage their fears and help rebuild their self-worth. None of these girls have come from healthy family situations so they were already vulnerable even before they got caught up with these thugs."

"So what can Sam and I do to help, they don't seem to like us," Sean offered.

"They don't trust you yet, give them time," said Reina, "you two just keep being yourselves but be sensitive when you're around them, keep your distance and speak gently when addressing them. It's okay to show them how to do chores, but let them make mistakes and encourage them along the way. No physical contact. They will be watching how you relate to me and Anya and Sheila."

"So what have you two been up to while I was away?" Sean invited Reina and Anya to fill him in on the events over the past couple of days.

* * *

"Where do you live and what is the purpose of your trip at this time of the year?" The customs officer stared into John's eyes.

"I live in Winnipeg and I've got some time off now so I thought I would visit some friends in Fairbanks. I've never seen this country but didn't realize it would be so cold this time of year." John maintained his composure as he answered the officer's question.

"What do you do for living?"

"I'm in shipping."

The officer continued to stare at John then handed him his passport and said, "Have a good trip."

* * *

"Well, we finished doing physical exams on all the girls and had some fun in between." Reina smiled at Anya. "Anya is a great help and eager to learn. She is a wonderful young lady who makes me proud." Anya blushed and Sean smiled at her. "I'm happy to report that the girls are healthy. All are suffering a level of malnutrition but Sheila is remedying that. Some of the girls are recovering from beatings and other abuse they received from those brutes (she refused to call them 'men'), but no broken bones. A couple of the girls are showing signs of severe sexual abuse but they will recover from their physical injuries. Their captivity and treatment by those animals has emotionally traumatized all the girls. They need to be constantly reassured of their safety and of our acceptance. We need to show that we love and care for them. They are fragile."

"Do Sam and Sheila understand their condition?"

"Yes, I talked with them. Sam and Sheila love the girls and can't do enough for them as it is. They just need to be sensitive to their moods, unusual behaviours and their needs and not take anything personally. Don't be surprised by outbursts of anger, sleeping difficulties including nightmares and tendencies to withdraw into isolation. The girls are learning with Anya's help to trust us, which is a huge plus for their recovery. They need to know that they can talk to us, not just Anya about their feelings. Anya also needs to heal. Even though she is a compassionate and kind young lady, we can't expect her to be a counsellor for the girls; she is going through her own healing. Already I am talking with a couple of the girls on a regular basis. We must be careful not to betray their trust. Anya has taken a very important initiative that will actually help the girls a lot in regaining a feeling of control in their lives; tell Sean what you did Anya."

Anya lowered her eyes as Reina spoke, then looked up at Sean. He noticed an unusual confidence in Anya as she began to speak. "Well, Sam and Sheila do a lot for us and I know the girls would like to help them where they can but they are shy because of their English and the strange surroundings. So, I arranged with Sam and Sheila to assign specific chores to the girls, like firewood, laundry, cleaning, meals and other stuff. The girls got to choose their job and they work in pairs and take responsibility for their work. It helps them to feel they can take charge over their lives. They are happy to be able to help and they feel the appreciation from Sam and Sheila. I think this, along with our other activities, will help us to get over the horrible things that we've been through."

Sean was quiet at first, staring at Reina and Anya. "You two are amazing! These girls couldn't be in better care. Thank you both. Oh, almost forgot." Reaching into his shirt, he handed the blood work report to Reina.

She quickly glanced through the pages. "It's a good report. These girls are doing well." Reina's face lit up as she continued to review the report. "Four of them are going to need to start a regimen of antibiotics, Celina, Irenka, Kazia and Tekla. Anya, these girls will take the same pill that you are taking. After a week or so you should all be fine. I'll start them tonight."

"Tell Sean what we made, Reina," Anya asked as she bounced on her chair and clapped her hands.

"Why don't you tell him," countered Reina.

"Sam and Sheila are having trouble with the girl's names so we made a name badge for each of us and a sign with our name for the door on our room. Sam cut us each a piece of wood and showed us how to carve our name then he put the signs on our door. Then we made a badge for each of us to wear every day. Sam cut pieces from the antlers of the moose he shot and we polished them and used a marker to put our name on them. After, we glued a pin on the back so we can pin it to our shirt. See." Anya moved closer and held her badge so Sean could see.

"Nice Anya – too bad you spelled your name wrong."

Anya quickly turned her badge so she could see it. "It's not wrong!" she asserted while glaring at Sean. When she realized that he was just fooling with her, she laughed and gave him a gentle swat on the knee.

"We also started practicing our English and learning more words. Reina reads us stories about Canada's North Country and we talk about the stories after. It's lots of fun and the girls look forward to our classes."

"You girls are a great bunch of students. I love you all," said Reina. "The girls have been very good about helping Sheila and Sam with chores and Sam and Anya took them on a short walk up the river one day. They couldn't go too far because they didn't have the proper clothes and boots like they do now."

"Speaking of classes, what are you going to do about your classes at the College?" asked Sean.

"I called the Dean and explained that an emergency had taken me away and I couldn't say when I would be able to return. He said he would cancel the fall classes and asked me to keep him posted so he could schedule the spring semester."

They continued to talk enthusiastically, sharing their adventures over the past couple of days. Nobody seemed to show any apprehension over their circumstances which both relieved and concerned Sean. Nobody asked whether Sean had found the men in the orange Kenworth.

Chapter 34

John's hidden tension began to release as he left the border crossing and drove into the darkness towards Tok where he planned to spend the night. The more he pondered the sight of the blonde girl at the White River Lodge, the more he was convinced she was one of his, the one that caused all the trouble. It made sense. No one had seen any sign of the girls along the highway. The Lodge was a logical stop for them and their kidnappers after escaping from them at Snag but they thought it was closed and vacant. He wished he had stopped to confirm his suspicions but he didn't have those same suspicions at the time. Besides, things would go sideways if anyone recognized him. No, it was better that he contact his client and take advantage of their organization's resources to track down and retrieve his missing girls. Sure, he'd take a cut in the payoff but with two less partners he would come out well ahead of the original plan.

It was 42 below zero when he arrived at the office building on Airport Way in Fairbanks. Ice fog generated by vehicle exhaust and the still open Chena River blanketed the area. He parked the truck and reluctantly shut off the engine before running to the entrance. The elevator doors opened as he stepped into the lobby so he punched the number three and waited. He walked down the carpeted hall and knocked on the door marked 314. An extremely attractive brunette opened the door, confirmed his identity and invited him to enter. He declined her offer of coffee while taking a seat on the expensive leather couch while she punched in some numbers on her phone. "Mr. Kozlov will be with you shortly," announced the brunette.

A short, stocky man in an expensive suit appeared from the hallway and greeted him with a smile while another, familiar man, stood close by. John stood and offered his hand. "Mr. Kozlov, I am John, we talked on the phone."

"Yes, yes, follow me."

Together they entered a lavish office overlooking the river valley, obscured in ice fog. The other man standing beside the door closed it after them then spun John around and pushed him face first into the wall. He removed John's pistol from its holster and released him before resuming his position against the wall, hands clasped in front and an expressionless, scarred face that stared at nothing in particular. Kozlov ignored him and didn't introduce him to John who recalled his face from the failed pickup at Snag.

"Carlos told me what happened. We have a deal, $260 thousand but you failed to deliver, what are you doing about it?" Kozlov stared at John from behind a massive desk.

John was still shaken but replied, "I'm pretty sure where the girls are hiding but I need help to confirm and get them back. I can't do it because they will recognize me. Once I know, then I can deal with their kidnappers and deliver them to you. I suspect whoever is holding them are just some do-gooders; I don't believe they are professionals. If you could loan me one of your men for a couple of days I'm sure I can deliver them within the week." John's voice betrayed his nervousness.

Kozlov continued to stare at him but didn't reply. After an awkward silence, he punched some numbers on his phone and spoke in Russian to whoever answered. He hung up and turned back to John. "I don't need your girls, I can get others."

John sighed, "But they are good ones, all young and attractive, 13 of them."

Kozlov interrupted him. "Sergio can go with you but I will deduct $20 thousand from our deal if you want his help."

John thought for a few seconds then, in defeat, muttered, "Okay."

"Wait until the weather breaks. Sergio will take you to a place to stay until then."

A knock on the door prompted the man by the door to open it. A tall, dark-complexioned man in his thirties, dressed in blue jeans and a pullover sweater, strode into the room and stood in front of the desk ignoring John. "Sergio, this is John," Kozlov swept his arm towards John. Sergio turned and nodded his head at John. "You will take him to the house where he will stay until the weather warms then you will go with him to find the girls. When he has them we will use the plane again to pick them up. We are done – let me down again and we're finished."

John rose from his chair. Sergio ushered him out of the office and down the hall to the reception area retrieving John's pistol from the other man as he left. In the reception area the brunette handed Sergio a key with a large plastic tag attached.

"Where is your vehicle?" Sergio spoke to him for the first time and handed John his pistol.

"In the parking lot next to the building," replied John.

"Good, you will follow me to the house. Here is my contact if you need anything." Sergio handed John a business card with his first name and a phone number imprinted on it.

They arrived at a large house and entered the underground parking garage. Sergio told John to write down the entry code so he could enter as needed. At the top of the stairs he pushed a card into a slot, pushed open a door, and entered a carpeted hallway. Sergio led John to a room at the end of the hall and used the key with the plastic tag to unlock the door.

"This is where you will stay. There are others that stay in the other half of this house, don't go there!" His glare reinforced the command as he handed John the key. "Come, you need to meet Wanda, she looks after the place. She will give you a special key to come and go. The others cannot leave without permission from Wanda or Mr. Kozlov."

Wanda looked to be in her forties, well groomed and, at one time, he thought, quite attractive. The heavy makeup failed to hide the scars of a life of booze, cigarettes and drugs. Her coarse voice testified to a hard life but she greeted John cordially and encouraged him to make himself at home. Sergio excused himself and left them alone.

"How long will you be here John?" she queried.

"Until the weather warms up. How long do you think that might be?" he answered.

Wanda laughed, "could be a week or three weeks but it's early for such cold weather so it might not last long."

A tall, impeccably dressed and perfectly proportioned young woman came into the room and joined them. She smiled at John who rose from his chair as she sat in the armchair opposite them crossing her shapely legs.

"John, this is Roksana. Roksana, meet John, he'll be staying with us for a few days." Wanda watched John approach Roksana and extend his hand. "We have a gentleman in our midst," she remarked. "You'll meet the others later; they live in the other half of the house – off limits to you. Help yourself in the kitchen or there's a roadhouse a couple of blocks away that serves good food. Sometimes we order pizza or Chinese but we'll let you know. There's a TV in your room or you're welcome to watch this one. The phone in your room is only for your use so don't let any of the girls try and con you." She handed him a key card. "That will unlock the front and basement doors. Make sure you are the only one that goes through them. Mr. Kozlov runs a tight ship and doesn't tolerate rule breakers."

John excused himself and went to his room where he turned on the TV and reclined on the bed. He found the weather channel where the forecast promised a break in the cold in a few days. His thoughts returned to the image of the blonde girl and the dog at the White River. If his suspicions were wrong he would be in deep trouble but if he guessed right his fortunes would change for the better. He would easily deal with the amateurs who held the girls. Finally, he'd deliver them to the waiting aircraft at the Snag airstrip. He hoped he was right.

Chapter 35

Anya's natural curiosity left her vulnerable but it also provided a door to experience and understanding. Her years of growing up in an institution had stifled her bright and eager spirit but did not destroy it. Now that she was no longer captive within the grey walls of the orphanage, she was free to bloom and grow. She seemed oblivious to her most recent past and the predicament that she and the girls were in; instead, she revelled in the new things that were part of her current life at the lodge. Maybe it was denial, her way of coping.

She and her best friend, Kazia, avoided the subject of their abduction and journey halfway around the world to this strange land. At night, they would lay in their beds talking about the events of the day and what lay in store for them tomorrow. Although they dared not look too far into their futures, they felt secure, cared for and loved by Sean, Reina, and their hosts. Perhaps one day they could dream of a future.

Activities like the firearms class made a difference for the girls. And, thanks to Sam and Sheila, they had settled into their sanctuary at the White River Lodge. They were beginning to relax, enjoying and growing in their freedom and the activities that Reina involved them in every day. Sean tried to participate in that same spirit of freedom and relief but knowing that an enemy still threatened kept him on constant alert.

Anya, Kazia and Tekla were practicing target acquisition in the dining room when suddenly Anya turned towards Sean not noticing that the pistol in her hand turned with her. "No!" Sean roared as he slapped the unloaded pistol away. He caught the reflex action of his other hand in time as it flashed towards Anya's throat. "Never point a gun at anything you don't want to destroy!" Sean's voice was firm, tinged with anger.

Anya shrank back at Sean's reaction to her carelessness. Tears welled up in fearful eyes. Kazia and Tekla looked on wide-eyed.

Sean mentally kicked himself as he touched her hand to reassure her. "I'm sorry Anya, I didn't mean to be so harsh with you, please forgive me," he pleaded. He offered her his bandana to catch the tear beginning to trace its way over her cheekbone. Partly regaining his composure he turned away, slammed his fist into his hand and moaned "God, I'm so sorry Anya."

Anya reached out and touched his shoulder. "I, I forgive you. You are right, but I'm still learning. I will try to do better; I want to do better." She was beginning to sob.

He turned to face her. "Anya, you always do your best and I really love that about you. It's my problem; I will try to do better." He glanced at the other girls. Sean was in a constant state of tension and it was affecting his relationships. "It is so important that handling a gun becomes instinctual but that only happens after lots of practice and, yes, you will make mistakes. That's why we are using unloaded pistols. Do you want to continue?" Sean's voice was now gentle and apologetic.

"Yes," the three girls chorused.

"We want to be able to shoot like you and Reina. Let's practice." Anya tried to smile as she holstered the pistol.

Together they continued their holstering, drawing and target acquisition drills. Anya was a natural but, like the others, she needed practice to develop her skill and muscle memory. She surprised Sean and Reina when she showed interest in their guns. They answered her questions and, along with Sam, proudly let her handle their various firearms. When some of the other girls showed interest, Sean asked Sam who was ex-military if he would help him offer a firearms handling course in their roster of daily activities. Sean gave advanced pistol training to Anya, Kazia and Tekla as they showed exceptional aptitude and interest. When the weather warmed, he and Sam would take them out to Sam's shooting range and let them shoot live ammunition.

Sam and Sheila enjoyed their houseguests and couldn't do enough for the girls. The girls in turn seemed to thrive on the daily chores that brought them closer to Sheila and Sam. Blanka was the exception. She seemed to have lost all spirit, her eyes emotionless. All were concerned for her, the youngest of the girls. None of the other girls knew Blanka before their abduction and Reina had minimal success establishing any history for her. Raised on a farm she didn't seem to have any family. Reina believed that she was little more than a slave to the owners. She was the only one who continued to awake in the night with nightmares.

Fortunately, her roommate, Danuta, had a kind and compassionate disposition and comforted her friend in the darkness. Sudden noises or unexpected touch startled her. She isolated herself, often sneaking off to her room where she would lay on her bed crying. The gifts of clothing she received seemed to perplex her. In contrast to the other girls, Blanka would only sit and look at the items and then, as if asking permission, she would stare with sad eyes at Reina. Reina would sit with her and go through the items individually as one might do with a toddler. Together, they carried the clothes to her room where Blanka carefully laid each item in a dresser drawer or hung it in the closet, mimicking Danuta. Danuta was her guardian angel and made a point of watching out for her, praying with her, encouraging her to participate and keeping Reina informed.

Reina and Sheila were spending time with Blanka and their attention and the prayers of others appeared to be paying off. She was fearful of Sean and Sam but in recent days Reina noticed that she would stay seated if one of the men happened to sit beside her at meals. At the morning breakfast, she actually sat beside Sam on her own initiative. Bozo was her best friend. She would often sit apart from the others lying beside Bozo on the floor listening to Reina read a story or monitoring an English lesson.

Blanka was sitting alone on the couch beside the airtight. She greeted Bozo with open arms as he and Sean came in from making the rounds of the

Lodge and the adjacent area. Sean smiled at her but said nothing as he continued towards the kitchen. "Reina, Sam can we meet in the dining room?"

"Something wrong?" asked Sam.

"No, no, we just need to talk." They sat at a small table beside a window where Sean could see the highway and out of earshot from the girls. The snow had stopped but the cold had settled in and there was almost no traffic on the highway. "I want you to know what I found out about those traffickers. There's only one now."

"No! You didn't?" cried Reina"

"No, not me. A guy named John Dubicki, probably the leader of the bunch, shot his two partners and left them at an old abandoned prospecting camp on the Teslin River along with the truck. I found out that he bought a red, 4x4 pickup from Bob and headed for Alaska. I never saw the truck so he must have been ahead of me. I bet he drove right by here."

"Now the police will be looking for him," said Reina. "If they catch him, our worries are over."

"Not likely. It will be a long time before anyone finds those bodies and highly unlikely that anyone would report those thugs as missing," replied Sean.

"Well, do you think he'll give up on the girls?" asked Reina.

"No, not a chance; they are worth a lot of money to him, even more now that he doesn't have to share it. I think he's meeting with his buyers. According to Trudy, he was asking questions about the girls when he was at the Chalet and probably elsewhere. She said he phoned Fairbanks while there. If I had to guess I'd say that we haven't seen the end of this guy."

"So we're still at risk. What do you think we should do?" asked Sam.

"If you'll let me use your truck Sam, I'll drive up to Beaver Creek and talk to Don and the border guys to see if they've seen that red pickup. If so, then I'll make up some story so as not to raise suspicions, and ask Don and Belle to keep an eye out and let us know if they see anything. That will give us a little warning if he comes back which I'm certain he will."

"No problem Sean," replied Sam. "So what do we do if he comes here looking for the girls?"

"That's my fear. Will we be able to protect them and ourselves for that matter? I would prefer to pre-empt any plans he might have but that's kind of hard when you don't know much about who you're dealing with and where they are. I do know what he looks like. Tall, dark with a scar on his cheek and wearing a dark blue nylon parka."

"Could we move the girls somewhere else, somewhere more secure?" asked Reina.

"That was my thought all along, that's why I had you bring the motor home. But, where can we hide 13 teenage girls? Not Whitehorse, too easy to find them there. My cabin would be great except that it's so small and I don't know of anywhere else that could house 13 young women without raising suspicion." Sean lamented.

"Your fishing lodge!" Reina almost shouted.

"Hey! You're not just a pretty face after all. Right under my nose and I never even thought." Sean's countenance brightened then turned to a frown. "It could work but I don't want to be on the run with these girls; this has got to stop and soon. I talked to Jay Morgan without divulging our situation and found out that there is a good chance the girls could stay in Canada legally. I guess the question is will this guy ever give up and, if so, when? He has money invested and he expects a good return on that investment. If he keeps pursuing them I'm willing to take drastic measures and I don't mean calling the cops."

"What do you mean by 'drastic'?" Reina's eyebrows furrowed as she glared at Sean.

"I mean that I don't want these girls always looking over their shoulder and if this guy comes for them he's not getting them without a fight. And I expect to win that fight."

Sam spoke up, "I'm not one to run from trouble and neither is Sheila. Just so you know, we're with you Sean, whatever you decide, but I say we stay put and let them come to us. I doubt whether they could surprise us;

the river's not frozen enough to cross and they're not bush people so they'll approach from the highway. They'll come with more than a pickup if they think they're getting the girls. I say we work out a plan to defend ourselves and wait to see what happens. I doubt they'll try anything in this cold so we've got some time."

Reina stared at Sean waiting apprehensively for his reaction to Sam's suggestion.

Sean looked at Sam. "You remind me of King David's commander Joab, only a few years older." He laughed. "David didn't run and hide when his enemies stole his family and the families of his fighting men." Sean spoke boldly. "No, he sought God and God told him to pursue the raiders; David obeyed and God gave him back his family and victory over the raiders. God has given these girls back into our hands and I know that He expects us to look after them. Let's all go to prayer and lay our predicament before the Lord. Remember Psalm 120, *"In my distress I cry to the LORD, that he may answer me."* Listen for what He has to say." He stood up, walked to the back door, threw on his parka and left.

Chapter 36

Anya and Reina sat on Reina's bed as Anya related the incident with Sean and the pistol. Reina could tell that something had happened but she didn't know what or how serious it was. She invited Anya to tell her what happened. After Anya explained what she had done, Reina understood Sean's anger. Her biggest concern was how the other things going on had aggravated his response. Reina told Anya that Sean was under a lot of pressure but she didn't give her any more details so as not to scare her. She reassured her that he didn't mean to hurt her and that he wanted the best for her and all the girls.

Sean walked along the riverbank with Bozo by his side. The air bit into the flesh on his face. His breath lay like a scarf over his shoulder and the snow crunched beneath his bush pacs. He was at home in the frozen wilderness of the Yukon. After half an hour, he entered a clearing where Sam had salvaged trees from a blow-down many years earlier. He sat on a tree trunk partly suspended by its roots at one end and branches at the other and stared at the white-cloaked mountains of the St. Elias range. His mind recalled Psalm 121, *"I lift up my eyes to the hills - from where will my help come from. My help comes from the Lord who made heaven and earth."* He sat in the frozen stillness, Bozo lying at his feet, recalling images of pathetic souls chanting hopefully to stone idols with mouths that didn't speak, eyes that didn't see and ears that didn't hear.

After an hour spent in communion with the living, sovereign God, Sean returned to the Lodge. He knew a perfect peace despite the circumstances. Getting the keys from Sam, he started the truck, letting it idle long enough to thaw the transmission oil and allow him to shift into first gear. The circulating heater warmed the engine but the gearboxes were another matter. He had to ride the clutch a little to get the drive train to turn and move the 3/4 ton 4x4 down the driveway. The frozen vehicle crawled towards the ploughed highway where he shifted to second then third gear and drove slowly, allowing the drive train to warm. At 45 degrees below zero metal was brittle and he didn't want to break anything.

He drove to the border crossing and stopped on the Canadian side to talk with Jerry who was on duty. Jerry recalled the red pickup and asked what interest Sean had in the truck. Sean lied, explaining that the driver was an old friend of Sam's. It seemed to satisfy Jerry. Jerry agreed to call him or Sam at the White River Lodge if the truck came through again. Sean thanked him and drove back to Beaver Creek to talk with Don and Belle asking God's forgiveness along the way.

The bell tinkled when Sean opened the door rousing Don to attention from his chair in front of the airtight. "Hi Sean, what you doing out in this weather?"

"Hi Don, not my choice, just doing Sam a favour. Have you noticed a red step-side pickup go by in the last couple of days?"

"Yup, he stopped for gas on his way to Fairbanks."

"Well, he's a friend of Sam's." Sean lied again trying to act nonchalant. "If you see him come by can you give me or Sam a call at the Lodge but don't let on. Sam's got a surprise for him when he stops in."

"No problem. You want gas?"

"It's filling, Stay put, I'll finish it off." Sean left to finish filling Sam's pickup.

When he returned to pay for the fuel, he asked Don about traffic on the highway. The answer was what he expected. Only a handful of vehicles had passed and most were of the commercial sort. Sean thanked Don and left.

As he drove past the junction, he noticed fresh, untracked snow covered the road to Snag. The day was bright with the fresh snow reflecting the arctic sun. Sundogs sat on either side of the yellow disc, a symbol of severe cold and ice crystals in the air. He turned into the driveway on his own tracks, there were no others.

Chapter 37

Reina was finishing her English lesson when Sean entered the living room dropping his armload of firewood into the wood box. Anya was intently explaining in Polish what Reina had been trying to explain in English. The class ignored him while Reina flashed a brilliant smile and threw him a kiss. He returned to the mudroom to hang up his parka and remove his boots.

Sean found Sam in the dining room reloading cartridges for his 30.06 with his simple but effective classic Lee Loader. Sam motioned for him to sit then slid a box of brass towards him. Sean took the cue and began knocking spent primers out of the bottom of the cases. He told Sam what he found out at the border and how he alerted Jerry and Don to call if they saw Mr. Dubicki come by, "I told them he was an old friend of yours." Sam looked up briefly and grunted his understanding ignoring Reina as she entered the room.

Reina approached Sean from behind, closed her arms around him and kissed him on the cheek. "Glad you're home and so is someone else. Be prepared. She wants you to know that the two of you are okay despite your *incident*."

"She *told* you?" Sean exclaimed, turning to face her.

"Of course she did. Now be nice." She tapped his nose with her finger. "I'm going to help Sheila with supper."

He resumed his work when suddenly a shock of blonde hair covered his face. Anya was behind him hugging his neck and letting her long hair fall over his head covering his face. "What you doing?" she simpered.

"Nothing, I can't see!" he pretended frustration.

"Ohhh, maybe Anya can help," came the feigned note of concern as she slid around to sit beside him on the bench. Sam was snickering to himself as he measured powder into the newly primed cases.

Anya took the hammer from Sean's hand and demanded to know what to do next.

"You're a mischievous clown and I love you for it." Sean gave her a squeeze and showed her how to remove the old primers while explaining what he and Sam were doing.

Anya had finished de-priming the box of shells when Sheila poked her head into the dining room. "Okay, Samuel, clean up your mess and get blondie to help you set the table."

"You two go ahead, I'll clean up. Good job Anya." Sean waved his arm towards the long table. Anya hugged his neck and kissed him on the cheek before joining Sam.

Sean retired to the living room and sat by the airtight. The girls had left to go to their rooms. His weary body and mind sunk into the old chair and the silence of the room. The stress of living with an unpredictable threat was taking its toll. He recalled his time in Israel where everyone lived with the threat of violence hanging over their heads; over time you got used to it but you never dropped your guard. His thoughts, periodically interrupted by popping sounds from the old heater and kitchen noises, swirled then settled. What did the Lord want him to do? He couldn't just sit around and wait – could he? That wasn't his nature but somehow the circumstances didn't seem to permit much else and that frustrated him.

Sheila came into the room with Bozo and sat on the couch drying her hands on her apron. "What are you thinking about hon'?" Her countenance expressed genuine but knowing concern. Sean shook his head and looked at the floor. "Frustrated aren't you? Can't stand waiting around not being able to do anything. Am I right?" He looked at her and nodded. "You make me think of David in Psalm 10 where he badgers the Lord for His apparent inaction 'Where are you Lord? Why are you hiding in these times of trouble? The wicked pursue the afflicted and the orphans; do something please.' But, let's remember that sometimes He wants you to be still and let Him work things out. You don't always have to be on the move. He pared down Gideon's army by quite a bit so Gideon couldn't take credit for what God was going to do. Likewise, with Jehoshaphat, He just told him to stand by and watch Him go to battle. We appreciate you Sean but try and be still and don't fret over evildoers." Sam entered the room and sat beside his wife. "We appreciate both you guys," she continued with a glance toward her husband. "I'm praying for you Sean but give God a chance." She gave Sam and Sean a hug and returned to the kitchen.

Sam and Sean gave each other a look of mutual appreciation. Words weren't necessary. The sound of many feet thundering from the stairwell interrupted their silent musing and came crashing into their peaceful sanctuary. Eleven giggling girls swarmed the room while Blanka lingered on the stairs. Some took up positions on couches and chairs while Danuta and Roza beckoned to Blanka who joined them and Bozo on the rug. Brygida and Celina lounged on the couch where Sam sat. Kazia and Tekla stood in front of Sean seeking his attention. He looked at them feeling guilty for his recent behaviour and questioning their intent but he remained silent.

The girls stopped their giggling and turned their attention to Tekla and Kazia. Tekla began, "Sean, the girls, they don't have much time with you like they do with Sam so they are shy. But Kazia, Anya, and me know you better. The girls want you know they like you. They say thank you for saving them from bad men."

Kazia interrupted, "Girls know how much you help look after Anya and them. Girls love you Sean."

Tears began to fill Sean's eyes. Reina, Anya and Sheila stood in the doorway smiling. At the appropriate time, Sheila clapped her hands and ordered, "Supper's ready, time to take your seats."

Sam and the girls stampeded into the dining room leaving Sean, Blanka and Bozo alone. Blanka stood and walked over to stand beside Sean. She reached up and touched his shoulder letting her hand slide down his arm. Sean smiled at her and she smiled back before running off to the dining room.

Sean slept soundly for the first time in a while but when he finally awoke, he scolded himself for being so out of it.

Chapter 38

Reina and Sean sat in the dining room talking over their coffee while the others cleaned up the breakfast dishes. The sun was still an hour away from showing its face. Despite its low azimuth at this time of year, it somehow contributed to the warmth of the lodge when it shone through the windows of the dining room. For now, though they relied on the Lord and a couple of light bulbs to illuminate their lives.

"I think we should plan on spending Christmas here," said Reina, "no matter how things turn out. The girls are doing so well and I don't want to interrupt their progress with another change. I have been surprised that none of them are showing any signs of homesickness."

"I understand. As for homesickness, I don't think they have a lot of fond memories of their 'homes' in Poland from what I hear. The routine that you have established seems to be helping a lot. They appear to feel pretty secure in their current home, even Blanka," Sean replied. "I hope it stays that way." He looked down at his coffee mug as Reina reached over and held his hand.

"We're all praying about that Sean. I've talked with Sam and Sheila and they would love to have us stay for Christmas." Reina smiled brightly hoping to distract Sean from the thoughts she knew he was pondering. "They have become so attached to the girls it will be a sad time when we have to leave."

"Okay, let's plan on staying until the New Year at least," Sean agreed.

"Since we're in this waiting mode, I would like you to join us during our reading time. It will give you more time with the girls and you have a good reading voice. Maybe you could even tell them some of your stories. What do you think?" Reina smiled an inviting smile while hiding her other motivation for the invitation.

"Okay, can I pick a book?"

"Sure, you pick. You know that most of these girls have never had a father in their lives. It is so good to see them developing a trusting relationship with Sam but I would like to see them get to know you better too. How do you feel about that?"

"Sure, I guess. I've already started to know them better since Sam and I started the firearms class. They are a great bunch of girls Reina and I really want to see them do well in life. If I can be a part of that then I'm all for it." Again, Sean paused and looked down at his coffee mug.

He looked up. "Reina, I need you to know that when I look at these girls I see Felicia, especially when I'm around Anya. Felicia would be about their age if she were alive today. In some ways I think I put up a wall so as not to get too close but I find that wall crumbling more and more. I guess I love them as if they were my own daughters. Do you think that is okay?"

Reina's smile was soft and understanding. "I do understand Sean and I love you so much for it. You go ahead and let that wall crumble; these girls need a man like you in their lives right now."

"Okay you two, break it up," announced Sam as he came into the dining room. "Time for our firearms class and I need to borrow your husband to be." He paused then said, "On second thought, Reina, would you like to give an introduction to shotguns since you're a bit of an expert with those?"

"Sounds like fun Sam. What have you got to show them?" Reina replied with enthusiasm.

"Well most of them are antiques that you've probably never heard of. Ever shot a Browning 'humpback' Auto 5?" Sam queried.

"No, but I know the gun, a classic. Not many autos out there so that one is a good candidate for introducing semi-auto actions. I suppose you have a pump. What about breaks and bolts?" asked Reina.

"You bet. I've got my classic 870 Wingmaster in 20 gauge and an old Mossberg 16 gauge bolt action. Still got my Cooey single shot break action in 12 gauge – my first shotgun; kicks like a mule."

"Well let's get to it – those are a fine bunch of guns to show the girls."

Reina went with Sam to gather up the guns and samples of ammo while Sean set up the chairs and blackboard for the class. The girls arrived on time as the dining room began to glow with the rising sun. Anya and Kazia sat in the front row as usual. Sean wrote 'Shotgun' across the top of the board and sketched a diagram of the interior of a shot shell then he wrote 'Gun' and 'Rifle' with a question mark. Anya was copying the same onto the writing pad on her clipboard but she added 'grooves' next to the word 'rifle'. Kazia leaned over and pointed to 'grooves' with a questioning look on her face.

Sam and Reina returned and laid the guns on the table parallel to the blackboard with their actions open. Reina displayed the shells on a separate table then Sam introduced her as the instructor for the day's lesson. He told the girls about Reina's proficiency with a shotgun and the many awards she had won over the years shooting trap and skeet. Irenka raised her hand and Sam invited her to ask her question. Reina already guessed what was coming.

"No, trap and skeet are not animals or birds – good question Irenka." Reina was in her teaching groove and had already anticipated another question sure to come. Sam was scurrying away to retrieve an object that would help with the lesson. Using the blackboard, Reina showed and then demonstrated with the Wingmaster how to shoot skeet and trap while Sam handed out some 'clays' for the girls to examine. "When the weather warms up you'll all get a chance to break one of these with a shotgun if you want."

"So who can tell me about a difference between a shotgun and a rifle?" Reina scanned her class ignoring Anya's hand in the air. Finally, confronted by 12 blank faces she gave in. "Okay Anya, tell us what you're thinking."

Anya's face beamed as she stood and addressed the rest of the girls. "The rifle barrel has grooves, żłobić, inside but the shotgun barrel is smooth inside."

"That's correct Anya. I'm sure Sam has already explained that these grooves in a rifle are what give a rifle its name. We call them 'rifling' and they are there to spin and stabilize the bullet as it travels down the barrel. Shotguns don't usually shoot single bullets; they shoot a lot of tiny balls called 'shot'." Sam passed around two bowls of 7 ½ and SSG shot. "There is one exception," Reina continued, "sometimes a shotgun shoots a 'slug' but it is only accurate over short distances unlike a bullet shot from a rifle." She held up a 12-gauge slug between her fingers then passed it to Sam who passed it on to the girls.

Sean sat off to the side with Blanka and Bozo. He smiled as he watched Reina capture and hold the attention of the class – and him. He marvelled at how attentive the girls were, including Blanka. He wondered if their past lives were so sterile that they wanted to fill up with anything that was good and unthreatening. It didn't seem to matter whether they were receiving instruction in firearms, the use of a kitchen utensil or simply sitting listening to Reina read a story. Instead of getting antsy while being cooped up inside during the cold spell, they enthusiastically entered into the activities of each day.

Chapter 39

The cold spell lingered. It seemed that even the fragile snowflake wanted to avoid the air at these temperatures. The river upstream of the lodge gurgled beneath a mantle of ice and snow before breaking into the open channel at the highway. Soon the entire river would sink into its icy bed for the next six months. The snow-laden spruce trees, frozen silent in the winter stillness, appeared apprehensive as if fearing a breath of wind or a scampering squirrel or marten might shake their snowy cloak from their boughs and expose them to the fierce cold. At these temperatures, even the wind refused to venture into the still forest. The only warmth in this Yukon scene came from the log building banked up with snow beside the White River.

A column of white smoke rose from the chimney straight into the sky until it was above the trees, and then dissipated in the chill air. Darkness shrouded the scene, except for the yellow glow of kerosene lamps that filled the back windows of the lodge. Inside, the crackling wood fire in the big black airtight in the middle of the lodge enhanced the ambiance of the lamps. A large graniteware canner simmered on the airtight, adding needed moisture to the dry winter air and providing a ready source of hot water in case the propane jelled.

Everyone had gone to bed. Sean and Bozo did their rounds outside before returning to the lodge. Sean stoked the fire for the night and blew out the last lamp. From the kitchen window, he looked out at the rising moon shining on the river. The snow sparkled in its cold light. He could see clouds in the distance advancing across the sky from the southwest. Yes, he thought, the weather is breaking. Already the 'little winds' were darting through the forest, stirring up the frigid air, breaking its grip on the land, but he didn't hear them as he climbed into bed.

The next morning at seven o'clock, the moon was gone and only the stars pierced the darkness. Sam was already up. He had opened the damper on the airtight allowing the sleepy fire to come alive. Flames roared up the chimney, burning out the accumulated creosote from the smouldering night fire. The metal heater and chimney squawked as they expanded in the heat. Sean met the freshly warmed air ascending the stairwell as he felt his way down the stairs in the dark as the others continued to sleep.

He joined Sam who sat in the glow of the kerosene lamp. They drank their coffee and relished the respite they and the girls would enjoy from hauling firewood and stoking fires, a constant chore when the temperatures got to forty below and colder. Highway traffic would pick up and Sean would be able to fly again. Now that they were staying for Christmas, he had some errands to run and no doubt Sheila and Reina had lists. Black thoughts began to intrude as he lingered in the warmth of the fire.

* * *

Anya snuggled into her blankets, listening to the fire crackling downstairs and feeling the warm air caress her exposed nose as it began to flood the bedroom. She whispered her thanks to God for the friends who had rescued her and brought her to this warm and peaceful place. She didn't know if her captors would return but she felt secure nonetheless. Anya believed what God said in the Bible, that she was His creation, the apple of His eye, much loved; she knew He cared for her. After she first read passages from Psalm 139 at Sean's cabin, she had read it many times afterward and it came to be her favourite Psalm. It spoke of how valuable she was as God's creation, made in His image. She had never felt valuable before. Anya trusted that God had sent her friends to protect her and the other girls and that she would be safe with them. Before she had gone to sleep, she had read Psalm 37 and she knew that she had a future and she trusted God to bring it about.

Outside, an occasional gust of wind and the sound of clumps of snow falling from the spruce trees aroused her curiosity. She hadn't heard these sounds before. What was happening she wondered? It was still too cold to get out of bed so she lay still allowing her mind to conjure its own explanations.

"Anya, are you awake?" Kazia whispered from her bed next to Anya's.

"Yes, Kazia, I have been praying."

"Do you pray for me Anya?"

"More than ever Kazia. God gave you to me as a friend before I really knew Him but I know He sent you into my life because He loves me. Do you know that God loves you too Kazia?"

"I think so. I talk to Him. Anya, you are an answer to my prayer, did you know that?"

"No, but why?"

"Even when we were in the orphanage together, God sent you to be *my* friend and to encourage and comfort me. When those bad men took us, I think God made sure that you would be with me and the other girls to help us. You are very brave Anya. What do you think will happen to us? Will those bad men come back and get us?"

"No!" Anya rose up on her elbow and glared at Kazia who peeked out from under her blanket. "God has given us protectors and He has a good plan for our lives. Reina helped me to memorize this verse in Jeremiah 29:11-13 and you need to memorize it too, all of us do. God *'has plans for you, plans for peace and not for evil to give you a future and a hope.'* You can read it all for yourself in your Bible. You read it Kazia and you ask God to help you believe it! It is His truth."

The cold was indeed breaking and the sounds from outside her window confirmed the warming trend. Overnight the thermometer had risen from forty-three below to a balmy twenty below zero. That explained why the airtight still had a few partly charred logs inside and why Bozo was so anxious to go out. Bozo was an outdoor dog except when it got colder than forty below. Not that he couldn't take it, he had a thick coat and a big bushy tail to cover his tender nose. The humans were the ones that couldn't bear to leave him out in such cold. When the cold weather first arrived, Blanka surprised everyone when she vehemently protested Sam's ushering Bozo outside for his evening constitutional. Once Sam reassured her that Bozo could stay in after he finished his business she settled down to wait for her friend's return.

* * *

John sat in the living room with Wanda, Kazlov's dual duty madam and 'bottom', drinking coffee and talking about girl business or 'the game' as Wanda liked to call it. "They have it pretty good here, it's a family, better than where most of them came from." She squished the remains of her cigarette into the already full glass ashtray. "Daddy Kazlov takes care of the necessities and makes sure they get out on the circuit which is pretty small in Alaska but the girls seem to like the change of venue."

"So what kind of money do these girls bring in?" John feigned a casual interest while probing to see if he had agreed to a fair price for the girls.

"Kazlov isn't hurting despite the overhead to keep the stable up and running." She lit another cigarette. "Once he turns out your girls he'll be making real good money and he's negotiating on some more. Foreign girls bring a premium – must be their accents." She laughed. "The quota depends on where they're working. Fairbanks is high dollar, lot's of high paid oil field guys, some executives travelling from out of state, but the tricks can be rough sometimes, that's why the high dollar. The seasoned girls have a quota up to two grand. The Juneau girls have high quotas too because they get the high paid government johns; lonely men away from home attending government meetings, courses and stuff."

They both turned at the sound of the door opening. Sergio came into the room nodding to Wanda but taking the chair facing John. "Weather's changing so we should plan on going. We'll take the van. I'll pick you up here tomorrow morning; be ready." He got up and left the way he came.

"Where you off to?" Wanda queried.

"The White River Lodge," John boasted.

Chapter 40

Reina and Sheila stood at the bottom of the stairs. Sheila called to the girls upstairs, "Come on you slow pokes, get a move on, daylights a wastin'." After being cooped up in the lodge during the cold spell they were all looking forward to an outdoor excursion. The rumble of feet in the upstairs hallway declared their enthusiasm for the planned outing. Reina and Sheila moved away from the stairwell as the mob descended en masse and crowded around them in the living room giggling and talking among themselves. They were dressed in their colourful parkas, mitts and scarves and shod in slick new bush pacs. They resembled models in an Arctic fashion show.

The two women led the way out the back door. Sean and Sam were changing the oil in the generator but turned to look at what was creating the commotion pouring from the lodge. Bozo bounded towards the girls sidling up to Blanka who was beaming at the attention he showed her. The two men waved and the girls waved back as Anya shouted, "We're going on a hike in the snow!"

"By the time they get back, their tongues will be dangling instead of wagging," said Sam.

"Should be pretty quiet at supper tonight," Sean enjoined. "Maybe we should take the snow machine and pack a trail to the lake for future hikes?"

"If this weather holds for a few more days why don't we hitch up the big sleigh and we'll all go for a wiener roast at the lake?" Sam suggested.

"Now they'd love that Sam, great idea. Wonder if Sheila's got any wieners hanging around?"

The men resumed their work on the generator as a big rig roared north along the highway.

It wasn't an Alberta Chinook but the air flowing over the St. Elias range was definitely heating up the White River Valley and scouring the cold air from its icy grip on the land. These short periods of relative warmth were a fringe benefit for those living near the western mountains of the Yukon. After prolonged cold spells, they invigorated the soul, relieved the onset of cabin fever and allowed a body to attend to chores neglected because of the frigid air. A snowstorm and another round of severe cold usually followed.

"You wanna go with me to the Creek? I have to get another couple of barrels of diesel while we've got this weather."

"Sure, let's do it." Sean accepted Sam's invitation.

The truck started with little coaxing. They loaded the empty barrels while the engine idled and warmed for the journey ahead. The wheels turned easily and gear changes were effortless as they pulled onto the highway. The rear wheels spun as the truck left the gravel and pulled onto the frosty pavement at the bridge approach. Sam pulled a lever and engaged the front axle. Traction wasn't a problem in the cold even on packed snow but now that the weather had warmed, driving habits had to change. The frost was coming out of the pavement forming a slick surface but Sam was well acquainted with the hazard.

The two men enjoyed Belle's company and her coffee and chocolate cake while Don filled the barrels with diesel. Belle talked up a storm about their upcoming trip outside to Arizona and all the plans she had. Don and Belle were not travelers so this trip was particularly intriguing to both of them. Their daughter had been instrumental in prying her parents from their home in Beaver Creek where they typically spent all their time except for occasional trips to Whitehorse or Anchorage. She tried to get them excited by telling them about all the things they would see and the activities that she felt might be of interest. They would spend most of their time in Phoenix with a few days in Vegas. Her Dad was especially keen to visit Las Vegas and "meet the showgirls" as he put it. A mule ride into the Grand Canyon was another important excursion on his list. She and her husband made the arrangements and planned to join them for a few days.

The bell over the door tinkled as Don entered. "You're ready to go guys," he stomped the snow from his boots and shed his parka and mitts. He poured himself a mug of coffee and joined his wife and guests. "Haven't seen that guy in the red pickup yet but I'll let you know if he comes by. Traffic will pick up now that the weather's warming."

After a time of visiting, drinking coffee and enjoying chocolate cake, Sean and Sam rose to leave. "Let's put that diesel on *my* tab Don since Sam's been so hospitable these days. I'll settle my account before Christmas so you have enough for the slots in Vegas." He laughed as the door closed and the bell tinkled.

Back at the Lodge, Sam backed the truck close to the generator shed. The two men wrestled a barrel to the tailgate of the truck then rolled it off into the snow. They grabbed the other one and did the same. They were stowing the last barrel in the shack when they heard singing in the distance. They listened, trying to make out the words. The girls' singing grew louder as they returned from their hike in high spirits but with weary bodies.

"Sounds like 'This is my Fathers World'. Kind of appropriate for our circumstances don't you think?" Sean joined in as he heard them singing the last verse, "*This is my Father's world Oh, let me ne'r forget that though the wrong seems oft so strong God is the ruler yet. This is my Father's world why should my heart be sad? The Lord is king, let the heavens ring God reigns, let the earth be glad.*"

Conversation at supper was much more vibrant than Sam had anticipated. Despite their weary bodies, the girls boiled over with enthusiasm telling about their day. Sheila reminded the more vocal girls that others wanted to share as well. Blanka pulled on Sam's shirtsleeve and quietly told him about the squirrel in a tree that scolded her and Bozo as they watched him jumping in the trees. He listened intently, watching with pleasure as her face reflected excitement over the experience and the opportunity to tell her story to an interested listener.

Bedtime came early, for the girls first, then Sheila and Reina. Sam and Sean enjoyed the rare quiet time reading by the fire.

* * *

John could hear Sergio's footsteps coming up the stairs from the garage. Wanda and the rest of the girls were still sleeping. He met Sergio as the door opened and they both returned to the garage where a 15-passenger van sat parked ready for their journey. Sergio handed the keys to John and motioned for him to take the driver's seat. The garage door opened and they drove into the morning darkness.

Chapter 41

After almost three hours of tense driving, John pulled into a roadhouse at Delta Junction for gas and a needed break. He was getting muscle spasms in his neck trying to keep the unwieldy vehicle on the icy road. The highway had become very slippery with the warmer weather and manoeuvring the long van along the winding road demanded all his concentration. The lack of weight in the vehicle aggravated its instability. Sometimes it would lose traction on the frosty pavement or in snow.

They paid for their gas and walked into the empty restaurant.

"Morning gentlemen, can I get you menus?" The waitress gave them each a smile.

"Two coffees will be good," Sergio replied.

She left them alone to retrieve the coffees. "How much farther is it," asked Sergio.

"We should be there by five or six if all goes well," replied John.

He could see that John was hurting from the drive. "You want me to drive for a while?" asked Sergio.

"That would be good. That van takes work to keep it on the road." John sounded relieved.

The waitress returned with their coffee. "You fellas southbound?" she asked trying to make conversation.

"Yeah," Sergio answered curtly hoping not to encourage conversation.

"Well you fellas be careful, the roads are awful." She got the message and returned to her bar stool and the small black and white television.

After she was out of earshot, Sergio asked with skepticism in his voice, "Are you sure they'll be there? It won't be good for you if they're not."

"I'm pretty sure we'll find them there. With all this cold weather I doubt that they would have gone anywhere else and they won't be expecting us." John tried to sound confident.

"So what's the plan?" Sergio asked.

"As I said, they won't be expecting us, and, they've never seen you so you should go in first and check it out. It's a highway lodge, closed for the season but, from what I found out, the owners, an older couple, still live there. You can make some excuse for stopping. I don't know if they took the girls but I'm pretty sure they're keeping them." John stopped talking as the waitress approached.

She refilled their coffee mugs and asked if they wanted anything else, retreating to her stool after receiving an abrupt "No".

John continued, "If the girls are there, and the old couple are the only others, then you can make up some reason to return to the van. Together we'll go in and get the girls. The old folks shouldn't give us any trouble staring down the barrel of a gun. We'll just tie them up and be out of there."

At Northway, they stopped for lunch and gas. Sergio was happy to turn the driving over to John even though the road was straighter and sanded in some places. In a couple of hours they would be at the Canada Customs border crossing in Beaver Creek, Yukon.

* * *

Sean saw the headlights first. He watched the blue pickup truck pull off the highway almost missing the driveway and skidding to a stop alongside the cable barrier. He alerted Sheila and Reina in the kitchen and ordered all the girls upstairs telling them to be quiet. Sam was finishing setting the tension on the new fan belt he installed on his truck when he saw the truck. He patted the pistol under his jacket and wandered over to meet the driver who was obviously in a hurry.

"Hello, what can I do for you?" Sam greeted the distraught driver.

"You've got to call the police or an ambulance, there's been an accident." The words spilled out of the driver's mouth as he trembled.

Sean cautiously approached the two men, his hand on the pistol in his parka pocket. Sam turned and told him what the driver of the pickup had just said.

"Where abouts?" asked Sean as he scanned the surrounding area for other persons or vehicles.

"Not far, maybe 15 minutes, on a curve this side of Dry Creek. It went off the road, rolled a couple of times and came to rest against some trees. I saw bodies!" The man's face stretched as his mouth hung open.

"How many? Was anyone injured?" asked Sean.

"Two, there were two, men. They weren't moving and I saw blood in the snow. I thought I better get help so I came here."

"I'll call the RCMP in the Junction and get some flashlights and a first aid kit." Sam walked to the Lodge.

"Did you see it happen?" Sean asked.

"No, I just came around the corner and saw the red taillights in the bush so I pulled over."

Sam came out of the back door of the lodge. "Okay, we're going back there. You drive your truck and we'll follow," ordered Sean.

"Can't raise the operator. Sheila will keep trying. Reina's coming in case she can help," said Sam.

"This guy thinks they're dead but it doesn't sound like he took a pulse or anything – too scared. You might not have much to do," Sean addressed Reina sitting between him and Sam in Sam's pickup.

"When it's cold, a person can have serious injuries and appear dead, but really they're still alive," counselled Reina. "We'll see when we get there."

The pickup in front of them pulled off the highway at a typical Yukon 'rest stop' - a 45-gallon garbage barrel and a trail into the bush. The white van was clearly visible in the moonlight lying on its side, its head and tail-lights now only faintly visible. The man in the blue pickup rolled down his window. "The bodies are on the other side, and you have to walk down there to see them. I'll wait here if you don't mind."

Sean took a photo of the scene from the side of the road and another of the skid tracks in the packed snow on the road. Reina carried the first aid kit while Sam and Sean used the lanterns to follow the tracks the man in the blue truck left in the snow. The van had rolled more than once. The vehicle, badly crumpled, had come to rest on the passenger side. The windshield lay a few feet away. Only one side window remained intact. Sean took more pictures.

He couldn't open the driver's door so he reached through the smashed window and turned off the lights and the ignition. Sam found a man in a brown sweater lying face down in the snow, his lower legs under the van. He had no pulse and there was no sign of breathing. The other man was some distance away lying face up with blood covering his face. Reina stopped, shone the flashlight on his face and called to Sean. She recognized him as the man that shot her. Together they approached him. She crouched to check for vital signs but found none. She checked her watch and wrote in her note-book. Sean noted the long scar on his left cheek and took photos of the man. "It's him, the one who shot me and took Anya." Reina's voice was dark and cold like the accident scene.

Sean put his arm around her, "You okay?" She nodded. Sean checked his pockets and went through the man's wallet confirming his name. He removed the Colt 45 from the holster under his jacket and left him in the snow.

He went to where the other man was lying and checked his pockets and wallet for any information that would help identify him and his purpose.

"Sergio Cardoza, sounds Portuguese," Sean spoke to no one in particular. He found some business cards; one with only the name 'Sergio' and a phone number and the other with a company name and contact information. He pocketed one of each before taking the Beretta from his shoulder holster. He took some more photos before going to search the van. There were no more bodies but he did find two passports, one American and one Canadian. He called to Sam and Reina as he read the name on the Canadian passport. "We'll give the guns and other stuff to the cops when they come; I don't' want to risk some passer-by pilfering anything this important as unlikely as that would be."

Before leaving the scene, Sam wrote on a piece of cardboard, 'Do Not Disturb – Police Contacted', and left it propped up on the van. It was doubtful that anyone would come by, let alone see the vehicle in the dark.

Back at the Lodge, they continued trying to reach the operator but to no avail. The man in the blue pickup, Tom Huntfield, from Haines Junction, finished his coffee and prepared to leave. "I'll stop at Koidern and D-Bay on the way and see if I can contact the cops, otherwise I'll see them in the Junction."

"Okay, we'll keep trying to reach them. Thanks for stopping Tom." Sean and Sam stood and walked with him to the door.

Chapter 42

The four of them watched his taillights disappear down the highway before turning and embracing each other with exclamations of relief. "Should we tell the girls?" Reina beamed as she addressed no one in particular.

Sean responded, "I think they need to know. Even though they don't *seem* to be worried about this guy, I think they are in denial and the news will be a great relief to them. Besides, this is a huge answer to prayer and they need to know that."

"I agree," said Reina as Sheila and Sam nodded in agreement. "These girls are living in a state of tension, never knowing if the 'bad men' will return and take them away. I think they need to hear the whole story Sean, including what this guy John did to his partners."

"Okay, you round up the girls Reina, I'll try calling the cops again."

This time Sean was able to reach the operator. She connected him to the Haines Junction detachment. He explained what had happened and that Tom was on his way south in a blue pickup. The constable knew Tom and his truck. They would stop at the Lodge and have them show the way to the scene. An ambulance would be following.

The girls sensed that something important had happened as they trooped down the stairs to the living room. Sam passed around tumblers of his cranberry wine. This, and the smiles on the faces of their hosts, served to confirm their suspicion that this was a special and probably a happy occasion.

"We have some very good news for all of you," Sean began, his arm around Reina's waist.

Reina continued, "You all know how much we've been praying for you girls, your protection and your freedom. Well God answered those prayers. You don't have to fear those 'bad men' anymore; they are no longer with us."

Sean continued, "I haven't told you everything that I found out since we brought you here because I didn't want to scare you anymore than you already were. You no longer have anything to fear and let me tell you why."

Sean told the girls how he found the two kidnappers, Wimp and Marik dead at the prospector's camp and how he had tracked John Dubicki to the Yukon/Alaska border. He explained that he was concerned that Dubicki would return and try to take them again but he didn't know when he might try and that's why he and Sam had been so cautious and alert. Anya helped with translation.

"Why didn't you call the police," asked Tekla.

"Good question Tekla. At first, I knew if we called the police you would all be sent back to Poland, and the traffickers that abducted you would get away to do it all again. They might even catch *you* again. This is something that usually happens in this horrible business and I wasn't about to risk your lives by calling in the police. After Dubicki killed his partners, I thought about involving the police. But, it would be difficult to prove Dubicki did it and you would still be sent back to Poland where you would be at risk again."

"Can we stay here with you now or do we have to go back?" Anya asked.

"Another good question. I have already talked to a friend of mine with Canadian Immigration without letting him know about you. He told me that people in your situation may be able to stay in Canada but they need a good lawyer, no guarantees. If successful, a local family, willing to care for you for at least a year, will help you adjust to your new home. But, if you want to return to Poland that is okay too and much easier to arrange."

"No!" the girls shouted in a chorus of protest.

Sam and the others stood with surprised looks on faces that quickly broke into broad smiles. "I think I speak for all of us when I say we kind of like you girls and hope you can stay around. Not necessarily here at White River, but not too far away that we can't visit," said Sam, "how about a toast?" He raised his glass. "To Him who loves you and to your future in His hands."

The celebration continued for almost an hour. The girls asked questions about their future for the first time. Since nobody knew what the future held for anybody, they just enjoyed talking about what they hoped it could be, somewhat like musing on what you would do if you won a million dollars. Sean noticed that Anya, unlike her usual self, had retreated to a couch in a melancholy mood. He touched Reina's hand and motioned towards Anya sitting alone on the love seat.

"Can we join you?" Sean asked as he and Reina sat beside her. "What are you thinking about Anya?"

She stared into Sean's eyes. "What will happen to me? I don't want to leave you." She turned to Reina, "do you think you might want to keep me?" Tears filled her eyes.

Sean and Reina held her in their arms as she sobbed, her body shaking.

Chapter 43

It was late; the girls had gone to bed. Sean saw the RCMP cruiser turn off the highway. He and Sam threw on their parkas and donned their boots meeting the two officers outside the lodge. They talked briefly, agreeing to lead the way in Sam's truck to the accident scene. Sean handed the two passports, wallets and handguns to one of the officers. "Didn't want them to get stolen while we were away from the scene; pretty unlikely I know but . . ."

The officers examined the scene and the bodies taking pictures and making notes. The interior of the van was empty except for a coil of clothesline rope, a couple of sleeping bags and some cold weather clothing and boots. Boxes of ammo for the pistols were in the glove box. The van had Alaska plates registered to Tanana Auto Inc. in Fairbanks.

The ambulance arrived as the officers finished interviewing Sean and Sam. The attendants spoke briefly with the officers before wading through the snow with their stretcher. "You are free to go and thanks for your help," the senior constable addressed the two men, "we'll stay at Beaver Creek tonight and see if Don can pull the van out tomorrow. If we need anything else, we know where to find you. Thanks again."

Sean and Sam took their time driving back to the lodge; it was almost midnight. They hadn't volunteered any information about the deceased John Dubicki or the girls back at the lodge. "I don't know about you but I'm feeling pretty good right now," Sam glanced over at Sean.

"I'm with you brother. I figured we could have been in a serious fight to protect those girls; not anymore."

"So who do you think that other guy was?" Sam quizzed.

"Good question. I don't know but if I had to guess I'd say he was either the client or he worked for the client. I thought that this Dubicki guy might try to get help from his client after he lost the girls."

"Do you think anybody else might come after the girls?"

"I guess it's possible but somehow I doubt it. Dubicki was the only one with a stake in them. His client would undoubtedly profit from them if he had them but I doubt he has any investment at risk; these guys never put any cash up front. I doubt that Dubicki told him where they were so first he'd have to find them. The time and risk he'd take trying to find and abduct them again wouldn't be worth it; it would be a lot easier to simply access his other suppliers. I suppose he could get mad and do something stupid. "

"That would be my guess too but just in case we should be on our guard."

"Always, my friend. Stay vigilant," Sean agreed.

Sam turned the truck into the driveway and parked at the back of the lodge. "I don't know about you but I need a nightcap," Sam offered as the two walked to the lodge.

Reina was still up, sitting on a couch in the living room. "Everything go alright with the cops?"

"All good," replied Sean. "They don't know anything about Dubicki or the girls. Want to join us for a nightcap?" He sat beside Reina on the couch.

"Sure, you know what I like Sam," she called after Sam who was on his way to the kitchen.

"Well, tell me what happened." She took Sean's hand and held it on her lap while giving him a quizzical look. Details, Reina always wanted the details.

The stairs squeaked as Sheila made her way down to the living room. She had heard the two men come in. "Sam, I'll have my usual," she called through the kitchen door.

Sean related the events at the accident scene while Sam thrashed around the kitchen searching for his prized bottle of Scotch whiskey and the other liquor. Sheila's habit of 'organizing' the kitchen now and then usually resulted in the temporary loss of his special bottle among others. He had threatened to relocate his liquor stash to his ammo and reloading cupboard but hadn't got around to it yet.

Sam returned to the living room with a glass of sherry, a tumbler of dark rum mixed with Coke and two others almost full of Scotch. The foursome sat quietly at first, sipping their drinks. Sam interrupted the silence by reflecting on what would have been an otherwise quiet winter at the lodge. He reassured Sean and Reina that he and Sheila had no regrets and explained how they came to embrace the situation and the victims. The death of the last bad guy had relieved a lot of the tension he had been under and he expressed his delight that the girls were out of danger. They loved the girls and were happy that they might be able to stay in the country. He spoke about how happy he and Sheila were that they had decided to stay for Christmas. Sheila was nodding her head in agreement as he spoke.

Sean and Reina expressed their gratefulness for how he and Sheila had opened up their home to the girls. "You two didn't miss a beat. You saw our need and accepted the danger that came with it, yet you both provided a loving sanctuary and a willingness to defend against the thugs who had victimized these precious girls." Reina nodded in agreement. Sean went on, "I'm proud to call you my friend and a brother Sam. I'm indebted to you and Sheila." He gave Reina a hug. "And to you my dear."

Sam and Sheila thanked Sean for his remarks, then Sam continued, "The girls are coming out from under the stress they have been feeling about being recaptured, but now they are concerned about their futures."

Reina responded, "All the girls have been sexually abused and are wrestling with their value as human beings. This is contributing to the anxiety they are feeling despite their new freedom. They can feel unwanted, useless and even ugly and deserving of punishment. I thank you and Sheila for helping them to cope with these wounds by accepting and caring for them the way you have. They feel your love."

Sean listened then interjected, "When I was overseas, I learned that this was a strategy used by traffickers. They would rape the girls, knowing what the trauma would do to their self-image. Asian culture and its religious underpinnings served to drive the girls into prostitution as they saw themselves having no other worth," Sean explained. "These girls are dealing with similar trauma but hopefully we have helped them to see their worth not just in our eyes but, most importantly, in God's eyes."

Reina added, "It is imperative that we keep affirming them over the next few weeks while we are together. Sean and I have talked about the next steps and they are daunting." She looked at Sean, inviting him to explain.

"I will talk to Jay again as soon as I can and explain what's happened, and then I'll talk with Ron Vance and see if he'll take this on," Sean spoke with purpose in his voice. "I want to talk with Ray too because we are going to need to find temporary places for these girls to live in the mean time. Temporary might even turn into something more permanent if the families are willing to become official sponsors."

Reina nudged Sean, questioning him with her eyes. "What?" said Sean.

She turned back to Sam and Sheila. "Sean and I have decided to get married right after Christmas. We want to have some of the girls come and live at my place; I have lots of room but it will be much more of a home with the two of us."

Sheila and Sam looked at each other. "That's great news! If this all goes as you are saying do you think Sam and I could host a girl?" Sheila's sheepish countenance invited a positive reply.

Reina glanced at Sean then turned back to Sheila. "You wouldn't be thinking of Blanka would you?"

Sheila and Sam both looked at the floor, then at Sean, then Reina. "What do you think?" said Sheila, pessimism in her voice, "I know she's really damaged and we're getting' on in years but she seems to be comfortable with us and she certainly likes Bozo. I know we aren't psychologists, but I have my counselling experience, and, even though we've never raised kids, we both love that little girl. We want to see her come out of this healthy and whole. We're willing to do anything to make that happen. Maybe I'm jumping the gun here. We will abide with whatever you think is best, but I just want you to know where we stand."

Reina smiled at the older couple across from them. "We've actually talked about this Sheila, and you are confirming our own thoughts," Reina spoke in affirmation. "Sean and I have watched Blanka develop a special relationship with you both, and, of course Bozo. What I find most amazing is how she is so comfortable with you Sam," she laughed. "You know what I mean. It is often very difficult for these girls to accept men in their lives. Blanka has definitely accepted you and seems to trust you." She turned to Sean. "What do you think?"

"I too have seen how Blanka has almost adopted *you*, cautiously I admit, but she definitely trusts you and feels comfortable with you. You'd be on the top of my list as a sponsor for this little girl, in fact, I would have great difficulty putting her with anyone else, given her fragility."

"Thank you guys for your confidence. I guess we'll just have to wait and see," said Sam.

"You guys can stay here all night for all I care but I'm going to bed," Reina kissed Sean and touched Sam's shoulder as she headed for the stairs. "Thanks for the drink Sam."

"Do the girls know they're staying for Christmas?" asked Sam.

"No, not yet; we should probably tell them tomorrow. I hope they'll receive it as good news," Sean answered. "I'm looking forward to seeing how the removal of this threat will affect them in the days to come."

"And us," added Sheila.

"Maybe we should go on that wiener roast at the lake that you talked about," Sean looked at Sam. "It would be a great outing and an opportunity for the girls to have some fun."

"Let's do it," Sam responded with eagerness. "We might have to use both snow machines to pull the sleigh with all that weight. What's the weather looking like?"

"Don't know but it should begin clearing and stay warm during the day," Sean replied. "I'll call Whitehorse weather in the morning; I expect to do some flying over the next few days so I need to check the forecast anyway. Been a good day Sam, I'm going to bed; thanks for the nightcap." Sean slapped Sam on his back as he left.

Sam and Sheila went into the kitchen and rummaged around in the freezer until they found some sausages, wieners and hotdog buns.

Chapter 44

It was still early. He lay in bed listening to Sam feed the fire. The aroma of fresh coffee flooded his room. Too good to ignore any longer, Sean climbed out of bed, dressed and made his way down the hall and the creaking stairs trying not to wake the others. He found Sheila and the coffee pot in the kitchen. Sheila filled three mugs and the two retreated to the warmth of the living room. Sam sat on a couch surveying the sky through the windows of the dining room. The blackness of the sky, studded with ultra bright stars and a brilliant shard of a moon, promised a day filled with brilliant sunshine.

Sean gave Sam and Sheila a puzzled look as they cocked their ears to the stairs. Someone was doing their best to be quiet as the stairs betrayed their efforts with groans and squeaks. Blanka's pale face showed itself from around the corner. Sam's grin was enough. The bathrobe-clad girl skipped into the room heading straight for Sam where she stopped in front of him looking into his eyes. "Can I sit with Sam?" He patted the couch cushion beside him. She sat, rested her head on his shoulder and closed her eyes. Sam gave Sheila a questioning look.

"Kinda confirms what we were saying last night, eh?" Sean smiled at Sam and Sheila.

Sam cautiously wrapped his left arm around Blanka's shoulders and gave a light squeeze. She didn't move. "Good morning Blanka; up early today aren't you? Is everything alright?" he spoke in a light tone not really expecting an answer from the timid youngster.

"I happy Sam; bad men gone but I worry so no sleep. Blanka has no house; no go Polska. Blanka stay with Sam and Sheila and Bozo; is okay?" She looked up at him with her innocent smile. His heart melted.

Sam's solicitous glance at Sheila spoke of his uneasiness. Sean just shrugged. "You are such a dear Blanka. Sheila and I love you very much and we would love to have you live with us," he paused to allow her to process his words, "we will do all we can to make that happen, but it may not be our decision, do you understand?" Blanka's puzzled look said she didn't understand. Sheila joined them on the couch.

The rumble of footsteps on the stairs betrayed Anya's inelegant entry. Sean raised a finger to his lips. Getting the message, she cringed in apology before looking at Sam, Sheila and Blanka then back to Sean. She stood in front of Sean. "Is okay?" She pointed to Blanka and then to him. Before he could answer, Anya was sitting at his side, her head on his shoulder. Sean hugged her and gave her a peck on the forehead.

"My dear Anya, good timing; maybe you can help Sam and Sheila. They are trying to tell Blanka that they love her and want to have her stay with them but the decision may not be entirely theirs. Can you help her to understand how they feel?"

Anya looked at Blanka and spoke to her in Polish. Blanka, in turn, responded in Polish with an obvious question. Anya must have answered to her satisfaction as Blanka snuggled into Sam and held his hand in hers. "Thank you Sam and Sheila; I love you."

Anya looked at Sean. "The other girls, they worry about where they will live. Can you and Reina talk to them?"

"Yes, Anya, after breakfast we will have a meeting. We want them to know that they will be looked after. Is that a good idea?"

"Oh yes, good idea; when is breakfast?"

Sean laughed as he gave her another hug. "Why don't you and I go in the kitchen and make breakfast; how's porridge sound?" Anya made a face but slid away, pulling on his arm to help him out of the chair.

Anya and Sean busied themselves in the kitchen while Sam and Blanka set the table. Reina had joined them. She and Sheila were enjoying their morning coffee by the airtight and delighting in how the two girls worked alongside Sean and Sam. Sam sent Blanka upstairs to dress and wake the other girls then joined Reina and Sheila. He explained the wiener roast that he and Sean had discussed and the meeting planned for after breakfast.

After breakfast, they gathered to talk about concerns the girls had. Anya helped to make sure that everyone understood the discussion. The girls had grown close to one another while sharing the trauma of their captivity and some, like Blanka and Halina, and Anya and Kazia, had formed close friendships. They knew they would be subject to a government immigration hearing. This concerned them, fearing that the process would separate them or place them in an institution. Their experiences with government in their home country were seldom positive. Sean assured them that they would live with families and not be placed in any institution. They wouldn't all live in the same house but they would live close enough to have regular visits with one another. He and Reina will ensure that they get to see each other and they will plan events where all can attend.

He told them that he would talk with his friend, Pastor Ray, and his wife, to find good families that would like to care for a girl. There might even be opportunity for two or more girls to live together with a family but it was too early to know for sure. He assured them that only good, caring families would host them and make sure they stayed safe. He and Reina would not let anything bad happen to them.

It seemed that all were at ease with what they learned. He told them that if the weather held he would fly to Whitehorse in the next couple of days to begin the process. When he returned, he might have more information to share with them. In the meantime, he told them that they were guests at the White River Lodge for another three weeks at least and they would celebrate Christmas with Sam, Sheila and Bozo. The girls turned to one another clapping hands, smiling and hugging one another.

Sam rose and announced the wiener roast at the lake while Anya tried to explain what that meant based on Sam's previous explanation. Everyone was to be ready by 11:30 for the sleigh ride to the lake. He encouraged them to dress warmly but noted that it would be a beautiful sunny day.

Sean and Sam worked at getting the snow machines running and topped up with fuel for the short trip to the lake. After an hour, both machines sat together idling in a cloud of blue smoke. The sleigh, built for hauling firewood, sat buried in snow. When Anya showed up wanting to help, Sean asked her to shovel the snow off the sleigh. He and Sam went to the workshop to make up another tug for the second snow machine, in case they needed to use both machines to pull it.

Anya enjoyed stretching her muscles in the clear air and finished her job quickly. She leaned on her shovel proudly inspecting her work before walking to the workshop to find Sean. The men appeared dragging a new tug, only this one was made of nylon rope. The tug on the sleigh was a solid steel bar. Since there was no one driving the sleigh, and therefore no brake, the bar prevented the sleigh from ramming the back of the tow vehicle on hills or when slowing or stopping.

The Arctic Cat had the biggest engine and widest track. Sean invited Anya to climb on the back before he pulled the machine over to the sleigh. He showed her how to hook the sleigh to the hitch and pulled it easily off the blocks Sam had placed under the runners to keep it from freezing to the ground. He towed it to the back door of the lodge and shut down the machine. He felt confident that the 'Cat' would be enough to haul its load over the level trail to the lake but the little Elan would provide extra muscle if needed. He lifted the back of the Elan with his left hand and applied throttle with his right to free up the frozen track. He showed Anya how to drive it and let her run it over beside the 'Cat'. Her broad, satisfied smile greeted Sam as he joined them. "Why don't you two take a run up to the lake on the 'Cat'?" he suggested, "that will break a trail and make towing the sleigh even easier. You could tow the toboggan up there at the same time in case the girls want to try sliding the hill later."

"Great idea Sam," said Sean. "Wanna come?" he said looking at Anya. "Maybe you can drive it back."

Anya did a little jump and clapped her hands. "Yes, that will be such fun, let's go!"

Sean showed Anya how to start the 'Cat' then the two of them drove to the workshop, picked up the six-foot toboggan and tied it to the hitch. Sam returned Anya's wave as Sean turned the machine onto the lake trail. The machine floated easily over the unbroken snow as they made their way to the lake less than a mile away. It was a bluebird day. The sun reflected off the distant, snow-clad mountain massif set in a royal blue sky and overlooking the lake. When Sean felt Anya was getting comfortable riding the machine he gave it more throttle until they were speeding along at over 30 miles an hour. He could feel her grip his waist a little tighter as she let out a yelp of glee, her hair flying in the wind.

They broke into a tree-lined bowl at the base of the massif. The 'Cat' coasted to a stop and Sean cut the engine. The small lake lay silent beneath a blanket of snow at least a foot deep. The two humans, frozen by the sudden silence, gazed at the wondrous scene before them. Anya whispered reverently in Sean's ear, "I have never seen anything this beautiful."

Sean led the way as the two trudged through the deep snow to the 'beach' at the north end of the lake. It was spring fed, cold and devoid of fish. In the summer, the lake was a favourite picnic spot and swimming hole for Sam and Sheila. Sometimes they would share the secret with guests staying at the lodge. The 'beach' provided a patch of sand and pebbles if one was inclined to sunbathe and in winter it received the full force of the winter sun. Sam had long ago constructed a lean-to, table and log benches to sit on.

"Let's dig out the fire pit and collect some kindling before we head back," Sean suggested. After kicking the snow away to expose the rock fire pit, they waded into the forest where the snow was not so deep. Sean showed Anya how to collect 'squaw wood' to start a fire. The pitch-laden twigs hung in abundance on the lower trunks of spruce trees and they soon had large handfuls of the fire starter. Sean cleared the remaining snow from the centre of the fire pit and carefully placed the tinder that would later create a blazing fire.

"Okay, let's get back. Do you want to drive it back?" Sean smiled at Anya betting he knew her answer.

Chapter 45

"Yes, yes, please let me try!" Anya pleaded, "I promise not to speed."

Sean laughed. *"What a girl!"* he thought. *"She's got Felicia's spirit alright, even lies like her."* He gave Anya a few pointers on how to drive a snowmobile, cautioning her that practice was the only way to become proficient. He advised her to take it slow to begin with, that way it won't hurt as much when things go bad. She acknowledged his remarks with a sly smile as she turned and took hold of the handlebars.

"Now lean into the turn." Sean coached as she struggled to turn the machine at low speed. He leaned with his own body to help her make the turn. After making a wide arc, Sean directed her to parallel their old track back to the lodge. She lined up the machine then gave it full throttle. The sudden lurch forward caught Sean off guard but he hung on and let her go. He wanted to see how fast she'd go before getting scared and slowing down.

Anya whooped in exhilaration as the machine gained speed and she felt the power she controlled, or thought she controlled. She didn't see it in time; the rise in the trail launched the 'Cat' into the air. When it landed, the skis sunk into the snow at an angle, throwing Anya and Sean into the soft snow. The machine continued a short distance along the trail finally losing its momentum and coming to a halt. Sean was relieved to see and hear Anya laughing out of control as she lay on her back in the snow. He walked over to make sure she wasn't hurt; instead, he found her celebrating her 'accident', thoroughly enjoying herself. He thanked God for the joy he saw in the girl who had known so much pain. He playfully threw a handful of snow on her face laughing as she sputtered and brushed it way with her mitt, then he helped her up. "That was so much fun; let's do it again!" she exclaimed.

Sam stood with Bozo and Blanka watching Anya guide the 'Cat' into the yard at a speed respectful of the multitude of structures that Sean hoped she would avoid hitting. She pulled it in front of the sleigh where she could re-attach the tug, and shut off the engine. Blanka and Sam clapped their hands as Anya took a bow and Sean wiped his brow in mock relief.

"Me and Blanka were getting the firewood boxed up. The others are getting the food and drinks together. Should be ready to go shortly. How was the trail?"

Sean and Anya laughed in sync, "Smooth as ever except for one large divot." Sean smiled at a puzzled Anya. "A hole in the snow," he added. She laughed again.

"I see," said Sam. "Sounds like you had a good time and no one got hurt."

Reina, Sheila and the other girls appeared through the lodge's back door with a couple of boxes of food, several thermoses of hot chocolate and some wiener sticks made from willow branches. "Well let's get this show on the road," Sheila commanded. "Where do you want us?"

Sean took Sam aside and whispered, "How do you feel about Anya driving the Elan with Blanka?"

"Okay with me if you think she's up to it," said Sam.

"Anya!" Sean's serious tone startled Anya thinking she was in trouble.

"I want you and Blanka to take the Elan and follow us on the trail. You drive Anya; do you think you can do that?" Sean tried to appear serious. Those looking on wondered if he knew what he was doing, not realizing that Anya had already driven the Elan *and* the 'Cat'.

Anya looked at a bewildered Blanka then turned back and said, "Sure, can we race?"

Sean laughed while the others joined in. "Sam will get you acquainted with it; not much different than the 'Cat' but a lot *slower*!" He emphasized 'slower'.

"Okay, let's get loaded. Sheila and Sam will ride shotgun with the girls on the sleigh, so find a spot and get ready to roll. I'll ride with Reina." Reina cocked her head questioning his last remark.

"Yeah, you're driving," he whispered. "It's good for the girls to see Anya and Blanka stepping out. They already look up to you as a very capable woman. You do know how to drive one of these don't you?" Sean laughed as Reina poked him in the ribs.

The hard-packed surface around the Lodge enabled the 'Cat' to gain momentum and easily pull the sleigh along the packed trail. Anya behaved herself, not wanting to frighten the timid Blanka who was hanging on tightly to Anya's waist while trying to smile. Bozo followed along behind. The girls in the sleigh talked and giggled the entire trip until they pulled into the lake basin. Reina made a wide loop and came to a stop facing back down the trail on her track. The scene stunned the girls into silence as they got up from the sleigh and stood in awe surveying their surroundings. None of them had ever been this close to a mountain and none had ever been in the wilderness.

At the picnic site the girls gathered around to watch Sam start the fire while Anya explained how she gathered the 'squaw wood' he was using to get the blaze ignited. Sheila spread out the food and drinks on the table. "We want the fire to burn really hot at first then we'll let it die down so we can roast our meat," Sam explained. The kindling caught with the first match. The fire came to life and began consuming the smaller pieces of wood Sam had carefully placed over the 'squaw wood'. "Why don't you girls take the toboggan up that hill?" He pointed to a slope next to the mountain face. "In fact, Anya, you show Blanka how to drive the Elan and let her tow a load of you on the toboggan over to the hill." Blanka beamed at Sam's show of confidence in her as she and Anya walked over to start the machine and hook up the toboggan.

Sean and Reina were walking on the snow-covered lake checking for signs of overflow or thin ice. The spell of cold weather pretty much guaranteed thick ice and it was early enough that overflow wasn't likely to be a problem but he wanted to be sure. Sam wanted to let the girls have some fun driving the Elan on the flat lake surface where they couldn't do much damage to themselves or the machine.

The four adults sat on a log in front of the fire drinking coffee, enjoying the bright sunshine and watching the girls playing on the hill. The screams of glee and abundant laughter echoed off the rock wall rising above the lake warming the hearts of those looking on. After an hour had passed Blanka and Tekla arrived on the Elan pulling the toboggan loaded with four weary girls. Some others trudged back to the fire trying to stay on the snowmobile track where walking was easier. Blanka waited until the girls got off the toboggan then turned back to pick up another load.

"We're hungry," said Tekla, "can we roast the wiener now?"

Sheila and Reina got the girls each a wiener stick then showed them how to skewer the meat so it wouldn't fall into the fire. Sean and Sam coached the roasting while Sheila and Reina prepared the buns with mustard, relish and ketchup. By the time Blanka returned with her last load the first shift were eagerly devouring the novel hotdog. The new shift received their instruction while sipping hot chocolate. As a final treat, Sam pulled out a plastic bag full of Polish sausage and invited the girls to sample his Yukon version of their national delight. Sam always made his sausage out of bear meat but he kept that information to himself.

Exercise and an unobstructed sun warmed the girls to the point where some sat in the snow eating their hotdogs and drinking hot chocolate while others perched on logs. Conversation covered a variety of topics but the girls were mostly curious about the wild animals that lived in the area hoping to see some. They had been learning about the Yukon fauna but had not met any of the critters mentioned in the stories they heard or pictured in the books Reina showed them. Sam told them that they weren't likely to see much because of all the noise they were making and that the best way to see animals was to find a comfortable spot, sit and wait quietly. He promised to take them out another time to see what they might find.

After everyone was full and rested, Sam invited the girls to each try driving the Elan on the lake. He appointed Anya and Blanka as instructors who were more than eager to show the others how it worked and instruct them on how to start and drive the machine. The amusing experiment went on for some time without injury or mishap much to the delight of the watchers and the participants. The highlight was watching smart aleck Anya get stuck in a drift of very deep and soft snow. She managed to bury the machine down to the ice surface, spinning the track trying to get out. Reluctantly she admitted defeat and called for help. Several of the girls slogged across the lake to help her lift and pull the machine out of the deep snow while Sean and Sam sat and watched. "Good for them," said Sam as he took another gulp of his coffee. "Been there, done that; now it's their turn."

The day's activities had exhausted the girls. Full of wieners and sausage they weren't interested in supper so Sheila put out some items to snack on if they were interested. They hung their wet outer clothing on racks, pegs and chairs around the lodge while some changed into their pyjamas. Others lounged on the furniture and floor in their long underwear drinking hot chocolate, reading, talking about the day and playing 'Old Maid'.

Reina turned to Sean sitting beside her. "This was a really good day. They'll sleep like a team of sled dogs tonight."

Chapter 46

"I'm going to Whitehorse today," Sean announced as he and Sam enjoyed their morning coffee.

"Let me know if you guys need anything. I want to get this immigration thing moving and get some of my own questions answered if I can."

"Probably a good idea, you've got the weather," replied Sam, "I'll get Sheila to put together a list. You taking Reina with you?"

"Yes, she wants to check on the house and take care of a few other things and she can help me out too."

Sam looked over his shoulder and whispered, "Would you do me a favour and pick up Sheila's Christmas present while you're there?"

"Sure will. What you got in mind?"

"Well, we're at the age where we don't need or want much but she has always wanted one of those Hudson's Bay parkas with the fur trim. Red, she likes the red ones. I think we did well enough this season that I can afford one now. I'll get you some money." Sam rose from his chair, wandered over to his ammo cupboard, and returned with a wad of bills.

"You bet Sam, I'll ask Reina to pick one up while we're there."

The sun was still below the horizon but the sky signalled her imminent arrival. Sean pulled the wing covers off TJ while Reina brushed away any lingering snow. He unplugged the electric heaters under the panel and the engine cowling and asked Anya to stow them in the small shack at the side of the airstrip. Anya got her good-bye hug then Sean and Reina climbed into the small plane. While the engine warmed, Sean pumped down the skis. Completing his checks he gunned the engine, taxied onto the strip then pushed full throttle. TJ jumped effortlessly into the air.

Arnie was waiting outside the hanger when TJ taxied onto the apron. Sean turned the plane over to his trusted friend and he and Reina walked to his truck idling in the parking lot. They drove to Bob's place to pick up Reina's Jeep. They agreed to meet later at Ray's office. Sean wanted to meet with Jay Morgan right away.

Jay leaned back in his high-back chair, his hands behind his head. "You're putting me on," he sneered, "this kind of stuff doesn't happen here!"

"I know it sounds crazy but I've got 13 traumatized teenage girls holed up at White River waiting on their fate. Go ahead, call Sam and Sheila, they'll tell you." Sean was getting frustrated. Jay didn't believe him.

Jay stared at Sean and Sean stared back. Neither man spoke.

"Okay, as preposterous as it sounds, I believe you because I know you. Besides, I can't for the life of me think of why you would pull such a stunt if it wasn't true."

"Thank you Jay; you'll soon meet some of the evidence. Now, these girls want to stay in Canada, so what's next?"

Jay sighed and threw his hands in the air. "This is serious stuff Sean. I can't just wave a magic wand and make them citizens."

"But you'll help us won't you? You'll facilitate instead of obstruct, won't you Jay? After all, you *are* a civil *servant*."

Jay smiled at Sean through the moment of silence that followed his remark.

"Yes, I'll *facilitate*. They will need temporary resident permits, which are good for six months and renewable. First, I want you to make an appointment with Ron Vance; if he is willing to take this on, your girls will be in good hands and he'll take it from here. He will work directly with my office. But, you need to see these girls placed in the care of families who are willing to sponsor and care for them until we can conclude the legal proceedings. Ron will help you with that paperwork. Have you got 13 families who will do this?" Jay looked skeptical.

"I'm meeting with Reina and Ray in a couple of hours. I don't expect that it will be a problem."

The two men rose from their chairs and shook hands before giving each other a hug. "Thank you Jay; you can give these girls a new life. God knows they need one." Jay rolled his eyes at Sean's optimism and confidence in him.

* * *

Kazia had been looking for Anya who wasn't responding to the calling of her name. She found her on her knees in her room. Kazia joined her, leaning on the bed alongside her best friend. She had noticed that Anya wasn't engaging with the other girls and seemed to be in another world during their English lesson. She put her arm over her shoulders and whispered, "Are you talking to God?"

Anya turned her sodden eyes to stare into Kazia's, "Yes, He can make it possible for me to stay with Sean and Reina. He can help all of us Kazia. You need to pray Kazia, share your heart. But, Kazia, even if He doesn't, He will take care of us. Never forget that my friend."

Kazia bowed her head joining Anya in her whispered prayers.

* * *

Reina walked through her house after shovelling snow off the walkway and the driveway. All was in order but she pushed the thermostat up to 20° C so she and Sean would have a warm house to come back to after their meetings. She called the College to touch base with her supervisor and let him in on her marriage plans. She allayed his fears by re-committing to the spring semester much to his relief. Next, she called Ray to arrange their meeting.

She set a mental itinerary that allowed her to pick up everything on Sheila's list before she met with Ray. Her own list included a visit to the pharmacy, the local print shop and Murdoch's jewellery store. She wanted to do some Christmas shopping but time would limit those plans.

* * *

"Mr. Vance will see you now Sean, please go in." Ron's receptionist was a fellow parent who served with Sean on the parent's school council where Felicia had attended school. He always admired Carol for her diligence in keeping informed and her willingness to speak her mind at the council meetings. She would make a great lawyer, he thought.

Ron met Sean at the door to his office taking his hand in a firm grip. The men were about the same age. Ron was married and had two teenage daughters. Sean thought this would be a plus for him taking the case. His reputation as a lawyer in the community was unsurpassed and Sean, through previous dealings, knew he could trust him. Ron had once retained Sean to introduce him to the shooting world and to go with him on his first moose hunt. Since then they frequently met at Fish and Game events and Ron sometimes shot his rifle at Sean's cabin. Years earlier Ron set up Sean's company but had not done any other legal work for him.

Ron listened while Sean first outlined the purpose of his visit and his conversations with Jay. Ron sat in rapt attention as Sean unfolded the events of recent weeks. Occasionally he would write on his legal pad. After almost half an hour Sean concluded, "I want you to keep the government from deporting those girls. I want you to get them legally admitted to Canada so they can apply for citizenship. Can you do it?"

Ron sat quietly looking at Sean and glancing at his notepad much like Jay had done. "Have you told the RCMP about the murders?"

"No, I know what they'll do; they'll get immigration to deport the girls. At least they won't let the scum bags get away since they're already dead; good riddance!"

Ron sensed Sean's hostility towards the authorities but he also understood where that hostility came from. "Does anyone know you found those two dead men?" Ron's serious demeanour hinted at the legal repercussions of his pending answer.

"Never mind those thugs, let's talk about the girls!" Sean was frustrated with the direction Ron was going.

"We *have* to talk about them *before* we talk about the girls," Ron was firm in his reply to Sean's obvious frustration. "Who knows about them?"

"Sam, Sheila, Reina and the girls." Sean accepted Ron's rebuke and answered his question.

"Listen, I'm going to take your case. I *want* to take this case. But, we have to let the cops in on this before we go any further." Ron anticipated Sean's reaction, raising a hand to keep him at bay. "Let me finish. They are unlikely to arrest you but they'll be pretty pissed that you didn't tell them about Reina and the two dead goons. They are supposed to be the heroes and they'll resent your actions. I'll make sure that the girls stay here but you have some work to do to help me make that happen; you okay with that?"

Sean didn't answer, instead he glared at Ron. Finally, he said, "Okay, *if* you protect those girls." Sean spoke firmly to make his point. "Thanks Ron; I trust you."

"Don't thank me yet, we have a monstrous immigration bureaucracy to confront but I'm thankful that Jay is on the side of those girls. That will potentially make a huge difference. We may also have an angry police sergeant to deal with."

"I don't' care about him, and his petty ego. What's next?" Sean asked.

Ron leaned across his desk locking his eyes with Sean's. "You *better* care about him; he's the law. I'm going to need a pretty substantial retainer Sean, $5000 now and another in a couple of weeks. Can you handle that?"

Sean took out his chequebook. "I'll give you a cheque for $10,000 right now. Let's get to work."

Ron punched a couple of numbers on his phone and asked Karen, his paralegal, to come in. He introduced her to Sean and gave her a verbal précis of the case.

"Okay, here's what we've got to do right away." Ron began to outline the things he needed Sean and Karen to do. When he was done, he dismissed Karen and his new client to begin their work. After they left, he picked up the phone and called RCMP sergeant Matt Dawson.

Chapter 47

Karen and Sean met for another half hour. She assured Sean that the girls would not be deported and handed Sean a large manila envelope full of legal forms. She asked if he had any other questions while handing him her business card. "Just one; could Reina and I adopt one of the girls?"

Karen smiled. "One thing at a time Sean." She reminded him to be back in the office with Reina at 4:00 pm to meet with the RCMP. As she held the door she asked if he new what valium was. Sean laughed and thanked her for her efforts.

Reina was already in Ray's office when he arrived. He gave her a kiss on the cheek and greeted his pastor with a hug before sitting in the chair beside Reina. He quickly reviewed his meetings with Jay and Ron and told Reina they had a meeting at Ron's with the RCMP at four.

"Sounds like you two have been rather busy lately. I hope you haven't got yourselves into trouble." Ray looked concerned after Sean's remark about the meeting with the police.

"No, *we* didn't get into the trouble; *it* came to us and 13 innocent teenage girls." Sean was still defensive after his meetings with Jay and Ron. "We are doing what we can to help those girls."

Reina interjected sensing the intensity in Sean's voice. "We need to find some families willing to take these girls in, at least temporarily while we pursue their legal entry to the country. If we are successful with immigration, they will need to live with a family for a year before they are free to be on their own. Of course we want only the best for these girls so we want to see them placed with appropriate families. We have some ideas but you know the families better than us so we need your help. Above all they need protection, acceptance and abundant love and care; all have been traumatized by their experience."

"Sam and Sheila will take one girl if immigration approves and Reina and I will take at least two," Sean added, "but that still leaves 10 who will need families. Jay said that if you, as a pastor, endorse the families there should be no problem making it work."

"We are getting married Ray," Reina announced.

"Well congratulations; Nancy and I have been getting a little impatient with you two." Ray admitted with a broad smile. He rose from his chair and gave them both a hug. "When's the wedding?"

"How's your schedule after the new year?" Sean asked.

"Wide open, you name a date and it's yours," Ray replied, "Nancy will be elated at this news!"

"Okay, we'll talk and get back to you soon." Sean looked at Reina who nodded in agreement.

"Let's get back to this immediate need. What exactly is this all about?" Ray questioned.

Sean and Reina took turns relating the story beginning with Sean's discovery of Anya on the road to his cabin. Ray remained attentive for the entire 20 minutes it took to tell the story.

"Wow!" He sat staring at the couple in front of him. After a pause, "You said you have some families in mind. Who are you thinking of?"

Sean nodded when Reina looked at him. "Roberts came to mind right away. They have Tahlia and a big house; they might even take *two* girls. Gatensby's don't have any children but they sure love them. Their house is a little small but no harm in asking. Jerry and Anne can never have enough kids around. They're a little far away but I don't think that's a problem and

I think they would jump at the chance to help. I know Connie lives alone but she raised two girls and just might welcome a young lady to keep her company. We all know she's a great caregiver."

"What about me and Nancy? Did you consider us?" asked Ray.

"Of course but we thought we'd wait to see how you responded. Now we know."

"Well, I like all your choices and have no problem with any of those families. Leave it with me. I'll get in touch with them and some others that come to mind and I'll get back to you. When will the girls be available?"

"Let's say January 2."

Reina and Sean thanked Ray and left for their meeting with the RCMP sergeant.

They got to the office early. Ron greeted Reina warmly and invited them into the conference room. Karen accompanied them and set up her recording equipment while the others gathered at one end of the long table. "Help yourself to coffee, there's water too?" he offered.

Reina poured Sean a glass of water before he could get to the coffee pot. As she handed him the glass, her eyes silently admonished him to stay away from any more stimulants. Ron explained that it was important to tell Matt everything that happened. "Technically, they could charge all four of you but Matt and I both know that no judge in the Territory would entertain it in light of the circumstances. Karen will record your statement for the record. The important thing is to get the events documented by the police so we can use it in our citizenship case." Ron paused, leaned across the table and looked into Sean's eyes. "Keep your cool Sean, the girls are no longer under threat by the police. Under *no* circumstances are you to talk about what you *might* have done had things not worked out the way they did."

Carol tapped on the door before opening it and announcing that Sergeant Matt Dawson had arrived. "Show him in," said Ron. He got up from his chair and greeted the Sergeant as he entered. "I believe you know Sean and Reina." Matt shook hands with both and took the seat beside Ron. "Karen will record our session and we'll provide you a copy for your records, if that's okay with you?"

"That will be helpful Ron, my thanks to you and Sean and Reina for meeting with me. I'm ready when you are." Matt sat back in his chair.

Ron introduced the statement venue, date, time and names of those attending then nodded to Sean. He began to relate the events beginning with his discovery of Anya on the road. After about a minute, he paused to note that Reina would be adding her own experience. He invited Ron and Matt to interrupt with any questions as he and Reina told the story.

Sean and Reina spoke for almost an hour. At the end, the Sergeant sat mute, overwhelmed with what he had heard. He broke his silence by addressing Reina, "How are you doing now Reina?"

"Oh, I'm fine. Dubicki was a lousy shot and Sean's a great first responder. God must have plans for me yet," she responded with a smile. "Thanks for asking."

"And the girls, how are they doing?" he pursued.

"Physically, they are doing well. Emotionally, they have a way to go; some more than others. Sheila and I are trained counsellors and my nursing background has helped. We are treating their trauma appropriately." Reina assured the Sergeant not wanting to risk police intervention. "Sean's experience working with similarly traumatized girls in Southeast Asia has helped."

"I would like to send a man over to recover the bullets from the wall in your kitchen," Matt asked. "Would tomorrow morning about nine work for you?"

"No problem," answered Reina.

"And Sean, would you be available to lead us to the place where those other two men and the truck are? I could pick you up at nine as well."

"I'll meet you at Reina's," Sean agreed. "If you want that truck to start you should bring a tiger torch, some stove pipe and jumper cables."

"So the girls are still with Sam and Sheila at White River?" asked the Sergeant.

Ron raised his hand and answered before Sean could say anything, "They are safe and secure. Jay Morgan at immigration is issuing temporary resident permits for them as we speak. I know you will want to speak with them but that will have to wait a few weeks if you don't mind. These girls, the victims, are still dealing with their trauma. Please remember that they come from a country where they see police officers as a threat. In fact, it might be wise to have a female officer, out of uniform, meet with them when the time comes, perhaps sometime after the New Year."

Matt could see that Ron and his clients were protective of the girls. He wisely decided not to pursue the matter any further.

Karen left to make a copy of the tape for Sergeant Dawson as the others engaged in small talk.

"Yes, we'll be at White River if you need us," Sean responded to the Sergeant's inquiry. "We're spending Christmas there. We'll be bringing the girls to Whitehorse after the New Year. If we're done here, Reina and I would like to go; we've had a long day."

"I'm done if you are Ron." The Sergeant looked at Ron.

"Yeah, you guys take off. I'll contact you if I need anything else. Don't worry, I'm highly optimistic that things will work out just fine." He looked at the Sergeant.

Sean and Reina thanked Ron and the Sergeant and left the office. Holding hands, they walked in silence towards Sean's truck.

"That went better than I expected," Sean said as he and Reina drove out of the parking lot. "I'm hungry, how about you?"

"Yes, I'm so relieved to have this whole thing off my chest. I have a lot of confidence in Ron getting the best deal for the girls," replied Reina. "I need a quiet place to relax and I could eat some crab legs; why don't we go to the '202'?"

"I'm with you." Sean turned left and pulled up in front of the 202 Club.

Reina put her hand on his leg. "I'm proud of you Sean, you did good with the policeman."

Chapter 48

Kathy welcomed them at the door and took their coats. The 202 Club was a favourite for both Sean and Reina. It held a special place in their hearts as it was the first place they had a meal together. They chose a small booth at the far end of the restaurant away from the other diners. The dimly lit restaurant complemented their mood and the candle on their table provided an appropriate finish to the quiet ambiance. The low light softened the coarseness of the aged building. Its crooked walls covered in salvaged boards, low ceilings and uneven floors appealed to the couple over the harsh glass and steel of some eateries.

They were holding hands across the table when Ian, the owner, approached and greeted them. "Reina, Sean, so nice to see you two again; it's been a while. How have you been?"

"Hi Ian," Sean replied, "it's good to be back. We're both famished but we'd each like to start with a red Dubonnet and a lemon wedge if you have any. Do you have crab tonight?"

"Please say yes Ian!" Reina pleaded.

"You bet," he laughed, "fresh order arrived today. You want anything else?" Ian waited while his patrons decided to order a plate of oysters Rockefeller as an appetizer.

"Okay, be right back with your . . ." Ian felt Kathy's presence. She stood behind him with two glasses of Dubonnet garnished with lemon. "Now that's service!" Ian stepped aside so Kathy could serve the drinks.

"I took the bet and I won," Kathy announced with satisfaction smiling at her husband.

Sean and Reina reviewed their day, rejoicing in the optimism they shared over the fate of the girls. Bouts of laughter erupted between bites of the flavourful oysters and sips of Dubonnet. They both felt the stress of the past weeks draining from their bodies as they talked. The conversation eventually turned to their wedding. They agreed on the format and the guest list but Sean deferred to Reina on the flowers. Reina deferred to Sean on the carrot cake. When the subject of the date came up they both went silent. Reina looked down at her drink but Sean just stared at her hoping she would look up. When their eyes met, they both spoke almost in unison, "Why are we waiting?"

Sean called Ray when they returned to Reina's house. Reina listened to the conversation deducing the conclusion before Sean hung up. "Okay, it's set, Sunday after service. How do you feel about that?"

Reina stepped up to him and hugged him close. "Perfect."

Reina retired early. Sean left for Ray and Nancy's where he stayed up reading and thinking about his plan. When everyone had gone to bed, he called Arnie at home. It was a long shot but worth the try. Did Arnie know of any aircraft that could stop at White River and pick up a passenger en route to Whitehorse? Later he called Sam and Sheila updating them and alerting them to his plan.

The next morning Sean met Reina at her house for breakfast before the officers arrived. Sean would be gone all morning but Reina would finish picking up the items on Sheila's list and a few on her own. She wanted to get her hair done but Sean protested. He loved her long hair and didn't want to see it hidden in some ziggurat perched on top of her head. She agreed to leave it down but she wouldn't back down on getting a wash and style. Her dress already hung in her closet. Reina always knew the day would come and had bought the dress during a trip to Mexico. When she saw it, she knew it was perfect. Sean's only suit hung in the same closet rather than at his cabin where he used to keep it. She convinced him that the smell of wood smoke failed to complement the garment unless he was wearing home-tanned moccasins.

Sean refilled their coffee mugs as the topic switched to the girls. They both wanted to house at least two of the girls. Anya and Kazia were the indisputable candidates. Anya had become a 'daughter' to both of them who, in turn, became like the parents she always longed for. Kazia and Anya shared a bond of friendship that made them like sisters. They didn't want to see them separated. Reina would relocate her office so each girl could have her own room. They agreed to house two more if Ray couldn't find families for all the girls.

The doorbell rang announcing the arrival of the RCMP officers. Matt Dawson introduced his two officers as Reina took their parkas and hung them in the entry closet. She led them upstairs to where the two bullets had lodged in the wall. She explained where she and her assailant were standing when he shot her and pointed to the dried blood on the floor. They followed her down the hallway where the smashed bathroom door testified to the violent capture and abduction of Anya. Lastly, she took them to the broken back door frame telling them how Dubicki had shot and killed Jesse pointing out the blood trail on the stairs where he had kicked the dog's body down the stairs.

One of the officers took pictures, measuring and scraping blood samples off the floor. The other dug the bullets out of the wall. "Do you know if your neighbours heard or saw anything that night?" asked the Sergeant.

"Not the ones on either side. The Wilsons were away visiting family in Alberta and Don, on the other side, works nights so he wasn't home either. He had a suppressor on his pistol anyway. I don't know about any others." Reina admitted.

"Okay, you guys done?" Matt addressed his officers. "Let's go then. Sean will take us to the other scene. Thanks for your cooperation Reina."

Sean kissed Reina goodbye, threw on his parka and joined the others outside. He rode with Matt in the pickup and the other two officers followed in a car. They stopped where the access track to the camp joined the main road. The two officers in the car brought their evidence kit and two body bags and jumped into the pickup box. The sight of the body bags reminded Sean of Service's 'Ballad of Blasphemous Bill'. He chuckled to himself.

Matt pulled the pickup into four-wheel drive and they turned onto the access road. The untracked snow was over a foot deep in spots but the truck had no problem making its way to the camp buildings. Everything was as Sean remembered it except for the blanket of snow. The Kenworth and trailer sat silent, shrouded in snow and ice. The door of the camp hung open as he left it.

"Can you drive that truck?" the Sergeant looked at Sean.

"Yeah. Did you bring a torch?" Sean responded.

"In the back." He waved towards the pickup.

"Give me a minute and I'll get the torch going." Sean set the end of the stovepipe under the oil pan of the Kenworth's engine and fired up the tiger torch. "This will take a while and it still might not start." Sean opened the lid on the Kenworth's toolbox, pulled out a can of starter fluid, and tucked it inside his parka. He joined the officers inside the building where the frozen bodies of the two men remained face down on the table in a pool of frozen blood.

After an hour of picture taking, measuring and thorough inspection of the Kenworth and the Sea Can, the officers retrieved the body bags. Sean had to stand outside to hide his mirth as the officers struggled to get the frozen, contorted bodies into the neat, rectangular bags. They finally gave up, loaded the frozen corpses into the pickup box, and covered them with a tarp.

Sean turned off the tiger torch then connected the jumper cables from the pickup to the Kenworth battery. He climbed into the cab and threw a couple of switches to get some current running from the batteries then turned the ignition key and pushed the starter button. The engine turned over but it wouldn't catch. He shot some starting fluid into the air cleaner mounted outside his window and pushed the starter button again. After cranking for a bit the engine fired but soon quit. He gave it another shot of fluid and tried again. This time it caught and continued to run. Black smoke puffed from the twin stacks into the surrounding forest. He set the idle and let it run to warm the engine and transmission and build air pressure.

"Do you think you can drive it out of here with all this snow?" Matt asked.

"Good chance. The good news is we've got dry ground underneath the rig for about 60 feet. I'll lock up both axles, back up to make the most of that dry ground, and see what happens." Sean replied. "If we have trouble we can hook a chain onto your truck. It might be enough between the two of them to pull this rig through the snow."

Matt and the others drove the pickup back to the main road and waited. Sean eased the rig back until his rear wheels met the tracks in the snow left by the trailer wheels. He selected a higher gear than usual; he wanted to gain as much speed as possible before he reached the snow-covered road ahead. He eased out the clutch; the tractor twisted with the torque and lurched forward. Sean kept the engine speed high as the rig ploughed through the soft snow and lunged onto the main road. Setting the brakes and the idle, he jumped out of the cab and walked to the police pickup where the officers were applauding his success.

"So, you want me to follow you back to town?" Sean spoke to Matt through the window as the others returned to their car.

"Yeah, we're finished here for now. Follow me to the compound and we'll park the truck there."

Chapter 49

Sean backed the truck into a spot in the compound near a power outlet, with easy access to the exit gate. He found the extension cord behind the passenger seat and plugged in the truck's engine heater in case they had to move it again. Locking the doors, he walked to where Matt was waiting with his ride back to Reina's house and gave him the keys.

"Have you talked to the guys at the Junction yet?" Sean was only making conversation, as he was certain that Matt had already been in touch.

"Yes, in fact we are meeting at the hospital morgue after I drop you," Matt replied. "I'm still puzzled that you didn't contact us sooner about all this."

"That's easy Matt," said Sean. "The track record of police intervention in sex trafficking is not very inspiring. The courts are even worse. *Defend the Law*' but to hell with the victims, foreign or domestic. Nothing personal Matt."

Matt knew that Sean spoke the truth and decided to drop the subject. He dropped Sean at Reina's house, thanked him for his cooperation and help and said good-bye. The phone was ringing when Sean opened the door. It was Reina. They spoke briefly; she wanted to meet him for lunch at the Sourdough Hotel. Sean hung up and dialled Flight Services to check the weather on the coast. Then he called the Sergeant Preston Motel in Skagway to reserve a room for a couple of nights. Lastly, he called Ray.

Sean pulled his Ford into the spot beside Reina's Jeep and walked into the hotel lobby. It was Saturday so the hotel guests were mostly Yukoners who took advantage of the warmer weather to come to town for their Christmas shopping. Tourists were a scarce commodity during the Yukon winter except when *Rendezvous* and the dog races started in February. Local hotels depended on a good summer season and the loyalty of locals to keep their doors open. Reina sat at a table against the wall sipping water from a glass through a straw. She smiled and watched him approach her table. He bent and kissed her before taking the seat opposite.

"How's it going?" Sean reached for a menu wedged between the wall and a ketchup bottle.

"I'm about done my shopping for now. I'll finish next time we come to town. Found a coat for Sheila in the red that she likes; Sam will be pleased. They even wrapped it so Sam won't have to. We need to talk about what to get the girls; I want each of them to get something personal that they will appreciate and want to keep. The pharmacy's out of a couple of things I wanted but we'll get by. I'm getting my hair done at two. How about you? Did you behave yourself?" she frowned at him.

"Always. The Sergeant even thanked me for my cooperation and help. I got the truck running and drove the rig back for them. Didn't even ask to see my license. Hey, what do you think about a honeymoon in Skagway?"

"Skagway! You read my mind." Reina was a master at sarcasm. They both laughed. Skagway, a small coastal town in Alaska, sported a population of about 50 souls this time of year. "You know me; I don't care where we go as long as we can be together for a few days and celebrate the beginning of our lives as husband and wife."

Sean took her hands in his and smiled. "That's just one of the things I love about you; you're so easy to get along with. We've got reservations at Sergeant Preston's for Sunday and Monday nights."

"Sergeant Preston's! Well that makes all the difference. How did you *ever* get a reservation?" her reply once again dripping with sarcasm. "Did you call Sam and Sheila yet to let them know the news and what we're up to?"

"Ah, no, I thought we could do that together tonight." Sean lied.

"Good, I want to talk to Anya too. She'll be so excited but I hope not too disappointed that she can't be here for the ceremony."

"Oh she'll get over it. She can watch the movie," Sean replied carelessly.

The couple ordered their food and talked about Christmas at the White and how much fun it was going to be. Reina had been going over in her mind everything she needed to make it a special time for the girls. Sean took advantage of a lull in her soliloquy to suggest that they take Anya and Kazia and fly to Fairbanks to do some Christmas shopping. Reina's eyes widened as she stared at him. "What a great idea. Can we really do that?" she exclaimed.

"If the weather cooperates, I don't see why not, it's only a couple hours away and the shopping is ten times better than Whitehorse."

"Oh yes, let's do that, the girls will love it." She paused in thought. "Oh oh, what about getting the girls across the border? They don't have any identification."

"Good point. Remind me to call Jay at home. He'll be able to give us something temporary that will work."

Reina's eyes shifted away from Sean and her mouth fell open. She glanced back at Sean then returned to stare at the young girl in the red parka who stood at the entry to the restaurant. Their eyes met and Anya and Reina ran into each other's arms squealing with delight.

Chapter 50

The threesome tried to eat their meal but excited conversation took priority leaving much of the food to cool. Anya had come to life since the demise of her captor and the reassurance that Sean and Reina would not abandon her. Her face beamed with happiness at the realization that she would be a part of the wedding of the two most important people in her life.

"I'm getting my hair done at two. Would you like to have yours done too?" Reina smiled at Anya.

"Oh can I? I've never done that," she replied bursting with excitement.

"Let me call Sally and see if she can work it out." Reina got up and went into the lobby to use the phone.

Sean stared at Anya. "What's the matter?" she said.

"Nothing, absolutely nothing Anya. I'm just overflowing with joy watching you bask in the life God intended for you. You're a wonderful young lady Anya, and it is a great privilege for me to know you."

Anya smiled, her face glowing as Reina re-joined them. "It's all set. Becky will do your hair while Sally does mine. So what style would you like?"

Anya looked thoughtful. "I don't know. I've never thought about it. Maybe shorter?"

Reina laughed. "They have lots of magazines and pictures of different hairstyles. You can look at them and Becky will help you pick a style that suits your hair and the shape of your face. It will be lots of fun Anya. I'm sure you will enjoy this experience."

"While you girls indulge yourselves I'm going to call Jay and then pop over to see Ted for a few minutes. I might do a little shopping but I'll meet you at your house around five. Is that okay?"

"That's fine," said Reina, "we are going shopping for a dress and shoes for Anya after we get our hair done. Let's plan on taking Anya to the 202 for supper."

Sean got up and walked around the table. He leaned down between his two favourite girls and hugged them before leaving. He paid the bill then used the lobby phone to call Jay. Jay agreed to put something together for Anya and Kazia so they could enter the US. He added that he had talked with Ron and encouraged Sean not to worry about the girls.

Sean drove to Ted's house. Ted ran a gunsmith business out of his basement as well as buying and selling firearms. They discussed the merits of different models of lightweight pistols hoping to identify one that would suit the small hands of his protégés. Ted retrieved a couple of examples from his gun cabinet to show Sean. Sean and Ted liked the CZ brand so when he laid the new CZ 75 compact 9 mm on the counter beside the Sig Sauer Sean's eyes lit up. He handled the pistol checking for weight, balance and grip all of which he liked. He slammed the magazine into place. As he watched the slide close on the snap cap he asked Ted about its capacity and if he could shoot it. Ted loaded the pinned mag with 10 rounds and led Sean to his basement 'gun range'. After emptying the magazine, he was sold.

"I want three of these Ted, can you get them before Christmas?" asked Sean.

"I've got two here. Let me check with T&Ds, they might have one, otherwise I'd have to get one from outside." Ted picked up the phone and called the other gun dealer in town. After some conversation and a lengthy pause Ted said, "Hold it for me Bill, I'll pick it up later this afternoon."

"So they've got one?" Sean queried expectantly.

"Yes, but it's used. Only about 50 rounds through it though so it should be good. I'll check it out of course."

"Great, I'll take all three. I'll sign the paperwork now, put them all in my name. Can I pick them up on Wednesday?"

"Shouldn't be a problem. I'll have them ready for you. Anything else?"

"I'm planning on going to Fairbanks in a week; do you think I will be able to find six magazines there?"

"Why don't you let me call Frenchy in Fairbanks? I'll have him order them for you. He should have them within a week? They'll be the factory 14 rounders."

"That's what I want. Do it Ted."

At the Muskrat Hair Salon, Anya and Becky flipped through the magazines together. Sally washed Reina's thick hair and Anya deliberated. After listening to Becky's counsel she settled on a chin-length style with sweeping bangs. She showed the picture to Reina hoping she liked her selection. Reina praised her choice eliciting broad smiles from Anya and Becky.

Becky massaged Anya's scalp as she worked the shampoo through her long hair. Anya revelled in the sensation almost falling asleep during the process. Later as she stared at herself in the mirror, fleeting doubts came and went. Her long hair had been with her for most of her life, now she was about to lose it.

She shuddered at the image that broke into her consciousness. The man was pulling her long hair as she screamed in fear and pain. The image disappeared as quickly as it came. Reina's eyes met Anya's as she turned seeking refuge in her friend. Reina had sensed something that she confirmed by the torment she saw in Anya's eyes. She reached over and gave Anya's hand a squeeze while saying a silent prayer. Becky too sensed Anya's distress. She brushed it off as the anxiety often felt by women about to substitute the familiar with the new. She encouraged her by sharing her own excitement over the prospect of Anya's new look. The cutting began. There was no turning back.

For the next half hour, Anya watched Becky's skilled hands transform the image in the mirror. She thought about how God was faithfully transforming her heart, her entire life. Reina stood at her side holding her hand as Becky cut and shaped the hair to frame Anya's face. A smile began to reflect back from the mirror. "I hope Sean likes it Reina."

"Never mind him. Do you like it?" said Reina.

"Oh yes, I do Reina. I look so different. Thank you Becky for helping me." Tears welled up in Anya's eyes.

Reina gave Becky and Sally a bigger than usual tip and thanked them for taking care of Anya so well. She in turn received hugs and congratulations on her upcoming wedding. The two left the salon and drove to a women's apparel shop that Reina was certain would have a dress for Anya. They browsed the racks of dresses gathering a selection of those that caught their eye. The choice came down to two that defied a final decision. In the end, Reina told the clerk that they would take both of them. Anya decided on the red one for the wedding. She and Reina both liked the lace sleeves and accents on the bodice. The clerk and three customers stopped and stared when Anya emerged from the change room. The fit was perfect. The fabric clung to her form and ended just above the knees. Nobody even noticed her calf-length grey wool socks.

* * *

Sean was frustrated in his attempt to find the right gift for his loved ones. Men weren't a problem; any good hardware or sporting goods store would yield just the right Christmas present. It was the women that caused him grief. He acknowledged that jewellery appealed to most women and he appreciated how it could complement their image but he was not inclined to shop for such accessories. In the past, Gina would draw his attention to something she liked and most often, he was happy to buy it for her. Now, as he wandered around Murdoch's he was hoping that something would grab his attention, something worthy of the woman soon to be his wife. He stopped in front of a display of birthstones. Reina's was an emerald so he asked to see some emerald jewellery. His eyes lit up when he saw the silver bracelet, ornately carved and studded with emeralds. Yes, he knew she would love it. He asked the clerk to gift-wrap it for him.

While he waited, he continued to browse the glass cases for ideas for Christmas. He and Reina wanted to find something personal for each of the girls. It had to be something they could treasure for the rest of their lives. He thought of Anya and the other girls. He guessed that they never owned a piece of jewellery. Perhaps jewellery was the answer. He went back to the display of birthstones and looked for September, Anya's birth month. The clerk returned with the wrapped gift and Sean asked her to show him some Sapphire jewellery. Much of what he saw appealed to him but no one item spoke to him. The clerk asked who he was buying the item for and he described Anya to her. She told him she had something he might like and disappeared into the back room. When she returned she was carrying a glass-covered box that she set on the counter. Inside were four silver necklaces each adorned with sapphire gems. The one in the middle spoke to him.

* * *

Reina and Anya were sitting in the kitchen when Sean arrived. Reina was explaining the arrangements she had made for Anya to stay with Ray and Nancy while she and Sean were on their honeymoon in Skagway. She didn't think it was a good idea for Anya to be alone in her house especially given the memories that were still fresh.

"Wow!" Sean stopped as he entered the kitchen. "Who's your friend?" he addressed Reina as she rose to give him a hug.

Anya blushed as she stood to greet him. He held her at arms length looking intently at the young face framed in the new hairstyle. "I love it Anya. You look terrific, such a flattering haircut. I'll bet you had a good time."

"I'm so glad you like it Sean, I was afraid you might not. I've never had my hair cut like that before. Becky was so nice to me. She helped me find this style and even washed my hair – it felt so good I almost fell asleep." Anya was beaming.

"And we found Anya a couple of cute dresses," Reina interjected. "They look great on her but you'll have to wait to see the one she's wearing at the wedding." Anya rushed off to her room.

She returned and held the dress up so he could see how it might look on her. The color complemented her eyes and the style suited her. Sean expressed his approval and gratefulness that she had found something she liked.

"Looks like you did some Christmas shopping, can we see?" Reina looked at the bags Sean had set on the floor.

"No, you certainly can't see. You gotta wait until Christmas morning like everyone else," he teased. "But, after seeing that beautiful new dress I think I should give Anya her gift now." He reached into the bag, drew out the little package with her name on it, and handed it to Anya. She ripped off the colourful paper and opened the royal blue velvet case as Reina leaned over to look.

She stood speechless looking at the silver, sapphire-studded necklace displayed on a satin background. "Oooooh," she moaned, "it's so beautiful. Is it really mine?"

"It's yours my dear," Sean replied, "with all our love. We hope you treasure it always. Now, I'm taking my two favourite girls out for dinner, maybe you should wear that new dress and your necklace Anya."

Chapter 51

Kathy greeted the three of them as they entered the 202 Club. Anya, radiant in her new dress and necklace, surveyed the room, distracted by the strange surroundings. She savoured the aromas coming from the kitchen as Kathy escorted them to their table. This was a new experience for Anya; she had never been in a nice restaurant before. It bore no resemblance to the dining hall at the orphanage.

Sean and Reina ordered their usual drinks while Anya, ignoring the drink menu, surveyed the restaurant décor. "You just order something you think you might like," Sean tried to get her attention. "If you don't like it then you can order something else."

Anya perused the menu while Kathy waited. "I don't know what to order, can I have some fruit juice?" Anya asked.

"Let's try this," Sean spoke to Kathy, "A Piña Colada for the young lady please; no rum." Kathy smiled and left to get the drinks.

Anya stared at the huge Alaska King Crab mounted on the wall across from their table. "Is that real?" she asked in astonishment.

"Yes it is; it's called an Alaska King Crab. They catch them in the Gulf of Alaska with big traps they lower into the ocean. It's a very dangerous job but the fishermen make good money. This restaurant specializes in serving King Crab; would you like to try it?" Sean asked.

"Oh, I don't think I could eat a whole one of those!" Anya exclaimed.

Sean and Reina laughed. "They won't serve you a whole crab, just some of the legs. Besides, they aren't *all* as big as that one. Have a look at the menu and decide what you would like." Kathy set their drinks on the table and waited to see if Anya liked hers. The smile on her face after her first sip told the tale.

Anya, sipping her drink, looked through the menu. "This drink is so good, I like it. What is the difference between an 'appetizer' and a 'main'?" she asked.

Reina explained the difference then invited Anya to try one of the oysters that she and Sean would be sharing as an appetizer. "What's an oyster?" Reina followed with a description. Anya made a face as if questioning their decision to eat one of them then resumed her perusal of the menu while sipping her Piña Colada.

Sean and Reina could see that she was struggling. "I know that some of the items on the menu may seem strange to you but be brave and try something. If you don't like your choice we'll get you something else. This is a new experience for you so enjoy it. You won't go hungry Anya." Reina tried to encourage her.

"Okay, I am going to have the steak and crab," Anya finally announced, "I don't know if I'll like the crab but I know I'll like the steak; is it made of moose?"

Again, Sean and Reina laughed. Reina reached across the table and took Anya's hand. "You are such a delight dear and no, it's not moose, it's beef. How do you want your steak cooked?" Anya stared blankly at Reina. "They will cook it however you prefer it. 'Rare' means that it's not cooked very much, 'medium' means it will be pink in the middle like the moose Sheila serves and 'well done' will have no pink."

"Medium then," Anya answered.

"Okay, when Kathy comes for your order she will ask you how you want your steak done and you tell her, 'medium'." Anya nodded.

Anya finished her drink so Sean ordered her another one when Kathy arrived to take their orders.

Kathy returned with a plate of oysters Rockefeller setting it between Sean and Reina. Anya leaned over to examine the creatures Reina had described. "Try one miss braveheart!" Sean dared her. He laid an oyster on her bread plate along with a wedge of lemon. "Squeeze some lemon juice onto it first. If it moves, squirt it again."

Anya shuddered and made a face but took the dare doing as Sean had instructed. She cut off a small piece of the oyster just in case it was gross and placed it in her mouth. As she chewed, her countenance reflected her satisfaction with the delicacy. She devoured the rest of the oyster and begged for another much to Sean's satisfaction.

The threesome bantered with each other as they enjoyed their appetizer. When they finished eating, Anya expressed her curiosity about the wedding ceremony. She seemed concerned about her role. While they waited for their orders to arrive, Sean talked about how God invented and ordained the institution of marriage. He explained how God used it in the Bible as a metaphor for His relationship with his people, the church. Reina explained how marriage ceremonies varied with different cultures. She described how couples married in Mexico then asked Anya how people got married in Poland. Anya didn't know; she had never attended a wedding.

Sean told her the wedding would be after the service at their church. Ray, who picked her up at Arnie's, would be the official who married them. Even though Ray was the pastor, he emphasized that he and Reina were marrying before God. They would pledge their vows to one another in His name.

Reina talked about the usual role of a bridesmaid but explained that, because the ceremony would be simple and non-traditional, she wouldn't have as many responsibilities. Anya was pleased to hear that she would be helping Reina in preparation for the wedding and after. She wanted to help. Reina told her that she would accompany her when she walked down the aisle to meet Sean at the front of the church. Sean reminded her not to trip on the way and Anya stuck her tongue out at him.

Kathy set the tray on the stand and served the plates of steaming food in front of each of them. She showed Anya how to use the special tools to crack open the crab legs and extract the meat then dip it in the bowl of melted butter.

Sean and Reina whispered to each other as they watched Anya devour her plate.

"What?" she demanded when she caught them staring at her. "What are you two saying about me?"

"We are just telling each other how much we love you and want you to live with us. Will you live with us Anya – will you be our daughter?" Reina's voice expressed their sincerity and purposefulness.

Anya wiped the butter off her chin and stared in disbelief at the two most important people in her life. Her mind struggled to interpret, *"Could it be true? They 'loved' her? They wanted to keep her and she would be their daughter?"* Her eyes filled with tears until they spilled over onto her cheeks. "No one has ever loved me." Blubbering through her tears, she reached across the table and joined her hands with her new 'parents'. "Are you true? Is it okay? You really want *me*!"

"Yes Anya. It's true and yes, we want *you*. It will be official after the new year." Sean squeezed her hand.

"Oh thank you, thank you. Yes, I will be your daughter. That means you will be my parents doesn't it?" her wet eyes pleaded.

Sean and Reina smiled at each other responding in unison, "Yes Anya, we love you and we will be your parents."

Chapter 52

Sean spent the night at Ray and Nancy's house as usual. He arrived at church early with Ray and helped set up for the wedding ceremony. Church members began arriving with pots and casseroles and desserts. The small church congregation was planning a potluck supper after the ceremony. Sean's friend and distant neighbour, MaryAnn, was providing the wedding cake. Her specialty and Sean's favourite – carrot cake with cream cheese icing. John would be taking pictures.

The word had gotten out and many of Sean and Reina's friends showed up to share in the celebration of their marriage. Ron Vance and Jay Morgan and their families were among them. Sean greeted them as they arrived apologizing for the sudden decision and lack of invitations. He kept a sharp eye out for Reina and Anya but to no avail. Had they forgotten? Maybe they slept in. He thought of Sam, Sheila, and the rest of the girls and wished they could share in this special day.

The time arrived for the service to start so Sean took a seat at the front anxious that Reina and Anya had not arrived. *"She wouldn't be late for her own wedding?"* he thought. Ray was walking to the front when he heard laughter coming from the back. Sean turned to see his beautiful bride greeting her friends as if she was shopping in a Mexican market. She made her way down the aisle smiling and laughing along with her friends. *"What?"* he thought, *"does she think she's on Mexico time."* Beside her was his daughter-to-be. Anya wore a stunning red dress accented with a blue sapphire pendant necklace.

His mind flashed back to images of the scrawny waif he found on the side of the road not that long ago. The two women joined him on his pew. Reina looked into his eyes and smiled a mischievous smile, "Thought I forgot huh?"

Ray was about to begin speaking when a commotion at the back of the church caused everyone to turn again. Sean's jaw dropped. Reina and Anya gasped. Sam and Sheila entered the sanctuary at the head of a procession of 12 girls and a dog. They had driven to Whitehorse in the motor home not able to bear being apart from their friends on this special day. Sean, Reina and Anya leaped up, still in shock, and rushed back to greet their friends from White River.

Ray welcomed them as he addressed the congregation. He explained their relationship to Sean, Reina and Anya and noted the distance they had travelled to be with their friends. People in the front pews made room for the new arrivals including Bozo.

Ray's message was brief and dealt with the institution of marriage. He closed with an invitation for all present to stay and celebrate with Sean and Reina. Reina and Anya retreated to the back of the church where they both received bouquets of flowers. Kazia gave Anya a thumbs-up as she passed.

Sean took his place at the altar checking his suit jacket pocket for the ring. As the music began, he turned and smiled. His beautiful bride wore a hand-embroidered, off-white cotton dress. She was smiling back at him. He had no doubts; Reina was his soul mate and soon, his wife.

Sean embraced his wife kissing her intently. Ray then presented Mr. and Mrs. Carson. The guests clapped and cheered. Reina threw her bouquet in the direction of the 12 girls, none of whom understood the significance of the gesture. The bouquet landed on a bewildered Celina who instinctively clutched the flowers to her breast. Another cheer went up as a puzzled Celina looked to her friends for an explanation of what had happened. Sheila leaned over and explained the significance of the event. She watched Celina's eyes widen with surprise and her face flushing red.

Sean and Reina posed for the usual pictures. Right after, Anya joined them for pictures of the wedding party. Sean suddenly interrupted the activity. "John, put on your wide angle. Anya, go and ask Sam, Sheila and the girls to join us for pictures." Anya slipped out of her heels and sprinted to the back of the church. She gathered her friends, entreating them to come and have their pictures taken.

"You can come too Bozo!"

Sean and Reina cut the carrot cake posing for more pictures then took their seats at the head table with Ray and Nancy. Anya sat beside Reina squeezing her hand all the while bursting with the joy of knowing she belonged to a real family with real parents who loved her.

The guests took their seats after filling their plates at the buffet table. Ray rose to give the toast to the bride and groom. He related the history of their relationship and joked at how long it took them to tie the knot. He rejoiced in seeing them finally marry invoking God's richest blessing on their marriage.

Sean rose to reply. He stood looking at his wife and daughter-to-be. He thanked Ray and Nancy for their friendship and perseverance while he found his way back from the tragedy in his life. "God saved me by His mercy and grace. He showed me how sin destroyed our relationship and separated me from His love. Then he showed me how Jesus made a way back to that love. He further demonstrated his unfathomable love by giving me Reina and Anya. Lifting his glass he invited all present to toast the Lord of Hosts and His gifts, Reina and Anya.

Ray stood to announce that the music was about to begin and the bride and groom would take the lead with a waltz. He apologized. Despite his efforts he couldn't find a Mariachi band anywhere in the Yukon.

Sean offered Reina his hand. As he escorted her to the dance floor, Joe's fiddle played the opening bars for 'Alejandra'. Nancy on the piano and Juanita on the violin joined in to play the traditional Mexican Waltz. Reina stood stunned; she hadn't heard that music since she left Mexico. Sean had arranged with three other men to join in the waltz where the bride would dance with each of them.

As they swirled across the floor, others joined in. Attentive young men, anxious to show off their dancing skills, enticed some of the girls onto the floor. It was a great excuse to meet the attractive strangers in their midst.

Reina hugged Sean at the end of the dance thanking him for the memorable surprise. They mingled with their guests all of whom had questions about the 13 young women that seemed to be such a part of the married couple's life. Sean urged them to be patient; an explanation would be coming. In the meantime, he urged them to make the girls feel welcome. He noticed that the young men were already doing their part, demonstrating their awkward hospitality. He also noticed Sam keeping a watchful eye on his charges.

Ray had already talked with some families about taking girls into their homes. He took the opportunity to introduce those couples to the girls. Sean and Reina were encouraged by Ray and Nancy's choice of families. They knew that they would provide exceptional care for their darlings.

Sam and Sheila joined Sean and Reina. Blanka and Bozo trailed behind. They congratulated their friends with hugs and words of blessing. Blanka wrapped her arms around Reina's waist telling her how beautiful she was. Sam explained how they had a meeting with all the girls and decided to make the trip. Everyone agreed that it was too important an event for them to miss. They drove to Haines Junction on Saturday night, stayed in a cabin at the Elias Motel, then drove to the church that morning. Sean and Reina expressed their appreciation and invited them to stay at Reina's house if they wanted. They thought that sounded like a good idea. It would give them a chance to show the girls around town after their isolation at the lodge.

Sean took a couple of bills from his wallet, passed them to Sam and told him to take the girls out for dinner on him and Reina. Reina gave him her Jeep and house keys. He told Sam that Jay, at immigration, needed signed passport photos for each girl so he could prepare their temporary permits. He asked if he could get them done while he was in town. Sam agreed, committing to leaving them at Jay's office. The girls began drifting over in small groups to congratulate them and get a hug from the newlyweds.

Reina tugged on Sean's sleeve to get his attention. She led him to where Anya and Kazia were busy talking up a storm after their separation for a whole two days. Kazia saw them approach and rushed to give them both a congratulatory hug. Anya's arm was around Kazia's shoulders as Sean pulled the two of them to his side. Reina joined the huddle with her arm around Kazia. "Did Anya tell you the news?" Sean asked even though he knew the answer.

"Oh yes! She is going to be your daughter! I am so happy for my friend. She will be a very good daughter." Kazia radiated her joy over her friend's good fortune.

Sean and Reina smiled at each other before Sean spoke. "Kazia, how would you like to be Anya's sister?"

Chapter 53

Kazia's face went blank. Anya squeezed her shoulder and looked into the expressionless face.

"We want to adopt you Kazia," Reina's voice expressed her love for the young orphan. "We want you to be our daughter. How would you feel about that?"

Kazia burst into tears, unable to speak. The huddle closed into a tight, silent knot of love.

Kazia looked at Sean and Reina, her face wet with tears, "Is true? You want *me* to be your daughter. Yes, yes, I love you guys so much. Thank you for loving me – and my sister – and all of us."

Sean pulled her into his chest and kissed her on the top of her head. He then held her at arms length while Reina wiped the tears from her face. "Thank you Kazia for blessing us. We love you. You will stay with Anya at Ray and Nancy's while we're gone. We'll see you again in a couple of days. Now the two of you go and have a good time." Sean and Reina gave each girl a final hug then slipped out the back door of the church.

* * *

The girls seemed to enjoy meeting the many wedding guests. Most of them participated in the reception festivities gaining confidence as they went. They seemed to enjoy the attention of the young men. Some accepted invitations to dance despite not knowing how. They had never learned to dance except children's folk dances. The guests made the girls feel welcome and at ease much to Sheila's relief. She was concerned that such a social engagement might overwhelm them. Instead, they responded well to the welcome they received. Sheila could see their reluctance when she and Sam announced it was time to leave.

Sam loaded some of the girls into the motor home while the others joined Sheila in Reina's Jeep. They drove to Reina's house where they settled for their brief stay. Sheila took six of the girls downstairs and showed them the beds and couches that they would sleep on. Then she had them help her gather blankets and sleeping bags from the storage closet. Sam gave the other girls their choice of the guest room, the couch in the living room and the floor.

It was going on six o'clock when they gathered in the living room. "Are you girls' hungry?" Sam asked. The loud response confirmed his thoughts. "Who has had pizza before, raise your hand?" The girls looked at each other some trying to describe the dish in Polish based on pictures they had seen but no one raised their hand. "Well, I think you'll like it; I hope you do because we are all going to the pizza parlour for supper." The enthusiasm of the girls spoke to their willingness to try the strange dish.

It had been a long day of travel and festivities and all went to bed soon after returning from their pizza supper. The Hawaiian pizza was definitely the favourite with the pepperoni coming in second. Sam and Sheila wasted no time retiring once the girls were secure in their makeshift beds. Sam was asleep when his head hit the pillow. Sheila lay listening to the muted whispering coming from the living room. Celina and Irenka were discussing whether they might get married some day while Natuzsa and Izabella listened. "Why would some man want to marry me, a whore?" lamented Celina.

"You are NOT a whore Celina!" Irenka admonished her friend. "Those men threatened and beat you; they forced you to do those things. It's not your fault. Reina talks to us all the time about this; you need to listen and believe her."

Celina began to weep, "I can't help it; I feel like a garbage can."

Sheila got out of bed at Irenka's outburst and went into the living room. The girls heard her coming and pretended to be asleep. "I know you're awake; I heard you talking. Now, *we* need to have a talk, especially you Celina." Sheila knelt beside the 17-year-old girl who was under a blanket on the floor beside Irenka. "Come here Celina. I want to hug you." Holding her in her arms seemed to accelerate the tears; Celina convulsed in Sheila's embrace. "*'Who is this that grows like the dawn, as beautiful as the full moon, as pure as the sun, as awesome as an army with banners?'* That is how God sees you Celina. He knows all about you. He knows your heart and He wants *you* to know His unconditional love and forgiveness. But, *you* have to forgive yourself and those who hurt you if you are to ever know His peace. Jesus forgave you, they beat Him badly before they hung him on that cross to die, yet, before He died He said, *'Father, forgive them for they don't know what they are doing.'* Believe me, I know how difficult that can be, ask Irenka, Natuzsa and Izabella. They have forgiven those men, an impossible choice, except for God's help. Forgiving can't change the past but it can change the future Celina."

"One day God will send a man into your life to love you. I know it's hard to feel loved after all you've been through, but you *are* loved my dear. Jesus died on that cross because He loves you. Sam, Sean, and Reina love you so much and so do your sisters. We love you because God made you and He wants you to have an abundant life." Sheila squeezed the young girl then looked into her red, tear soaked eyes, "Let's ask God to help you forgive and love yourself. You can't do it on your own but God wants to help you, He wants your life so He can give it back to you under His great care. If you believe that then you ask Him to help you." The other girls gathered around their friend.

Celina spoke softly, her voice quaking with sobs. "Please help me Jesus, I know I don't really know You but I want you to be my friend and to help me forgive those bad men. Thank you for dying for me so that I might have good life. Thank you for the friends you sent to rescue my sisters and me. And God, someday I would like to be married if You can find a man who will have me." Sheila kissed Celina on the forehead and the other girls joined in a group hug.

* * *

The passport photos were first on Sam's list after breakfast. Sheila supervised clean up after a breakfast of scrambled eggs, bacon and home fried potatoes. The girls got ready to go while Blanka hugged Bozo and told him she'd be back soon. Sam drove all the girls to the photo shop at the mall. When they were done Sheila led them on a tour of the mall while Sam delivered the signed photos to Jay. It was a small mall by southern standards but it fascinated the girls nonetheless. They stopped in the food court and had hot dogs and Cokes for lunch before making their way to the museum. Sam had called his friend Charlie and arranged for a private tour of the museum normally closed during winter. He called and invited Ray and Nancy, Kazia and Anya to join them.

They spent over three hours going through the museum. Charlie, Sam and Sheila kept busy telling the girls about all the things they were seeing. The full body mounts of various Yukon wildlife left the girls in awe, especially the stuffed moose. "Is he real!" asked an astonished Blanka. The history of the gold rush was Charlie's favourite. He had worked in the Dawson gold fields and his stories and humour kept the girls in rapt attention even though they missed most of his jokes.

Ray suggested that they all have supper at the Chinese restaurant where they served an extensive buffet. A quick poll revealed that none of the girls had ever had Chinese food but all were up for the experience. The girls thanked Charlie for showing them so many things about the Yukon and for telling good stories then they all left for the restaurant.

Anya and Kazia went home with Ray and Nancy after thanking Sam and Sheila for including them in their day. The rest of them returned to Reina's house where Bozo, looking for his supper, greeted Blanka. Sam searched through Reina's video tape collection and found the movie 'Anne of Green Gables'. Reina had read the story to the girls. It had profoundly affected some like Anya, Kazia and especially Blanka. Sheila knew the girls would enjoy the movie and get a glimpse of early maritime Canada at the same time. Sam noticed how the music seemed to mesmerize the girls as they sat, eyes glued to the screen. They were all in tears when Matthew died but by the end, they were rejoicing with Anne as she reconciled with Gilbert and began to make her own way in the world.

Chapter 54

The newlyweds changed at Ray and Nancy's house then drove to Arnie's where TJ sat plugged in. Sean unplugged the extension cord and completed his walk-around as Reina loaded their gear through the cargo door. The sky was a deep blue typical of skies under northern high-pressure systems. Reina climbed into the left-hand seat and started the engine. She did her instrument checks while Sean talked on the radio to flight services about the weather forecast and current conditions in Skagway then filed a note for their short trip to the Alaska coastal town. Switching frequencies, he requested clearance to taxi. Reina gave the plane some throttle and proceeded to the end of the runway where she completed her run-up and waited for take-off clearance. Sean leaned over to kiss his wife. Their headset microphones clashed and they broke out in laughter as the tower announced their clearance for take-off.

The little plane climbed out in the still, clear air. The snow-covered Coast Mountains marked the horizon ahead of them. Reina climbed to 4500 feet and levelled out. She planned on flying through the White Pass and this altitude would give her lots of room above the rocks given the clear air. It was a short flight, less than an hour, but enough time to get nervous about landing. She had never landed at Skagway before and she knew it could be tricky depending on visibility and wind conditions. Current conditions promised clear air and a gentle on-shore breeze right down the runway. With these conditions, Sean insisted that she fly so she could get her Skagway badge with a minimum of trauma. Reina had over a thousand hours of pilot-in-command time with over 200 of those in TJ on wheels, floats and skis. But, she knew that in the north it wasn't just about hours with the stick. Mental fortitude, experienced judgment and humility ranked high on qualifications of a good bush pilot. Thanks to Sean's coaching, she had tested her skills in many unique situations and this would be another one.

Reina guided the little plane down the steep, snow-free and narrow valley of the Skagway River. As she began to level out, she turned west to bring the airstrip into view. Flight services, the windsock and the surface of the ocean at the end of the runway confirmed the light head wind. She dropped 20 degrees of flap, made a straight-in approach, flared and touched down like a pro'. She took a sly peek at Sean to see his affirming smile while taxiing to the tie down ramp.

They tied down TJ and cleared customs without incident then walked with their light packs to the motel a few blocks away. The manager was watching television when they entered the office. He got up and greeted them, "Afternoon, welcome to Skagway. Where you folks from? I'll bet you're our newlyweds Sean and Reina, from Whitehorse." He mispronounced her name. "Of course I've got the honeymoon suite reserved for you although reservations weren't really necessary – you're our only guests this week." He laughed.

Sean signed the register and paid for their room asking about places to eat.

"The hotel is the only restaurant open in the winter – food's really good. George's General Store has a small selection of groceries, beer and wine. Only a few of us stick around here through winter, come again in the summer when things are really hopping. You'll find a hotplate and dishes in your room but the fridge is on the fritz – sorry about that. There's a tape deck and some cassettes for music – hope you like the selection."

Summer in Skagway was too busy for Sean so he rarely visited at that time of year. Spring and fall, when the tourists were gone, were much more appealing. He and Reina checked into their 'suite'. It differed little from the other rooms he had occupied at the motel although it did have a couch, table and counter with a sink and cupboards. The bedroom was separate from the main room. The place was cold so Sean turned up the electric heat. Checking the bathroom, he discovered that the window was open so he shut it. Skagway, because of its location on the coast, was always a lot milder than interior locations. Temperatures were often above freezing during the winter months.

"Well Mrs. Carson, I don't know about you but I'm awfully nervous about this new arrangement. What do you say we take a walk to George's and get us some booze to ease us into our new relationship?"

Reina punched him playfully then threw her arms around his neck looking into his eyes. "I'm not the least bit nervous Mr. Carson," her seductive voice got Sean's attention. "Wanna go to bed?"

Both of them had fallen asleep after exploring their new relationship as husband and wife. Sean's stirring woke his wife who lay with her long black hair draped over his chest. He stroked her hair as he lay thinking how blessed he was to have such a wife. He hoped she felt the same way about him.

Reina rolled onto her shoulder and he leaned down to kiss her. "I love you so much Mr. Carson; thanks for picking me to be your wife." She looked intently into his eyes.

"My pleasure Mrs. Carson. I love you more than you may ever know and I'll do my best to make you believe it. In fact, I was thinking of inviting you to have dinner with me at the best restaurant in town." They both laughed and hugged each other.

The two friends, now husband and wife, took abundant pleasure in their new relationship. During their brief honeymoon, they enjoyed freedom from any serious responsibility other than total devotion to each other. They bought a box of four wine coolers at Georges and took them back to the motel where they left them outside their door to cool. Later when Sean went to retrieve them, they were gone. He was furious. How could a town with fewer than 50 people harbour a wine cooler thief? After he calmed down Reina convinced him to pray that whoever took them would know their guilt and turn from his wicked ways. Sean had some other prayers in mind but he kept them to himself.

Sean browsed through the tape library in their room and found John Denver's album 'Gold Collection'. Reina knew he liked the artist but she wasn't familiar with his songs. "Reina, I want to dedicate this song to you and I want you to remember to play it whenever we go through tough times because we will – more because of me than you. I wish I could sing it for you but pretend John is me." He pushed the play button and 'My Sweet Lady' began to play.

Their time together went quickly but they promised each other to do something more special after the New Year. Now it was time to leave. Their thoughts returned to Whitehorse where two daughters-to-be waited on their newfound parents-to-be. Reina had never had children but she was confident in her ability to cherish the two young girls God had put in her life. She and Sean had spent a lot of time deliberating over their commitment and vowed to trust God to make them into the right parents for two precious girls who had missed so much in their young lives. They probably would have only a few years together but during that time they were hopeful of building relationships and characters that would endure.

Reina touched down at the Whitehorse airport and taxied to Arnie's ramp. They unloaded and asked Arnie to top off the fuel and tie down the small plane. They would be back tomorrow morning to fly out to the White. Sean stopped at Ted's on the way to Ray's to pick up the pistols. Ted had the registrations and the three pistols in their cases wrapped together in brown paper.

The girls, excited at the arrival of their new parents, had been ready to go since breakfast. They both sat on the window seat watching the sky for the little yellow plane. "There it is!" Kazia shouted turning her sister's face in the direction of the plane. "Come and see," she beckoned Ray and Nancy to come and verify the siting. Every few minutes they would run to the window overlooking the driveway and look for Sean's truck. A loud screech announced the arrival of the truck. Grabbing their backpacks they gave Ray and Nancy hurried hugs and thanks for letting them stay with them then disappeared down the stairs to join their parents for the ride to their new home.

After welcoming hugs, the four of them squeezed into the cab of the truck. "We'll unload at the house but I have to see Jay about the papers for the girls then I'll be home. What do you want to do for supper?" Sean asked Reina.

"Let's stay in tonight, pick up a pizza and we'll beat the girls at Monopoly. Anya and I are taking Kazia shopping for a few new clothes since she's in town, is that Okay? Reina looked to Sean for his approval.

"Sounds like a plan. I'll pick up the pizza. Where are the girls going to sleep?"

"They'll have to share the bed in the guest room; you won't need it – I hope!" she glared at Sean and laughed. "We'll fix up their rooms when we return from the White after Christmas."

Sean met Jay in the lobby of the Federal building on the way back to his office. He had the paperwork for Anya and Kazia that would allow them to cross the border into the USA. He also had the temporary permits for the rest of the girls. Sam had brought the photos by before he left for home. Sean gratefully received the large brown envelope thanking Jay for his help in making everything come together.

Now that Kazia had consented to becoming a member of his family, Sean decided to stop at Murdoch's again. The same clerk was behind the counter. Sean asked if he could see the sapphire necklaces again. Kazia's birth month was the same as Anya's. She presented the glass-covered case as before only with two new necklaces on display with the others. Sean, with no hesitation, spotted the one he knew was for Kazia. He waited while the clerk wrapped it as before.

He knew the girls would still be shopping so he stopped at a small coffee and sandwich store across the street. Jimmy Jackson was sitting alone at a table so Sean took his coffee and joined his old friend. Jimmy was a member of the White River Indian Band. A Northern Tutchone native his people mostly lived around Beaver Creek and Burwash Landing. Sean hired him most years as a fishing guide. He knew the lake better than anyone did and because of his talent, he made good tips from his clients. He also looked after Sean's equipment and made sure the other guides didn't abuse it.

"Hi Jimmy. What you doing in town? Sarah with you?"

"Hi Sean. No, she didn't want to come, things to do at home. I'm doing my Christmas shopping and picking up some medicine for my brother. Billy's on the trap line now but he plans to come home for Christmas. What's up with you?"

"Well Jimmy, I just got married." Sean realized that he had just energized the moccasin telegraph and the entire northern Yukon would get the news in short order.

"Reina and you finally tied the knot? Good for you! Congratulations Sean; she's a fine lady and a good bush girl. You gonna live at her place or yours?"

"At hers. We're going to need the space."

"You planning on starting a family?" Jimmy laughed.

"Not quite. I'll explain another time. We're staying with Sam and Sheila at the White over Christmas then back here after the New Year. You and Sarah and Billy should come by at Christmas," Sean paused, "Billy getting any fur?"

"I talked to him on the HF before I came up here and he's doing good with the marten. Got a wolf and a lynx too." (Southerners when going north say they are going 'up north' or, if southbound, 'down south'. Not so with local people who travel the waterways. People often travelled on rivers before they built roads. They go 'up' when going against the stream and 'down' when going with the current no matter what compass direction it repre- sents. If you're travelling from Dawson to Whitehorse you're going 'up' to Whitehorse even though it's south of Dawson.)

"Great, that long fur brings a good dollar these days. So, you coming to work for me again this summer? You're my best guide Jimmy, hate to lose you."

"Thanks Sean. I'd sure like to, you're a good boss. I'll get back to you before the ice goes out if that's okay."

"No problem Jimmy. You know that Sarah is always welcome too. I've always got work for her if she wants it. Well, gotta run and pick up a pizza for supper. Good to see you Jimmy, say hi to Sarah and Billy for me and Reina."

Sean walked over to the post office to pick up his mail. As usual, the box was empty except for a couple of bills that could wait. He walked to his truck and drove to the pizza parlour a few blocks away. He ordered an extra large pizza anticipating two extra large teenage appetites then read the paper as he waited. He read a story about the bodies found at the prospector camp; their origin remained a mystery and the investigation was ongoing. Another story reported on the rollover south of Beaver Creek but made no connection to the other incident. The article identified the men as John Dubicki of Winnipeg and Sergio Cardoza of Fairbanks. There were no next of kin to notify.

* * *

Kozlov laid the newspaper on his desk, picked up the phone and punched a number, "Tell Carlos I want to see him."

* * *

Reina was in the kitchen getting glasses out of a cupboard while plates warmed in the oven. He could hear the girls in the guest room down the hall giggling and talking. Sean put the pizza in the oven then hugged his wife.

"I saw Jimmy at the coffee shop. Sarah was at home. He's doing some Christmas shopping and getting some medicine for Billy. Billy's on his trap line but coming out for Christmas."

"I'm surprised he still goes trapping with his bad heart," said Reina. "He'll probably die out there."

"That's all he knows," said Sean. "He'd rather be out there with his dogs than cooped up in a rest home or hospital. Can't say I blame him."

Reina rolled her eyes. "Why don't you call the girls for supper?"

Sean walked part way down the hall and shouted, "Hey you ruffians, get out here and eat your supper."

Chapter 55

Kazia had never ridden in an airplane and Anya's only experience was her trip from the White to Whitehorse in a Twin Otter. Their excitement grew as they drove to Arnie's for their trip back to the White River Lodge. Sean parked the truck and asked the girls to help carry the gear. In the office, Arnie greeted Sean and Reina complimenting them on their wedding ceremony that he and his wife had attended. When he saw Anya, he greeted her as if she was a long time friend, "Hi Anya, really like your new haircut. Who's your friend?"

Anya blushed. She took Kazia by the arm and brought her over to meet Arnie. "Arnie, this is my sister Kazia, Kazia, this is Arnie, he looks after Sean's, I mean Dad's, airplane."

Arnie looked quizzically at Sean who only shrugged his shoulders. Arnie shook Kazia's hand, "Nice to meet you Kazia. Have you ever flown in a small plane before?"

Kazia looked at the floor. "I've never been in an airplane."

Sensing her nervousness Arnie said, "Oh, well you'll love this trip, you've got two experienced pilots on board and some beautiful country to see on your way to the White. Why don't' you and your sister go and have a look at TJ. I'll help with your gear."

Arnie threw on his parka, grabbed a duffle bag and followed the two girls to the plane. Sean and Reina brought the rest of the gear. Arnie gave them an enthusiastic tour of the aircraft giving them lessons on aerodynamics and piloting in the process. Reina called the girls to help her stow the gear in the back of the plane while Sean and Arnie talked about the weather.

When the girls finished helping Reina, Sean called them over. "I'm going to do what we call a 'walk-around' and I want you to come with me and pay attention because you might have to do it yourselves some day. We want to make sure that everything is in order on the plane before we put it in the air."

Anya interrupted, "I thought Arnie looked after your airplane."

"That's right, he does and I trust him to do that. But, a pilot is ultimately responsible for his aircraft and its passengers. Even though Arnie has made sure that TJ is ready to fly, I still have to do my own checks."

Sean led them around the aircraft as he checked everything from engine oil to control surface movement. Kazia stalled at the wheel-skis, squatting to examine them. Sean explained that sometimes if the snow was too deep on a landing strip he would pump the skis down so they were below the wheels and they could land safely. She nodded her understanding.

"Now Kazia, I want you to sit in front with Reina." Sean wasn't sure how Kazia's stomach would respond to her first flight and sitting up front would lessen any motion sickness she might experience. "Reina will fly to Burwash where we'll take a short break before we trade places and continue on to the White. Anya, you and I will sit in the back."

"Really!" came a sarcastic retort.

"You're already starting to sound like your mother," Sean said with a smile.

The newly formed family climbed into their appointed seats and fastened their seat belts. Sean helped Kazia with her headphones. Reina started the engine and did her checks while waiting for clearance to taxi. She filed a note as they taxied towards the threshold of the runway and confirmed that her passengers could hear through their headsets. Kazia glanced over her shoulder at Anya looking for reassurance from her best friend. Anya laid her hand on her sister's shoulder giving it a squeeze. "This will be lots of fun Kazia, you'll see." Anya tried to sound like a veteran flier. Reina smiled at Kazia, reached over and gave her hand a squeeze. Sean watched Kazia tense at the sound of the roaring engine as Reina pushed the throttle for take-off. Reina was fully aware of her nervous passenger and exercised smooth, slow manoeuvres as she climbed out in a turning bank to the west. Kazia looked down at the Alaska Highway and the church where her new parents were married.

The clear blue sky contrasted with the snow-white earth below. Winds flowing over the St. Elias Mountains could make their trip a lot more interesting but today the air was still. Kazia's first flight should be a gentle one. Reina pointed out various landmarks and other features as they flew along about 2000 feet above the ground. The plane encountered some occasional but mild turbulence as they approached Haines Junction. Kazia tensed whenever the plane jolted. Reina asked Kazia if she would like to fly. Kazia looked at Reina in disbelief. Reina explained how to hold the 'stick' or wheel and to rest her feet on the rudder pedals. Reluctantly Kazia took hold of the wheel. The little plane began to climb but Reina gently coached her how to bring it back to level flight and keep it there. "Good Kazia," Reina spoke into the microphone, "now let's try a turn to the left. You'll push slightly on the left pedal as you gently turn the wheel to the left keeping us level." Kazia followed her instructions and the plane made a partially coordinated turn. "Okay, now turn to the right and straighten out when the DG reads 310." She pointed to the instrument on the panel. Kazia obeyed and rolled out after overshooting their heading. "Well done Kazia!" Sean and Anya added their praises over the intercom. "Now, when we get close to that narrow part of the lake you are going to begin a descent into Burwash."

Kazia followed Reina's finger with her eyes locating the narrows on Kluane Lake. "Can you see Burwash Landing?" Reina asked pointing to the small village on the west side of the lake. Kazia located the village and nodded her head. "Okay, now push the wheel forward gently and we'll begin to go down." Kazia obeyed as Reina trimmed for their descent. After losing a thousand feet of altitude, Reina reduced power and announced, "I have control now Kazia. Well done." Kazia released the stick and leaned back into her seat relieved but pleased with herself. Reina's strategy worked perfectly, Kazia was so intent on flying the airplane she never felt any motion sickness.

Reina executed a smooth landing and taxied to the fuel storage area where she spun the plane around to face the runway and shut down the engine.

Removing her headset, she pointed to the outhouses and invited the girls to take a break. The temperature was colder than Whitehorse but the light breeze made it feel even colder despite the bright sunshine. Sean used the HF radio to call Sam and advise on their ETA while the girls walked around stretching and debriefing Kazia on her first flying experience.

Now that Kazia had some positive flying experience, Sean decided to be a little less gentle on their final leg. He climbed out on take-off at a much steeper angle than they had at Whitehorse turning sharply onto their heading and levelling off a thousand feet above the ground. "Okay Anya, your turn." Without hesitation, she grabbed the wheel and immediately put the plane into a climb. Sean brought it back level with his stick then released it. "Gently my dear; pretend she's a kitty for now." Anya smiled at him and nodded. "Now I want you to push the pedals one at a time while flying straight and level." The plane yawed left then right in response to Anya's input with her feet. "Good. Now let's turn left using your left pedal and turning the wheel gently to the left. Keep the nose steady in relation to the horizon." Anya executed a smooth, coordinated turn. They practiced a few more turns then Sean pointed to the Donjek River ahead. "I want you to steer for the bridge at the river and begin a slow descent keeping the nose of the aircraft lined up on the bridge." She brought the plane down to about 500 feet above ground when Sean announced, "I have control. Great flying Anya, I think you're a natural. Everybody keep your eyes open and you might see a moose." They flew over a flat, boggy landscape littered with small lakes. "On your right coming up." Sean banked the plane so everyone could see the cow moose and her calf feeding on willows at the edge of a pond. They saw three more moose before they buzzed the Lodge at the White River to announce their arrival.

Sam parked at the end of the strip. Sean alerted Kazia to watch as he pumped down the skis. After a short, smooth landing, he pulled up to the fuel tank, and shut down the engine. The girls were first out, running to Sam for their hug then on to the Lodge to tell Sheila and their friends all about their trip. Sam and Reina unloaded the plane into the pickup while Sean topped up the fuel tanks. "You guys go ahead; I'll put TJ to bed and see you later."

Sam and Reina drove to the Lodge and unloaded the cargo and gear. The girls swarmed Reina expressing their happiness to see Mrs. Carson. "Where's Mr. Carson?" said Tekla with a broad smile.

"He's on his way. He's just putting his beloved airplane to bed," said Reina. All the girls laughed at her expression.

The girls, reliving their experiences in Whitehorse, dominated the conversation over lunch. There was some debate over the ranking of the boys they met at the wedding but nothing was resolved. They teased Celina asking if she had found her husband yet. All of them wanted dance lessons after watching some beautiful dancing by some guests at the reception. Hawaiian pizza and sweet and sour chicken balls won the vote for best new food experience. Blanka uncharacteristically gushed about her experience with the stuffed moose at the museum vowing to see a real one someday. All expressed sheer delight over the news that they were very likely to receive permission to stay in Canada. They treasured their new temporary resident permits pinning them on the wall above the headboard of their beds. They were doubly encouraged with the news that Sean and Reina chose to adopt Anya and Kazia as their daughters believing that they too would someday have the same good fortune.

Chapter 56

After lunch, Sam and Sean took Anya, Kazia and Tekla outside to do some pistol shooting with live ammunition. The girls were excited to put their training into practice not realizing the challenges that awaited them. Sam had set up a pistol range by his woodpile with the stacked wood as the back-drop. Their training target was set up at 10 yards from the shooting bench. The two men reviewed safety procedures with the girls then waited until they put on their glasses and ear defenders. Sean handed Anya his loaded CZ with a round in the chamber and the safety off. Anya took the pistol in her strong hand, engaged the safety, laid her trigger finger alongside the trigger guard and pointed the gun at the ground down range. She released the mag' putting it into her pocket and pulled back the slide. She caught the ejected cartridge in her left hand and checked the chamber. "Clear," she announced pointing the gun downrange and looking at Sean for his approval. Sam looked at Sean, "I say she gets an A+".

"Good girl, now load it up and kill that bulls eye," Sean commanded.

Anya put the pistol at the ready with a full mag' and one in the chamber, safety on. Taking an Israeli stance, she thumbed off the safety, aligned her sights and controlled her breathing before firing her first shot. The recoil and noise surprised her but she regained her composure and fired the remaining 10 rounds. With the slide locked back, she dropped the mag', set the safety and checked the chamber before announcing she was clear and setting the pistol and empty mag' on the bench.

Sean walked over and hugged her shoulders. "That was about perfect Anya; well done. Let's go get your first target and see how you did." Except for one 'flyer' she had put the other 10 bullets in a four-inch group around the bull's eye. "Now that is definitely a keeper. You should be proud of that my dear. Take a bow." Anya faced her audience, held up her target and took a bow to their enthusiastic applause. Sean dated and signed her target as a keepsake.

Kazia and Tekla completed the same drill. Their performance surprised Sean and Sam. Both agreed that teamwork and diligence in practicing dry fire drills while cooped up during the cold spell accounted for their remarkable performance. They spent a few minutes debriefing the girls then spent the next couple of hours coaching the girls through 110 rounds each. The girls proudly displayed their targets on the windows in the dining room.

Chapter 57

Over morning coffee, Sean told Sam of their plans to take their daughters to Fairbanks for some Christmas shopping. He noted that he would be picking up some contraband at Frenchies and asked if he needed anything. Sam suggested some .223 ammo. "What contraband you have in mind?"

"I ordered some factory magazines for the pistols I got the girls for Christmas. As you know, they aren't welcome in Canada thanks to brain dead, milquetoast politicians. They hold 14 rounds instead of the magical 10 rounds that are declared legal."

"Don't get me going," Sam acknowledged Sean's comment. "If they spent more time on the criminals, like Dubicki, instead of chasing law abiding gun owners we would be a lot better off. I'm just happy that most of the cops up here look the other way.

"Yeah, except for four digit Dennis," added Sean. Yukon gun owners despised Dennis who loved to use his authority as an RCMP officer to make life difficult for them. Consequently, they did everything in their power to publicly mock him and emasculate his authority. He shot off one of his fingers when a semi-auto pistol "got away on him" but he'd never admit it.

The weather continued to be favourable with temperatures hovering around 20 below during the day. Christmas was less than two weeks away and cold weather could arrive at any time. The forecast was for more of the same with no major systems likely to disrupt things for a while. Sean decided to take advantage of the weather and leave for Fairbanks tomorrow if Reina and the girls were up to it.

Reina came into the room in her housecoat and sat beside Sean on the couch. He got up and poured her a cup of coffee from the pot on top of the airtight. "Anya was sure proud of her shooting yesterday wasn't she?" she looked at Sean then Sam.

"I didn't think she'd ever get to sleep the way her and Kazia and Tekla were carrying on last night," said Sean. "They're all good little shooters right out of the box; a testament to their diligent practice. We'll up the ante after we get back from Fairbanks if the weather holds. Are you up to going tomorrow?"

"Sure, fine with me and I think the girls will be excited to go. I was thinking of letting all the girls do some shot gunning today, what do you think?" Reina's eyes sought support for her plan from the two men.

"Sure, might as well while the weather holds," said Sam. "You plan on easing them in with the twenty?"

"Exactly. We'll set up a few targets so they can see how the shot spreads then some bottles and stuff. Later we'll throw a few clays just for fun," Reina said. "We'll finish with your Cooey twelve just so they can have the experience."

The sound of feet on the stairs brought their conversation to a halt. Sheila came into the room. "Morning," she greeted the others as she poured herself a cup of coffee. "Girls are still sleeping; they've had a lot of excitement last few days."

"I think it's done them a lot of good, don't you?" asked Sean.

"You know it," replied Sheila. "I think that knowing the last of their kidnappers is gone made a huge difference and the trip to Whitehorse really sparked some new life in them. Even Blanka is coming out of her shell and Celina is doing so much better."

"Sean was just saying that he and Reina plan on taking their daughters to Fairbanks tomorrow while the weather is still good," said Sam. "If you need anything, better give Reina your list."

"Yeah, let me know Sheila, I'll be happy to pick up anything you want as long as it's *legal*," she glared at Sean as Sheila smiled knowingly. "We were just talking about letting the girls shoot some shotguns after breakfast."

"Speaking of which, I better get something going before the mob comes down," Sheila took her coffee and retreated to the kitchen with Reina close behind.

After breakfast, Sean helped Sam with the guns and ammo then they filled some plastic bottles with water and set them up on top of the woodpile. Sean staked some pieces of cardboard at different distances from the bench while Sam went to get the clay launcher out of the shed.

Reina arrived with her class of 13 excited girls. She reviewed basic safety procedures and used the Wingmaster to demonstrate gun handling. Without warning, she tossed the gun at a shocked Danuta. "Never, never do that!" she firmly admonished her class as Danuta, who had caught the gun, stood confused pointing the gun at the ground. "Good catch Danuta, now show us how to clear it." The gun was not loaded. Danuta stepped forward, muzzle towards the ground down range, and then demonstrated what she had earlier learned in class. Sean and Sam looked at each other with raised eyebrows.

"Now give the gun to Brygida," ordered Reina. The exercises continued with each girl getting the opportunity to receive, clear and safely pass on the gun to another. Luiza passed the gun to Reina. "Now I want you to reach inside your parka and find your collar bone. Do you all feel it?" Reina waited while the girls located the bone. "Now move your hand in and feel that soft pocket below your collar bone. Do you feel it? That's where you are going to place the butt of the gun just like you practiced in class." She demonstrated, using her cheek to help guide the butt into the pocket. "Now remember to pull the gun into that pocket, there should be no space between the butt and the pocket." She continued, demonstrating the proper stance to take when shooting a shotgun. "Now, unlike a rifle, you can effectively shoot a shotgun from the hip but you're not going to be as accurate. You would only shoot a shotgun like this for tactical engagements," she held the gun at her side to demonstrate. "But, if you ever shoot from that position you better hang on tight."

Each girl shot at a cardboard target. Even though the recoil surprised them, their training and their thick parkas mitigated the impact. They checked out the shot patterns on the cardboard then took turns shooting a bottle. The water explosion delighted them when the load of number four shot hit its mark.

The girls were handling the recoil of the 20 gauge without difficulty. Now was the time to introduce the more powerful 12 gauge. Reina held up the old Cooey and reviewed how to use a break action gun then loaded and cocked it. "Ears on," she shouted before firing the gun at a one-gallon ice cream pail. The girls took turns shooting the lightweight gun that kicked like a mule. All expressed their desire to practice with the 20 gauge instead.

Reina shouted, "Pull!" Sam let a clay go and she dropped it with precision. She turned to face the girls. "Looks easy doesn't it? Well it's not but it sure is fun. The most important thing to remember when shooting flying birds or any other moving target is to keep your eyes on the target. Unlike shooting at a cardboard target or a bottle on the woodpile, you don't want to be sighting along the barrel of the gun. This takes practice, lots of it. If you want to develop any skill you have to practice, there is no other way. Anya, come over here and see if you can knock down one of these clay pigeons."

Anya took the gun, pushed three shells into the magazine, racked the slide and shouted, "Pull!" Sam let go a clay and Anya blew it to pieces. Her smile challenged the brilliance of the morning sun as she looked back at the other girls with a side-glance at Sean. The next two clays escaped into the surrounding forest unhurt. The rest of the girls took turns with mixed success. Kazia and Luiza were the only ones to hit two of their three clays. Reina congratulated the girls on their performance promising more practice sessions for those interested. She dismissed them to hunt for the orange coloured clays that escaped.

Luiza sat beside Reina at lunch exploring the sport of trap and skeet shooting with the champion sitting next to her. "Maybe you teach me Reina?" her voice was weak and tentative as if she might be asking too much. Luiza worked 12 hours a day in a factory in Poland and lived in the employee dorms. She, like most of the girls had lost her parents early in life growing up with her grandmother in a small apartment. As a child, she led a sterile existence with school being the only diversion that gave her any pleasure.

Reina smiled, put her arm around her shoulders and pulled her close. She looked into the young girls eyes. "Luiza, I would *love* to teach you. I think you have a knack for shot gunning and if you work hard at practice, you can be a very good shooter. Did you know that your name means 'famous warrior'? That means that you are a brave fighter and you're good at over-coming obstacles."

Anya listened as Reina spoke then she spoke to Luiza in Polish. Luiza's face lit up and she gave Reina a grateful smile. "Thanks Anya," Reina smiled at her daughter.

Dance lessons were on the agenda for the afternoon. Sam and Sheila, like Sean and Reina, enjoyed dancing and were happy to share their skills with the girls. They decided to introduce the classic waltz and the two-step leaving the modern teenage gyrations for the girls to explore on their own at some other time. They wouldn't bother with the more exotic and difficult dances like the cha cha, tango and quick step. They cleared the 'dance floor' by moving tables and chairs to the walls in the dining room.

Sheila and Sam demonstrated a waltz to Shostakovich's 'Second Waltz' with some minor flourishes. Sean and Reina danced to Tchaikovsky's 'Waltz of the Flowers' from the Nutcracker Suite. They hoped to introduce this musical story to the girls over Christmas. Sean demonstrated the formal invitation to the lady and how to escort her onto the dance floor. The girls sat enthralled, many with tears in their eyes as they watched and listened. They had not been exposed to much in the way of music and knew nothing of the masters and their compositions, let alone modern music genres. Sean made a mental note of this gross deficiency in their lives. He told Reina that he was introducing an hour of music appreciation into the girls' routine every day when they got back from Fairbanks.

That night at supper, Sean put on a tape with some instrumental 'dinner' music softly playing in the background. He thought back to his days growing up in a house filled with music. None of his family had any musical talent but his parents loved music and dance and it rubbed off on their son. He recalled his father coming home with his first LP record, the Nutcracker Suite. Later his father bought one of those huge floor stereos with built in speakers. He and his Mom would dance around the living room trying not to trip on the shag carpet. It was a privilege to grow up in a home filled with music.

He attributed his love of music not only to its constant presence in his home but to Mr. Magee. Mr. Magee was his grade seven music teacher. He recalled that September day when he found himself sitting in Magee's music class for the first time. *"This year you will learn to appreciate music,"* he ordered. *"When you come to class you will sit quietly with your head on your desk and you will listen."* For the rest of that year Sean sat in Mr. Magee's music class and he listened; listened to Tchaikovsky, Pete Seeger, Bach, Bing Crosby, Hildegard von Bingen, Patsy Cline, John Cage, Giovanni Gabrielli, Doris Day, Cab Calloway, The Mills Brothers, Brahms, Mozart, Grieg, John Coltrane, Louis Armstrong, Lerner and Loewe, B. B. King, John Phillip Sousa, Elvis Presley, Itzhak Perlman, Billie Holiday, Sarah Vaughn, Irving Berlin and countless others. Grade seven didn't advance his knowledge of music theory but he learned to appreciate the variety, the deficiencies and the magnificence of music and its artisans. And, he learned to discern.

These girls had missed something he took for granted. He intended to remedy their situation and add another important dimension to their lives.

Chapter 58

The flight to Fairbanks took a couple of hours. Reina and Kazia in the back seats talked most of the way taking time out to read from a book of Wordsworth's poems. "Do you think clouds are really lonely Reina?" Kazia stared into the almost cloudless sky. Sean flew or at least tried. Anya was by his side and insisted on taking control so she could 'practice'. Along their route, he tested her whenever he spotted another aircraft, defying her to point it out. She was still learning to identify familiar objects from this new perspective. She found it challenging but Anya thrived on challenges. Between navigation lessons, they played a game of spotting airstrips of which there are many in Alaska. Time flew by.

"There's Fairbanks up ahead, can you find the airport?" Anya scanned the landscape before them by sectors as Sean had taught her but she didn't get far, she spotted it immediately, or so she thought.

"There, I see it, on the right, starboard, over there," she pointed excitedly at the Wainwright military base airfield.

"Are you sure? Check your map. Does it look right?" Sean pointed to the airfield marked on his WAC chart.

"No, that's not it, it's on the wrong side of the city," she lamented while continuing to scan the ground around her. "I see it, over there, that's it!"

"It's really embarrassing when you land at the wrong airport Anya. If we land at the wrong place I'm blaming you!" Sean glared at Anya. "Check your ADF; where is it pointing?"

"Yes, I see, it's pointing where I showed you. That's it Dad, we won't be embarrassed, I promise."

Sean chuckled, contacted the tower and gave his position and intention to land.

They cleared customs then taxied to the Warren Air Services hangers and shut down at the fuel tanks. "Okay, let's unload and take our bags into the office and meet Al." A young man came out of the office and asked if Sean wanted fuel. He seemed distracted by Anya and Kazia as they disembarked but he eventually got Sean's affirmative. Al Warren was behind the counter and greeted Sean. Al was one of the foremost Helio Courier pilots in the north, at one time working for Air America in Southeast Asia. Sean had chartered Warren Air in the past for some of his clients and he and Al knew each other.

"Been a while, how you doing Sean?" Al shook Sean's hand.

"Been good Al. Got married. Al, let me present my wife Reina and my two daughters, Anya and Kazia." Al smiled and welcomed Sean's family shaking hands with each.

"I'll look after TJ for you. Got your car outside ready to go and they're expecting you at the Travelodge." He handed Sean the keys.

"Much appreciated Al; you're better than a travel agent. Can I get a couple of business cards from you for the girls in case we get separated?" Al handed the cards to Sean. "Tell me, do you know what's playing at the auditorium right now?"

"No, but I can find out pretty quick. Usually some traditional Christmas concert this time of year." He picked up the phone and dialled. "Thanks Julie; hang on will you?" He turned to Sean. "Nutcracker is being performed by the group out of Anchorage. They are very good; want me to check if tickets are available?" Sean nodded. "Yeah Julie have you got four good seats for tonight? Okay, I'll take them." Sean gave Al his credit card. "Thanks Julie, you're a good girl." He hung up the phone and turned to Sean and his family, "Julie's my niece. Good to have contacts. Your tickets will be waiting for you at the box office tonight. Show starts at seven."

"Thanks Al, you make things easy. Okay ladies let's go get settled in our teepee and have some muskrat stew for lunch," Sean teased. Reina and his daughters pretended to gag.

Sean always stayed at the Travelodge when he visited Fairbanks; it was quiet, out of the way and the restaurant was above average. He signed in at the desk and grabbed a couple of business cards for the girls after introducing them to the desk clerk. Reina escorted the girls into their room while Sean dropped their gear in the room across the hall. Neither girl had ever stayed in a hotel before so Reina acquainted them with the facilities and the rules. "You two get freshened up and we'll meet you in the restaurant downstairs in 10 minutes."

Over lunch they discussed their itinerary for the next couple of days and asked their daughters what they wanted to do. They were content to go with the flow as they knew nothing about Fairbanks or Alaska for that matter. Sean would drop them off with Reina at the Chena Mall while he conducted business with Frenchy.

Sean and Reina had discussed what to get the girls for Christmas but didn't settle on anything specific. They would see what their shopping spree turned up. Reina and the girls only had casual clothes with them so Sean suggested they pick up something nice to wear to the ballet that evening. He noticed they didn't argue with him. He would buy a sports jacket and wear a clean pair of newer jeans.

Frenchy had his mag's ready. He inquired about rubber grips, holsters and belts for the compact CZs. Frenchy produced two pairs of grips, three holsters and belts. Sean bought a box of 200 rounds of .223 ammo for Sam. He stocked up with a thousand rounds of 9 mm and a couple of boxes of .45-70 for himself. As he browsed the store for ideas for Sam's Christmas gift he spotted the Carhartt jacket. Sam definitely needed a new chore jacket and this one would be perfect. Reina had told Sean about her conversation with Luiza and shared her intention of giving Luiza her Ithaca Featherlight

20 gauge for Christmas. With that and the three pistols in mind he added a shotgun vest, a box of 20 gauge shells and four sets of ear defenders and shooting glasses to his pile of stuff before paying the bill.

He met Reina and his daughters at the coffee shop in the mall. They were already loaded down with shopping bags. "Looks like we'll have to charter a Herc' to get all this stuff back home." Except for Reina, the girls had no idea what he was talking about so his attempt at humour died a quick death.

Reina squeezed his knee and smiled. "Did you get what you wanted at Frenchy's?" Sean nodded. "We got talking about your jewellery suggestion and thought about getting the girls each a ring with their birthstone. Sam knows how to size them so we could just make sure they were big enough."

Kazia added, "And can we get them each a pair of *new* jeans and a blouse? I know they would love that and Anya and I can help with the sizes."

"Okay with me. Can we get the rings here or do we have to go downtown?"

"Oh, let's go downtown, we want to see what it's like," Anya enthused.

"Okay, tomorrow we'll go downtown. Let's see if we can find the jeans and shirts here then go back and get ready to go out for dinner and the ballet. I need a sports jacket too."

They filled the trunk of the car with bags and packages and drove back to the hotel. Sean had a shower and lay on the bed in a bathrobe supplied with the room. He watched the local news and weather while Reina showered and dressed for their special evening. She looked stunning in her red dress and heels as she stood in front of the mirror brushing her long black hair. He got up and helped her with her gold necklace made from Klondike River placer gold whispering in her ear that he wanted to stay in instead of going out. She elbowed him in the ribs. He retreated to finish dressing.

Sean knocked on the door of the girls' room. The door opened and two beautiful young ladies stood awaiting his affirmation. "Have you two seen a couple of young girls named Anya and Kazia?" His eyes searched the room behind them as if looking for his daughters. Noting their frowns, he quickly adjusted his focus to stare at his daughters. "You two are gorgeous!"

He thought Reina and the store clerk did well in their choice of attire and accessories.

Sean had picked a restaurant located on the banks of the Chena River because of its historic motif and quality food. The maître d' found a private table for the family by a window overlooking the river. The interior décor held Kazia and Anya spellbound as they made their way to the table. It reminded them of their museum tour in Whitehorse but, unlike the museum, this was a wonderfully aromatic restaurant. Anya wondered if they served crab.

After dinner they drove to the auditorium. It was three quarters full as the usher showed Sean and his family to their seats. Julie had done well for them; they were centered five rows back from the orchestra pit. The girls devoured their programs and asked questions as the orchestra tuned. "This is like a story," said Anya speaking to her sister beside her.

"It *is* a story," said Sean leaning over to speak to the girls, "but it will be told with music and dancers. A French author named Alexander Dumas adapted a story written by E. T Hoffman almost 200 years ago, The Nutcracker and the Mouse King. Peter Tchaikovsky, a very famous Russian composer, wrote the music that tells the story. Read the synopsis at the back of your program then, if you close your eyes, you can imagine what is happening as the story unfolds."

The girls were entirely silent through the first act; in the past, only sleep had ever succeeded in inducing such a state. Sean and Reina delighted in watching their eyes flit among the dancers dressed in their colourful costumes while their ears captured the astonishingly rich, melodious music that raised goose bumps on their bare arms. The two girls were enraptured.

At intermission, their silence abruptly ended and the two girls burst into a verbal review of the events that had so forcefully captured their entire being. The family made their way to the lobby where a display of nutcrackers lured the girls away from their parents. Sean and Reina watched as Anya and Kazia each caressed and examined the vividly painted wooden 'toys'. "I know what you're thinking," Reina squeezed her husband's arm, "go and buy them one. It will be a wonderful memento of their first ballet."

While they waited for the next act to start Sean introduced the girls to some of the musicians in the orchestra. They were happy to discuss their instruments and tell how they came to earn a place in an orchestra. Anya was intrigued with the sound of the French horn. She asked why the musician would sometimes place his hand in the bell and listened attentively to his explanation. Kazia expressed her admiration for their talent and thanked them for making such beautiful music.

The second act began and the girls once again left the real world for somewhere far away in time and space. The first strains of the waltz of the flowers interrupted their attention. They looked at their parents exclaiming, "That's *your* dance!" Sean and Reina nodded, smiled and held their index fingers to their lips.

On the way back to the hotel, the girls sat in the back seat recounting the highlights of what they had just experienced. Rather than go directly to their rooms Sean recognized the need to wind down and led his family into the almost empty cocktail lounge taking a table near the wall. The waitress came over, complimented the girls on their dresses and took everyone's order. Anya wanted a Piña Colada and persuaded her sister to have one too. "Hold the rum," Sean added.

When she returned and served the drinks, the waitress remarked on the 'dolls' the girls were holding. "Oh, they are not dolls," Anya responded, a hint of indignation in her voice. "This is the brave prince from the land of sweets who Clara rescued from the evil mice."

Kazia joined in, "We just saw the story at the auditorium. It's called the Nutcracker Suite. You should go."

"Well maybe I will just do that." The baffled waitress retreated to the bar.

"Her skirt sure is short," observed Anya as she watched the waitress leave.

Sean almost spit out his rusty nail when he burst out laughing.

Chapter 59

Sean tapped on the door of the girls' room as he and Reina walked down to the restaurant for breakfast. They joined them a few minutes later dressed in their usual blue jeans and sweatshirts.

"We sure enjoyed last night," Kazia addressed her parents. "Thanks for taking us to the ballet; I'll never forget the wonderful time we had."

"Yes, Mom and Dad, I had a wonderful time. Thank you," Anya echoed her sister's sentiments. "It seems so strange to call you Mom and Dad. It is okay?"

"It is very okay! You are our daughters and you are most welcome for last night. It was a blessing just to see you two enjoying yourself so much," replied Reina.

"And thank you for being thankful. You are two exceptional daughters," Sean added.

After breakfast, they retrieved their parkas from the room and assembled in the lobby. Sean took the long way to downtown as part of his tour of the city. He told them how wild the town was during the building of the Trans Alaska Pipeline. There was lots of drinking and sometimes gunfights. Stories abounded of snowploughs scooping up passed out drunks and dumping them on the river ice. They stopped at the old riverboat, which was closed for the season, and Sean talked about how important rivers were during the early days.

He parked and they spent the morning walking main street browsing the different shops they encountered. They found a jewellery store that specialized in gold jewellery but also had a large selection of birthstone rings. Sean went through the list and the girls selected a ring for each of their sisters back at the White. Reina suggested getting one for Sheila too. Sean had each gift wrapped with a small card attached identifying the recipient. They had lunch at one of the old hotels better known for its bar but also its good food.

After lunch Sean drove to the university. He wanted the girls to see what a university was like in case they chose to attend one someday. He also wanted them to see the caribou and muskoxen that the biology department used in their research. The hairy muskoxen fascinated the girls. Sean bought them each a pair of mitts made from qiviut, the soft under wool of the musk ox. The library was their last stop. Anya loved to read and the sight of floor after floor of shelves lined with books overwhelmed her. The girls learned how to use a computer to find almost any book they wanted. Before leaving, they had coffee in the cafeteria sitting with students at a long table. Anya and Kazia engaged some of the students with questions about their lives and studies at the university. When it was time to leave, Sean reluctantly dragged them away from their new friends.

On their way back to the hotel Sean and Reina discussed taking the girls to a movie that evening. Sean checked with the front desk to see what was playing. The perennial Christmas favourite, Sound of Music, was playing at one of the theatres. Sean and Reina broached the suggestion over supper and the girls expressed their enthusiasm for such a venture.

Like their experience with the Nutcracker, the story and the music enthralled the girls. The fact that it was true added to their interest. "She was such a beautiful lady and he was very handsome and brave," Anya pronounced on their way back to the hotel. "Those Germans were very bad people."

Sean corrected her, "You must remember Anya that it was the Nazis who were bad. Not *all* Germans were Nazis; many of them, like the Von Trapp family, resisted or fled the Nazis. Some even helped those, like Polish people, who the Nazis persecuted. I have good German friends in Whitehorse who you will meet some day. They make good sausage."

The next morning they checked out and loaded into the rental car. The girls had to hold their packs on their laps as the trunk was full from their shopping spree. Al greeted them as they entered the office. He listened patiently as the girls enthusiastically told him of their adventures while Sean and Reina unloaded the car and transferred their booty to the plane. Sean paid his bill, thanked Al again for taking care of them so well, and wished him a Merry Christmas.

They landed at Beaver Creek and cleared customs. The customs officer knew Sean and Reina and treated their arrival as a time-wasting formality. Sean refuelled and they carried on to the White. Sam greeted them as usual helping to unload their treasures. "So which one of you is Santa Claus?" he laughed. "Sheila's got some fresh Christmas baking in the Lodge for you."

The two girls ran to the Lodge. The rich aroma of fresh-baked cookies greeted them when they opened the door. They rushed into the living room where everyone was sitting around drinking hot chocolate and eating colourfully decorated cookies. Throwing their parkas on the table, they joined their sisters on the floor helping themselves to the plate of cookies glad to be 'home'.

"Welcome home." Sheila passed them each a mug of hot chocolate. "Now, tell us all about your adventures in Fairbanks."

Reina and Sean, not wanting to interrupt the story of Anya and Kazia's adventures, waved at Sheila and the girls as they crept past carrying bags and boxes upstairs to their room. Sam followed with his load. "So what's happening Sam, anything exciting?" Sean asked as he navigated the stairs blinded by boxes in his arms.

"Been pretty quiet. Sheila's got the girls collecting stuff and making Christmas decorations. We've been waiting for you to get back so you can make your famous Christmas cake." Sam loved Sean's Christmas cake and looked for a package under the tree every year. This year he might get to see how he put the delicacy together.

In their room, Reina passed Sam a large box of ammunition.

"Thanks dear, appreciate you picking this up for me."

"We'll get right on that Christmas cake Sam," Sean laughed, "In fact, I'll start marinating the fruit and nuts this afternoon. Tomorrow morning we'll put it together and bake it. I'll have to make a pretty big batch this year." He had picked up all the ingredients in Fairbanks as supplies were scarce in Whitehorse.

"You guys have fun on your trip?"

"We sure did Sam. Just seeing how much the girls enjoyed themselves made us so happy. I don't think they or us will ever forget their first visit to Fairbanks." Reina's eyes watered as she expressed her delight over the trip. "Let's go downstairs and listen to the story before it gets too far along."

The girls were still fervidly describing their Nutcracker experience when Sean, Sam and Reina joined Sheila on the couch. The two wooden nut-cracker souvenirs were making their rounds through the audience followed by qiviut mitts. Sheila served mugs of hot chocolate to Sam, Sean and Reina. As she passed the plate of cookies she whispered, "Better take two, I don't think they're gonna last much longer." They listened as the girls relived their trip for another hour answering questions from the audience along the way.

When the story telling was over, Sean leaned over to Sheila, "I'm going to start my Christmas cake if that's okay Sheila?"

"No problem Sean, just ask if you need anything. Are the girls helping?"

Anya's ears perked up, "Oh yes, he needs all the help he can get," she announced as she led some of the girls into the kitchen her arms full of grocery bags.

"Cheeky little imp isn't she?" Sean winked as she walked by. Sheila and Reina went back into the living room where Reina gave Sheila her version of the trip.

Sean, Sam and the girls spent the rest of the afternoon cutting up fruit and nuts and mixing the concoction in two large bowls while Christmas carols played on Sam's stereo. Sean had been making his Christmas cake for years and no longer needed the recipe. Besides, it only invited questions when he deviated from the directions. Sam retrieved the rum, bourbon and brandy trying a sample of each to make sure it was still good. "Sean's Christmas cake can be used as fire starter and it's even been known to start a diesel in cold weather," Sam lied to the trusting helpers. Some of the girls were curious and asked if they could try some of what Sam was drinking. Sam was happy to oblige filling liqueur glasses half full with the spirits and inviting the girls to try some. The two men laughed at the girls' reactions to the liquor.

After a supper treat of the Colonel's chicken that they brought back from Fairbanks, the conversation turned to Christmas. Sam asked if anyone wanted to describe Christmas in Poland. Celina volunteered, giving a description of a celebration that resembled a Canadian Christmas in many respects. She spoke of a custom important to Polish people involving a piece of unleavened bread called 'oplatek'. They share the wafer around the table at the start of Christmas dinner and everyone is to forgive each other for any hurts they have caused. She asked Sheila if they could try to make some oplatek. Celina didn't know how. Sheila said they would check the encyclopedia together and see if they can find a recipe.

Sam explained that tomorrow they would go and hunt for a Christmas tree but tonight they would finish making the decorations that would adorn the tree. Some of the girls popped popcorn to make popcorn strings while the others made chains from coloured paper. When the popcorn was ready, Sheila brought out bowls of cranberries that she and Sam picked in the fall. She distributed needles and thread and some girls began making their strings of popcorn accented with the red cranberries. Others worked with spruce bows, ribbons and cones making wreathes and other ornaments to hang around the dining room, on the door of the Lodge and on the tree.

Later, Celina and Irenka lay in bed talking about their most memorable Christmas in Poland. Irenka remembered the only Christmas where she received a gift. "It was before my parents were killed. I was only little, maybe five or six years old. One night when Papa returned from working at the factory he had something special hidden in his overcoat but he wouldn't let me see. I forgot about it after a few days. On Christmas Eve, after sharing the oplatek, and eating our supper of beetroot soup, we sat by the coal stove because we didn't have a tree. Papa and Mama hugged me and told the story of the birth of Jesus. After the story Papa handed me something wrapped in a piece of red cloth."

"What was in it Irenka? Tell me!" Celina had been listening intently but now she was growing impatient.

"I will tell you but you must wait until I finish." Irenka was firm in rebuking her friend. "I remember them smiling at me as I struggled to untie the string in the warmth of the fire. I can still see their faces and feel the warm fire. I miss them Celina. I had never received a gift before and I liked not knowing what was in the package but at the same time I was excited about what I might find inside."

"So am I," said Celina impatiently.

"The string finally came off and I unfolded the cloth very carefully on the floor in case whatever was inside fell out and broke. Then I saw it. I was so happy. It was a small bag like a purse with a handle. It was made of red felt with a green and yellow felt flower my Mama sewed on the front and it was full of hard candies that looked like little coloured jewels. That night in my bed, I was so happy I cried. I thanked Jesus for being born and for being so good to me and giving me parents to love me and take care of me."

"Oh Irenka, you are such a wonderful friend. Thank you for sharing your special Christmas with me," said Celina. "I hope this Christmas is just as special for you. You know that God loves you and is taking care of you now don't you Irenka?'

"Yes Celina, I do and I thank Him every night before I go to bed. I thank Him for giving you to me as a friend too Celina. I'm tired dear friend, can we go to sleep?

"Yes, let's go to sleep. Good night Irenka."

"Good night Celina. God bless you."

Chapter 60

Breakfast time was full of conversation about Christmas trees and the imminent outing to find one. None of the girls had ever cut their own tree and many of them had never grown up with a tree at Christmas time. The discussion turned to who was going to cut down the tree when they found one. Although everyone wanted the honour, everyone knew that wouldn't be possible.

Sheila announced that they would have a contest to see who would get to cut down the tree. It took three people to cut it down, a faller, one to trim the branches so the faller could swing her axe and another to steady the tree so it fell in the right direction. They would have a quiz; the first person to raise their hand and get the correct answer would win a place among the three.

Sheila posed the first question as the room grew silent. "In what country did the Christmas tree become a part of the Christian celebration of Christmas?" Six hands shot into the air. Anya was first. "Okay Anya, what country?"

"Germany!" she shouted.

"Yes, that's right Anya." Everyone applauded the winner. "Okay you are one of the team. Now, in what town was Jesus born?" All but Blanka raised a hand. Natusza was first.

"Bethlehem!" she shouted when Sheila pointed to her.

"Of course Natusza would get the answer to that question. Did everyone know that her name means 'Christmas Day'?" Sheila looked at the surprised faces. "Okay Natusza, you and Anya are on the team. Now here's a difficult but important question. Why did God come to our world as a man?"

Anya raised her hand first but Sheila reminded her that she already had her turn. The rest of the girls were pondering their answer when Danuta raised her hand. "Okay Danuta, do you think you have the answer?"

"Because God wants us to be part of His family. But, because of our sin we can't. Sin brings death. We are all sinners and we need a Saviour; someone to pay the penalty for our sins so that we might have life. It was a merciful act of a loving God unwilling to punish human beings. That's why Jesus came." She stated her answer firmly then quoted John 3:16 from the Bible, *"For God so loved the world that He gave His only Son that whoever believes in Him shall not perish but have everlasting life."*

Everyone applauded her answer, "Well done Danuta, excellent answer. You are on the team with Anya and Natusza. Now team you have to decide among yourselves who will do what task but you have time to decide. Let's be ready to leave after lunch." The girls took their dishes into the kitchen where those on dish duty went to work. The others joined Sam and Sean where Sean was about to prepare his famous Christmas cake.

Sam put on the Christmas music while Sean uncovered the bowls of marinating fruit and nuts and invited Sam and the girls to smell the liquor-soaked mixture. "This is the key to a good cake," he chuckled as he watched the girls respond to the penetrating smell of rum, bourbon and brandy. He listed off the ingredients he needed and set the girls to gathering them while he prepared another couple of bowls. Sean had quadrupled his usual recipe hoping that his cake would appeal to most of the girls. Even if it didn't, he and Sam could live off the nutritious, high-density survival food for weeks.

"Halina, would you take those molasses containers and put them beside the airtight to warm?" thanks dear. "Rosa and Brygida you can measure and mix up the spices while Sam and Anya prepare the other ingredients. Kazia, Danuta you can help me with the loaf tins. Do you know where Sheila keeps them?" Kazia and Danuta placed eight loaf pans on the counter and Sean showed them how to grease the brown butcher's paper with lard and line each pan.

The girls took turns mixing the thick, heavy batter until the ingredients were well blended. "I think we should wear a gas mask when we're doing this," said Anya crinkling her nose at the powerful smell of molasses and liquor. Everyone laughed.

Sean guided them as they ladled the mixture into the loaf pans and arranged them on the oven racks. "Okay, it's going to be a while before they're done so while we're waiting let's have a look at the recipe Sheila found for making oplatek. How do you say that word?" Anya corrected his pronunciation. The item was nothing more than an unleavened cracker-like biscuit like the Jewish matzo bread but Sean had never made anything like it. In the end, the recipe was simple and everyone worked in pairs to produce their own oplatek complete with creative embossing or carving in the dough.

Sean arranged the loaf pans on cooking racks to cool as Reina and Sheila prepared a simple lunch of roast moose sandwiches on homemade bread. The girls devoured the lunch excited to get dressed for their Christmas tree hunt.

In the city you still have to search for a tree, but it's like looking for the perfect pearl pendant in Tiffany's where they're *all* perfect. It doesn't really matter which one you pick. Not so in the wilds of the Yukon. Finding the perfect Christmas tree in the vacant vastness of the Yukon landscape seems at first an imprudent challenge. Yet it was these repeated challenges over the years that helped tell the true story of Christmas for Sam and Sheila.

The three winners finally decided who would do what as they trudged through the snow with the others. Bozo bounded into the open forest after a fool hen flushed by the commotion of their arrival. "What is that?" shouted Kazia pointing to the grouse sitting in a spruce tree.

"Maybe it's a partridge in a pear tree," Sean remarked. The girls groaned. "Actually, It's a spruce grouse," said Sean as he helped some of the others locate the bird in the tree. "We call them 'fool hens' because they are so easy to sneak up on and kill. If you are ever lost and hungry, this bird could save your life. Because he's so stupid you can sneak up and knock him out of the tree with a stick." The bird sat still in the tree blinking at the girls trying to get a good look at him as they walked by.

Bozo broke trail for the tree hunters as they made their way through the deep snow. Armed with a Swede saw, axe and a rope, the falling team followed Bozo in their quest for the perfect Christmas tree. Heads tilted back as the girls scanned the tops of the trees. The perfect tree strangely preferred to reside closest to the sky. Young trees of six or seven feet were often skinny and sparse and rejected by the hunters. But, as they grew to 20 or 30 feet tall, the tops seemed to fill out. It was among these tops that their hope lay.

Snow was beginning to fall. Sean kept a watchful eye on the south sky. After an hour, they had passed judgement on eight trees, selecting three for final evaluation. Necks straining, the falling team circled the base of each tree, viewing it from all angles and noting the many imperfections. Finally, everyone agreed on a sturdy spruce with a bushy top. Danuta was ready with the axe, moving in to remove the lower limbs so Anya could swing the axe and fall the tree. Anya examined the tree with Sam's help, determining where it should fall. She waved everyone away from the drop zone. Sam coached her as she made the undercut in the five-inch thick trunk. She started to make the back cut but stopped her swing and turned to the others standing and watching her. "Blanka, come here and cut down our Christmas tree." Blanka stood with a surprised look on her face. Anya beckoned the girl with her mitt as others urged her forward. Sam came over and showed Blanka how to hold and swing the axe reminding her to shout 'timber' when the tree was ready to fall. She was a strong girl having worked on a farm and her blows with the sharp axe soon brought the tree to the verge of falling. Natusza and Danuta pushed on the trunk causing the tree to lean in the direction they chose. Blanka administered a few more blows then shouted "Tim---ber!" as the tree came crashing down to the frenzied applause of those looking on. Bozo barked with satisfaction. Blanka turned and thanked Anya while Sam hugged her around the shoulders and congratulated the smiling young girl.

The girls sat in the snow, drinking hot cocoa and nibbling on buttery, homemade shortbread and chocolate-coated 'tingalings'. They were satisfied with the object of their quest and turned to talking about the events surrounding that special time of year. Bozo lay curled up, oblivious to the falling snow forming a blanket on his thick coat. After severing their trophy from the rest of the tree, Danuta attached the rope and several girls began to drag it through the snow. By this time, the snow was falling heavily. Getting the tree was a memorable Yukon Christmas tradition for the adults probably because it always started out to be such a daunting quest. Yet, hope bloomed with each step until they finally found their prize. But, this was not the end.

That evening, they installed the tree in the living room of the old Lodge beside the White River. They decorated the limbs with baubles, including some glass bells from Sam's childhood and the decorations the girls had made. The final garnish included gingerbread men and cranberry and popcorn strings. On Christmas Eve they would light the candles perched on the boughs. Sean stood looking out the dining room windows at the snow falling heavily.

Anya sat thinking about the day's events. The rest of the tired crew lounged in the dimly lit living room drinking mulled wine. They gazed in wonder at the tree born and raised in the Yukon wilderness. It bore all the scars of its harsh existence, but now it stood transformed into a thing of beauty.

She stood. "Can I make a toast?" Anya looked at Sean who nodded his approval. "I've been thinking about what we did today as I look at this beautiful tree. We acted out the story of Christmas." Puzzled faces looked on expectantly. "God sent His only Son to bring *us* out of the wilderness of sin and transform us into *'a new creature in Christ Jesus.'* He has made *us* beautiful. Jesus is God's ultimate gift to mankind but, like any gift, you have to receive it. I hope you all reach out and accept His Gift if you haven't already? To Jesus." Anya lifted her glass and all drank to the toast.

* * *

There was only one motel worth staying at in Tok. He parked the Suburban, left it running and walked through the door of the motel office. "Have you got a room for the night," Carlos addressed the young man behind the counter then waited while the clerk took a key from the board and laid it on the counter.

"Just the one night?" he asked.

"Yah. How much? I'll pay now." Carlos withdrew a money clip from his pocket and began counting out the bills.

"Fifty. You can register here." The clerk turned the book and offered Carlos a pen.

Chapter 61

The sun had risen and its low angled rays silhouetted the figure on the highway. "There a man; he walking on driveway!" Blanka turned to Sheila. She pointed to the figure making his way towards the front of the Lodge with Bozo at his side.

Reina and the girls were involved in their English class. Blanka was getting a plate of cookies from the kitchen. The girls quickly gathered at the windows to watch the rare and unexpected visitor approach.

"So there is, must have car trouble to be on foot," replied Sheila. "Go tell Sam and Sean."

Blanka left the plate of cookies on the counter and bounded out of the kitchen and out the back door into the yard where Sam and Sean were cutting firewood.

Sheila opened the front door and stood watching as the man approached. He was dressed appropriately for the weather with a heavy parka, mitts and boots and carrying a small backpack. "Good morning, nice day for a walk."

"Not for me it isn't," the man responded gruffly, his voice slightly accented. "My car's broken down about a mile up the road. I saw your sign when I drove past but I took a chance that someone would be around since I wasn't having any luck catching a ride."

"You headed to Alaska then? Come in and warm up. My husband and his friend are just coming in from doing chores, maybe they can help you." She ushered the man through the door into the dining room. "Can I get you a coffee while you're waiting? Have a chair."

"Yes, I can do with a coffee." The man removed his boots, leaving them and his bag at the door, and hung his parka on the back of the chair before sitting down. His eyes followed Sheila as she retrieved the coffee pot and a mug seemingly oblivious to the crowd of female eyes staring at him from across the room.

"Do you take cream and sugar?" she asked.

"Yes, thank you. Nice place." His eyes scanned the room and came to rest on the English class standing silently across the room studying the stranger. He mentally counted 13 young girls and an adult female.

Reina watched closely as the man entered the dining room, his Hispanic features drawing her particular attention. He was a large, husky man with black hair and a pockmarked face. When her eyes met his she motioned for the girls to take their seats and approached him with an outstretched hand. "Hello, I'm Reina. Sorry to hear of your misfortune but Sam and Sean are pretty good mechanics and should be able to help you out." She smiled at the stranger.

His hand swallowed Reina's as he returned the gesture. "Yo soy Carlos," he responded knowingly in Spanish, "Tu´ eres mexicano?"

"Si, ahora Canadiense. And you? Where are you from?"

"I am from Spain but I live in Alaska."

Sean and Sam hung their parkas in the mudroom and made their way through the living room and into the dining room. The entry of the two men cut the conversation short. Sean's suspicious eyes told his brain all it needed to know as they automatically 'cleared' the room and the outside surroundings visible through the dining room windows. "Hi, I'm Sam and this is Sean," Sam held out his hand. "We're closed this time of year but always here to help. What can we do for you?" The two men joined the stranger across the table while Sheila brought them each a mug of coffee and sat beside her husband. Anya had quietly left for her bathroom break.

"Lot more people here than I thought," he remarked. "I wasn't sure there'd be anyone here. Just how many are there of you?"

Sean and Sam successfully hid the warning lights that flashed brightly upon hearing the question. "Just us, one big happy family," Sheila offered innocently before either man could respond, "we have friends visiting from Poland." Sean mentally scolded himself for leaving his pistol in his parka.

In what seemed like one well-orchestrated movement the stranger pushed back his chair, rose to his feet and withdrew a large handgun from under his jacket. The girls screamed in unison when they saw the pistol. "Shut up!" he shouted as he pointed the pistol first at the men then at the girls. "All of you, on the floor, face down, now!"

"Do as he says, everything will be okay," shouted Sean as the stranger swung his arm and pointed the pistol at him. He traded glances with Sam and reluctantly joined the others on the floor.

The stranger retrieved his bag and withdrew several pairs of handcuffs. "Put your hands behind your back," he ordered Sam and Sean. "You," he glared at Sheila, "put these on them." Sheila obeyed while she prayed. "Now, take the bag and put the rest of them in cuffs starting with the Mexican."

Anya was returning from the upstairs bathroom when she heard what was happening. She froze at the top of the stairs listening. *"No God, this can't be happening,"* she prayed silently. *"Please Lord show me what to do."*

Sheila went from girl to girl reassuring them they would be safe but telling them they had to remain calm and do what the stranger said. Sam got Sean's attention and motioned towards the counter a few feet away from where they were lying. "Shotgun," he whispered. Sean rolled on his side, slipped the handcuffs so they were now in front of him and rolled toward the counter. The stranger had his back to the men as he supervised Sheila. He turned in time to see Sean awkwardly trying to pull the shotgun up to shoot when a shot rang out and shattered a window off his right shoulder. He fired at Sean then turned to address the unseen threat now crouched boldly in his sights but it was too late. Two more shots rang out in rapid succession. The stranger crumpled to the floor.

The screaming stopped as the girls watched the stranger fall and his pistol slide across the floor. Reina entered attack mode but to no end; when she reached the stranger it was clear that he was dead, shot twice in the chest. She looked up to see Anya resuming an upright stance from her crouched position, staring at the stranger's body while holding Sean's pistol pointed at the floor.

Sean emerged from behind the counter clearly in pain. Reina and Anya ran to him, Sheila close behind with keys to the handcuffs. "I'm okay. My shoulder." he rolled his left shoulder towards Reina. Sheila quickly released him from the cuffs. "Are *you* okay Anya?" Sean tried to look into her eyes as he gripped her shoulder with his good hand."

Slowly her head came up and her eyes met his. "You said you would never leave me Dad."

Chapter 62

Sam took the shotgun and checked outside for others who might be lurking nearby but there was no sign of anybody else. He had the foresight to take some photos of the scene before he dragged the body out the front door and into the snow. It would be a while before the cops showed up and he didn't want a dead body further traumatising the girls. Sheila cleaned up the blood and put the stranger's belongings into garbage bags that joined him in the snow.

Anya finished stitching the wound in Sean's shoulder like Reina had taught her. Reina and Sheila attended to the distraught girls. He watched her as she worked seemingly unfazed by what had just happened. *"Must be in shock."* He thought. Sam covered the wound with a large dressing when she was done. "It's only a flesh wound Sean, like a cut from a chainsaw," said Sam, "you'll be good to go in no time thanks to this here nurse." He smiled at Anya.

"Thanks Sam. You're a brother like no other. I appreciate you Sam." He hugged Sam with his good arm.

"Anya?" She looked at him with eyes full of love and concern. "You saved my life." The father and daughter held each other in silence for a long time. Sean felt a deep peace as he held the girl from the side of the road that had stumbled into his life not long ago. Out of the love that had grown for this lost one, he had promised to protect her. He promised never to leave her but he always seemed to fail. God was showing him that he couldn't keep that promise on his own. He bowed his heart and silently committed his promise to the One who *could* keep it.

Reina and Kazia stood in the doorway watching." You did good Anya," announced Kazia as she approached her sister. "You saved all of us. You are a true warrior my sister." She and her mother joined Sean and Anya in each other's arms.

"How is your shoulder?" Reina admired Sam and Anya's handiwork.

"It's sore but no worse than a big cut. It'll heal fine in a few days." He kissed his wife in thankfulness for her safety. "How are you doing?"

"I'm good and the girls are settling down. Sheila will stay with them for now."

Sean asked Sam to call the RCMP, then he and his family retreated to his and Reina's bedroom. Reina had assumed Anya was in shock but she was wrong. "I'm fine Mom, I know what I did and I'd do it again; I know why I did it and I'm happy that all of us escaped that bad man. None of us ever want to go back to the hell those men put us through." She turned to Sean, "I told you I wanted to learn how to shoot, thank you for teaching me so well."

"You saved your father's life, my husband, thank you Anya." Reina turned to Kazia, "How are you doing Kazia?"

"I'm like Anya Mom, I'm so thankful that Anya saved Dad and was able to help us. It's too bad that evil people die when they could choose to live but it is their choice. We were all so scared Mom; I kept remembering us in that old building and the steel box. I would rather die than go back to that."

Sean and Reina looked at each other. "I don't think we have to worry about these two," said Sean, "what do you think?"

"I have to agree but I want you both to pray about this and talk to your Dad and me if anything starts to bother you. Do you understand?" She looked at her two daughters.

"Okay Mom, we will," the two girls replied in unison.

"I want you to keep an eye on the other girls too. You let me know if you think any of them are struggling with what happened. Will you do that?" The two girls nodded. "Okay, come here, let's pray."

After their prayer, Sean turned to Anya. "I have a question for you Anya. How did you get down those creaky old stairs without any of us hearing you?" Sean queried his daughter.

"I didn't. I knew they would make noise so I climbed out a bathroom window and dropped into the snow piled around the Lodge and came in the back door. I knew you kept your pistol in your parka pocket so I found it and snuck through the living room until I could see you all in the dining room."

Sean shook his head in amazement at the resourcefulness of his daughter.

When they came downstairs, Sam told Sean that the constable from Haines Junction was in Beaver Creek and would be arriving within minutes; an ambulance was on its way. Sheila was talking with the girls in the living room attempting to assess their emotional condition. Reina and her daughters joined them.

"They all seem to be fine Reina and I don't think it's shock. I think they are *relieved* over what happened. Tell me if you think I'm missing something."

Reina looked at the girls. "Is Sheila right? How are you doing? Blanka, tell us what you are thinking."

"It okay Reina. Anya did the good thing. She save us. She is very brave girl. Thank you Anya."

The other girls quickly joined in thanking Anya for saving them. Anya flushed red as Sean entered the room.

"Are you okay Sean?" The anxiety in Tekla's voice testified to her genuine concern. She and the other girls gathered around Sean as he stood with his arm in a sling.

"Thank you, all of you. I am better than fine thanks to Anya. I have a small wound in my shoulder. I have to wear this sling for a while so I don't move too much and open the wound. Most of all, we want you to know that if you find yourselves struggling with what happened this morning, you must tell us. Do you all understand?" All nodded their understanding. "Now the police will be arriving soon. They will probably want to talk to each of you alone. You have nothing to fear from them; you are not in any trouble. I want you to do as they say and tell the truth about what you saw. Do you understand?" Heads nodded once again.

"He's here," Sam announced.

Chapter 63

Life at the Lodge was returning to normal. None of the girls exhibited any sign of emotional trauma related to the shooting. They soon engaged in their former routines. Every night after supper they gathered to talk and share how they were doing. Preparation for the upcoming Christmas celebration happily displaced any brooding over recent events.

The police were content with the statements they secured and were now busy trying to identify the victim. They deemed that Anya acted in self-defence and didn't lay any charges. Sean requested that Sergeant Dawson in Whitehorse be involved in the investigation given the history behind the event.

Sam stood with his coffee mug in his hand looking out the dining room windows at the new fall of snow. A fresh snowfall seemed to make all things new. He watched the pickup cross the bridge, turn into the driveway and continue into the yard leaving deep tracks in the new accumulation of snow. With all the excitement, he forgot to put the cable back up. The truck belonged to Jimmy and Sarah Jackson.

Sheila met them at the door ushering the couple inside. The girls, recognizing the visitors as friendly based on Sheila's welcome, gathered in curiosity about the newcomers. Sheila introduced them collectively knowing that Sarah and Jimmy had little hope of remembering their individual names.

"Can you stay for coffee?" Sheila could read the concern in their faces as she led them into the dining room.

"Is Reina here Sheila? We need her help. Billy's sick in the back of the truck," Jimmy asked.

"Reina!" Sheila yelled upstairs. "Halina, go find Sean and Sam, they're out in the yard somewhere." Reina entered the room alert to the urgency in Sheila's voice.

"Billy's sick and he's in the back of Jimmy's truck," Sheila reported with concern in her voice.

Sean and Sam came in with Halina. "Billy's sick in the back of Jimmy's truck. Come with me," ordered Reina as she threw on her parka.

Jimmy joined them as they went out to the truck. He pulled back the tarp covering his brother lying in a sleeping bag in the open box of the pickup. "Get me some aspirin and a glass of water," Reina ordered Sean who immediately ran to the Lodge.

Sheila invited Sarah to take a seat while she sat in the chair opposite her, the girls joining them at the table. "Roza can you bring some cups and a plate of cookies? Blanka, bring the coffee pot please." Sheila acknowledged Sarah's obvious surprise and curiosity at meeting the girls. "I suppose you're wondering where all these girls came from?" She hoped to distract Sarah from Billy's condition.

"Yes, are they relatives or school kids?" She smiled at the girls sitting next to her.

"It's a long story Sarah but they are all from Poland and they will be staying with us over Christmas. They are a lovely bunch of young ladies and a big help to me around here." Roza placed the plate of cookies on the table.

"You sure have a beautiful tree Sheila," Sarah spoke softly.

"Yes, isn't it magnificent for a Yukon tree? The girls found it, cut it down and decorated it. Have you and Jimmy got yours up yet?" Sheila filled Sarah's mug with coffee and slid the cookie plate close to her.

"No, we were going to but Billy got sick."

"So what happened?" Sheila was concerned knowing that Billy had a heart condition.

"He called Jimmy on the HF and Jimmy went to get him with his snow machine. Billy only uses dogs and he was too sick to come in on his own. He stayed the night at our place but he seemed to be getting worse so we brought him here to see if Reina can help him. Jimmy met Sean in Whitehorse so he knew she was here with you guys."

Reina and the men came into the lodge. "It's not really urgent but Billy still needs to be in the hospital. He's okay for now but Jimmy will drive him to Whitehorse. You should probably stay here Sarah. Billy will need the room in the cab; he can't ride in the box all the way to town."

"Sam will drive you home Sarah," Jimmy looked at Sam who nodded his agreement. "Sean, I know this is a lot to ask but Billy's dogs are still at his cabin. Do you think you could drive them in for him?" Jimmy looked apologetic.

"Sure can Jimmy, not a problem, you leave them to me, they'll be fine." Sean tried to put him at ease.

"Thanks Sean. I'll make it up to you. I better get moving." Reina passed him a bottle of pills and a jug of water as he left.

"Sarah, you might as well stay for supper. Sam will drive you home after," Sheila offered.

"I have to feed our dog, but I guess he can wait a while," Sarah thanked Sheila.

Reina joined them at the table pouring herself a mug of coffee. "Thank you Reina for helping Billy and congratulations on your marriage. Jimmy told me." Sarah smiled.

"Thank you Sarah. Yes, it all happened very fast. We decided on the wedding two days before," Reina smiled back at Sarah. "Did you meet our two daughters?" Reina waved Anya and Kazia over.

"This is Anya, she started all this." She hugged her daughter around her waist. "And this is Kazia, her sister." Reina drew Kazia to her with her other arm around her waist.

"We are pleased to meet you Sarah." Anya's smile reflected her sincerity.

"We are so glad you like our tree. Maybe you and your husband can visit us together when Billy gets well. I think Sam would let you bring your dog. He could play with Bozo." Kazia innocently extended Sam and Sheila's hospitality to Sarah.

Sarah was impressed. "I am pleased to meet you too. I am happy that my friends found two nice daughters like you."

"Can we pray for Billy?" Anya looked at Sarah then Reina.

"You sure can," said Sarah, "thank you for asking."

Anya and the others bowed their heads as Anya asked God to give Billy good doctors and medicine and to heal him.

Sheila asked Sarah to tell the girls about her life in the Yukon, where she was born and raised and how she met Jimmy. All sat in rapt attention to Sarah's story of how she grew up near Snag where Sean rescued the girls. She told them about the log cabin her father built and where she lived until they moved to Beaver Creek. Her father trapped animals and sold the fur to get money to buy things like flour and salt and ammunition but sometimes he would get short-term jobs. She helped scrape and stretch the hides for sale to the fur buyers. Her mother made mitts and moccasins out of moose skin and decorated them with felt and beads. Sometimes she would sell them to the truck drivers and others who drove the Alaska Highway or to the men who worked at the Snag airfield. Some of her favourite memories were when her family hunted muskrats in the spring and split and dried fish at their fish camp. They didn't have snow machines in those days but they had dogs that packed in the summer and pulled a toboggan in the winter.

"Did you go to school when you were young?" asked Izabella.

"Oh no," said Sarah. "There were no schools in this area at that time. The missionary at the church taught us how to read and he let us borrow his books. I learned a lot just by reading books. The men at the airstrip used to read to us when we were little."

"Me too," said Anya. "I think I learned more from reading books than from our school at the orphanage. Mom and Dad teach all us girls many things too. So do Sam and Sheila."

"My Mom and Dad taught me lots of things too," said Sarah. "Not things that will get me a job in Whitehorse but I never wanted to work in town. I liked living in the bush."

Sheila interrupted, "Okay, who's on the meal crew today? We have a guest so let's see what we can put together for lunch and decide on supper." Several of the girls made their way to the kitchen while Sheila encouraged Sarah to sit and talk with the others.

Sean and Sam finished repairing the broken shackle bolt on Sam's truck. They stood beside the airtight in his shop wiping their hands with dirty rags. "I'm thinking I should plan on two days to run Billy's dogs in. What do you think Sam?" Sean respected Sam's knowledge of the area and often sought his advice when he first set up his fishing lodge and guiding business. Sean had visited Billy at his cabin once by air landing on the lake and another time on a snow machine. His experience on the trails was limited to the short time he spent with Billy on his trap line. He knew the dogs, a good team, and he hoped they remembered him.

"I think that's a reasonable estimate given the snow conditions and weather. Jimmy's snow machine trail will help a lot even after this snow-fall. Watch out for overflow at the springs; better to go around this time of year. You shouldn't have to break trail and you can travel pretty light." Sam's response was encouraging. "You can overnight at Stewart's cabin, way better than sleeping under a lean to. We should finish up, lunch must be ready."

The savoury aroma of moose and barley soup and fresh baked biscuits welcomed Sean and Sam as they entered the mudroom. Sheila had shown the girls how to make soup out of just about anything but this was one of her specialties. Kazia had taken the lead on this pot under the watchful eye of the chief cook. They joined the others in the dining room.

Sean spoke reassuringly with Reina who sat next to him expressing her concern that he was overstressing his shoulder helping Sam. "I'm fine. It's healing great; now let's enjoy our soup and these freshly baked biscuits before they get cold." She smiled and gave him a squeeze.

After lunch they sat at the table drinking coffee. "Are you okay with this?" Sean wanted to make sure Reina was comfortable flying TJ back from Billy's cabin and leaving him there. Anya, sitting beside her Dad, was listening. Finally, she broke in during a lull in their conversation.

"I want to go with you Dad. You need the company and someone to change the dressing on your wound; I promise I won't be a bother. Please let me come."

Her request surprised Sean. He looked at Reina who was shaking her head in the wrong direction for Anya's liking, "Hey, why not?" Sean looked at his wife. "This would be a great experience for Anya. It's only a couple of days, she's light and doesn't eat much so no problem on the trail. Maybe she could drive and I'll just go along for the ride. Remember my shoulder."

Reina glared back at him. "What if something happens? Anya wouldn't know what to do. She's never done anything like this especially in the winter. I don't think this is a very good idea."

"Well this is a great chance to introduce her to bush life. Look dear, it's only a couple of days, it's not very cold and what could happen? She's a very responsible and capable young lady. If we get held up for any reason you can come and get us on Sam's Cat, it's not that far. Let her go Reina." Sean pleaded while Anya mouthed a long, silent 'please'.

Reina looked lovingly at her new daughter whose eyes feigned anguish as she pleaded with her new mother. "You are so stubborn young lady."

"Just like your Mother." Sean muttered under his breath.

"I heard that!" Reina poked Sean in the ribs then sighed in defeat. "Okay, but you better take good care of her out there. Don't go taking unnecessary risks; just come straight home, no side trips!"

Anya jumped up and threw her arms around her Mother's neck, "Thank you, thank you, thank you Mom. I love you." Reina melted into a pool of gratefulness for the daughter God had given her. Anya ran off to tell her sister and the others what had just happened.

"You know that she doesn't have a clue what she's in for, don't you." Reina faced Sean.

"I know, but, that's how they learn. I . . . sorry, God won't let anything bad happen to her." Sean tried to reassure his wife.

"I know you won't." She hugged him. "She's in good hands and not just yours."

"We'll plan on leaving tomorrow at first light," said Sean. The two put their heads together and committed the trip into God's hands.

Chapter 64

It was 10 in the morning and the eastern sky was beginning to brighten with an ominous red tinge. "You got your long johns on little lady?" Sean addressed Anya as she came down the stairs. The thermometer registered 20 below, balmy for that time of year.

"Yes, and I've got my pack with extra socks and stuff like you said. It's not *that* cold you know." There was a hint of protest in her voice.

"Anya, you don't know what cold is!" Sean retorted. "Let's go."

"You're taking the Five-Stars with you?" Reina questioned him on their way to the plane.

"We've got the room and I know you don't want your little darling getting cold," he smiled.

The flight to Billy's cabin took slightly longer than usual as Sean flew low along the trail he would be taking on their return trip. Jimmy's snow machine trail was faintly recognizable under the blanket of new snow. They passed over a large bull moose browsing willows near the springs. "Oh too bad Blanka couldn't have seen him," Anya exclaimed. Sean was watching the sky ahead of him. A change in the weather was coming but he kept his observation to himself.

The lake and Billy's cabin came into view as Sean approached at about 200 feet above the ground. The dogs were on their feet looking skyward straining at the chains attached to the doghouses that they rarely used. *"Anticipating a meal of frozen fish and some warm water,"* Sean thought. There was no wind but Sean surveyed the field of snow covering the lake for evidence of over-flow. He spotted a 'spider hole' at the far end of the lake but he was confident that the surface next to the cabin was dry. It was still early enough in the season that the risk was low. To be safe he came in parallel to the shore allow-ing his skis to sink into the snow but maintaining flying speed. He circled back and examined his tracks for signs of water; there were none.

He landed on the field of soft, deep snow. While taxiing he kept his speed up making a wide loop to turn back on his tracks. Reina's take off would be much easier and quicker on the packed ski tracks than if she had to plough virgin snow. He stopped and shut down the engine abeam Billy's cabin.

They unloaded some of their gear onto the short pulk that Sean kept in the back of the plane. Anya shouldered her pack and pulled it through untracked snow up to her knees. Sean grabbed his rifle and he and Reina brought the rest of the gear. He caught her in time as she parked the pulk and ran to meet the dogs.

"Stop Anya!" he shouted. "Wait there, don't approach the dogs." He caught up to her and explained the danger of approaching chained teams of sled dogs. "These guys are pretty good but most sled dogs, especially native teams, are not pets. They work for a living and they can do you serious damage. Every year you hear of someone, usually a child, getting mauled or killed by dogs."

The shocked look on her face told Sean that she got the message. "I'll introduce you later."

The interior of the cabin was still slightly warmer than outside. Sean opened the cast iron door on the barrel stove and found remnant hot coals in the ashes. He placed a pile of kindling on the coals and dumped a small amount of kerosene-soaked sawdust from a tobacco can onto the pile. Reina came in with an armload of split wood from the woodshed and started a fire in the cook stove. Anya wandered around the small cabin examining items hanging on walls and the rough furniture scattered throughout. She was par-ticularly curious about the stretcher boards propped against the walls covered in some kind of animal skin. "Those are marten skins. Kind of like a weasel only a lot bigger," Reina explained. "Anya, fill the kettle with water will you?" Reina pointed to the five-gallon crock at the end of the kitchen counter.

Reina had a fire going in minutes. She removed one of the larger stove plates and slid the kettle over the raging fire beneath. "I'll check the cache for dog food." She disappeared out the door.

The kindling in the barrel stove was burning brightly so Sean added some split wood. "Come over here Anya and see how to start a fire. Now I need some larger logs that haven't been split like these ones in the wood box. We'll use these ones first but you need to go out to the woodshed and bring in some more. I need the wood box full." She nodded and left to find the woodshed passing her mother on the way.

"Billy's got lots of whitefish in the cache. I brought enough for the dog's supper and breakfast; left them in the entry. They're probably pretty hungry. The toboggan looks fine; it's in good shape," Reina checked the kettle. "We should get a couple of pails of water or you might run out before you leave. Anya's going to want a bath." She chuckled to herself waiting for the reaction.

Sean, kneeling in front of the barrel stove, turned to glare at his wife. "A bath! Are you nuts? No way is she having a bath, this isn't a vacation."

Reina stood laughing, enjoying her successful suckering of her husband. "Just kidding." Anya came in struggling with an armload of large pieces of firewood. She dumped them into the wood box and retreated for another load.

Anya helped her Mother prepare buckets of water for the dogs while listening to her caution about approaching the animals. "Now I want you to grab five fish and I'll bring the water buckets." They walked to where the dogs were lunging at their chains. "Now throw a fish to each dog, away from their bowl." The dogs immediately attacked their overdue supper while Reina poured warm water into each of their bowls. She watched as the team of malamutes made short work of their fish. "There, you just scored some points with them."

Reina carried the empty buckets to the lake. They followed a faint trail leading to a snow-covered box about a hundred feet from shore. Brushing off the snow, she turned over the insulated box uncovering a hole in the ice. She broke through the thin layer of ice using the chisel that had been lying against the box. Reina let Anya fill both buckets with the dipper she brought with her.

The cabin had warmed considerably by the time they returned with their buckets of water. Anya poured them into the crock while Reina joined Sean at the window overlooking the lake. "What are you looking at?" she asked searching the lake surface for some object that had his attention.

"Oh, nothing," he lied. He knew what was coming but he didn't want to alarm his wife.

"I should be going. You've got meatloaf to warm up for supper with potatoes and veggies. Apple crisp for dessert. There's some moose and veggies for you to make a stew for the trail. The kettle's boiled so you can make some coffee." She hugged her husband as Anya joined them. Reina put her arm around her daughter. "You two have a great time together. Take care of your shoulder and I'll see you in a couple of days. Don't you be late for Christmas!" She kissed Anya and Sean.

Father and daughter walked Mom to the plane. The engine started and Reina gave a thumbs up through the window. They watched from the shore as the engine warmed and Reina did her checks. She blew a kiss and advanced the throttle. TJ and Mom disappeared over the trees and into an ever-darkening south-western sky. Sean put his arm over Anya's shoulders and the two walked back to the cabin.

"It will be dark soon so we should split some wood and make sure Billy's got a good supply for when he comes back." Sean steered Anya toward the woodshed. He showed her how to select and split logs so as not to have to fight with knots. The straight grained pieces he pitched into a separate pile that he split into kindling. Stopping now and again, he watched proudly as his daughter made short work of the 16-inch long pieces of wood cut from the spruce and tamarack that surrounded the lake. When they finished they both loaded their arms with split wood and kindling and walked to the cabin. The dogs lay curled up in the snow as the sky grew darker, clouds hiding the waning December sun. Sean tried to hide his concern.

After supper, Sean prepared a Dutch oven of moose stew for the trail and let it simmer while they played a game of crib by the light of a kerosene lamp. Sam had taught most of the girls how to play the game but he refused to play with Anya because she always beat him. Sean put her in her place by winning three of the four games they played.

"Have you ever heard of Louis Lamour, Anya?" Sean pulled one of Billy's collection off a shelf.

"No, who is he?" she asked standing in her long underwear brushing her teeth and spitting into the slop pail.

"He writes books about the old west, cowboys and such. Come over here when you're done; I'll read to you and let Louis broaden your mind." Sean leaned against a pillow on Billy's homemade couch. Anya bounded over to the couch, pulled the quilt over her and snuggled close to her Dad happy to enjoy his undivided attention. Sean read for an hour but Anya wouldn't let him stop. Her pleading to read just one more chapter continued until they finished the book.

He tucked her into the Five-Star and kissed her goodnight before going to the window looking over the lake. The snow fell heavily, whipped about by the wind. The sight confirmed his nagging suspicions that began with the red-tinged sunrise. After loading the barrel stove he climbed into his own Five-Star and quickly fell asleep. It would be well before sunup when they would begin their journey.

Chapter 65

As expected, the storm was gone when Sean awoke the next morning. He pushed the door closed with his elbow, stomped the snow off his boots and dropped an armload of firewood into the wood box. The cook stove crackled and heat from the freshly revived barrel stove flooded the room. He hung his parka on a peg in the mudroom and began to fill the buckets with warm water for the dogs.

Anya sat on the edge of her bunk trying to wake up. The gloom that filled the cabin challenged the kerosene lamp beside the stove. "Why is it so cold in here?" she muttered. She got up and shuffled over to a partially frosted window where she could see the thermometer. "Thirty eight below!" The snow and wind had smoothed the rough edges of the yard and its structures as if someone threw a white blanket over it; she could barely make out the forms of the dogs lying under the blanket. She retreated to her bunk and began dressing.

"We had a storm come through last night," Sean explained turning up the wick on the lamp over the stove. "I'm afraid we're in for a cold spell. Lousy timing." She joined him beside the cook stove hugging him around the waist as he melted some kind of white fat in a cast iron frying pan.

"What is that, it smells funny?" She twisted her nose.

"Bear fat. Billy's doctor told him to stay away from bacon so he uses it instead of bacon fat for making stuff." Sean's nonchalant reply ignored the contradiction in Billy's rationale. "I need you to feed the dogs like Mom showed you. I'll finish making breakfast." Anya retreated to the mudroom donning her bush pacs, parka and mitts. Obediently she picked up the bucket of warm water and left the cabin. The frozen air stung her face as she threw the dogs a fish and filled their bowls with steaming water.

Back in the cabin, she joined her Dad at the small table next to the stove. A steaming mug of coffee sat beside her bowl. The mug warmed her hands and her heart as they bowed their heads to give thanks, ask for Billy's healing and ask God for His blessing on their trip to the White. Sean filled her bowl with hot oatmeal littered with small black crowberries. He pushed the tea towel-covered plate towards her. "Eat up. Your body is going to need this." Sean spread raspberry jam on his piece of bannock eating it in thought-ful silence.

In good weather, they could make it home in two days. This wasn't 'good weather' and under normal circumstances Sean would wait until there was a break in the cold. As it was, he knew that it was likely to get colder before it got warmer and Christmas was coming. He was beginning to doubt his decision to allow Anya along on the trip. He was pretty sure he knew what his wife was thinking.

He poured himself another mug of coffee. Anya was intent on eating her breakfast, paying him no attention. *"We'll leave today,"* he thought. *"What? In this cold!"* His conscience protested. *"We must leave today or we'll be late for Christmas. Could they make it home for Christmas?"*

Anya and her Dad cleaned up the dishes and put them away on the open shelves. "Roll up our sleeping bags and put them in their bags. I'll get the rest of our stuff together," Sean directed Anya to her task while he packed their food in a duffle bag.

The five dogs lay curled up in the snow, their noses in their tails. Like coiled springs they respond quickly when called to work but for now they were content to rest. Nakina was Billy's prized lead dog. He chose her from the litter born to Lobo and Mandy five years earlier. Lobo was the largest Malamute in the country weighing 140 pounds. Nakina, his daughter, came in at 110 pounds. Malamutes are the Mack trucks of the north, built for steady hauls of heavy loads over miles of trail without complaint. The smaller Siberian huskies were the sports car sprinters mostly used for sport racing and tourist gigs.

Sean loaded the toboggan while the dogs danced on their chains in anticipation. Anya arrived with the two large sleeping bags. He placed the Dutch oven full of hot stew on a folded canvas tarp at the bottom of the toboggan and laid the sleeping bags over top. She would be riding, at least for a while, and the bags would provide a comfortable place to sit while keeping the stew warm, for a while. He tucked her snowshoes, the new kind made of metal and synthetic materials with built in ice cleats, into the front of the toboggan. "Go and shut down the stoves, empty the slop pail, kettle and the water crock and blow out the lamp. We're ready to go." Sean put the harnesses on the dogs and clipped them into the tug while Anya completed her tasks.

The cold pierced their cheeks as if someone was driving icy nails through their skin. Anya lay on top of the load with a canvas tarp pulled up to her neck. Sean walked ahead breaking trail in the newly fallen snow. Sometimes a tree would let out a loud 'snap' shattering the silence gripping the land. Sean's moustache, constantly bathed in warm, moist air from his nostrils, mingled with his beard and froze his mouth shut as if to guard the silence. The stillness and pall of a winter dawn cloaked the land and its inhabitants. Nothing moved but the toboggan, the dogs and him.

His eyes squinted in their quest to discern the trail, a narrow path through the frozen spruces. He felt like the friend of Robert Service's 'Blasphemous Bill MacKie' who *"blundered blind with a trail to find through that blank and bitter land."* With each step his snowshoes rose in victory only to fall in defeat beneath the 12 inches of fresh, fleecy snow that hindered their progress. The dogs laboured behind, tongues lolling from their mouths as they strained against the lethargic toboggan. Dogs know nothing about thermometers but their instinct told them this was foolishness. Yet, their loyalty and obedience masked their apprehension over the terrific cold that froze their breath and covered their fur with a fine, icy dust. They pushed on.

He could feel sweat soaking the wool underwear beneath his shirt. *"How can a man sweat in this cold?"* he thought. Such cold is a creeping terror deserving respect lest the prideful man succumb to its stealthy advance and final grip. Wool clothing like good judgement is a traditional defence against the cold. Unlike many of his friends, Sean liked wool. Perhaps it was his Scottish heritage but he wallowed in wool. His socks were wool, his underwear, shirts, inner gloves and mitts were wool. Even his daughter was clothed in wool. Wool, even when wet, keeps you warm.

The appearance of the orange orb in the southern sky was a welcome sign. The ice crystals floating in the air restrained its energy yet it spurred both man and dogs to renewed effort. Their burdens lightened under its dull glow. They made good progress along the flat valley floor. In a few hours, it would sink below the horizon to resume its winter slumber and leave them again shrouded in a darkness that magnified the cold a hundred fold.

Arriving at Bear Springs, they picked their way through the trees to avoid getting soaked in the overflow. These springs were a welcome source of refreshing water in the summer but a deadly trap in the winter. Should man or beast fall through the deceptive sheet of thin ice and snow that covered them, it meant almost certain death from freezing. Having successfully manoeuvred past the hazard they stopped at the edge of a large moose meadow to rest and receive the full, albeit meagre, warmth of the sun.

Anya was happy to be moving her body. Sean checked her face for frostbite then had her retrieve the tea billy, bannock, sugar and tea from the toboggan. He showed her how to set the anchor used to keep the dogs from running off should some mad hare happen by. The dogs lay among the trees in the deep snow while Sean built a fire. The hot tea and bannock rejuvenated his body and mind convincing him that they wouldn't make Stewart's cabin at their current pace. They would be camping out their first night. He decided to keep the news to himself for now. Instead, he tried to remember how far along the trail they had to travel to find Billy's campsite.

On the next leg of their journey Anya rode the runners at the back of the toboggan. When the cold penetrated her clothing she would step off the runners and maintain a brisk walk behind the toboggan warming her body in the process before again hitching a ride courtesy of the malamutes. She watched her Dad; he kept a steady pace ahead of the team, his exertion keeping him warm. The dogs pulled steadily along the broken trail. The arctic sun disappeared behind the western mountains after its brief visit.

Darkness enveloped the land and a fragment of a moon rose to cast its light upon the snow. "How much longer to the cabin?" Anya shouted at her Dad. There was no reply.

Sean made out the shape of the lean-to ahead as they climbed up a familiar east-west trending ridge. Men and game used the ridge as a travel route. It boasted an open pine forest with abundant firewood, grassy slopes and elevation where the coldest air refused to linger. He stopped in front of the lean-to. Turning to Anya, he placed an ungloved hand over his mouth until the ice thawed allowing him to speak, then announced, "We camp here tonight."

"What?" she walked to where he was standing. "We're sleeping *here*? Where's the cabin? It's too cold to sleep out here. We don't even have a tent!"

Sean took off his snowshoes and handed one to Anya. "Use this as a shovel and clear away the snow in front of the lean-to. When you're done, go and collect some firewood."

After staking the dogs among the trees, he spread the tarp over the frame of the lean-to. Anya stacked the firewood beside the ring of stones she uncovered from under the snow. She stood waiting for her Dad to light the fire. "Where's the fire?" Sean looked at her, his face and beard crusted with ice.

"You want *me* to start it?" she protested. "I've never started a fire in the snow."

"But you know how don't you? Remember the picnic at the lake?" Sean waited for her response.

"Oh yeah, I've got to get some squaw wood first." She trudged off to collect the fine tinder she would use to start a blaze. Returning with a good bundle of twigs she duplicated what she had learned at the picnic and soon had a roaring fire brightening their campsite and their moods.

"We're going to need a lot more firewood than that." Sean pointed to the small pile of sticks remaining. "Come with me, I'll show you." The moon and northern lights in the crystal night sky lit their way as the man and his daughter walked into the dark forest together. Sean showed Anya how to pull down enough standing or leaning dead wood and drag it to the fire. Afterwards they gathered fresh spruce boughs for their bed.

Anya threw the dogs a frozen whitefish for supper while she filled their bowls from the big billy hanging over the fire. Sean retrieved the Dutch oven buried in the toboggan and placed it on a bed of coals to thaw the partially frozen moose stew. After supper, they reclined together in front of the fire on their sleeping bags savouring their mugs of sweet tea. They watched the northern lights "*rippling green with a wondrous sheen*" as Robert Service once wrote. Their progress for the day was slow as Sean had expected. It had been only eight hours since they left Billy's cabin but it felt like 12. It was a good day but at this pace they would need three more days to get home.

The arctic night gripped their little camp. A shroud of cold covered a land that seemed to have died. Except for the popping and cracking of the fire, all was still. Such sounds somehow enhanced the warmth that radiated from its hearth and flooded the cozy lean-to. Father and daughter lay close together on top of their thick sleeping bags and mattress of spruce boughs. Anya was surprised how warm and content she felt in the tiny shelter. She grew drowsy in the heat from the fire. Sean watched her nod off a couple of times before jerking back to consciousness.

"I think it's time for bed young lady." He gave her a gentle hug. The dogs were sleeping on their beds of snow, noses buried in bushy tails. Sean banked the fire with large logs then stripped to his long underwear. He hung his outer clothes on the rope stretching across the lean-to and spread his parka on top of his bag for extra warmth. "Don't sleep in your clothes, you'll regret it," he admonished Anya as he climbed into his sleeping bag.

Anya followed the example of her Dad pulling the bag over her head. Sean pulled the folds of the bag off her face and peered into her sleepy eyes. "You did great today Anya." He kissed her on the forehead as her eyelids slid shut. "Good night Anya, I love you." Sleep came quickly, a refuge from the frozen, lifeless arctic night.

Chapter 66

Dawn was hours away but their day had begun. Sean pushed a couple of logs into the embers where they soon burst into magnificent orange flame. The warmth and glow of the fire contrasted with the cold grey background faintly illuminated by a shard of a moon hanging in the blackness. Snatching his clothes from the overhead cord, he dressed for the day leaving Anya to sleep a little longer.

He fed the dogs while the tea billy struggled to come to a boil. Breakfast consisted of bannock warmed on the rocks beside the fire and chunks of bacon fried in a pan. His activity eventually woke Anya who peeked from the opening at the top of her bag. "Good morning Anya, sleep well?" he asked. "Were you warm enough?"

"Oh yes. I was warm all night. I had a good sleep. This is a very good sleeping bag," she remarked. "I have to pee." She climbed out of the bag sitting on top of it as she dressed in clothes warmed by the morning fire. "It's too cold, my fingers are already freezing; where is that cabin you promised?" Sean ignored her.

They ate their breakfast while reviewing their progress on the trail. Sean still planned to reach the White in time for Christmas but he expected another night on the trail. Stewart's cabin would be their next stop. Sean told the story of John Stewart while they washed down the bacon fat-soaked bannock with strong coffee. Stewart built a small log cabin and barn on Kluhini Creek

60 years earlier. It was one of several cabins strategically positioned along his trap line. John was long since gone but nobody knew where he went. Over the years, those who lived in the country maintained the cabin. In 1953, he had an exceptional catch, and marten, in great demand, brought a good price. The story goes that he left his dogs with Pierre Lavoi for the summer, took the cash, and boarded a Canadian Pacific Airlines DC3 in Whitehorse. John hadn't been 'outside' since he arrived in the Yukon. Well, he never came back and nobody knows where he went or what he got up to.

Sean was confident the day would be shorter providing the trail didn't hold any surprises, but he didn't tell Anya. He handed her some pieces of bannock instructing her to keep them inside her parka for snacking. He did the same and the two began breaking camp.

They started down the trail, off the ridge and into the blackness of the valley forest. The dogs pulled exuberantly causing the harness bells to tinkle. They knew the trail; perhaps they knew more.

Sean seemed to float as his five-foot trail snowshoes glided over the deep, soft snow in the valley bottom. His strides seemed almost effortless after the night's rest and a hot breakfast. It felt good to be moving again. The fur trim on his parka soon formed an icy mass as his warm, moist breath made contact. Without a doubt, it was 40 below and probably colder. Anya was snug under her tarp in the toboggan. The cold had an edge like a skinning knife and cut to the bone. There was something mysterious about 40 below. It was if the physical world underwent a subtle transformation. Those who lived in this pathetic land could sense the change and their bodies and minds went on alert at the presence of the frost fiend. Sean knew you could die at 39 below but, somehow he believed the odds were much greater at 40 below.

The sun appeared shortly after 10:00 o'clock and, like a coffee break, revitalized their bodies and minds. They mushed on along the flat valley floor making better time than the previous day. Sean was certain they would spend the night in the comfort of Stewart's cabin. Maybe this was the reason behind the unusual energy of the dogs, perhaps they knew they would make it.

They made a brief stop at the edge of an open meadow for lunch and tea. Anya asked if she could break trail with her new hi-tech snowshoes that she had yet to try. Sean agreed but warned her that the dogs might run over her if she was too slow. Anya set the pace as they continued down the trail through more open country. Sean was impressed with her stride and stamina. The sky had cleared allowing the winter-weakened sun to do its best. By mid afternoon, the pace was slowing. Anya needed a break so Sean traded places with her. The sun disappeared behind the hills into a western sky painted gunmetal blue and tinged with pink. Soon after, the moonless sky turned black. They plodded along in the gathering darkness beneath a velvet sky studded with a million stars.

Yes, the dogs were right; they knew they were spending the night in the barn at Stewart's cabin. The cold grew more and more intense as Sean and the dogs fought the fatigue brought on by seven hours on the trail. Another hour he mused. Good dogs, Billy had good dogs, loyal and hard working animals that thrived in the wilderness. Sean stopped the team and stepped out of his snowshoes. Flipping his beaver mitts behind his back where they hung on their sissy strings, he went back to give each dog an affectionate rubbing of their frosted ears. When they started out again, he could feel the energy in the team. They knew about the straw filled barn and he knew about the airtight stove in a cozy cabin.

Yelping in anticipation the dogs confirmed that the cabin was at the bottom of the next dip in the trail. They pulled up to the barn where Sean unclipped the dogs from the tug. As he opened the barn door, they pushed him out of the way rushing in to stake a spot in the straw before rolling around in some kind of dog ecstasy. He and Anya laughed at their antics and left them to their revelry while they fetched gear from the toboggan and walked to the cabin.

The door to the cabin was unlocked in dutiful compliance with northern hospitality. Sean lit the hurricane lantern hanging next to the door. Its weight told him the previous tenant had topped it up before he left. The wood box was full with a stack of kindling piled neatly beside it. If you used another man's cabin, you always left it better than you found it and NEVER without firewood! The fire was soon blazing fiercely in the airtight. The creaking sounds of warming metal filled the one room cabin. Sean grabbed the axe and the bucket by the door and trudged through the deep snow to the creek with Anya at his side. Within minutes, he had a bucket of clear creek water garnished with chunks of ice. As they headed back to the cabin Sean pointed out the column of white smoke and fiery embers rising from the Yukon chimney straight into the frozen air. "That tells me it's real cold," he said. Standing on the stoop in front of the cabin door, he glanced at the thermometer, wishing he hadn't. It registered 52 below zero.

The one room cabin continued to warm. Sean started a fire in the cook stove while Anya retrieved dog food and the rest of their gear from the toboggan. Tonight was special. They had achieved the halfway point for travel in this weather. A night in a cabin and barn was a welcome respite from sleeping in a snow bank or under a lean-to. No stew tonight – moose steak for him and Anya and cooked mash and moose fat for the dogs.

Dog dinner began to simmer in a large pot on the airtight. Anya lit the oil lamp on the table and unrolled their sleeping bags spreading them over the chairs in the cabin to warm. Someone had built a kitchen table from logs. Split logs formed the top, it's once rough surface now smooth from years of use. Four chairs were store-bought and two others were fashioned from poles. A soft cushion and afghan-covered backrest adorned a couch made of logs. A split-log bench stood against the wall next to the door. There was only one bed. It was big enough for two and boasted a 3-inch thick foam mattress guaranteeing an uninterrupted sleep once it thawed.

Sean showed Anya how to set their socks and the liners from their bush pacs on the drying rack hanging over the airtight. He explained the importance of keeping socks and liners dry and told her to put on her spare socks for the evening.

Anya insisted that she change his bandage. "Mom told me you'd be stubborn but to beat you with a stick if necessary," she frowned at him. Sean smiled and agreed while protesting that the wound was doing fine. He sat patiently while she swabbed the wound with peroxide and applied a new bandage. He silently admitted that it felt better as he slipped his long underwear back onto his shoulder and donned his shirt.

After their supper, Sean checked on the dogs in the barn. They were sprawled in the hay enjoying their dog dreams. He loaded his arms with firewood and walked back to the cabin where he replenished the wood box and stoked the airtight. Anya was browsing the collection of books left by a hundred wayfaring strangers over the years. "That Louis Lamour guy sure is popular around here," she remarked. "Let's read another story before bed. We can take turns this time."

Sean poured two mugs of tea before settling down to read with his daughter. As Anya snuggled beside him under the afghan, he found himself reliving memories. Perhaps it was fatigue but a tear rolled down his cheek. Anya's concerned and puzzled look helped him regain his composure. "I'm fine," he squeezed her shoulders with his left arm setting his tea on a stump beside the couch. "My daughter and I used to do this. I'm weeping with gratitude Anya. God has given me another daughter and I am so thankful to have you as my daughter Anya." She kissed him on the cheek and hugged his neck.

They took turns reading for at least an hour by the light of the kerosene lamp. Anya loved to dramatize her reading but despite her exuberance the sound of the crackling fire was restful and they soon began to doze in its warmth. They wouldn't finish the book tonight, their bodies were crying out for sleep. Anya eventually fell asleep on his shoulder. He closed the book and gently carried her to her sleeping bag. She never woke.

Sean stoked the fire then peered out the window trying to read the thermometer with his flashlight. The temperature had climbed to -43. He climbed into his sleeping bag where he soon joined Billy's team in dreamland.

Chapter 67

The Yukon wilderness in winter is a great silent and lone land where frigid darkness obscures summer's musical score. It's as if the land had stopped to pray. Darkness dominated the arctic winter at this time of year. The absence of light and heat from the sun for over 18 hours a day drove the land and its inhabitants into a multitude of silent refuges. Trees stood stark, brittle and motionless as if afraid of breaking. The grouse buried himself in the snow. The mouse sought her refuge in a grassy nest at the base of the snowpack. Squirrels curled inside their nests and went into a state of torpor. The bear sought out his den early knowing what was to come and slept through the agony of winter. For Sean and Anya, a warm cabin and a pile of firewood brought relief and safety from the killing cold.

There was no dawn but Sean rolled out of bed by force of habit. He stoked the fire and climbed back in to wait for the cabin to warm up. He could hear Anya's gentle breathing as she lay beside him sleeping peacefully. Hungry bellies beckoned as he donned his bush pacs and parka and walked to the barn. The air felt warm. He made a mental note to check the thermometer. Each dog got a fish and a bowl of warm water. Sean and Anya would get a pot of oatmeal studded with dried crowberries and cranberries harvested before the snow.

He checked the thermometer as he opened the cabin door. It had warmed up. The thermometer registered 30 below and it was his guess that by afternoon it would be up to 20 below. Anya was still sleeping. He leaned over her and whispered in her ear, "Hey sleepy head, the dogs are waiting for you."

She opened her eyes, turned onto her back and muttered, "Dogs, what dogs?" Her eyes closed again.

"Oh no you don't," said Sean. "Anya! Time to get up. Breakfast's almost ready. Get up and get dressed."

She moaned, opened her eyes and smiled up at Sean, "You are so mean to me."

They sat together at the table enjoying their porridge and talking about the change in temperature. Anya munched on a large piece of browned bannock lathered with butter and marmalade. The hot coffee went down smoothly banishing her early morning lethargy and stimulating a desire for a second cup. "Hey, we didn't finish the book did we? I must have fallen asleep," she confessed. "Do you think we can take it with us and finish it tonight?"

"I don't think anyone will miss it," replied Sean. "Under better conditions we could make it to the White in one day from here but even though it seems to be warming we still have to break trail. Be prepared for another night of sleeping in a lean-to."

Sean had no idea what the trail had in store for them today. The Bible says that a man makes his plans but the Lord orders his steps, only for His purposes. He didn't have much of a plan but he was hoping that the Lord's purpose was to have them home for Christmas. He figured two days to the White if they had to break trail all the way. That would put them in on Christmas day, perhaps in time for turkey dinner. The dogs were doing well despite the cold. The toboggan was staying together and, although he knew better, he was driving the outfit.

They left Stewart's cabin in darkness. It would be a good two hours before they'd see the sun. The trail while unbroken was mostly level and wound through open pine forest. Life was returning to the land as the temperature continued to rise. They even heard a squirrel bark. Light from over the eastern horizon began to open up the land even more and the sight of the sun signalled a tea break. Already they had reached the junction with the Koidern trail.

Sean stopped so suddenly that Anya had to apply the brake on the toboggan. The dogs rested in the snow while he walked on to see if his eyes were playing tricks on his mind. It was real. Before them was a packed trail. A couple of snow machines had come out of Koidern west bound on the White River trail. They would be home for Christmas!

Their speed more than doubled on the packed trail. Sean rode the runners. Anya rode on the load as the dogs pulled with a lively gait, harness bells jingling a new tune. The sun shone especially brightly that afternoon. At mid-day tea break, they lounged on spruce boughs in their shirtsleeves. Already they had reached the campsite Sean had chosen for the night but the day was still young. Indeed, God had a purpose and they were the beneficiaries.

Sunset, instead of robbing them of their zeal, renewed their drive to reach their loved ones for Christmas Eve. The ocean of stars reflecting off the snow provided sufficient light to guide their progress. They were finally on the home trail and making good time. The sounds of the crystalline snow rushing past the toboggan runners and the rhythmic breathing of the dogs invigorated Sean. In his mind he could see the Lodge on the White.

They stopped atop the ridge overlooking the highway and the Lodge. The windows of the log building glowed amber and a plume of white smoke rose against the black sky. Anya turned to Sean with a smile, "We made it!" Nakina sent a throaty howl into the darkness followed by yips and whines from the team. "Mush", Sean commanded and the dogs launched down the trail to 'home'.

The dogs showed no sign of slowing as they entered the yard barking and yipping as they went. Anya gripped the ropes suspending the canvas basket preparing herself for whatever upset was coming. Sean shouted 'easy' as he applied moderate pressure to the brake. They drifted in a lateral slide as they passed the back door of the lodge. Billy and Sam stood heralding their arrival. Sean yelled 'whoa' and the dogs slowed to a walk finally coming to a full stop by Sam's workshop tongues lolling and dripping saliva.

Billy was first on the scene greeting his beloved lead dog and the others in turn. Anya stood beside her Dad watching Billy attend to his team when Sam arrived. "Merry Christmas!" Sam hugged Anya and Sean welcoming them 'home', "You two are a welcome sight for some sore eyes." Reina came running from the lodge still in her slippers and embraced her husband and daughter together.

"I knew you'd make it, but I still prayed for you." Her eyes began to water. "Let's get in out of this cold."

"I've gotta help Billy stake the dogs. You and Anya go in, I'll be in soon." Sean kissed her. "It's good to be back."

Sean and Billy unclipped the dogs in silence and staked them at the edge of the clearing next to the woodpile. Sean retrieved their water bowls from the toboggan. "There's some fish up front Billy," he pointed as Billy walked to the toboggan. "I'm sure glad to see you back Billy. How you feeling?"

"Feel good. Doc gave me different medicine. Thanks for taking care of my dogs Sean."

Anya walked across the yard with a bucket in each hand. Sean directed Billy's attention. "There's my helper Billy. Her name is Anya." Anya approached the two men. "Anya, this is Billy and these are his dogs."

She set down one bucket, shook off her mitt letting it hang on the sissy string and shook Billy's hand smiling brightly. "Good dogs Mr. Billy. I brought them some water." Billy walked with her towards the dogs his arms full of frozen fish.

They unloaded the toboggan and brought everything into the lodge with Billy's help. A corporate 'Merry Christmas' greeted them as they entered the living room. Kazia ran to embrace her Dad expressing her excitement to have him home. Jimmy and Sarah stood by politely waiting their turn to welcome Sean and Anya from off the trail.

Sheila and Blanka brought Anya and Sean each a tray with a hot supper. It was close to seven o'clock; they had been on the trail for almost 11 hours. They devoured their meal in short order then sat back to enjoy their coffee and Christmas cake. Anya fielded questions interspersed with her narrative of their adventures on the trail. The dogs got more credit than her Dad did for bringing them home safely but Sean didn't notice; he sat beside his wife in quiet admiration of the wonderful daughter that blessed their lives.

Chapter 68

The weather had warmed to a balmy -22° but was retreating once again as darkness gripped the land. Falling snow reflected light from the living room window. Sheila and Sam served platters of Christmas baking with mugs of mulled wine to wash down the cakes and cookies. Sheila and the girls had been busy baking and were proud to show off their accomplishments. This was just one part of Christmas Eve tradition at the White River Lodge. Another was the lighting of the candles on the tree. The time had arrived and Sam invited each of the girls to take part. He explained that after they had lit a candle they were to tell the others about one thing they were thankful for over the past year.

Blanka was the first volunteer. Sam handed the once reserved and petite girl the lighting stick as she sought out a candle on the lower branches within her reach. She turned and smiled at everyone then turned back to the tree and lit a candle, "I thankful for many things but I only pick one so it is Sam and Sheila. They love me and good to me." Blanka smiled and took a bow. Everyone applauded.

One by one, the girls took their turn lighting a candle and sharing their gratefulness. Anya took her turn at the last. A tall girl, she chose a candle near the top of the tree. "This is going to sound strange but I thank God for all that has happened in my life over these past four months. Yes, a lot of it was very painful and sometimes, like you," her eyes panned her sisters most of whom were sitting on the floor, "I thought I would die. But, when I gave my life to Jesus, he kept His promise. He helped me to forgive those who hurt me and even those who took my parents from me so many years ago. Now I have new parents and even a sister." She looked at Sean, Reina and Kazia sitting on the couch and smiled. "I have a family and a life that I never knew could be." The room erupted in exuberant applause as she joined her family on the couch.

Sam rose from his chair. "Thank you Anya. We are all happy for you and your family. Now it's time for the rest of us to light a candle. Sarah, come on over and light a candle." He beckoned to Sarah with his arm. She expressed thanks to Sam and Sheila for being their good neighbours. Jimmy took his turn reiterating his wife's sentiment but adding his thanks to everyone who prayed for his brother Billy. Billy expressed his thanks for the doctors and nurses at the Whitehorse General Hospital for their care of him.

Sean and Reina were next. Sean had been wrestling in his mind with what to say. Like the others, he had much to be thankful for and identifying one thing was not easy. Reina took the lead, confident in her choice. "This is not a problem for me although I have many things to be thankful for." She lit the candle next to Anya's. "But, this year I am especially thankful for the wonderful man that God has given to me as a husband. As you know, I sometimes wondered if it would ever happen but now it has and I thank God for His gift to me. And, just like our God, He threw in a bonus; now I have two lovely daughters to go along with my man."

Sean intercepted his wife as she returned to the couch and led her back in front of the tree. He lit the candle next to the one Reina had lit then turned to face the others, his arm around Reina's waist. "Isn't this lady gorgeous?" Reina blushed and leaned into her husband. "She's my wife by God's grace and I am grateful that she counted me worthy to be her husband. But, I want to thank God for all of you and for what He has done to rescue you from evil. He has given you all a hope and a future. You can't see that future but know that God will walk beside you through whatever comes. I love you all."

Sam and Sheila stood together. They lit two candles as they had done every Christmas on the banks of the White River for over 40 years. Sam began, "We have always led quiet and peaceful lives here on the White River but when Sean showed up that day with 13 young ladies under his arm our lives changed forever – and, we're so grateful." He and Sheila looked at the girls through tears in their eyes. "Thank you for letting us serve you girls and watch you heal and blossom into who God made you to be. Thank you for being our friends. We love you." The girls surrounded the couple thanking them for the shelter and care they offered in their time of need. Blanka remained, standing between them as the others went back to their places.

Everyone began to retire to their rooms but Sean and his family stayed until they were the only ones left in the room. "You two go on to bed. Anya and I have some unfinished business." The three women looked at Sean and each other trying to understand the ominous announcement. Sean laughed. "We have to finish a Louis Lamour book we started last night."

Chapter 69

Despite the darkness, it was Christmas morning, a symbol of light. The top floor of the lodge resonated with the sounds of gleeful shouts and laughter punctuated by the sound of footsteps racing up and down the hall. Sean and Reina lay in each other's arms with puzzled looks on their faces. A lot of celebrating was going on.

Suddenly, their half-open door burst open. Anya and Kazia raced into the room, stockings in hand. They landed on the bed eager to share their uncharacteristic morning joy. "Well Merry Christmas to you too," said Sean. The girls in their flannel pyjamas wedged themselves between he and Reina. They began pulling items from the wool stockings they had 'hung by the chimney with care' the night before to show their Mom and Dad.

Kazia, knowing the way to her Dad's heart, poked a dark chocolate truffle into his mouth. Anya fed her mother slices of Mandarin orange. "See my beautiful watch," Kazia rotated her wrist so all could see the glistening gold timepiece decorating her wrist. "Anya got one too." Anya proudly displayed her new watch holding it above her head admiring it as if it were a hundred carat diamond. Sean and Reina fawned over the gifts that, too their own delight, seemed to enrapture their daughters.

"What did you get?" Anya asked excitedly as she looked around for her parent's stockings.

"Oh, nothing," said Sean, "we were bad this year so Santa didn't give us anything."

Puzzled looks appeared on their faces before they realized Sean was teasing them. "You *are* bad," Anya glared at him before crawling off the bed. She found the two socks lying on the floor at the foot of the bed. She retrieved them and passed them to Reina and Sean. They laid them aside. "What are you doing! Aren't you going to look inside?" Anya was frantic; she had little patience with mysteries and her parents knew it. "You have to look inside. There might be a present for you." She grabbed the two socks and put them on their laps. Anya and Kazia had each bought a gift for Sean and Reina while they were in Whitehorse thanks to Sheila's inspiration and Sam's small loan. They had been waiting for this moment but their parents were not cooperating.

Sean and Reina smiled at each other and picked up the socks stuffed with candy, an orange and two small mystery packages. Sean began slowly unwrapping one of the truffles while Reina began to peel her orange. Anya snatched the truffle from Sean's hand, "You can eat that later. Why don't you open your present?" She sighed heavily as her and Kazia raised their arms in frustration.

"You go first Reina," said Sean.

Reina tore the paper and unwrapped her present as the girls, full of tension, looked on. The paper had hidden a small black rectangular box. "Open it, open it!"Anya and Kazia were bursting with excitement. Inside was an airline ticket to Lihue, Kauai. "What is that? That's not a present!" declared Anya.

"It certainly is Anya," Reina declared as she leaned over to kiss Sean. "Thank you dear. I can't wait."

The two girls looked at each other perplexed. What was this strange piece of paper? Reina could see that they didn't understand having never seen an airline ticket before. She explained, "When a couple gets married they usually go on a honeymoon. We only went on a short honeymoon knowing that we would have a *real* honeymoon later. Sean and I are going to Hawaii for two weeks after Christmas."

"Is that in the Yukon?" Kazia broke in.

"No," Reina laughed. "Hawaii is a group of tropical islands in the south Pacific Ocean, a long way from here and a lot warmer."

"Can we come," Anya had that pleading look in her eyes again.

"No you can't!" Sean quickly put an end to the inquiry. "You will both stay with Ray and Nancy and you *will* be good."

Anya put on her best crocodile pout but suddenly regained her composure when Sean and Reina both began to open identical packages in their stocking. Inside was a blue velvet box. "Not another pair of earrings!" Sean lamented with a dramatic sigh. Reina chuckled as she watched the puzzled reaction of the girls to his remark. They knew he didn't wear earrings. Together they opened their box as the two girls leaned forward almost blocking their view of the rings. They pulled the shiny gold rings from the satin slot and examined them closely. Two gold nuggets from some Yukon creek dominated the top with the names of their daughters engraved on each side of the band; the year appeared at the bottom. "Is this in case we forget your names?" Sean and Reina wrapped their arms around their daughters pulling them close. "We will *never* forget you two precious nuggets of love. Thank you Kazia, Anya; we will wear these always." The girls wore brilliant smiles at the appreciation of their gifts.

Sheila and Sarah had been the first ones up and they were on a mission. The smell of fresh cinnamon buns lured the upstairs tenants to the main floor where they gathered in the living room in their pyjamas and housecoats. The girls were in awe of the huge pile of colourfully wrapped gifts surrounding the base of the tree where none had been on Christmas Eve. Some stole close to read the names on tags then retreated quickly to whisper in the intended recipient's ear. Their focus shifted when Blanka and Luiza arrived with mugs and pots of coffee and hot chocolate. Sarah and Sheila followed close behind with a huge tray of the aromatic, iced buns. Bozo manoeuvred through the bodies scattered over his carpet trying to get close to the buns.

The Christmas season was laden with traditions going back to childhood, at least for the adults. The same couldn't be said for most of the girls. To them, many of the celebratory events memorializing the birth of Christ were a new experience and a delightful one. Perhaps the traditions they were experiencing would bind to their own lives and, ultimately, to their future families. They might even be the catalyst for developing their own traditions.

Christmas morning could devolve into chaos in homes with young children as most parents could attest. Although there were no young children present, the novelty of the situation for most of the participants suggested the need for an orderly distribution of gifts. Sam played the part of Santa. He handed out packages so that *all* could savour the joy of receiving and opening a gift. Blanka was first.

Her eyes grew wide as she stretched out her arms to receive the large box wrapped in green paper with a red ribbon and bow. She held it on her lap running her hands over the paper and touching the bow as if reluctant to destroy the thing of beauty with her name on it. She glanced up at a smiling Sam and Sheila both of whom gave nods of encouragement. Sean snapped a photograph. Blanka carefully removed the ribbon and bow setting them aside as personal treasures. The paper came off swiftly. Separating the tissue paper inside the box revealed a deep blue dress. Blanka stood and held the garment against her body to show it off to an audience expressing their collective approval. She beamed a grateful smile. "It is so beautiful. I have never had anything so beautiful," she whispered. "Thank you."

"For a beautiful young lady Blanka," Sam spoke with reverence to the young girl who was becoming more and more like a daughter to him and Sheila.

Sam announced that he was going to pass a gift to each of the girls but he asked that they wait and open their gifts together. The girls waited in obedience until he gave the signal to open them. At first they seemed more interested in the indigo-blue velvet boxes that held their gift but upon opening the box and seeing the ring inside their expressions changed. Sam explained that the stones represented their birth month but that the rings were a symbol. They were to remind them that they were God's creation, fearfully and wonderfully made, the apple of His eye. The girls gathered together with Sheila showing off their ring to the others and admiring their beauty. Sam offered to resize their ring if it was too tight or loose.

Kazia melted into a puddle of tears at the sight of her silver and sapphire necklace draped on a background of dark blue velvet. The pistol protégés, Anya, Kazia and Tekla dutifully cleared their new pistols before holding them up for all to see. Once they finished opening the companion gifts of a holster, belt, shooting glasses and ear defenders, they strutted around the room showing off their gear.

Luiza, baffled by the long box wrapped in blue tissue with gold ribbon and bow, looked around the room as if trying to verify that it was hers to open. "Open it Luiza," said Reina. "It's for you." The shy young girl unwrapped her gift and opened the box. Inside was an Ithaca Featherlight 20 gauge pump shotgun. Tears overflowed onto her cheeks as she went to embrace Reina and thank her. "I know you're going to be a champion Luiza," Reina whispered in her ear.

Sheila modeled her new red coat with fur-trimmed hood. She stood alongside her husband in his new Carhartt chore jacket. The girls scurried back to their rooms to try on their new jeans and blouse. They reappeared shortly after, strutting like models showing off their new outfits, watches and rings.

Jimmy and his family were surprised to each receive a gift. They all loved Sean's Christmas cake so he gave them each a loaf. Billy got a bonus, a box of .45-70 ammo for his bush rifle. Jimmy got a card with a hand-made coupon good for a 10 percent raise if he decided to work for Sean the coming summer. Sarah received a bottle of Sam's cranberry wine, her favourite.

At Sean's request, Sam handed Reina her gift last. Another velvet box was under the paper only this one was black and too large to contain a ring. Flipping the lid she gaped at the exquisitely engraved silver bracelet studded with emerald stones. "This is gorgeous Sean! You have amazing taste," she cooed.

"I saw it and immediately thought of you in your housecoat," he replied to his wife sitting on the floor in her pyjamas and housecoat.

Chapter 70

Christmas dinner, prepared with many helping hands, boasted two turkeys, yams, brussel sprouts, mashed potatoes and superb gravy that only Sheila could manufacture. Sean prepared his signature stuffing that included fall-picked wild cranberries complemented with pieces of tart apple. His Christmas pudding, a recipe from his mother's kitchen, was a tradition with his own family that he was proud to share with friends. Ironically, the foundation of the pudding included carrots, Sean's vegetable nemesis. He could only abide the vegetable when presented in the form of a cake or a pudding.

Reina and Halina set the 'table' made up of three rectangular tables butted end to end. Halina, gifted with an artistic bent, garnished the red tablecloths with sprigs of spruce and candles sitting in spruce cone sconces that she and the girls fabricated. Sheila's best set of Chinaware could only handle 12 settings so Reina filled in with the 'restaurant grade'. A potpourri of silverware graced the table. Halina took pride in finishing their creation by folding green napkins and placing them next to each place setting.

The feast left the participants lethargic, lounging in the living room. All were at peace, talking quietly among themselves. Some discussed the coming days when they would leave the White River Lodge and move to Whitehorse. Sean and Reina detected the nervous anticipation that animated their thoughts and conversation. Their hearts went out to the girls. Blanka would stay at the Lodge with Sheila and Sam but the other girls had yet to meet the strangers who would care for them in the months to come. They were confident that Sean and Reina would watch over their placement but the unknown still left them anxious.

Sam and Sheila's hospitality and their cozy, peaceful home had contributed much to the healing the girls had undergone. They had felt safe and secure, worthy and loved; would they know that same peace in their new homes? Reina and Sheila's regular counselling helped them to deal with the effects of their trauma but it would only be by the grace of God that they would know total freedom. Now they faced a new, potentially traumatic experience. Who would be there for them now?

Sam and Sheila had tried to encourage the girls in their private conversations with them. They reminded them of Sean and Reina's oversight that would ensure they came under the care of only the very best guardians. When questions and concerns arose they addressed them and gently laid them to rest. They explored expectations and responsibilities in relation to potential realistic scenarios while reassuring the girls that Sean and Reina would be close by if needed.

They had talked to all the girls about their immediate futures, counselling them on the various options that they could pursue while adjusting to their new 'families' and environment. All the girls had attended school in Poland but most had never completed the equivalent of high school and the quality of their education seemed poor. Reina and Sean felt confident in their identification of the 'intellectuals' in the crowd who might want to pursue further education. Most had not given a lot of thought to their futures but all wanted to marry and have a family. Many of the families they would be staying with home-schooled their children but a few sent their teenagers to the local high school. The college where Reina worked part-time offered a program for students who partially completed high school granting a high school diploma upon completion and preparing them for college entrance. Both Anya and Kazia were contemplating enrolling in that program but they were still unsure of their future careers, if any.

They would leave on New Year's Day; the very name of the day foreshadowed an auspicious new chapter in their lives. Nobody wanted to think about leaving White River Lodge and its gracious owners. All the girls looked to Sam and Sheila as parents and they called the Lodge their home. The people and the environment had contributed immensely to their emotional healing and growth as young women. The significance of their time on the banks of the White River would forever be a part of them.

Reina would drive most of the girls in the motor home but Sean would take three with him in TJ. Choosing the three involved another contest to see who would win a place in the plane. Anya came up with the contest. In the end Halina, Celina and Irenka won seats on the flight to Whitehorse. None had ever flown in an airplane.

* * *

The weather moderated after Christmas providing opportunity for some outdoor pursuits and another picnic at the lake. Luiza and Reina spent some time shooting Luiza's 'new' 20 gauge. The pistol protégés took the opportunity to break in their new pistols. Sean and Reina discussed getting the girls involved in shooting clubs in Whitehorse. They knew that such involvement would let them further develop their skills while introducing them to the local community. Sean was pleased to see his two daughters developing a passion for a sport he loved and could share with them.

On New Year's Eve, the girls began to pack. Although they owned few personal items, packing their belongings in their individual duffle bags turned out to be a melancholy time. Some fell into paroxysms of weeping which often triggered the same response in their roommate.

Others, seeing or hearing the heartbreak, rushed to console their sisters. Celina wept uncontrollably despite Irenka's attempt to console her. Suddenly she broke from the arms of her friend and rushed downstairs and into Sheila's arms. Sam stood by helplessly holding back tears of his own. He would dearly miss the girls he had come to love.

It was New Year's Day. Sean and Sam sat in silence drinking their coffee beside the airtight as they did most mornings. Words were not necessary. Each man somehow knew the words buried in the heart of their friend. Reina padded down the stairs with Sheila joining their husbands in the dimly lit living room. The two women respected the silent cocoon that enveloped the two mourning men. The sound of bodies stirring above them alerted the two women who retired to the kitchen to start breakfast.

The sombre mood dominated the breakfast gathering, the usual cacophony of voices replaced by the sound of utensils clicking against Chinaware and Bozo's dog sounds as he lay on the floor in his own blissful world. "I'm sad like all of you but we need to start looking forward to what comes next," Anya broke the silence. "We can come back and visit and I know Sam and Sheila will visit us when they come to Whitehorse. I will never forget you guys and your house of refuge for me and my sisters. Please try to understand how thankful we all are to you. We love you both so much." Anya's remarks elicited applause and more monologues of gratefulness directed to Sam and Sheila. Sean quietly rose from his chair, leaned toward Reina's ear and whispered that he was going to start the motor home so the diesel could warm up.

"See you at home!" shouted Anya as she and Reina stepped into the motor home after loading the girls and their duffle bags. Everyone waved as Reina pulled out of the yard, onto the Alaska Highway and turned south. The others retreated into the lodge except for Sean who went to check his airplane for the upcoming flight.

Chapter 71

"Where do you get all these girls." Arnie watched as the three girls climbed out of the airplane. "If I didn't know better I'd say you were up to something."

Sean laughed but otherwise ignored his comment then introduced the girls to Arnie. He shook their hands and helped carry their duffle bags to Sean's truck idling in the parking lot. "Reina and I are going to Hawaii for our belated honeymoon so won't see you for a couple of weeks," Sean addressed Arnie. "Take care of TJ and maybe I'll bring you a can of macadamia nuts." The two men laughed as Sean climbed into his truck with the three girls.

They stopped at the corner grocery store that was always open. It was small but they kept a good selection of items. The girls, entranced by the rows of stocked shelves, stopped to read labels and gaze at the bins of vegetables and fruit. Sean filled a couple of hand baskets with important items that would carry them through the next couple of days. He pulled into the driveway at the house and shut off the engine. Reina and the rest of the girls wouldn't arrive for another couple of hours. The girls helped carry the duffle bags and groceries into the house. Sean turned up the thermostat and showed the girls where to put the groceries while he made a pot of coffee. "You can sleep where you did last time but don't get too comfortable because you'll be meeting your foster families tomorrow." He watched the girls go quiet. "Tell you what, you put your bags away and we'll have coffee together and plan something for supper." The girls smiled weakly and left to put away their bags.

Sean put out some mugs, cream and honey on the table. He found some oatmeal cookies in the cookie jar and arranged them on a plate. The three girls came back with dower looks on their faces and stood facing him. His heart broke for them. "Come here," he beckoned with open arms. They came together in a group hug. "I know you're scared but try not to worry," he spoke softly. "It will be strange at first but be patient and be yourselves. You will be safe with your new families and you'll learn to love each other. Reina and I will be right here if you ever need us." He paused, "Lord, please help these girls to be strong and teach them to trust You. Now, let's sit and have our coffee and figure out what to cook for supper." The girls smiled and took their seats at the table.

Reina arrived in the motor home at four o'clock. She had stopped to fill up the fuel tank and announced her arrival with a brief blast of the air horn. Halina, Celina and Irenka went ahead of Sean to greet Reina and their sisters. They were anxious to reunite and share about their first airplane ride. Sean embraced his wife then helped unload the vehicle as the girls hauled their bags into the house. "Supper is in the oven," he said to Reina, "should be ready in an hour."

"What's for dessert?" she teased him.

The girls sought out their previous sleeping spots and left their duffle bags before assembling in the living room eager to share their travelling experience. Sean and Reina sat at the kitchen table. "We're meeting with the families tomorrow at the church. Immigration vetted and approved all Ray's choices and so did I. They are all quality families Reina and I know you'll agree," he sighed. "The girls are still scared but what else can we do."

Reina reached across the table and held his hands in hers while looking into his eyes. "Nothing, we have to leave them in the Lord's hands and trust in Him. Let's pray."

Anya and Halina set the dining room table after Sean installed the extension pieces. Celina and Irenka arranged the food in serving bowls and placed them on the table. When all was ready Sean invited everyone to take a seat. He asked Halina to invoke the blessing and he wasn't disappointed. She concluded by acknowledging her confidence that God would continue take care of her and her sisters.

Chapter 72

Ray scheduled the meeting for ten in the morning. The motor home pulled into the church parking lot at 9:45 full of anxious young women and all their possessions. Most of the foster families had already arrived. They milled about seeking reassurance from one another in their own anxiety over what was about to happen. Ray and Nancy had prayed for days over how to pair the girls with their family. On a wall, they pinned 5x7 photographs of each girl above the name of the family she would join. In three cases, families had agreed to take two girls.

The girls entered the room looking at the faces looking back at them. They recognized most of them from the wedding. Some families stood with their children including some with teenagers who the girls had previously met at the wedding. Ray got everyone's attention and gave a short introduction reiterating the purpose behind placing the girls with different families. The nervous girls crowded close to Sean and Reina as they waited.

Ray asked the foster families to invite their assigned girl or girls to join them. He and Nancy placed Celina and Irenka together with the Thompson family whose children were no longer at home but lived in Whitehorse. Natusza, and Izabella would live with the Roberts family and their teenage daughter Tahlia. Luiza joined the Jackson family; Ron Jackson and his teenage son Jeremy coincidentally belonged to the same shotgun club as Reina. Halina stood beside Lorna Scroggins, her husband Jason and their teenage daughter Sophia. Lorna owned the flower shop in town. The Wilson's stood beside Tekla. They had spent some time together at the wedding sharing their mutual interest in shooting. Jerry and Anne Wilson lived out of town, they still had two pre-teen children at home who they homeschooled. They were both handgunners. Ray and Nancy believed that Roza was the right fit for the Wagner family and it became clear that they were correct. Roza was already busy conversing with the Wagners and their 13-year-old daughter Becky. Danuta and Brygida joined Ray and Nancy. Their daughter Nanette was ecstatic over having two older sisters in their home.

Anya stood beside her father, her arm wrapped around his. Kazia and Reina stood together with their arms around each other's waist. They watched the girls relaxing as they talked with their new families. Ray and Nancy looked pleased at what they were seeing. Ray called for quiet, "I would like to pray for us as we embark on a new season in your lives. Be assured that God is in this and He will accomplish His purposes in us. Trust Him." All bowed their heads as Ray prayed over them. When he was done he turned to Sean and Reina, "Do you two want to add anything?"

"We are so grateful for you offering to take our beloved girls into your homes," Reina said.

Sean added, "Please take special care of these precious lives that have become so much a part of us. May they endear themselves to you and your families as they have done to us. Thank you." He turned to his own family, "What do you say we take a drive and have lunch at Spirit Lake? I think God has everything under control here." Anya and Kazia shrugged their shoulders, open to try whatever their Dad had in mind.

"I like that idea," said Reina, "a little alone time wouldn't hurt any of us. Do you girls like pierogis?"

"Really? They make varenyky here?" Anya and Kazia were beside themselves with joy. "Yes, we like very much, they are very Polish food."

After farewell hugs and words of encouragement to their sisters, they joined their parents in the parking lot. "We'll pick up Reina's Jeep, then I want to drop the motor home at Bob's on our way."

Sean and Reina sat in the front seat holding hands as they drove south to the lake sharing happy thoughts over their new circumstances and dreaming of their futures. Anya and Kazia sat silently in the back seat looking out the windows at the land that had become their new home. Their gaze periodically shifted to the couple in the front seats as if to verify that they were still there, the parents who loved them and promised never to leave them.

They felt secure in their new home and relationships but the future, like all futures, was uncertain. The peace they now enjoyed allowed exploratory thoughts about what God might have in store for them. Both were apprehensive about entering the community in which they now found themselves fearing the culture shock that most certainly would touch their young lives. The teen years were awkward enough without the added stress of trying to fit in but, thanks to Sean and Reina, they were secure in the knowledge of who they were. They had learned much about Canadian society during their months at the lodge and during their brief time in Whitehorse but they knew that their acculturation was only beginning. Sean and Reina were sensitive to their feelings and needs and excursions like this one were welcome, especially under the umbrella of their caring parents.

Sean turned off the Carcross Road and parked in front of the small building sitting at the side of Spirit Lake. The long, thin lake now covered in ice and snow sat at the base of a steep mountain slope. Sean explained to the girls how it got its name and dared them to shout at the mountain to see if the 'spirit' shouted back. They both giggled, unsure of whether to try it or not and debating over what to shout. Anya cupped her hands in front of her mouth and shouted her name. She smiled at her Dad as a faint echo returned. The effect was more dramatic in the summer when there was no snow to absorb the sound waves. Kazia mimicked her sister delighting in the echo of her name. Sean shouted, "What's for lunch?" Anya answered her father and the 'spirit' shouted, *"varenyky!"*

Over lunch, the conversation settled on what the girls had been thinking now that they were settling into their new home and family arrangement. They confessed that they would miss each other now they were getting their own bedroom but promised to get over it. Anya expressed her desire to learn to drive and to fly Sean's airplane. Kazia was less interested but she thought it would be good to learn to drive a car. Sean promised to look into driving lessons when he and Reina returned from Hawaii. Both expressed concern about being alone while Sean and Reina were working. Reina laughed, "Sean doesn't work! He plays." Sean mocked her laugh and told the girls to ignore her.

"Have you thought anymore about going to school?" Reina asked. Kazia seemed most keen on the idea but was unsure whether she was capable of learning the curriculum. She wanted to know how she would get to and from school and how many students would be in the class. Reina assured her that the classes were usually small, only 15 to 20 students and that either she or Sean would drive her to and from school at least at first.

Sean told Kazia that she was a natural student and while at the Lodge he was often amazed at her capacity to learn and reason. "You will have no difficulty my dear," he spoke reassuringly. "You speak good English, you love to read and you formulate your thoughts well before making statements. I have full confidence in you Kazia."

Reina added, "It will be different at first and it will take a little time to get comfortable but you will do fine Kazia. I hope you decide to do it. What about you Anya?"

Anya was listening. "I would just like to work at a job but I think if I went to school it would be better. I would be with others my own age and I would learn more about being a Canadian and living in the Yukon. I think I would make some friends too. It is so good to be free."

Sean and Reina were pleased with what they were hearing. They too thought it would be a good move for the girls to complete the high school program. It would allow them to become more comfortable in their new environment, build their confidence and give them time to think about other options. If they chose to carry on in school, they would have that option and if they decided to enter the workforce, they would be much better prepared.

"School won't start for a couple more weeks but if you want you can come to the College with me tomorrow and I'll show you around. I have to meet with my boss about my spring classes." Reina smiled.

The girls looked at each other and nodded enthusiastically. "Yes, that would be fun and it would be good for Kazia to see the school and the class-rooms," Anya replied excitedly.

"Good. After breakfast we'll go. Sean has to meet with Ray and Nancy then his friend at immigration. Maybe we could meet for lunch at the Roadhouse afterwards?" Reina looked at Sean.

"Sounds good to me. What do you say I invite Ray and Nancy and Danuta and Brygida to join us? After all, you'll be spending some time with them while we're away."

Anya pouted at the thought of the upcoming separation from their parents. "Can't we come with you guys? We'll be miserable without you around and nobody will want to be with us. What if we die? How would that make you feel?" Her drama was well crafted but transparent.

"Oh, quit being so silly. You're not going to die and you won't be miser-able. You'll probably forget all about us in a few days." Reina tried to override the emotions with some reason.

Anya's face reddened in defiance. "Forget about you!" she exclaimed attracting the attention of the waitress. "We will *never* forget about you. We will miss you!"

Reina turned to her husband hoping for rescue. "And, yes, we will miss you both very much but you can't come. End of discussion." Sean's eyes emphasized their position on the matter.

Chapter 73

Their 'real' honeymoon on Hawaii's garden island suited them both. This time they had an entire 12 days together almost without interruption. For three days they managed to keep their erratic but persistent thoughts to themselves thinking they would fade away. Hoping they would.

During dinner at a nearby restaurant, Sean wondered aloud how their two daughters were doing. Reina offered no comment. "Do you think about them Reina?" he asked.

"Always!" she confessed laying down her knife and fork and locking her eyes with Sean's. "I can't keep them out of my mind; they're always there, sometimes more than at other times. But, don't' worry, I always leave room for you."

"Thanks, you're a sweetheart. I'm glad I'm not alone with my thoughts. I really miss them Reina. I know it's only been three days." He shook his head and took a sip from his cocktail. "Don't' get me wrong, I am thoroughly enjoying our time together."

She reached across the table and held his hand in hers. "So am I Sean, but I can't help missing our two daughters, they have become such a part of us. Sometimes I wish they could be here to share in our fun. Well, some of our fun."

Sean laughed and squeezed her hand. "Love you girl." Had Reina just sent him a coded message?

They finished their meal on the patio beneath Tiki lamps and palm trees enveloped in the warm tropical evening. They walked back to their two-bedroom, spacious ground level condo along lamp-lit paths that wound through tropical vegetation. Sean fixed them each a tall, rum-based fruit drink and they retired to their patio a couple of hundred feet from the beach.

"You slap me if I'm crazy to even mention this." Sean's tone was serious but humble. "What do you think about flying the girls over for the rest of our time here?"

Reina smiled at her husband who was preparing to dodge incoming. "I don't think you're crazy. That's why I married you - you have such great ideas."

They both laughed and squeezed hands across the table. "I'm going to call Ray right now; it's still afternoon in Whitehorse."

"You know that now we won't be able to sleep tonight," Reina admonished him.

"Really. Maybe we can come up with something to do so we don't get bored." his smile teased.

Reina was right, neither of them slept except for a brief period before the sunrise.

* * *

Their flight was due at 8:35 that morning. Sean showered then dressed and made coffee. Reina wasn't far behind sharing his excitement at seeing their girls again. They sat on the patio listening to the birds singing, content with their decision. Together they talked over coffee about what they wanted to do when the girls arrived. "I hope they'll be okay during their travels," said Reina. "I don't like the idea of them alone at the Vancouver airport between flights."

"Ray talked to the agent and made sure that the girls got VIP treatment especially during the layover in Vancouver." He wanted to reassure Reina. "He said Amanda was on duty southbound so they were in good hands. She would manage the handoff at YVR putting the girls up in the lounge until their connecting flight."

"I'm so glad Ray was able to get seats. This is a busy time of year for travel to Hawaii." Reina noticed Sean looking a little sheepish. "What did you do?"

"You're right, there weren't any spaces left," he confessed, "except in first class."

Reina put down her coffee cup and glared at him. "You didn't?" Sean cowered. "No more toys for you this year!"

Sean and Reina watched through the large glass windows in the arrivals lounge. The girls were part of the first group to disembark on the air stairs. They each carried a daypack, their heads swivelling trying to take in their surroundings while anxiously looking for the familiar faces of their parents. Two Hawaiian women, arms ladened with leis, placed fragrant lei over each girl's neck and gave them each a welcome kiss on the cheek.

Sean caught Anya off guard. She didn't see him come in from her side. He lifted her off her feet as he swung her around in a welcoming hug. Kazia got the same treatment before Reina was able to join in the welcome. The girls jumped up and down in excitement repeatedly hugging and kissing their parents while prattling about their surprise trip. They had no luggage so Sean herded his family through the crowd and into the parking lot where he had parked their bright yellow rental Jeep.

Anya begged her mother to let her sit with her Dad in the front seat – she won. The drive back to the condo would take less than 15 minutes. Anya and Kazia revelled in the warm air blowing through their hair in the open Jeep. "What a beautiful place is this," she effused. "Thank you for letting us come here. We missed you so much." She and Kazia had grins from ear to ear as they locked arms with the parent next to them. Neither showed any sign of fatigue from the long flight.

Alani was finishing putting their condo back in order when they arrived. She had become friends with Sean and Reina. They met her and her brother at the nearby Hawaiian church. Reina introduced her daughters to Alani who was two years older than the girls. They made an immediate connection.

Anya invited her to join them for supper after clearing the offer with her parents. It was evident that Anya's offer surprised Alani but she graciously accepted. Sean stepped in and told Alani to bring her brother along if he was free. Alani lived with her brother Kana who worked in a local scuba shop. Their mother had died of cancer five years earlier. They never knew their father who abandoned the family when they were very young. They had no other family.

The girls had breakfast before landing so Sean poured them each a cup of coffee while he and Reina picked at a large plate of sliced fruit in the centre of the table. They spent the next hour listening to their daughters recount their journey and the experiences they enjoyed along the way.

Neither girl had clothing appropriate for the climate so they decided to go shopping. Afterwards, Sean suggested they go to lunch at a nearby hotel with a patio restaurant on the beach. While they discussed plans for the day, Reina retrieved a tube of SPF 30 suntan lotion. She educated the girls on the power of the sun at that latitude and the importance of protecting their fair skin. Their jeans and long-sleeved blouses provided ample protection for now. Anya loved the coconut fragrance of the lotion and needed no further urging to apply it to her minimally exposed skin.

The girls, dressed in flip-flops, white shorts and short sleeve blouses, attracted attention wherever they went. Their bleached white skin and fashion sunglasses branded them as tourists but their admirers didn't seem to care. They felt self-conscious in the midst of so many brown-skinned natives and other bronzed bodies. Reina encouraged them that they would all have nice tans before they left.

The maître d' at the restaurant greeted Reina and the girls with hibiscus blossoms. He placed them in their hair then offered to take a photo of the family. Sean kibitzed that they would be back in a week for another photo only with tanned bodies. He showed them to their table at the edge of the covered patio overlooking the bay. Rather than the menu, the girls focused on the surfers lying on their boards in their colourful board shorts waiting for the next wave. Mahi-mahi was the special as usual just like veal cutlets in the Yukon. Sean chose the Lau Lau with Hawaiian salt listed as the other special. He didn't want to spoil their appetites for the supper he planned with Alani and Kana as their guests.

After lunch, the foursome drove up the island to see the sights and learn about the garden isle of Hawaii. They stopped at beaches along the route to wade in the warm ocean water and get some sun while watching the wind surfers off shore. By mid afternoon they were back at the condo where the girls tried on the various outfits they bought, modeling them for their parents. Sean particularly liked the sundresses the girls chose but the more elegant full length dresses were the ones they planned to wear to dinner. Neither girl had ever owned a bathing suit so Reina coached them on appropriate styles steering them away from the string bikinis. Both had chosen brightly patterned, one-piece suits that modestly flattered their figures. Sean could see that they were shy about showing them off so he tried not to pay a lot of attention while still complimenting them on their choices.

Alani and Kana arrived at the condo on time. Alani was dressed in a long floral-pattern dress hanging on one shoulder. A bright yellow hibiscus garnished her thick, dark Hawaiian hair that hung below her shoulders. Kana, dressed in white slacks and flowered Hawaiian shirt, thanked Sean and Reina for inviting him and Alani. Sean introduced him to Anya and Kazia. He was Alani's younger brother by a year, close to the same age as Anya and Kazia. Kana, visibly taken by Anya's beauty, tried unsuccessfully to avoid staring at her.

They walked along the Tiki torch-lit paths to the five-star restaurant that Sean had chosen to celebrate his bride and the arrival of his daughters. Along the way, Kana stopped the party and offered to replace the flowers in the hair of the three women with fresh ones he had just picked. He reserved Anya for last. Facing her, he removed the wilting hibiscus blossom, "You are much too beautiful to wear that old flower. Allow me." The dim light hid Anya's reddening face. Sean and Reina exchanged smiles.

The maître d' escorted the group to a table set apart from the other diners and with a view of the ocean. He must have sensed the attraction between Anya and Kana as he sat them together across from Sean and Reina. Anya, for once, seemed tongue-tied choosing to bury her face in the menu as they awaited their drink orders. Kana took his cue offering to explain the different dishes while helping Anya to pronounce their names. Kana leaned close to Anya as he inspected her menu and pointed to the different offerings. At one point Anya turned to face him and they almost bumped noses.

The warm tropical night made it easy to linger long over their meal and conversation. Anya and Kazia listened intently as Alani and her brother shared stories of growing up in a small village on the Island. The villagers cared for them after they lost their mother until they were old enough to take jobs in Lihue. Alani was proud of her brother who managed the Scuba shop and one day hoped to own the business. Anya and Kazia were curious about Scuba diving so Kana happily explained the sport and invited the family to come by and try it out. The look on the girl's faces told Sean and Reina that they should take up Kana's offer.

The next morning they drove to the Scuba shop where Kana and his staff were finishing outfitting a group of tourists for a day on the reef. Kana waved when he saw them drive up and walked over to meet them. "Good morning," he smiled, his gaze lingering on Anya. "Come on over and we'll get the theory lesson over before we go to the lagoon. Do you girls know how to swim?"

"A little," they replied looking at each other with some apprehension. Neither girl had even owned her own bathing suit until yesterday.

"Not a problem. I guess the water is a little hard most of the year in the Yukon," he laughed. "This is just an introduction but we'll have you swimming in no time. I understand that you and Reina are certified already," he looked to Sean and Reina.

"Yes but we want to tag along if that's okay," Sean replied.

"No problem. Happy to have you. Have you all got T-shirts?"

"No, we didn't bring any with us. Why?" answered Reina.

"The sun. A T-shirt will help protect their back and shoulders from burning. No problem, with this free lesson you all get free T-shirts," he laughed.

Kana spent the next hour familiarizing the girls with the equipment they would be using and going over safety measures and basic hand signals. When he was done he got each one a T-shirt, fins and mask with snorkel. One of his helpers loaded the tanks, regulators and weight belts onto a small trailer hitched to a quad and the group walked down to the beach. He first introduced the girls to snorkelling. They stayed in a calm part of the lagoon where they saw lots of fish. Here they practiced diving and clearing their snorkel when surfacing. Returning to shore, he, Sean, and Reina helped the girls into their scuba gear. They practiced breathing through the regulator before they got into the water. Sean took photos of the girls in their outfits. Kana led them into the lagoon where they sat on the sand underwater and practiced breathing with their strange equipment. When they were comfortable, he led them toward the reef. Sean and Reina followed. Kana used his underwater camera to take photos of the girls feeding the fish.

Although they only spent a little over an hour in the water, the girls were ecstatic with the experience. They thanked Kana for showing them how to Scuba dive and promised to learn how to swim before they came again. He printed off certificates for each of them to keep as mementos of their introduction to Scuba diving. "I give swimming lessons too you know," he offered. Anya looked at her Dad seeking approval to accept the offer.

Sean nodded, "How about later in the afternoon Kana?"

"That will work nicely. Say around three?"

Anya and Kazia both leaped with delight, clapping their hands in anticipation.

Chapter 74

The men in suits walked towards where the family sat on the patio having a light lunch. Reina motioned to Sean whose back was to the men, "We have some visitors."

Sean turned and stood to greet the strangers. One looked Hawaiian, the other Asian. Both men flashed badges identifying themselves as FBI agents. "Is this young lady your daughter sir?" The Asian agent nodded toward Anya.

"Yes. Is there a problem?" Sean moved closer to Anya.

"We have a warrant for the arrest of Anya Carson. Are you Anya Carson?" The Asian man addressed Anya.

"Yes, but I haven't done anything," replied Anya before looking to her Dad. Her hands began shaking as she rose from her chair and stood beside Sean hanging onto his arm.

"What are you talking about? She hasn't done anything. Why would you arrest her? Let me see your ID again."

The agents produced their badges once again for Sean to view. The Hawaiian held the warrant that they were serving so Sean could read it. Sean examined each item carefully. Anya clung tightly to her father's arm, her face flushed with fear. "Murder? Are you nuts! That guy tried to murder *us*. She defended us. The police didn't lay any charges. It was self-defence."

"Sir, she is alleged to have murdered a US national. We are only serving the warrant and taking your daughter into custody. The court will adjudicate the case. You can make representation before the judge."

Reina had joined her daughter and held Anya tightly in her arms. "You can't take her! She didn't do anything wrong. What's going on?"

The Hawaiian agent took handcuffs from the pouch under his jacket and approached Anya as he recited her rights. Sean stopped the agent by moving into his path. He stared into the man's eyes. The agent met his glare, "Sir, you don't want to do this. If you try to obstruct us we will be forced to arrest you as well." Sean didn't move at first, then stepped aside and let the agent pass.

"Dad!" Anya screamed, "Don't let them take me Dad. I didn't do anything wrong."

The agent pulled Anya away from Sean and Reina by her arm and began putting the handcuffs on her. She stood unmoving, bound in steel; tears flowed like a tropical rainstorm. She pleaded for the men to let her go, gulping for air between deep sobs. Her family tried to comfort her. "She will be held in custody at the courthouse until her detention hearing on Friday. Depending on the outcome of that hearing, she will be transferred to Anchorage, Alaska. There, she will remain in custody pending a preliminary hearing and possible Grand Jury. You can visit her at the court house during normal visiting hours." The agent led her away.

Sean, Reina and Kazia stood staring at the two men leading Anya away. She was looking over her shoulder, eyes pleading for rescue. They loaded her into the back seat of a car and drove away. Sean slumped into a chair. The defeat and helplessness he felt inflamed his anger to the point of catatonic rage. That old feeling of guilt assaulted him once again. He clenched his fists. *"No! This is Your problem Lord, I'm only Your servant. Tell me what You want me to do. She's in Your hands, not mine,"* he thought. He reached out and drew his wife and daughter close to him. "Try not to worry. She's safe in God's care."

Alani had heard Anya's cries and arrived with her housekeeping trolley. Stunned by the scene on the patio, she ran over to the family to learn what had happened. Sean looked up at her confused and inquiring face. "I need a lawyer Alani. The best and I need him now."

"I will call our pastor. He will know who to call. What has happened Sean? Where is Anya?"

"Anya has been arrested. It's a long story. I need a lawyer Alani. Please call your pastor and if your church has a prayer chain, pray for Anya."

Alani ran into the condo and called her pastor. Sean hugged what was left of his family. "It's going to be okay," he murmured, "Anya is so scared. Let's pray."

Alani rejoined them. "The lawyer will call here in a few minutes. Your family is on the prayer chain."

"Where is the courthouse Alani? Is it far from here?" Sean asked.

"Oh no, 10 minutes in your Jeep. I can give you directions."

"Reina, Kazia, look at me. Everything will be okay. I need you to drive to the courthouse and stay as close to Anya as they will let you. She needs to know we're near her. Find out what you can. I'll wait here until the lawyer calls then I'll join you. Can you do that?" Reina and Kazia nodded. The phone rang as they hugged one another.

Sean left the others and went to answer the phone. "Hello, this is Sean Carson."

"Sean, this is Burton James. Pastor Jim asked me to call you. He said it was urgent. What can I do for you Sean?"

Sean spent the next few minutes explaining what had just happened. He only hinted at the incident at the White River Lodge suggesting that they meet and he would explain more fully.

"I will meet you at your condo in a few minutes. Stay put and don't worry. I might be bringing a colleague with me." He hung up and dialed another number.

* * *

Anya sat on the steel mesh bench in the bare cell. They had taken her clothes and dressed her in orange coveralls. She sobbed quietly as she poured out her heart in prayer. "I'm tired God. Will I ever be free? You seem to give me moments of pure joy with people I love and who love me then I am dragged away again to one kind of prison or another. Please God, loose my bonds, set me free. I would rather be dead than to live my life as a prisoner." She fell on her side and curled into the fetal position as her body convulsed with sobs. As she lay there, she thought of her Lord, His capture, imprisonment, torture, death and resurrection. *"What was true freedom,"* she thought. The passage from Galatians came to her mind, *"It was for freedom that Christ set us free; therefore keep standing firm and do not be subject again to a yoke of slavery."* Yes, despite her circumstances, she was free; He had come *"to set the captives free."* She would forever trust God for her life. She sat up and leaned against the concrete wall. Her lips parted and smiled as her tongue tasted the salt of her tears.

* * *

Sean poured himself a large glass of Scotch and fell onto the couch. "What is going on? Hasn't this girl been through enough? God, I don't understand. I need your help. Anya needs your help. Let her know that you're with her Lord, and Lord, while you're at it, give this lawyer all he needs to get Anya out of this mess. Thanks, I trust You."

A tall man in expensive casual slacks and a flowered sport shirt stepped onto the patio followed by another in shorts, a tee shirt and sandals. The tall man looked like a middle-aged athlete with sandy hair and a deep tan. The other man was shorter, dressed even more casually, like a surfer. He was of a similar age and equally fit looking. The tall man waved at Sean through the patio doors. Sean walked out and greeted the men, motioning for them to take a seat at the patio table. "Sean, I'm Burton James. Call me BJ. This is my friend from Honolulu, Sam Gervais." The shorter man extended a hand that Sean eagerly grasped and shook. "Sam's on vacation but the Lord may have put him here for a time such as this. Sam is an international criminal lawyer."

Sam leaned forward and looked into Sean's eyes. "Even though I'm on vacation Sean I want you to know that I will help any way I can. I need to hear the details behind what just happened. I understand that your 17 year old daughter has been arrested for a murder that she allegedly committed in the Yukon, Canada?" He queried Sean with his eyes.

Sean sighed and sat back in his chair. "Will this ever end? Will she ever know peace in her life?" he mumbled as he stared at the waves breaking on the beach. He turned and faced Sam. "This is a long story Sam but I'm getting pretty good at telling it. I'll give you the short version up until when the so-called murder took place, then I'll fill you in with the details. Ask any questions you have along the way." Sean related the story from the beginning providing details about the day the man came to the Lodge on the White and tried to re-capture the girls. He made sure he understood what Anya had done and what the police had concluded.

Sam listened, watching Sean relate the events surrounding Anya's life in the Yukon. His eyebrows arched when he heard how she had shot the man at the Lodge. "How many witnesses were there to the shooting?" he asked.

"Sixteen, not counting Anya," Sean replied. "The police took statements from everyone. I don't know if they looked into the background of the guy. He was from Fairbanks, Alaska as far as I know."

"Sixteen witnesses?" Sam was incredulous. "Who was in charge of the investigation?"

"Matt Dawson. He's the sergeant based at the Whitehorse RCMP detachment."

Sam sat in silence thinking about what he had just heard. After a few minutes he said, "Sean, I think I know what's going on here. This may simply be the action of an overzealous federal prosecutor, possibly abetted by an incompetent law clerk. Why he would try and pull such a stunt, especially on a minor, is beyond me. It has to be a mistake. You think this dead guy was involved in organized crime?"

"Yes. I think the entire series of events surrounding the kidnapping of these girls is sponsored by organized crime operating out of Alaska. Do you think they are behind this?"

"No I don't, but, if you decide to retain my services, I will be looking into the possibility. I think this is simply an incredibly stupid and naive action by some junior prosecutor and his staff."

"Stupid or not, is this a legitimate arrest? Can they actually arrest Anya for something that happened in Canada and for which she was exonerated?" Sean was desperate to understand how this could happen.

Sam watched Sean trembling in his confusion and helplessness. "Under international criminal law it *is* possible. Unusual, but possible. Under what we call the 'the passive personality principle' the state may look to the nationality of a victim to determine jurisdiction. It may assert jurisdiction over persons and events outside the state's territory on the basis that its citizen has been harmed. I think that's what is happening here. A warrant has been issued for Anya's arrest but it can only be served on US soil. Unhappily, you chose to vacation in the USA which makes her vulnerable. I need to do some research to find out what exactly is going on."

"Please, do whatever you have to. My daughter has already been traumatized beyond what any youngster should ever have to endure. It is only by God's grace that she has endured and thrived this far. I want to retain you Sam. Sorry to spoil your vacation."

Sam laughed. "I'm concerned for your daughter Sean; she is my priority. I will call my office and get them working on this. BJ, can you drive us to the courthouse?"

Chapter 75

Reina and Kazia greeted him at the door of the courthouse. "They won't let us see her yet. It might be another hour."

BJ came over and Sean introduced him to his family. "We want you to know that we are already working on Anya's situation. The good news is that the Lord got here before us. My good friend over there," he pointed to Sam who was talking to someone at the counter, "is an international criminal lawyer. I know he doesn't look like one but he's on vacation. His staff in Honolulu are already working on the case. Try not to worry."

The four of them sat in the lobby waiting for permission to see Anya and watching Sam as he spoke with different people. After half an hour, Sam joined them. Sean introduced him to Reina and Kazia. "I'm waiting to see the judge who will oversee her detention hearing. I'll try to get her released before the hearing."

"Mr. Gervais?" The woman at the counter called out to him. He quickly excused himself, turned and walked back to the counter.

"The judge will see you now sir." She invited him to follow her.

Another half hour passed before Sam reappeared with the judge. She was a short, attractive Hawaiian woman dressed casually but not as casual as Sam. The two of them approached Sean and his family. She smiled as Sam introduced her.

Her voice was soft, full of compassion as she spoke, "I am so sorry that your daughter has been taken into custody. Sam and I agree that there is good reason to believe that this is all a mistake and I know he will do his utmost to uncover the details. While he is working on the case, I am issuing a release order for your daughter. Sam has agreed to be her custodian."

"Oh thank you judge!" Reina clasped her hands in relief. "Does that mean she doesn't have to go to Alaska?"

The judge looked at Sam before answering, "That will depend on what Sam discovers."

"When can we see her," asked Reina.

"Very soon. She is changing out of her prison clothes now."

"Anya!" Kazia let out a whoop and ran into the arms of her sister as she appeared from behind a steel door. Sean and Reina, close behind, raced to join in the group hug. Anya wept in her relief as she melted into the embrace of her family.

"Let's get out of here," Sean ordered, "but, Anya, first you need to meet your lawyers."

Sean led Anya over to the two men and introduced her. Their hearts went out to the young girl who greeted them with red eyes, dishevelled hair and a dejected countenance. Both men encouraged her to be patient and to pray.

Sam turned to Sean. "I will call you tomorrow morning Sean. I should know a lot more by then. We can only do so much at the moment with the time difference."

"And I'll drop by your condo in the morning if that's okay?" asked BJ.

"We'll have the coffee on BJ," said Sean, "thanks for everything."

"Thank you for helping me," Anya addressed the two lawyers as she leaned weakly into her father's embrace.

* * *

Anya rode in the back of the Jeep comforted by her mother's embrace. She was exhausted. Her emotions had almost expired and her mind was too tired to think. Sleep would be a welcome relief but for now, she rested in her family's love and care, a gift that she knew came from God.

"I just want to go to bed. Is that okay?" she looked at her Mom and Dad for approval.

"Come with me," said Reina as she led her to her room. The two of them lay on the bed in each other's arms until Reina could hear her daughter's metered breathing confirming she was asleep. Reina gently slipped off the bed and shut the door on her way to the patio where Sean and Kazia waited.

"She's sleeping."

Chapter 76

Sean didn't sleep. He paced the beach all night, praying aloud for Anya and the two lawyers. Prayer was the only answer to his own impotence in the circumstances. *"Trials do indeed test your faith,"* he thought. He thought of the three men facing the fiery furnace. They trusted God no matter what happened. Could he?

He sat with his back against a palm tree watching the sunrise. *"It was Reina,"* he thought. He could tell by the rhythm of her steps as she approached from behind the tree. She sat beside him and handed him a cup of coffee as she kissed him on the neck. "You okay?"

"Yeah. Been praying. Feel so helpless otherwise. Why does she have to go through this? Every time she gets a break, something else happens. Leave my girl alone Satan!" he shouted into the dawn, "You don't know who you're messin' with."

Reina put her arm around his shoulders and leaned close. "Lord, you know how helpless we feel. You know our love for Anya and we know Your love for her. Please Lord, set her free from this latest captor and flood her with Your peace. Help us all to trust You and to rest in You no matter what the outcome."

Sean and Reina both turned at the sound of footsteps. It was Anya. "Good morning Mom and Dad. Isn't this just the most beautiful sunrise. Did you sleep well? I sure did." She wedged herself between her parents sitting on the sand. "Everything is going to be fine – don't worry. I love you."

Sean and Reina leaned into their daughter, each taking a hand in theirs. "Yes, sweet girl, everything will be fine. We love you."

* * *

BJ arrived at eight. The two girls ate their breakfast together in the condo while Sean and Reina talked with BJ over coffee on the patio. Their story fascinated him. He asked a lot of questions and made a point of reminding them of how God had brought them through considerable trials already.

It was close to nine when Sam appeared on the path leading to the condo. He joined them on the patio. "Good morning folks," he smiled brightly as if he didn't have a care in the world. Thought we should meet in person instead of by phone. Where's Anya?" he looked around and spotted her and her sister in the condo. "Why don't you bring them over? They are going to want to hear the news." Sam knew more than he would share but he wanted to encourage his clients as much as he could without giving them false hope.

Sean and Reina smiled at each other in anticipation. "I'll get them," said Sean as he sprinted for the open patio door. "Anya, Kazia, come and join us. Sam has some news."

The two girls slid off their stools and pranced onto the patio where they greeted their guests. "You seem to be in much better spirits today Anya," observed Sam.

"Oh yes Mr. Gervais. I know how much I am loved and I trust God with my life. I think He sent you to help me. You might even be an angel Mr. Gervais but you don't fool me."

Sam laughed loudly as the others joined in. "An angel! Well, you must be sure to tell my wife about that when you meet her."

Sean, anxious to hear the news, interjected, "So what have you found out Sam?"

"Well, I'm sorry to say that the warrant is legitimate and Anya was legally arrested. She will have to attend her detention hearing on Friday." Everyone, except Anya, slumped in despair at the unexpected news. "She could still be sent to Anchorage for a preliminary hearing but I'm hoping to avert that move."

Sean interjected again, "Is this all a mistake or will she have to go to trial?"

Sam didn't answer right away. He was watching Anya who was smiling at him. "I don't understand you young lady. You are unusually composed given your predicament."

"I have an angel fighting for me. There is nothing to worry about. Besides, I've never been to Anchorage."

Reina and Sean shot her angry glances.

Sam smiled back at her then turned to answer Sean. "Let's call it an error in judgement. As I said, the warrant is legitimate but the circumstances underlying it are questionable. I am of the opinion that the presentation of the facts of the matter was deficient. In fact, the facts may have been mis-represented, albeit unintentionally. My staff are in the process of vetting my suspicions."

"So what's next?" asked Reina.

"Let me finish," urged Sam. "We have to be cognizant of the personalities involved in this matter. If I am correct, then we must tread softly and allow the perpetrator to save face gracefully. Lawyer's egos can be daunting. We don't want to incite retaliation by carelessly challenging a poor decision."

"What a crock!" exploded Sean. "My daughter goes to prison because we might hurt some feelings!"

Reina reached for his arm pulling him back into his chair. "Stop it Sean! Sam knows what needs to happen. Let him do his job."

Sean's outburst surprised Sam. He responded in a modulated voice, "You surprised me Sean, but I shouldn't be surprised. You are Anya's father and I understand your anger over this situation. I am with you Sean and with

God's help we'll get your daughter back. Let me try things my way first. If we fail then I am quite prepared to play hardball and I have the team to do it."

The phone rang. Reina left to answer it. "It's for you Sam." Sam excused himself and went to take the call.

"I'm such an ass sometimes," Sean confessed before his family and BJ. "Please forgive my outburst." He looked at Anya. She smiled at him but said nothing.

Sam returned a few minutes later and took his seat. "That was my office."

Sean interrupted, "I'm sorry Sam. I was out of line. Please forgive me and do your job. If it happens again follow my wife's lead and tell me to shut up." He leaned over and kissed Reina. "Thank you dear."

"You're forgiven Sean," said Sam, "Now let's get on with this business. My staff tell me that my suspicions are well founded. The judge who issued the warrant didn't have all the facts. They are putting together a new brief that contains *all* the facts. You want to see Anchorage Anya? You will get your chance. Can you be ready to go later this evening?"

Chapter 77

The Astra SPX business-class jet sat on the tarmac, its navigation lights glowing in the tropical night. It was after midnight when Sam ushered Anya and Sean onboard. He and his executive assistant followed. The co-pilot pulled the door shut and rotated the locking lever. She welcomed all onboard and gave a brief pre-flight briefing before returning to the cockpit.

Anya looked at Sean seated next to her as the engines started. He smiled and gave her hand a squeeze. She squeezed back but neither said a word. Reina and Anya had gone shopping for an outfit appropriate for meeting and seeking the favour of a federal prosecutor and possibly a federal judge. Reina selected tailored navy blue slacks, a brocaded white blouse and a short wool jacket for her daughter. She loaned Anya her string of pearls and pearl bracelet. For now, she travelled in jeans and a sweatshirt reserving her new outfit for their arrival in Anchorage. Her navy blue, wool pea coat hung in the suit rack with coats and jackets belonging to the rest of Sam's entourage. It was still winter. She relaxed and felt the rich leather seat hug her torso as the jet lunged down the runway and launched into Hawaiian airspace.

* * *

The chime announced that they would be landing in half an hour. Anya rubbed her eyes, unbuckled her seatbelt and sought out the restroom. When she returned, she tapped Sam on the shoulder before taking her seat. "Is this okay?" She turned in place so Sam could pass judgement on her outfit.

Sam turned to Rebecca, his EA, seeking her counsel. "I think that will be just fine Anya. Don't you agree Sam?" Sam nodded his agreement.

Sean leaned over as Anya took her seat. "Good morning my dear. You look great. How are you feeling?"

"Oh I'm feeling fine Dad. I had a good sleep and I am excited about our meetings. I know that God is with us. Don't worry Dad, everything will work out."

It was still dark when they touched down at the Anchorage International Airport. "We'll go for breakfast at the Hilton," said Sam, "We've got lots of time before our meeting at ten. I want to go over our plan and make sure you are comfortable with our approach. If all goes well we should be out of here by this afternoon. Let's pray."

The limousine pulled up to the hotel entrance. A doorman opened the car door and Rebecca and Anya stepped onto the pavement. Sam and Sean followed. The foursome made their way across the lobby towards the restaurant. "Good morning Mr. Gervais, Ms Rebecca, nice to see you again. Are you staying with us or just passing through?"

"Good morning Julie. Just here for the day if all goes well. Can you find us a private booth?" The hostess led them to a spacious booth next to the fireplace. "Splendid Julie. Remind me to leave you a tip." Sam laughed along with Julie.

The waitress arrived promptly and poured coffee for everyone. "Do you have real orange juice?" asked Sean.

"Oh yes sir. Squeezed in our kitchen. Would you like a glass?" Sean nodded. "Anyone else?"

After breakfast, Sam asked for everyone's attention. He waited until the waitress topped up their coffee cups and left before speaking. "In a few minutes you will meet a colleague of mine, Gerald Henderson. Gerald and I sometimes work together. He is local and knows the lay of the land and the personalities we will be dealing with. He will brief us on what we are likely to encounter and suggest strategies that will help us achieve our objective." Sam turned to see Gerald coming towards them. He rose and greeted him with a hug and slap on the back. After introductions, Gerald joined the group. The waitress arrived with a cup of coffee and a menu.

"Just coffee. Thanks." He smiled at the server. Gerald was Sam's age, over six feet and built like a football player. He served in Special Forces but retired into the law profession in his hometown. "So you're the reason for all this excitement?" he smiled at Anya, "Pretty good with a handgun I hear."

Anya smiled back as her face began to flush. "My Dad taught me," she said proudly.

"Good job Sean. That's what dads are for, training their kids up to face this world effectively and for God's glory." His eyes locked with Sean's. Sean nodded in affirmation while subtly signalling his acceptance of Gerald as part of their team. "So let me tell you what you're up against."

Gerald spent the next half hour briefing Sam and his team on the pros- ecutor's office and the background of the particular prosecutor who started everything. "Alex Johnson is young and inexperienced for sure. But, he's a good man, ambitious, he wants to do a good job. He does exactly that in most instances. Like the rest of us, he relies on his staff. Sometimes they let us down. Experience can play a key role in sniffing out stuff that ain't right, but without that experience, stuff can get by you. I'm sure that's what hap- pened in this case but you'll have to convince Alex of that. He doesn't want a defective arrest warrant on his record."

Sam and Rebecca were following Gerald's remarks closely, making notes on their legal pads. "I have no doubt that we can provide enough facts to convince Alex that the warrant is defective. It sounds like he might be open to our presentation of those facts. We will essentially do his homework for him and leave it up to him to approach the judge to rescind the warrant. If he comes before the bench with the right attitude he could even score some points for his career."

"I think that approach will work except for one thing. He's not going to want to be burned twice so he'll want to vet your work. Make it easy for him," replied Gerald. "He's not the type to go after his para' but he'll hold her to account. He might even use her, with special oversight, to vet your work just to demonstrate that he hasn't lost confidence in her. Don't go after his assistant or him. Just make your case." He paused and looked at Anya. "I think that bringing Anya with you is brilliant. She will put the icing on the cake. He won't be able to resist taking a second look at the case."

"Will you be coming with us Gerald?" asked Sam.

"No. Actually, you and I have a meeting on the Alberto case after lunch if you can make yourself available. I know it's last minute but the ambassador knows you're here and he's adamant. Besides, you can write off this trip on that case." Gerald smiled.

"I don't think that should be a problem. We'll be having lunch here so pick me up." Sam addressed Gerald then turned to Rebecca. "Rebecca, I'll need you to brief me on the Alberto case. I'm sure enjoying my vacation." Rebecca smiled while the others laughed.

Chapter 78

The receptionist ushered Sam and the others into the conference room. "Mr. Johnson will join you shortly. There is coffee and water on the side table. Please help yourself. Can I get you anything else?"

"Thank you. We'll be fine," said Sam.

Alex Johnson entered the room. He looked younger than his thirty-one years. A tall man, he was dressed immaculately in an expensive, dark blue pin striped suit. He introduced himself and made the rounds shaking hands and smiling at his guests before taking a seat at the head of the table. "I hope you are not suffering unduly from our cold weather. Let's work to get this matter settled so you can get home to those warm tropical breezes." He smiled broadly. "I understand that we have a rather urgent matter before us this morning and I believe I may be responsible for its urgency. Let me be clear, if anything is out of order I want it remedied and I'll do my best to make that happen." He glanced at Anya and smiled with the intent of putting her at ease.

Sam nodded his understanding before addressing the prosecutor, "Thank you Mr. Johnson."

"Alex please. May I reciprocate?"

"Thank you Alex. By all means, we appreciate your gesture," replied Sam as he looked around at his team who were nodding their approval.

"Alex, I sense that you are a man of integrity." Sam made friendly eye contact with Alex. "Of course I checked out your history and it supports my assessment. You have a record attesting to your devotion in getting at the truth through our legal system and bringing justice home to victims and their families."

Alex smiled, "Thank you Sam. I return the compliment. Your record too testifies to your honest diligence in pursuing justice."

Sam scanned the faces of his team then turned back to Alex. "Alex, even though this is the first time I've met you, I trust you. Let me cut to the chase." He paused. "That young lady," he swept his hand towards Anya, "Anya Carson, has been arrested for the alleged murder of a US citizen on Canadian soil. It is our contention that the facts underlying the application for the arrest warrant are deficient and do not accurately describe the events surrounding the matter. We believe the warrant is defective."

The room was silent to the point of awkwardness. Alex stared at Sam. "Show me Sam. What have we missed?" His face showed genuine concern.

"Rebecca?" Sam turned to his EA.

Rebecca removed a document from her briefcase. "This is a copy of our brief." She passed the report to Alex. "With your permission I will summarize and take any questions you may have?" He nodded his permission.

Alex listened attentively without asking any questions. When she finished, Rebecca turned to Sam who nodded his approval. There was silence in the room again as Alex flipped through the brief. Sean and Anya began to squirm awkwardly glancing at each other with anxious eyes. Had Sam erred in his assessment of Alex Johnson?

Alex pressed a button on the phone beside him, "Brenda, send in Erin."

A young woman in her twenties entered the room and walked to stand beside Alex. "Erin, some new information has come to light on the Carson case." He handed her the briefing report. "Will you look into this for me and verify this new information?"

"Yes sir. Right away." She took the report and left the room.

Alex stood and addressed Sam, "I have no reason to doubt your findings Sam despite my direction to Erin. I believe I have made a grave error. Sixteen witnesses you say?" He turned to face Anya. "Anya, I am sorry for the pain and suffering this has caused you and your family. I hope you can forgive me."

Anya smiled at the prosecutor. "I forgive you. You are an honest and courageous man and I accept your apology. Thank you. Does this mean I don't have to go to jail?"

The others joined Alex in laughing at Anya's question, thankful for the break in tension. "Not if I have anything to say about it my dear. Sam, I will apprise the judge of our error and seek his leave to rescind the warrant. If possible, I will take care of this today. How can I reach you?"

"Thank you Alex." Sam rose and the two men shook hands. "We appreciate your graciousness in responding to our presentation. You can leave a message at the Hilton until mid afternoon. After that you can leave a message with my office."

Chapter 79

The foursome stood quietly in front of the elevator doors. Sam pushed the button for the ground floor. The doors opened. When they closed, the sedate group erupted in hugs and cries of jubilation over the promise of Anya's freedom.

"Thank you Sam and Rebecca," Anya hugged the two lawyers.

"You are most welcome young lady. I appreciate your faith in us but most of all in our Lord. You are a wonderful example to us all." Sam beamed as he held Anya's shoulders and looked into her happy face. "Let's go back to the hotel. We'll make a few phone calls and have lunch."

Sean called the condo when they arrived back at the Hilton. He held the receiver so Anya could hear the screams of joy coming from her mother and sister. Sean told Reina that Sam had invited the family for dinner at their vacation rental and they should touch down at the Lihue airport around five.

* * *

Sean and Anya sat at the patio table while Reina and Kazia got ready to go for dinner. "Are you a happy girl Anya?" asked Sean.

"Oh yes Dad. It's all over isn't it? God has truly released me from my bondage. I am forever free."

He looked at Anya who sat smiling confidently in the afternoon sunshine, her hair animated by the breeze. "Young lady, with your faith, you are free indeed."

* * *

JoAnna, Sam's wife, was dressed in a floor length casual dress in an Hawaiian floral print. She was tall and slim sporting a cream plumeria in her raven black hair. She introduced herself and welcomed her guests into the spacious home overlooking the ocean. "Oh it's not ours; we just rent it when we're on vacation," she commented as she watched her guests taking in the home's grandeur. "Come, let's sit on the terrace. Here's Sam now."

"Welcome," Sam greeted his guests. "JoAnna, did you meet our guest of honour tonight?"

"Yes dear. You mean Anya I presume?"

"Yes indeed. She had a recent revelation that I think you might enjoy hearing. Can you tell my wife what you observed Anya?" Sam was smiling broadly.

"Well, Mrs. Gervais, I told your husband that I thought he was an angel sent by God to rescue me." Anya smiled at JoAnna.

"Now that is quite the revelation!" said JoAnna, "let's hope it doesn't go to his head and bend his halo." Everyone laughed. "I was so pleased to hear that you were set free from that legal faux pas my dear, especially after hearing some of the rest of your story and that of your sister."

"God loves me Mrs. Gervais. I will always trust Him no matter what happens. I am a very happy girl with a good family." Anya got up from her chair and hugged Sam around his neck. She kissed his cheek and thanked him for being such an angel. "Now I can say I've kissed an angel," she announced.

Sam turned and kissed her on the cheek. "Now you can say you were kissed by an angel."

"Let's all sit and I'll get the drinks," Sam gestured to the chairs and couches on the terrace. "Anya, what would you like?"

"Do you have a Pina Colada? Kazia and I really like them."

"Hold the rum," interjected Sean.

Sam returned with a tray of drinks. After serving his guests, he sat beside his wife. "So I know you must be curious about what happened." He looked at Reina and Kazia.

"Well, it was as I suspected. A junior prosecutor and his assistant missed some important facts and acted in haste. Unfortunately, their actions caused considerable trauma to your daughter, and the rest of you, for which he is extremely apologetic. He made his apology directly to Anya at our meeting. The warrant has been rescinded and Anya is free to move about the USA without fear of prosecution."

"Well you know how grateful we are for your help Sam," said Reina. If you ever feel the need for a trip to the Yukon be sure to stay with us. You and JoAnna are most welcome.

"Thank you. You never know. I'm just sorry the girls missed out on their swimming lessons."

"Oh that's been taken care of, "said Sean, "tomorrow at nine, Kana is picking them both up for a full morning of lessons and practice."

Chapter 80

Back home, life together as a family began to take on a rhythm. Anya's latest experience as a prisoner engendered a remarkable confidence that her parents and sister were quick to recognize. She had experienced a profound growth in her faith; her confidence was not so much in herself as in her Lord.

The girls looked forward to going to school, much to the relief of Sean and Reina. Their relationships as a family grew stronger every day, so strong that others expressed wonder at how Sean and Reina were able to absorb these two foreign orphans into their own relationship. Few people knew the dark history of their daughters believing them to be simply the product of a foreign adoption. Until the girls were comfortable with sharing their kidnapping experience, they would manoeuvre around the curiosity seekers. The unspoken question, was, *"Why would anybody adopt two teenage girls?"*

Sean and Reina knew the answer. It was simple; they had fallen in love with them. Now as they watched the foster families care for the others they saw the same thing happening. These unloved and abused girls captured the hearts of their foster families and bonds of love were forming. Every Sunday Sean and Reina witnessed the growth occurring in their lives and the peace in their hearts. Spring was coming to the Yukon and a new life was being born in these girls.

Reina kept busy with her language classes, filling in at the hospital as time permitted and need arose. She made a point of meeting with the girls once a month to monitor their adjustment to their new family and to counsel them on any problems they were experiencing. Anya and Kazia enrolled in Reina's daytime Spanish class. Kazia was curious about Reina's nursing profession and had spent time with her at the hospital learning what it meant to be a nurse. Anya was happy learning to speak Spanish and practicing on her new Spanish-speaking friend from Honduras. School to Anya was a pleasant social diversion that satisfied her thirst for both knowledge and human relationship.

Sean enrolled both girls in driver training when they returned from Hawaii. He felt it better that they learn from a stranger than from him or Reina. He made a point of occasionally debriefing them on their progress. Kazia wasn't interested in flying so he enrolled Anya in the local flying school with the stipulation that Hans would be her flight instructor. Hans was a commercial bush pilot but also instructed in his spare time, which he had a lot of during the winter. Sean held Hans in high esteem as a pilot and trusted his girl to learn from him.

The family joined Tekla and her foster parents at least once a week at the pistol range. It soon became a special night for both families meeting for dinner before going to the range. The girls met other young shooters who, impressed with their proficiency, invited them to join the Tactical Shooting League starting in May. The girls were keen to participate and Sean was encouraged to see their enthusiasm. Sam would be proud.

Kazia and Anya were enjoying making their bedrooms into their personal space. Reina helped them choose the wall colors, curtains and bedspread. She promised to make them each their own quilt. Sean had bought a small desk and chair for their rooms hoping to encourage diligence in completing their homework. Now that they were attending school, they had accumulated a small wardrobe that they proudly kept in the closet.

Sean and Reina had made sure to get prints of various photographs they had accumulated over the past months. They put together an album for each of the girls so they could look back on their journey. The day Anya invited her Dad to see her room he found himself sitting beside her on the bed holding the picture frame that was on her night table beside her Bible. In it was the photo of him, Jesse and Anya sitting on the woodpile at his cabin.

Sean spent his time gearing up for the summer guiding and fishing season. He already had enough clients booked for fishing trips and a few for backpacking trips. If Jimmy Jackson was coming back, he could take on more clients but he never knew until the last minute if Jimmy was coming on. This never bothered Sean, he didn't *have* to work but he enjoyed it and with Jimmy things just went a lot easier.

He was preparing to attend the annual spring Fish Guides convention in Las Vegas when Reina told him she couldn't go after all. They really needed her at the hospital. She and Sean agreed that her obligations there should take priority in this case. Reina suggested he take Anya instead. "She wants to work with you this summer and this would be a great opportunity for her to see the full scope of the fish guiding business." The words had just left her mouth when she realized the implications of her suggestion. She stopped abruptly and put her hand on his arm. "I'm sorry Sean. I shouldn't have suggested that. I wasn't thinking." Her eyes searched his.

The suggestion had indeed brought back memories for Sean. "No, it's okay Reina. You know it might do me good to take her. The memory will be forever with me but the pain is gone and God has redeemed my loss with a beautiful wife and two wonderful daughters. I'll ask her."

"I think I already know the answer you'll get," Reina smiled.

"Anya!" Sean called down the hall and waited.

"Coming." He could hear stocking feet padding down the hall.

"Sit down young lady." Sean's stern countenance put her on guard. He enjoyed teasing her. Anya sat down, a worried look on her face.

"I have to go to a guiding convention in Las Vegas. You want to come with me?"

Her confusion was evident in her face as she looked to her Mom for explanation. Reina nodded towards Sean. "He wants you to say yes Anya."

Anya turned to her father and almost shouted, "Yes! Oh yes. I will go Dad. I won't be any bother and I'll catch up on my school work when we come home I promise."

"I hoped you'd say that." Sean smiled at his wife as Anya hugged his neck.

Chapter 81

It was dark when the plane landed in Las Vegas. Anya stared out the window marvelling at the city of lights surrounded by the pitch-black desert. On approach, Sean pointed out the 'strip' and the hotel where they would be staying. Anya had led a protected life and her naivety put her at risk in a town like Vegas. He had spoken to her about the city and its reputation alerting her to the hidden hazards and her need to stay aware and alert as she enjoyed herself. Despite the abundance of light, darkness lurked beneath the glittering façade.

Sean arranged with the Bellagio for a limousine to pick him and Anya up at McCarran arrivals. *"Why not?"* he thought, *"this was Vegas and Anya was a daughter of the King."* Reina and Kazia had taken special delight in making sure that Anya's attire was appropriate for her premier arrival in Las Vegas. She wore the designer jeans, rhinestone belt, embroidered blouse and Bolero jacket that Reina first bought her the previous fall. Reina loaned her a plain silver necklace, dangly silver earrings and a simple silver bracelet for her wrist. She had spent some time under Reina's tutelage learning to walk in her high-heeled shoes but for travel she wore ankle length black leather boots. Reina made Sean promise to take her to a quality women's clothing store and buy her a special outfit for the dinner and dance evening put on by the convention hosts.

Sean spotted the long white limousine parked in front of the sliding doors of the arrivals lounge. The driver approached them as they stepped onto the sidewalk. He confirmed their identity and offered to carry their luggage. Sean nodded his approval for Anya to let him take her small suitcase. She watched the man place their bags in the trunk of the vehicle and questioned her Dad with her eyes. "Yes, this is our ride honey." The driver stood holding the rear door for them as they approached the gleaming white car.

Once seated, the driver asked if they needed to make any stops on the way to the hotel. Sean declined. Anya was overwhelmed with the opulence of the limousine's interior. "Sure beats your truck Dad," she remarked.

Sean laughed and pointed out the window to a man standing beside another limousine. "That man is a movie star. You might see him in a movie some day. Lots of celebrities spend time in Vegas."

The limousine joined the river of Friday night traffic on the 'strip'. Although it hindered their progress, it gave them time to see the sights. And, what sights they saw! After 20 minutes, the driver pulled up to the front doors of the hotel. A man in uniform opened the door for Sean and Anya and welcomed them to the Bellagio. He directed them to the check-in desk and promised to have their luggage delivered to their room.

Anya stared in wonder at the richness of her surroundings and the variety of people moving through the lobby. Sean had booked a suite so Anya would have her own room. She gasped when Sean opened the door to the suite. They entered a spacious room on the 12th floor with a huge window overlooking the 'strip'. Their luggage was sitting just inside the door as the doorman had promised. A queen size bed stood against one wall with a couch, chairs and tables taking up the rest of the room. Sean led the way to her room complete with a king-size bed and en suite bathroom. "Look at that bed!" she exclaimed. "Our whole family could sleep in it!" He smiled and hugged her around her shoulders.

After unpacking and freshening up, they took the elevator to the convention registration centre. Despite his absence in recent years, Sean recognized a few people and made a point of greeting them and introducing Anya. He picked up their name badges and the convention package then led Anya toward a couple of men standing off by themselves. They spotted him coming and the older man strode towards Sean, "Well if it isn't Sean Carson.

So great to see you again Sean." He wrapped his arms around Sean slapping him on the back.

The two men separated and Sean pulled Anya to his side. "Joel, I want you to meet my daughter, Anya."

Joel shook Anya's hand smiling at the attractive girl standing before him. He expressed his delight in meeting her then turned to the young man with him. "Anya, Sean let me introduce my son, Jason." Both greeted Jason but Jason lingered longer as he shook Anya's hand.

"We just got in. Are you two up to getting a drink and catching up?" Sean asked.

"Love to Sean, it's been a while." Joel was genuinely appreciative of Sean's invitation while trying to hide his curiosity about Anya.

The foursome found a table in the quiet cocktail lounge and ordered drinks. Anya had her usual virgin Pina Colada. She sat between her Dad and Jason. Jason was at least six feet with broad shoulders, a slim waist and thick dark hair. Anya noticed that his hands were strong and calloused. He was dressed casually, like his father, in jeans and a cotton shirt open at the neck. His bright green eyes that shone from a strong but gentle countenance captivated her. She turned to engage him in conversation, "Do you work as a guide Jason?"

Jason met her gaze. His response stalled. Anya's deep blue eyes and golden blonde hair distracted him. This was the most beautiful fishing guide he had ever met. "Yes, sorry, it's just Dad and me now that Mom's gone. She died of cancer a few years back. Of course I miss her but life goes on and I know she's with the Lord and He is looking out for me. How about you? Do you work with your Dad?"

Anya watched him as he spoke and tingled at the sound of his rich, mellow voice. She thought it sounded sexy. "Oh no, but I might; God knows. I'm finishing school right now but I hope dad let's me help this summer. I'm learning to fly but I've never caught a fish." She felt relaxed and at ease as she spoke to him. She didn't feel shy like she usually did when speaking to strangers.

"You've never caught a fish and you're at a fish guide convention!" he chuckled. "Well if you ever need a guide I'm available." He smiled. He wasn't mocking her; instead, he looked at her with tender eyes that told her he was serious about his offer.

"Where do you live Jason?"

"Alaska. Do you know Alaska?"

"Not really. I've been to Fairbanks." She paused. "And Anchorage."

Joel and Sean were engaged in catching up on past events in their lives but they were both pleased to see Anya and Jason getting along so well. Jason was Joel's only child now 20 years old and working with him in the guiding business. Sean told Joel how he had remarried and acquired two teenage daughters leaving out some of the details. Joel recounted the loss of his wife and the dark time he and Jason had gone through afterwards. They too had missed a couple of conventions but now they were back in the saddle and looking forward to the coming season.

* * *

Before meeting Joel and Jason for breakfast Sean talked to the hotel concierge about getting an evening dress for Anya. He recommended a shop just off the strip giving him directions on a sheet of paper. "After breakfast I want to catch a couple of sessions then we'll go and get you a dress and go for lunch." Anya eagerly agreed. After breakfast, Jason offered to chaperone Anya around the exhibit room while their fathers took in the presentations. Anya tried not to betray her enthusiasm over the offer but Sean could see that she had made up her mind. He gave his approval and set a rendezvous time and place before thanking Jason for the offer and admonishing him to take care of his daughter.

The woman at the dress shop suggested three different dresses to Anya. Sean tried to hide his choice until Anya had made hers. She tried on all three, parading in front of mirrors and admiring customers. Still, she was having difficulty deciding between two of them. Sean's restraint finally caved. He made it very clear that she should buy the long black one that she was wearing. He noticed the clerk nod in affirmation. Anya hugged his neck. "I like it too. Thanks for helping me Dad." The clerk showed Anya some small clutch purses and gave her a few pointers when she discovered that this was her first formal affair.

Over lunch, Anya gushed about the good time she had with Jason. He began by introducing her to the gear associated with the fish guiding business. During her tour, she learned more than she could ever remember about how to catch a trophy fish. The exhibitors were more than happy to talk with the beautiful fishing guide from the Yukon visiting their booth. Time flew by. "He invited me to have coffee with him this afternoon during the break. Is that okay Dad?" She batted her eyes leaving Sean no alternative but to say yes. He was happy for his girl and he knew that she was in good and trustworthy company with Jason.

Anya spent over an hour getting ready for the banquet and dance. Sean had arranged for her to get her hair tuned up at the salon in the hotel but then came the rest of the preparation. It was a semi-formal affair. Sean wanted his daughter to remember the event so he bided his time looking out the window while she fussed in her room. He wore a rented tuxedo only because he needed to keep pace with his daughter and didn't want his princess escorted by a pauper. As it turned out, he needn't have bothered.

There was a knock on the door. Sean got up and opened the door. Jason stood on the other side dressed in a black tux, sapphire blue cummerbund (pleats up) and bow tie and patent leather shoes. "I've come to escort Anya to the banquet," he said.

Sean looked at him then turned to see Anya coming from the bedroom. "Um, she must have forgotten to tell me you were her escort." Sean looked back at his daughter now looking very guilty but stunning. The two men stared at the elegant blonde-haired princess in her black, half shoulder dress with silver and sapphire accessories holding a tiny silver sequin purse. "Anya, your date is here." Sean kept his cool as he kissed her on the cheek and handed her off to Jason. "I'll be down soon. You look gorgeous honey. Don't spill soup on that dress." He closed the door.

Chapter 82

"Oh, you are gorgeous in that dress Anya," Reina's eyes were filling with tears as the three women looked through the photos Sean had taken during their trip. "I am so happy that you had such a good time. Who is this young man you're standing beside?"

"Yes Anya, who *is* he!" added Kazia.

Anya blushed and looked down at the floor. "His name is Jason. He's the son of a friend of Dad's. He was my escort for the dinner and dance on Saturday night."

"He's so handsome. How old is he? Can he dance? Where does he live? Does he have a brother?" Kazia was excited to learn more of her sister's relationship to the young man.

"Oh yes, he is a good dancer." Anya seemed to suddenly come to life. "We had so much fun Mom. He's 20 and lives in Alaska with his Dad; they are fishing guides. Dad said we might visit them someday and he invited them to visit us whenever they could."

Reina and Sean had privately discussed Anya's response to Jason and men in general. They were sensitive to the response of both girls to the men in their lives. Both were encouraged by the ease with which they both socialized with men. Anya's response to young men her own age was also encouraging beginning with Kana and now Jason. Her self-assurance and willingness to engage socially heartened her parents. Sean shared how she entered into conversation with Jason without reserve and how both of them agreed to a 'date' without any intervention from him; in fact, without even telling him!

* * *

It was mid-March and already Anya was ready for her first solo flight. Hans had called Sean throughout her training to brief him on her progress. He considered her an outstanding student with an aptitude not only for flying but for the mechanical aspects of the machine itself. For this reason he had made a point of challenging her more than he would another student. She never failed to meet the challenge. He deliberately left a gas cap off on one occasion but Anya discovered and fixed the problem. Another time he shut off her fuel when she was preoccupied with training manoeuvres. She took the sudden shut down of the engine in stride trimming the plane for an emergency landing while scanning the cockpit for clues to the problem. She brought the engine back into operation in record time scolding Hans for playing tricks on her.

Hans was confident in releasing her for her first solo flight so he called Sean to let him know. He knew he would want to be there for this important step in her training. Sean called Reina at the college to see if she could get Kazia out of class and both of them meet him at the flight school. In half an hour they all assembled to watch out the windows of the building as Anya and Hans taxied onto the apron. They watched Hans get out and say something to Anya before shutting the door and walking away. Anya taxied back toward the runway as Hans entered the building. "That's one special girl you've got there. She'll do fine." And she did. Later her family greeted her with congratulatory hugs and Hans presented her with a small, engraved lapel pin honouring her achievement.

Learning to drive a car seemed to take longer than learning to fly an airplane. Road conditions and instructor availability slowed the process. By the end of March the girls were ready for their road test. Of course, Sean and Reina were there to cheer them on. It was a beautiful sunny day with no snow on the roads. "They will be so disappointed if they fail," said Reina.

"Fail?" Sean objected. "I will be surprised if those two fail. They take things like this so seriously. Five bucks say they both pass?" Sean held his hand out to clinch the bet. Reina, having second thoughts, declined. After the tests, the girls came bounding in from outside waving the paper that certified their successful completion of the driving course. They waited at the counter while the clerk prepared their temporary licenses. Beaming, they showed them to their parents before tucking them away in their wallets. "So who wants to drive home?" Sean asked.

Anya turned to her sister, "Kazia, you can drive, you're a way better driver than me."

Kazia slapped her sister on the arm. "I am not! We're *both* really good drivers, but I'll still drive."

"Let's make a short stop on our way. Your Mom and I have to finish some business at the Jeep dealer," Sean announced as he climbed into the back seat with Reina. "You know where it is?"

"Oh yes, Mom and I have been there to get her Jeep serviced," Kazia replied.

Kazia pulled into the dealership lot and Sean and Reina got out. "You two can go home and we'll see you there within the hour. You want pizza for lunch to celebrate?" The look on their faces answered his question.

Reina ordered the pizza over the phone while Sean finished the paperwork. The salesman led him and Reina into the shop where their new Jeep Grand Cherokee was waiting for them. Until now they had only seen their new vehicle in pictures as it had to be ordered from 'outside'. Reina climbed into the driver's seat admiring the vehicle interior as Sean joined her on the passenger side. "I think I'm going to enjoy driving this," she remarked as she headed for the pizza parlour.

The girls, excited about having pizza for lunch, didn't notice the new vehicle and never asked how their parents got home. The conversation centered on their adventures learning to drive and those that were yet to come. Sean impressed on them the reality that experience played in becoming a good driver or pilot and promised to help them gain that experience. "Now don't think you can drive our Jeep whenever you want, after all we need transportation too." He watched their faces as Reina turned to hide her smile.

The expected reaction didn't materialize. "Oh, we understand Dad. Maybe we could drive your truck sometimes?" said Anya.

"My truck! Are you crazy? Do you think I would let you drive my truck?" Sean feigned serious offense at Anya's suggestion.

Their faces expressed shock at Sean's response. "Oh, okay, I didn't think you would mind," Anya responded timidly.

Sean and Reina's laughter told the girls they had been the victims of the joke and they joined in the fun. "Just kidding. Of course you can drive my truck. But, your Mom and I would like to see you drive your own vehicle as much as possible." Sean watched the puzzled look appear on their faces.

Reina added, "We just bought a new Jeep and we thought we'd keep my old one and let you two share it. Do you think you can do that?"

The puzzled looks morphed into happy smiles as the girls hugged each other. "Oh yes, we can do that can't we Kazia?" Anya replied looking to her sister nodding her head in affirmation. "Thank you for trusting us, we love you. Can we see the new Jeep?"

Chapter 83

The day finally arrived for Anya to take her flight test. Hans had already taken her through a pre-flight test and knew she was ready for the final. Sean, a little nervous but full of confidence in his daughter, tried to avoid offering advice or coaching as he watched her cope with her own anxiety. Anya picked at her breakfast, an obvious sign of her concern over the imminent test. Despite his better judgment, Sean reiterated the importance of having a good breakfast especially before going flying.

"I know Dad!" Anya shot back. "Leave me alone. I'm okay,"

Reina squeezed Sean's hand under the table and he squeezed back with an apologetic look on his face. "I'm sorry Anya. I love you." The tone of his voice comforted Anya as she continued to pick at her meal in silence.

Anya drove herself to the airport after receiving a silent send-off replete with hugs of comfort and reassurance from her family. Her family followed an hour later picking up coffee on the way. It was a bluebird day, ideal for a flight test. Spring was still on its way in the Yukon but it would be several weeks before leaves began appearing on the trees. It was a windy time of year but today the air was calm. Sean and his family walked into the flight school. Hans was sitting in front of the windows, a coffee cup in his hand and his feet stretched out before him, basking in the warmth of the morning sun streaming through the windows. He stood when he saw the Carson family arrive greeting them all with a friendly handshake and a smile. "She'll be another half hour I expect. She's got Dave as her examiner. He's tough but fair and as long as she keeps her mouth shut she'll do okay," he chuckled. Sean and the others laughed aloud at his remark.

Sean and Hans talked about Anya's flying aspirations while keeping an eye on the sky. She had often shared her plans with Hans and her family. Despite her enthusiasm for flying, she understood and appreciated the willingness of her family to indulge her in what was becoming a passion. Sean knew that she wanted to fly floats, especially with the open water season on the horizon. Over the past month, she had been reading books on the subject. They only whetted her appetite for the real thing; she wanted that float endorsement. Sean knew that Hans would soon be back flying commercial but he needed to ask anyway. Hans was a premier float pilot and even though Sean's own float skills and experience rivalled those of Hans, he still wanted Anya to learn from someone other than himself.

Hans listened as Sean made his case. "Tell you what Sean, you get TJ on floats and make her available to me and I'll teach your girl how to fly the water but only when I've got the time," Hans paused, "You know I shouldn't be doing this, but Anya is exceptional and she deserves the attention. She's gotta be available though, no schedules, I call and she's here or she doesn't fly."

Sean smiled at Hans and extended his hand. "You've got a deal as long as Anya is willing to abide by your conditions. We'll talk to her after she gets her license."

Sean and Hans looked at each other, surprised looks on their faces. "Reina, Kazia, watch this!" Sean pointed out the window. The little plane was too high for landing on the threshold. What was she doing? Suddenly she slipped forward, kicked straight and touched down only to take off again. "Did you see that?" Hans almost shouted. "Even Dave sees her potential. He never asks a student to pull a slip on a flight test."

The student pilot and examiner, both stone-faced, walked into the flight school lounge. Dave was still writing on his clipboard. Anya glanced at her family trying to smile but looking like she was about to cry. "Is this your family Anya?" Dave asked gesturing to the Carson family lined up expectantly.

"Yes." Her voice trembled.

Dave nodded to the family then turned to face Hans. "You always do good work young fellow, I can always count on you, but this time . . ." Dave paused and looked back at Anya frozen with apprehension, "you had help. This girl is a natural. Anya, I'm proud to give you a full pass with honours young lady. Take a bow." He reached out to shake Anya's already shaking hand.

Hans rose and gave Anya a hug. "I too am proud of you Anya. Congratulations."

Anya dissolved into another of her rare, speechless moments as she sighed in relief radiating her joy. Her family embraced her, heaping praise on a much-loved daughter and sister. She closed her eyes and silently thanked God for His blessings in her life.

Hans joined them for lunch at the Chalet. Anya had regained her voice and was bubbling over with emotion at the reality that she was now a licensed pilot. She had done it! She kept getting up and hugging everyone around the neck in grateful enthusiasm.

When she settled back in her chair Hans said, "Hey girl, what was that slip all about?"

"Oh that. Well, I thought we would be landing but he told me to maintain altitude so I did. Then he asked me what I would do if I was too high to touch down like on a normal approach. I told him I'd go around if I could or slip in. That's when he said, 'Do it!'" Anya paused, "I asked him if he really wanted me to slip and he confirmed so I did. You know how much I like that manoeuvre." Hans looked at her and shook his head. "What?" she said.

"Well this seems like a good time to present you with a graduation gift," said Sean as Reina took a small gift-wrapped box from her purse and handed it to Anya. She tore open the paper and opened the case inside to find a pair of Ray-Ban, brown-tint, polarized aviator sunglasses. "You're not just a pilot, now you can look like one!" He snapped a picture as she modeled them for everyone.

By the time their orders arrived, she had mellowed enough for Sean to tell her about her next training session. She began to protest over spending more money on her training. "I'll go to work and earn money to pay for my training, I promise. You don't have to do this," she pleaded. "You have already been so good to me."

Sean and Reina looked at each other. Sean could see that Reina needed to speak to her daughter. "Anya, we love you and Kazia and we love to see you embracing new things in your lives, possibly even careers. We want to support you as best we can. You are both very responsible girls willing to pull your own weight but it gives us great joy to be able to help you along your way."

Sean added, "Your mother is right. Besides, this is all a plot." Anya looked puzzled. "We're investing in you now so that you will take care of us when we're old and wrinkled and need help getting into the airplane." Everyone laughed. "Even Hans wants to invest in you as long as you are willing to meet his conditions."

Anya looked around the table at the people who loved her. "I guess I still have a problem believing that I'm worth it. But I promise to work on it. Thank you for showing me that *you* believe I'm worth it. Yes Hans, I accept your conditions and I won't let you down. I'm honoured to have you as my instructor."

Epilogue

She blew out all 27 candles with one breath to the applause of all in attendance. Jason leaned over and kissed his wife on the cheek. "Years only add to your beauty my dear; don't ever stop getting older." Anya turned and kissed him back as he held her in his arms.

"It's our turn," declared four-year-old Danny as he and his little sister, Anika, pushed their father out of the way so they could hug their mother. "Happy Birthday mother!"

The 'big room' in Sean's fishing lodge was more colourful than usual with the birthday decorations. Joel had flown in from Alaska and Sean had flown Sam, Sheila and Blanka in for the occasion. Sheila and Blanka made the cake while Jimmy and Sarah did kitchen duty preparing the baked lake trout dinner. Two clients, invited to join in the celebrations, could only guess at what all these people meant to each other.

Sean and Reina sat beside each other on the couch arms entwined watching the scene before them. Outside the window behind them, the deep blue of the lake complemented the yellow willow and poplars. Sean's mind cast back to that first summer he brought Anya to his fishing lodge.

They had sat on the deck listening to the loons. "Those birds make that sound?" she whispered in disbelief. "What wonderful music. It makes my skin tingle." That evening they paddled the canoe to a small bay. Together they sat quietly on the still water watching the birds. The female, carrying her two youngsters on her back, ploughed a furrow in the glassy water as she swam. The male appeared from behind a small island and joined his mate offering one of the chicks a small fish in his bill.

Anya stared, following the birds with her eyes. Sean, from the back of the canoe, could hear her faintly sobbing. She was remembering that day at Sean's cabin where she gazed in fascination at the photograph of the bird in the encyclopedia. It was then that he first told her about the birds carrying their young. She had cried then too out of longing for someone to love her and carry her through her pain.

"I guess it has been 10 years," Sean looked at his wife. "Time has the wings of a falcon. I can't keep up anymore."

"Don't be so hard on yourself. Most young guys can't keep up with you." Reina squeezed his arm. "She is a beautiful mom isn't she? I'm so happy for her Sean."

"Just like you my dear. You've been such a good mom to both the girls for the short time they were with us; and after." Sean kissed his wife.

His thoughts once again retreated in time. Tears began to slide down his cheeks before hiding in his beard. Anya walked over to her parents and noticed the tears on her dad's cheeks. "You're such a cry baby Dad," she teased. He reached up and pulled her onto the couch where they hugged each other close.

"I love you so much Anya. You have no idea how happy it makes me to see you and your family together like this. Excuse my tears but I can't help it; they are tears of extreme joy my dear. I like to think that God cries right alongside me when He looks at what's become of the daughter He rescued 10 years ago."

"I understand Dad." She looked into his eyes. "I love that you cry. I love it even more when you cry over Kazia and me." She kissed him on the cheek tasting the salt in his tears. "Soon it will be Kazia's birthday. Too bad she is so far away," lamented Anya.

"We'll give her your love dear," said Reina. "We're leaving next week. It's been nine years since we all visited Ben and Sydney in Cambodia."

After that first winter, Anya and Kazia had both returned to school to start a course in emergency medicine. Anya, after her first season flying floats and learning the guiding business, decided to continue to work with her Dad but the emergency medicine course fit nicely with her plans. Kazia was leaning towards the medical field considering going on to train as a nurse.

That fall after Anya and Kazia had started their course, Sean, Reina and the Wilsons took the three girls to their first tactical shooting competition in Juneau. Joel and his son Jason hosted them in the large home that they used as their base of operations. Jason and Anya had kept up their relationship by writing letters to each other over the summer while she worked with her Dad at the lodge and Jason worked with his Dad out of Juneau. This was the first time they had seen each other since Las Vegas. The guiding season hindered opportunities to visit so Anya and Jason were thankful to be together again. Jason and his Dad spent Christmas with the Carsons and they all went to Vegas again the next year.

Sean had taken his family to Cambodia after Christmas with a stop in Hawaii for some R and R. He hadn't seen Ben and Sydney for several years and he wanted his girls to experience Asia and meet his dear friends. Kazia was so captivated by what Ben and Sydney were doing, she spent much of her time working alongside them when she wasn't travelling around the country with her sister and parents. When it came time to leave, Kazia, smitten by the people and their culture, vowed to return and join them. She moved to Cambodia that summer after graduation. Since then she continued to work with Ben and Sydney helping girls caught in the sex trafficking business.

Arnie offered Anya a job flying charters with his Cessna 185 on wheel skis during the winter months. She jumped at the opportunity to advance her hours and gain more experience. He started her out flying freight to see if she could handle the loads both in the air and on the ground. Her perseverance impressed him so he started her flying passengers as well as freight. It wasn't long before the blonde female bush pilot began to earn a reputation among the locals. By spring the blonde bush princess had made her mark.

Anya continued to live at home working alongside her Dad during the guiding season. She and Jason saw each other as often as they could. The following winter Jason asked her to marry him. They wed in the spring. Sean and Reina offered the guiding business to them on the condition that they kept Sean around to do a little guiding and maintenance. They both jumped at the opportunity. This freed Joel up to sell his operation and retire while putting a good deal of cash in his son's pocket.

Anya and her sister had kept in touch with the others all of whom established roots, thanks to their foster families, and stayed in the Yukon. Every five years they had a reunion at the White River Lodge courtesy of Sam and Sheila. Luiza and Reina saw each other frequently while sharing their passion for shot gunning. Luiza had become a champion just as Reina had predicted. Anya was the first to marry but Celina and Danuta followed shortly after. All the girls married and had children except for Kazia and Blanka. Blanka, the shy one, had stayed with Sam and Sheila at the lodge. Charlie Johnson from nearby Koidern worked for the highway department. He often stopped at the Lodge for coffee and meals and became her best man-friend over the years. The two of them enjoyed canoeing and fishing and Charlie made a point of inviting Blanka to go moose hunting with him. Last month he asked her to marry him. She said yes.

Kazia had always excused her status as a single woman by claiming to be too busy to marry despite Sydney's admonitions to take time for herself. Despite her preoccupation with the ministry, she had developed a friendly relationship with a Canadian missionary over the past two years. The two were beginning to spend more time together and Sydney had hinted in her last letter that *"things were moving along splendidly."* Sean and Reina were understandably anxious to meet the young man.

Every fall Reina and Sean would spend a month or so at the cabin. It was a special time for them both. Together, after cutting firewood, they would sit on the shore of Pancake Lake absorbing the fading warmth of the late afternoon autumn sunshine listening to the chickadees. Memories of the early days of their relationship came to life and they laughed and talked sharing their lives and love for one another. As the sun's rays settled onto the tops of the mountains, the air cooled and they would retire to the cabin. There they would start a fire in the kitchen stove and plan their evening meal sitting at the table.

As the woodpile grew, Reina would watch Sean, his countenance transforming from peaceful to pensive. *"Would she come? She always did."* She knew his thoughts. He missed his Anya more when he was at the cabin where it all began. In the evening, he sat in his overstuffed chair, a framed 5 x 7 photo on the table beside him, John Denver singing softly in the background. He treasured that photo of him, Anya and Jesse sitting on the woodpile.

The strains of his favourite Denver song, "Perhaps Love", played in the quiet ambiance of the cabin; the words played in his mind.

The tape ended. Reina got up to turn it over. Sean returned to his book. As he read, he occasionally looked up to stare at the door before glancing at Reina knitting or quilting before turning back to his book. *"She had to come soon; they were almost done getting firewood."*

The morning sun rose later each day. Its brilliance, magnified in the clear autumn air, made up for its tardiness. The sun's warmth stirred the mist covering Pancake Lake sending it back into a deep blue sky while uncovering the vibrant yellow willows and poplars surrounding the lake. Sean and Reina sat at the kitchen table talking over coffee and watching the unfolding scene through the bay window. Reina understood how Sean anticipated Anya's visits to the cabin every fall. She had always been a bright light in his life just as his Felicia had once been. They both knew and understood a little better the grace and love of God because of their presence in each other's lives.

He turned his head, listening, "Did you hear that Reina?" They both went still, listening intently. Sean rose from his chair. "She's here. That's her truck on the road." He threw on his jacket and slipped into his boots tucking the laces inside instead of tying them. Reina joined him at the driveway as the truck pulled into the yard. Anya stepped down from the big Ford 4x4 her broad smile and bountiful blonde hair shining resplendent in the morning sun.

"Hi Dad. See, I didn't forget. I'll never forget."

The End

Printed in Canada